PRAISE FOR MARGARET LUCKE
AND HER NOVELS

"Margaret Lucke is an exceptional writer."

— MARCIA MULLER, Grand Master, Mystery Writers of America

"Margaret Lucke writes with style and confidence."

— MOSTLY MURDER

"Margaret Lucke has found a new twist on haunted houses, as well as presenting an intriguing mystery mixed with romance."

— CHELSEA QUINN YARBRO, award-winning creator of the Saint-GERMAIN series

"A mystery, a fantasy and a love story, imaginative and cleverly crafted. A page-turner, worth losing sleep to keep reading. What more can a reader want?"

— RITA LAKIN, author of the popular Gladdy Gold mysteries

"Mystery, romance and ghosts come together in this first-class tale."

— ROMANTIC TIMES

"A fascinating blending of romance, mystery and the paranormal."

— FUTURES MYSTERY ANTHOLOGY MAGAZINE

"I was drawn into Claire's story from the first page and could hardly put the book down for wanting to know what could possibly happen next."

— FALLEN ANGELS REVIEW

HOUSE *of* DESIRE

ALSO BY MARGARET LUCKE

FICTION

Snow Angel

House of Whispers

A Relative Stranger

NONFICTION

Schaum's Quick Guide to Writing Great Short Stories

Writing Mysteries

AS EDITOR

Fault Lines: Stories by Northern California Crime Writers

HOUSE *of* DESIRE

A CLAIRE SCANLAN HAUNTED HOUSE NOVEL

Margaret Lucke

OAKLEDGE PRESS

ISBN 978-1-939030-06-1

This book is a work of fiction. Names, characters, places, and incidents are either the products of the author's imagination or used in a fictitious manner. Any resemblance to actual persons, living or dead, events, or locales is purely coincidental.

Cover photos by Charles Lucke

Oakledge Press
Hercules, California
www.oakledge-press.com

In memory of artist and author

BETTE GOLDEN LAMB

I miss you, dear friend

CHAPTER

1

Roxane came down the spiral stairs to the third floor and risked a glance back up into the tower. The space at the top was deeply shadowed, but through a corner of a window high above she could see a sliver of twilight sky. No hint of movement, no sign that anyone—especially not that disgusting beast Thaddeus Burnham—was about to descend in pursuit of her.

Sighing with relief, she stepped into the big storage room, empty now, which shared the third floor of the house with a warren of small bedchambers.

A trill of lively music rose from a lower floor. She froze, her hand on the banister. Had she not escaped after all?

She hurried to the front window. The age-darkened pine floorboards creaked under her soft kidskin shoes, and her sweeping hem stirred a powder of dust into the air. Her breath caught as she raised the sash and looked out onto Octavia Street.

What year was she going to see?

If she were still in Chez Celeste, in 1896, horse-drawn carriages would be traveling on the street. Her heart lifted when, instead, the lanes were filled with those strange metal boxes that could move on their own.

Across the way she saw an ugly building that resembled a tall warehouse made of glass. Her friend Granny Jo had told her it was an apartment house. Roxane found it hard to believe that anyone would choose to dwell in such unappealing accommodations, but right now it was a welcome sight. It confirmed that she'd succeeded in slipping out of her own time and into what she thought of as the Future House.

The buildings across from Lady Celeste's parlor house were other Queen Anne mansions, equal to Chez Celeste in grandeur and elegance. According to Granny Jo, they'd been torn down to make room for the unsightly glass block. Progress, Granny Jo had called it, which left Roxane shaking her head.

Leaning out the window, Roxane watched one of the metal conveyances pull to a stop in front of the house. A young man in a flapping blue jacket ran forward to open its door, and two women alighted onto the sidewalk. They were costumed in gowns not unlike Roxane's own. This was strange. Usually the people she saw in the Future House were oddly dressed—imagine, ladies attired in trousers. Who had ever heard of such craziness?

The pale dress worn by the brunette was several years out of vogue; Roxane would never be allowed to go out in a garment so unfashionable. She nodded in approval, though, at the fair-haired woman's modish gown, as lovely as a jewel. If Lady Celeste could see it, she'd be eager to learn the name of the woman's seamstress. But Roxane had no intention of letting Lady Celeste in on the secret of the tower stairs.

Roxane sighed. She was fortunate to have this place to escape to, but coming here tonight reminded her how lonely she was.

The first time she'd stumbled into the Future House, she had encountered the ancient lady who invited Roxane to address her as Granny Jo. Roxane was flattered; she'd never known her own grandmothers, nor much of any family. Though ill-assorted and far apart in age, she and the old woman became fast friends—the finest friendship Roxane had known. Granny Jo had the most amazing stories to tell, and she enjoyed having an audience. The other people who visited her house never noticed Roxane. To be honest, most of the time they seemed oblivious to Granny Jo as well.

Then one day she arrived to find that Granny Jo had disappeared, and so had her possessions. Most likely she had died, which made Roxane sad indeed. Since then the Future House had been empty.

Until tonight.

The sound of a fiddle rippled upward and set Roxane's feet to tapping. The musicians must be down in the ballroom. Oh, how she would love to dance—so long as her partner was someone other than Thaddeus Burnham.

A babble of voices reached her ears, sounding like the rush of water over stones in a brook back home in Missouri. A peal of laughter beckoned her. Why not go down to the parlor? She was wearing her best gown and a beautiful necklace.

But she had just run away from Lady Celeste's birthday festivities to escape a man's unwanted attention. There was no telling who was attending this other party or what they were celebrating. Her wisest course would be to stay away from the merriment below.

Despite that sensible decision, she glided out of the storage room as if she were being pulled on a string. The music and laughter grew louder, more enticing.

She tiptoed through the hallway, passing her own bedroom, the place where, in Chez Celeste, she slept and often plied her trade, should the customer be unwilling to pay for one of the grander chambers on the second floor. One time while in the Future House she'd peeked behind the closed door and found the tiny room empty of everything but memories and dust.

At the top of the steps to the lower floors, Roxane hesitated. She brushed her hands over her hips, smoothing the lilac silk of her skirt, then fussed with the lace that was designed to draw men's eyes to her bosom.

Did she dare venture down the stairs?

2

"Whoever invented the bustle ought to be shot."

Savoring the taste of her murderous words, Claire tugged at the padded pleats and gathers on her rear end. The thick lump of satin had made sitting awkward and uncomfortable, even in the cushy leather seat of Tess McMillan's Mercedes Benz. Emerging from the car into the soft air of the September evening, Claire could feel that the whole bulky arrangement had shifted askew.

"Impressive, don't you think?" Tess said. She dropped her key into the waiting palm of the parking-service valet.

"Not exactly the word I'd use." Claire gave another yank, and the complicated features of her long skirt fell into place. "I can't believe women used to wear this kind of thing all the time."

She envied her boss's 1890s gown. Instead of a ridiculous bustle and a train that dragged along the sidewalk, it featured a long gored skirt, slim at the hips and wide at the hem. Its champagne color nearly matched Tess's hair, and even with the poufy leg-o'-mutton sleeves, she looked tall and regal. Of course, Tess always looked tall and regal.

The only good thing about her own dress was that its pale mauve color made a good backdrop for her cherished amethyst necklace.

Tess said, "By impressive, I meant the house."

"Oh. Of course."

Claire gazed at the Victorian manse in front of them: three stories of whimsy made of wood. Peaks and gables jutted up. Bay windows protruded out. Shingles, spindles, frills, and furbelows covered every surface. At the corner, a round tower rose above the roofline. It had windows peering in all four directions and was topped by a conical roof like a witch's hat.

The place was an architectural version of the nineteenth century's overwrought ladies' fashions. And it sadly needed paint.

"The Burnham Mansion," Tess said, stepping aside to let two gentlemen in tailcoats and top hats reach the front steps. "One of San Francisco's historic treasures. It's shabby now, but imagine what it will look like if we get the chance to fix it up."

We meant the Bay Area Preservation Alliance, called BAPA for short. Tess was on its board, one of her many civic engagements. The mystery to Claire was how Tess ever found time to manage her real estate firm, BayCrest Properties, where Claire was an agent.

"This party should help BAPA's cause," she said, but Tess was already climbing the steps that led from the street to the garden, then up to the entrance portico.

Claire followed, tripping on her ruffled hem. The last time she'd worn a gown with a train was at her wedding. She hoped this evening wouldn't turn out as badly as her marriage had.

The fundraising ball was launching BAPA's campaign to save the Burnham Mansion. Tess had bought ten tickets and doled them out to her agents, urging them not only to attend but to wear Victorian-era dress. And when Tess spoke, agents listened.

She'd invited Claire to ride with her, saying, "We need to chat." About what, she hadn't specified, which made Claire nervous. She'd been hired on a three-month trial basis, and that time was almost up. Back in June, in the first days of her job, she had sold a large oceanfront house—but so far that was her only success in her brand-new career. Was Tess planning to give her a pep talk? Or chide her for her lack of sales—possibly even let her go?

Maybe her boss just didn't want to be embarrassed by having Claire show up at the Burnham Mansion in her lime-green jellybean, a Volkswagen that did not say *successful Marin County real estate agent.* Tess had spoken little on the way here, focusing on heavy traffic. Claire would have to stay in the dark until the drive home.

When Claire reached the porch, Tess was chatting with a tall, lean man whose thick blond hair was touched with gray. He looked completely comfortable in his tux, as if he wore one every day.

Her heart skipped a beat.

Tess said, "Claire Scanlan, meet Simon Thatcher, executive director of BAPA. Claire is my newest agent, Simon, with a very promising career ahead of her."

Simon's smile put a silver light into the gray eyes behind his glasses. He shook Claire's hand with a warm, firm grip. She wished she didn't have to let go.

"Welcome, Claire. Tess told me about your success in selling that house on the coast. Congratulations."

"Um, yes, I …" Claire tried to remember how to speak. He wouldn't be impressed if she reverted to her middle-school awkwardness, and she realized she wanted very much to impress him.

He leaned forward, as if sharing a secret. "I hear the place was haunted."

Claire forced herself to laugh. "Rumors, gotta love 'em."

She had nothing to gain by telling Simon, or Tess for that matter, about the strange and disturbing things that had happened to her in that house. Whatever she'd encountered—a ghost, a spirit, some otherworldly phenomenon she had no name for—she never wanted to experience anything like it again.

Simon said, "That's one worry we won't have here." He added, with a chuckle, "Unless Josephine is hanging around."

"Who?"

"Josephine Burnham," Tess explained. "She was born in this house in 1906, hours before the famous earthquake struck, and lived here all her life. She died a few months ago."

"Wow. That means she lived here for well over a century."

"And she was proud and independent for every minute of it," Simon said. "There's no other house in the city like this, a historic mansion that's been in one family's hands for so long. Imagine what a fine museum it will make."

"If we succeed in buying it," Tess added.

"Who owns it now?" Claire asked. Along with music and the buzz of conversation drifting through the open doorway, she heard voices raised in argument. Neither Simon nor Tess seemed to notice.

"Josephine left the house to her grandchildren," Simon said. "Unfortunately, they disagree about what to do with it."

"One wants to live here and the others want to sell," Claire guessed.

"Living here would cost a fortune. Josephine nearly went bankrupt trying to keep the place going in her final years. As you can see, she left a lot of work undone."

Tess interrupted. "We raised what we thought would be enough to buy the place, and the grandchildren were ready to accept our purchase offer. The money coming in tonight was supposed to go toward making repairs and setting up the museum. But at the last minute a developer stepped in. He's made an offer that, frankly, we can't match."

Simon nodded. "Not unless our fundraising succeeds beyond

our wildest dreams. So now the heirs are split. One grandson is on our side. The other is pushing to take the extra money and run. Their sister hasn't made up her mind. I'm hoping tonight will earn us her vote."

Claire said, "At least they agreed to open the house for the fundraiser."

Tess snorted. "By the time the developer appeared on the scene, it was too late to cancel it."

"What can a developer do?" Claire asked. "Isn't the house a historic property?"

"Sadly, it's never been put on any official list," Simon said. "But being a registered landmark would give it only limited protection. Just one more hoop for someone to jump through before tearing it down."

"What a crime that would be," Claire said.

"Speaking of crime, here's George." Tess waved to a heavy, florid man who was huffing and puffing up the steps.

Oh great. George Pugh was Claire's least favorite of the agents at BayCrest Properties. Why Tess put up with him was a total mystery. Well, not total. There was a family connection; he was a brother-in-law or something. But there had to be more to it than that. Tess didn't suffer fools gladly, yet she risked her company's reputation to keep this idiot ungainfully employed.

The image of politeness, George greeted his boss and shook Simon's hand. Then he swatted Claire's bustle. "Hey, girl, nice rump."

Before she could retort, he disappeared into the house. On his way he stepped on the puddle of satin that was Claire's train, leaving a dark blotch on the pallid fabric.

Claire glared after him until Simon reclaimed her attention.

"Go in and have some champagne," Simon said. "The bar's in the parlor, the buffet is set up in the dining room, and there's dancing in the ballroom downstairs." He smiled warmly at Claire. "Be sure to save me a dance."

Claire was out of practice when it came to flirtatious smiles, but she did her best. "As many as you'd like."

—·—

The music grew louder as Claire and Tess stepped into a large, crowded foyer that was paneled in rich, dark wood. A hallway extended straight ahead; Claire glimpsed a kitchen at the far end. To their left, people flowed through wide archways into an oversized parlor and dining room. On the right-hand side, a magnificent redwood staircase rose to the second floor.

What would it be like to live in a house so grand?

Claire noticed a girl of about eighteen standing on the stairs, in front of a huge stained-glass window. Her hands grasped the carved balustrade as she watched the crowd with a look of puzzlement. Her antique dress, in a rich lilac hue, was styled more like Tess's elegant gown than Claire's bustle-burdened folly. And her jewelry …

Claire's hand flew to her amethyst beads.

Her good luck charm, a gift from her mother. More than a gift—a legacy. Her parents had died in a car crash when she was a baby. She and her older sister were raised by their Grandmother Scanlan. On Claire's sixteenth birthday, Gram had presented her with her mother's strand of purple crystals. It instantly became one of her most precious possessions.

"Look." She nudged Tess. "See that girl's necklace? It's just like mine."

"Which girl?"

"On the stairs." She pointed discreetly. "Not exactly the same, but close."

Claire caught the girl's eye and was surprised to see her mouth drop in alarm.

Tess gave Claire an odd look. "There's no one on the stairs. But I love that necklace on you."

"But …" How could Tess not see her?

"Come on, let's find Mirabelle Burnham. You can help plead BAPA's case."

Tess swept into the parlor. Claire scurried to keep up, clutching her skirt close in a vain attempt to keep it out of people's way. At the doorway she glanced back at the stairs.

The Amethyst Girl was gone.

"There's Mirabelle," Tess said. "By the windows, with her brothers."

They worked their way through the crowd, dodging guests in formal attire who carried champagne flutes and plates of hors d'oeuvres. Claire glanced around, taking in the features of the room—a plaster medallion on the ceiling, elaborate moldings, faded wallpaper, and scuffed hardwood floors.

Tess's destination was a round bay at the far corner. Claire guessed it was the base of the witch's-hat tower. Tall, uncurtained windows gave a view of the street and the weedy side garden. The three people standing in the bay were speaking to each other at normal volume, but their scowls and jabbing gestures made it clear their discussion was heated. They broke it off abruptly when Claire and Tess reached them.

"Hello, Tess," said the woman who apparently was Mirabelle Burnham. A smile flicked at the corners of her mouth, but hot spots of anger colored her checks. Hunching her shoulders, she stepped forward, putting distance between herself and the men.

She had short blond hair and would have been pretty if she didn't look so uptight. Instead of a Victorian gown, she wore a silver flapper dress covered with sequins and fringe.

"Mirabelle, Marc, Richard—so good to see you." Tess shook Mirabelle's hand and nodded to the tuxedoed men. "Thank you for allowing us to hold this splendid event. Meet Claire, one of my agents. She'll be working with me to make the house sale go smoothly."

This was news to Claire, though she knew BayCrest Properties would represent BAPA as the buyer's broker—if the transaction went through.

The two men spoke at once.

"Great to have you aboard," began the taller, darker-haired brother—Marc, if Claire had kept Tess's brisk introductions straight.

"No offense, but the BAPA sale's not going to happen." Richard—stocky, red-faced, balding—crossed his arms. "Is it, Ellie?"

Mirabelle bit her lip and pushed a stray wisp of blond hair into her 1920s-style headband.

"Is it, Ellie?" Richard repeated, his tone more stern.

"Nothing's decided. You know that." She looked away from him, past Claire's shoulder, and her face lit up. "Oh good, here comes Peter with my drink."

Claire twisted to see the newcomer, then stepped back in surprise, tangling her feet in her train. The lanky, fortyish man coming toward them was Peter Mortensen. His tux and the two champagne flutes he held made him look rakish and debonair.

Peter stopped short when he saw her, then came forward and handed Mirabelle one of the crystal glasses. "Claire! What are you doing here?"

Mirabelle moved close to Peter's side and placed her hand on his arm. "You two know each other?"

Something about the blonde's demeanor and Peter's panicked look made Claire think twice about how she should answer.

Before she could speak, Peter said, "Claire's an old friend of my family's."

Okay, if that's how he wanted to play it. "How are you, Peter? I didn't know you took an interest in historic houses."

"Well, I—a professional interest. I'm here representing the firm." He saluted Claire with his glass and took a gulp of champagne.

Claire nodded. Peter was a partner with one of the city's top real estate law firms. It made sense that he could be involved in BAPA's effort to acquire the mansion.

Mirabelle looked hurt and confused. "A professional interest? Is that all?"

"Come on, Ellie, let's go hit the buffet. Nice seeing you, Claire." With his hand on Mirabelle's back, Peter guided her away from the group.

Marc and Richard excused themselves, too, and wandered into the crowd, leaving Claire and Tess alone in the window bay.

"You know," Claire said, "I could use a glass of that champagne."

"Bar's over there. Let's go." Tess started to move toward it. "So you know Peter Mortensen. That could be helpful, you're being a family friend—"

Claire sighed. Tess never made it easy to tell her less than the full truth. "More like a family member. Peter's married to my sister."

"Really?" Tess looked thoughtful as they queued up at the bar. "Do you suppose Ellie Burnham knows he's already spoken for?"

"Good question," Claire said. "I'm wondering that too."

3

"C'mon, Claire." George pulled her toward the dance floor. "What fun is it being a wallflower?"

More fun than dancing with you. Claire bit her lip to keep from saying the words aloud. She tried to slide her hand from his clammy grasp but he clutched it harder.

She'd spent the early part of the evening chatting with some of the other BayCrest agents. When they decided to leave, she'd come downstairs to the ballroom, hoping to find Simon.

Where a lesser house would have a basement, the Burnham Mansion had a vast open space with a high ceiling and a hardwood floor perfect for dancing. As men in tuxes and women in long gowns swirled around, Claire had stood near the band, tapping her feet and wishing she had a partner. Then the gods played one of their perverse jokes—they granted her wish by setting George in front of her, his face flushed and sweaty, his manner insistent.

"I told you, George, I'm not in the mood to dance."

"Sure you are. I can see the longing in your eyes." He yanked her hand. The sudden movement threw her off balance and she lurched forward.

Catching her waist, George spun her around to face him. He shuffled his feet in an awkward box step, counting under his breath—"One-two-three, one-two-three"—in a rhythm that bore no relationship to the music.

"George—"

He pulled her tight against his ample midsection. "You know what they say, baby. When it's inevitable, relax and enjoy it." His hand squirmed around in her bustle and squeezed her rear end.

"Stop that!" Twisting away, Claire stumbled out of her shoes. She felt around with her stocking feet, trying to find them under her voluminous train. She shook one free, only to have George kick it and send it skidding across the floor.

"Oops. I'll get that." He let go of her, finally, and scuttled after the shoe.

Claire fished its mate from under the fabric. She tried to sit on one of the folding chairs along the wall to put it back on, but her bustle took up most of the seat, leaving her perched precariously on the edge. How the hell had Victorian women managed to live normal lives dressed like this?

George came back and jammed the runaway shoe onto her foot. "Just like Cinderella's glass slipper. Guess that makes me the handsome prince." He grabbed her wrist. "Okay, princess, let's pick up where we left off."

"Not on your life," Claire muttered.

A deep voice behind George said, "May I have the pleasure of this dance?"

Simon? Her heart quickened. But when she looked up it was Peter, her brother-in-law, who extended his hand toward her.

"Love to." Claire led him through the crowd, as far away from George as possible. "Thanks for coming to my rescue."

Peter held her stiffly in proper ballroom-dancing position, as if they were kids taking lessons. "You didn't look like you were having a good time. Who is that guy, anyway?"

"One of my real estate colleagues. Can you believe it?"

He shook his head, then said, "Look, Claire, I want to talk to you about—well, about tonight."

"Yes, you looked surprised to see 'a friend of the family.' " Claire made a show of surveying the crowd. "I don't see Cassandra anywhere."

"She's home with the kids."

"Why didn't you bring her? She'd love an event like this."

"I'm talking business all night. Cass would be bored out of her mind." He twirled Claire around.

"That's right, you said you're here in a professional capacity."

Peter nodded, looking grateful to change the subject. "My firm represents Harding and Boyer, the development company that wants to buy this house."

Claire stopped short. "Wait—your client's the developer?"

"Sure, what did you think?"

"This is BAPA's fundraiser. I assumed you were working with them. Why are you here, if you're on the other side?"

Someone bumped into her. She pulled her train out of range of people's feet and let Peter ease her back into the flow of dancers.

"Hey, it's not like we're spies," he said. "We paid full price for our tickets, and gave BAPA a generous donation besides. It's a fine organization, does a lot of good."

"But you're trying to snatch the house away from them."

"Look at it this way—we're giving the owners a better deal."

"And what does your client get?"

"The chance to develop the property, of course."

"Develop it how?"

"Condos. This is a residential neighborhood, and a prime location. San Francisco needs more housing."

"You'd tear down a beautiful historic mansion to put up condos? How could you?" Nearby couples turned to glare at her, and Claire realized her voice had become shrill.

"Hey now," Peter said soothingly. "Who said anything about

tearing it down? Harding and Boyer's design will incorporate the main architectural details."

"What about BAPA's plan to make the house a museum?"

"You know that's pie in the sky, Claire."

"Won't the Burnhams get tax benefits if they accept BAPA's offer? The difference between the sale price and the market value could count as a charitable donation."

"Even if the heirs donate the house outright, BAPA can't afford it. The old lady, Josephine, really let the place go. They'd have to take care of decades of deferred maintenance before they could open it to the public."

Peter seemed more relaxed now. Claire had danced with him only once before, at her sister's wedding, and she'd forgotten how smoothly he could move. Back then she'd been a starry-eyed twenty-year-old, and if she hadn't been so thrilled for Cassandra, she might have been tempted to fall for the bridegroom herself. Fifteen years ago—so much had changed in all their lives.

She said, "I heard the Burnhams haven't reached an agreement about what to do with the house."

"True. Richard and Marc are on opposite sides."

"And Mirabelle?"

Peter's gaze slid away from her. "Ellie hasn't made up her mind. Each brother is trying to persuade her to his point of view."

"And your job is to use your charm to convince her to go with the development option."

"My charm?" He offered her a self-deprecating smile. "You're giving me too much credit."

"Oh, you can be very charming, Peter, especially when you think it will get you something you want."

But Peter had quit listening to her. He'd stopped dancing, too, and was looking at something across the room. Then he recovered and spun her around. Claire caught a glimpse of

Mirabelle, the silver fringe and sequins of her flapper dress shimmering as she came toward them.

A moment later, Claire felt a tap on her shoulder. Mirabelle said, "May I cut in?"

———◆———

To Ellie's dismay Peter didn't gather her into his arms right away. He smiled at her but turned to watch his previous dance partner cross the floor, bustle swaying. Ellie assessed the competition—lustrous brown hair that curled at the nape of her neck, a figure that was slim yet more curvaceous than Ellie's own boyish shape. Maybe the billowing dress created that effect.

"That's your family friend, isn't it? Claire somebody."

"That's right." Peter stretched his arm along Ellie's waist, and a zing of electricity shot through her.

She settled one hand on his back and he wrapped her other hand in his. She sighed with pleasure. Though they'd been lovers for several weeks, this was the first time they'd danced together.

Yet something wasn't right. Peter guided her easily in time to the music, but he didn't pull her closer. In fact, he wasn't giving her his full attention. It was as if someone else occupied the narrow space between their bodies.

Who was Claire?

Ellie's stomach knotted. "How close a friend?"

Or was she something more? Ex-girlfriend, ex-wife? Peter hadn't told her much about his past, but she didn't delude herself that she was the first woman he'd loved.

Her own romantic history didn't bear talking about—long spells of loneliness broken by brief involvements with disappointing men. She'd fallen hard for the last guy, who kept promising he'd marry her as soon his divorce came through.

They'd even started to plan their wedding. Yet he kept making delays and excuses. Finally she discovered he'd never filed the divorce papers. She'd thought she'd never get over her heartbreak.

Then Peter came along and healed it.

"Claire's just a casual acquaintance." His lips brushed Ellie's hair. "Unlike you. Nothing casual about my acquaintance with the beautiful Ellie Burnham."

Ellie leaned against his shoulder, closing the gap between them. "I have an idea," she murmured. "Let's go back to my place right now."

"You want to leave the party already?"

"We've put in our appearance. No one will miss us. If you want more champagne, there's a bottle in my fridge."

Peter released her to look at his slim gold watch. "I'm supposed to meet Simon Thatcher and Daniel Harding in the library in a few minutes to discuss a few things."

Ellie stiffened. "What things? Why wasn't I invited? Will my brothers be there?"

"Just an informal chat. Simon has an idea he wants to float. No need for you and your brothers to be bothered unless his plan turns out to make sense, which isn't likely."

"How long will it take?" As much as she loved this house, she was eager to have this evening end. The strangers ogling her grandmother's home, the quarrel with Marc and Richard, the odd way Peter was behaving—it all made her uneasy. But she would feel fine once she and Peter were alone.

"Tell you what," Peter said. "I know how hard this event is for you. Let me put you in a taxi and send you home." When she started to protest, he placed his fingers on her lips. "As soon as I've taken care of business here, I'll come right over. I won't be long, I promise. That way you won't have to wait around getting bored, and your brothers can't pick any more fights."

"Not tonight anyway." Ellie sighed. "Okay, let's call a taxi."

"Good girl." He kissed her forehead lightly, but Ellie could have sworn he looked around first, as if worried that someone was watching.

4

Glancing at her wrist, Claire remembered that, in the interest of authentic costuming, she hadn't worn a watch. It must be getting late though. The party was winding down, guests drifting away. She was ready to leave but had to wait for Tess.

Her boss was in the library behind the dining room, conferring with Simon and some others, trying to come up with a solution that would let BAPA purchase the Burnham Mansion and create a museum. Whatever strategy they devised, she hoped it would work. Condos! What could Peter and his client be thinking?

She cruised past the buffet for the third time. The food was spread on a huge oval table with carved wooden legs, the only item of furniture she'd seen in the house besides the rented bar and folding chairs. She imagined a family gathered round this table for holiday dinners, Josephine the matriarch sitting at its head.

The chocolate truffles were gone, no surprise, but the caterer was setting down a fresh tray of bite-sized lemon tarts. Claire popped one in her mouth, enjoying the explosion of sour and sweet on her tongue.

The library door opened and Peter and Simon burst out, clearly in the midst of a heated argument. They aimed for the buffet table, but when Peter spotted Claire there, he scowled and veered away.

Simon glared at Peter's retreating back, then came up beside her. He inhaled deeply and ran long fingers through his thick gray-blond hair. "Drat," he grumbled. "No more truffles."

"I recommend the lemon tarts," Claire said. Interesting how her heart quickened as he stood close.

He looked startled; apparently he hadn't noticed her. "Ah. Good advice." Then he smiled. "You're Claire, Tess's associate."

She smiled back—winningly, she hoped. "The party looks like a grand success." Except for his fight with Peter, that is, but that didn't seem like the right subject to bring up.

"Yes, it's gone well." He'd calmed down and was giving her his full attention. "The tickets sold out, even at the pretty penny we were charging for them, and our guests seem to be enjoying themselves. A few media people came, so hopefully we'll get some favorable coverage."

"Good. I'd much rather see this place go to BAPA than a developer."

Simon picked up a tart. "Tess speaks highly of you, Claire. I'm glad you're on our team."

"What does that involve—being on the team?" Not that it mattered as long as it helped her get to know Simon.

"Tell you what, I'll call you tomorrow and we'll talk about it. Right now I have go make nice with a couple of our major donors before they leave."

"You must know almost everyone here. Who's the girl with a necklace like mine? I'd like to talk to her." The question wasn't simply a ploy to get him to linger. Okay, yes it was, but she was truly curious. She'd kept an eye out for the Amethyst Girl all evening but hadn't seen her again.

"Your necklace is beautiful. But I didn't see anybody wearing a similar one." Simon fingers grazed her shoulder, much too briefly. "Sorry I didn't get a chance to claim that dance. Next time, for sure."

As she watched him go into the parlor, her hand went to the spot he'd touched. Next time—hopefully very soon.

She reached for another lemon tart, then decided she'd better resist. But when she tried to step away from the table and its temptations, her awkward skirt refused to budge. She tugged it and—*ri-i-i-ip*. A shiny black leather shoe was planted on her train. It had held the dress in place as she moved, pulling a ruffle away from the hem. Just what the damn dress deserved.

The man whose foot was in the shoe was deep in conversation with the Burnham brothers, unmindful of her plight. She tapped his arm.

"Excuse me, you're standing on my dress."

"What? Oh, I'm sorry." He stepped aside, releasing her.

She hauled the train beyond reach of his shoes. "It's okay."

"No, I mean it. I really do apologize. I usually don't tear off a woman's clothes before I meet her."

He smiled. A good-looking man, with dark hair and warm brown eyes. But no competition for Simon.

"To make things worse," he added, "I see my clumsy foot left a stain."

Claire looked down at a black smudge that George had inflicted on the ruffle. "Actually, someone else did that."

"Even so, I'm responsible for some damage. Let me pay for the mending and dry cleaning."

"That's not necessary."

"I'm Daniel Harding. Who am I apologizing to?"

"Claire Scanlan. Wait, Harding? As in Harding and Boyer, the developer?" Her favorable assessment slipped a notch.

"Guilty. I hope you won't hold it against me." He took a silver case from his pocket and handed her a business card. "When you get the dress cleaned, send me the bill."

"Really, there's no need. But thank you for offering."

She drew open the tasseled cords of her reticule, the tiny drawstring bag that hung from her wrist. She and Tess had borrowed their outfits from a community theater, and the costume manager had insisted that this was what a proper Victorian lady would use to carry her essentials. Instead of a perfumed hankie, Claire's contained her comb and lipstick, some cash, and a few business cards. She slid Daniel's card in and gave him one of her own.

Tess came up to them. "Oh, here you are, Claire." She and Daniel exchanged brief nods, as if they'd met before and weren't quite sure they liked each other.

"Shall we leave?" Tess asked her. "I'm ready to call it a night."

"So am I," Claire said, which was half true. It was too late for a dance with Simon, but she wasn't eager for Tess's promised chat. To Daniel she added, "Nice to meet you."

"Pleasure's mine," he said warmly.

"Let's go," Tess said. Quick strides carried her out of the room. Encumbered by excess fabric, Claire had trouble keeping pace.

Reaching the foyer she saw the Amethyst Girl standing on the grand staircase. At last!

"Go on, Tess," Claire called. "I'll catch up."

She dragged her dress up a couple of steps. "Hi, I'm Claire Scanlan. I couldn't help noticing your necklace—"

The girl spun around and rushed up the stairs.

"Wait! I just want to talk—"

Why did the sight of Claire upset her? Was it the necklace? Claire hurried after her, but by the time she maneuvered herself and her dress up to the second floor, the Amethyst Girl had disappeared.

The doors to all the rooms stood open, and the ornate overhead light fixtures were ablaze; the guests had been invited to come up and see more of the house that, with their support, BAPA hoped to preserve. Now all was empty and still.

Claire stepped into the pink, high-ceilinged bedroom where Josephine Burnham had spent her nights for so many decades. The room was cold as ice. She shivered and rubbed the goosebumps that suddenly rose on her arms. Funny—she wasn't aware of such an intense chill earlier when she took the tour. She also hadn't noticed the rocking chair in the window bay, but there it was, with someone in it rocking gently. The Amethyst Girl?

Claire moved toward the chair. "Hello?"

The rocker vanished.

She pressed her fingers against her eyes and shook her head. What had just happened? She couldn't blame the champagne; she'd had only one glass. It was a shadow, a mirage, a trick of the nighttime lights beyond the window …

Something brushed past her; she caught a whiff of perfume—flowers mixed with spice.

"Welcome, dear."

"Who said that?" Claire whirled around. No one there. The whisper was so faint that she couldn't be sure she'd really heard it. But this room was giving her the creeps.

"Don't be afraid."

She ran back into the hall.

This couldn't be happening. Not again. What had happened when she sold the coast house was bad enough, but that was a one-time thing. There had to be rational explanations for tonight's illusions. The whisperer must be the Amethyst Girl. The rocking chair had emerged from her overactive imagination. Simon's joking about haunted houses had set up her mind to play games.

Heart pounding, she peered into the other rooms. A bathroom with a claw-footed tub. Three smaller bedrooms with faded floral wallpaper. They were all empty—no furnishings, no curtains. No ghostly rocking chairs. No young lady wearing a necklace like Claire's.

Where had she gone?

Claire was about to give up when she heard shuffling footsteps overhead.

A flight of service stairs, boxed in and narrow, opened off the hallway. One branch led up and another went down, probably to the kitchen. Earlier tonight a velvet rope had hung across the staircase to keep guests from venturing farther. Now it dangled to one side.

The Amethyst Girl must have gone up there.

Claire glanced around, saw no one to stop her from following. Her skirt was wider than the steps, which made the climb awkward. She reeled in her pleats and ruffles and tried not to trip.

Reaching the top, she listened for a sound of movement, a whispered voice. Nothing.

A naked bulb burned overhead, creating aisles of light that penetrated partway into the surrounding rooms. They were small and plain compared to the ones below, and smelled of dust. Servants' quarters, she guessed.

No sign of the Amethyst Girl.

The last room, at the front of the house, was different—a large open space. Pine-plank floor, wood-paneled walls, a dark vault above formed by the underside of the roof. A few feet from the door, the path of light from hall bulb dissolved into shadows. Streetlights outside backlit the wavy window glass but did nothing to brighten the room. An open window let in a cold draft.

The girl had to be in here. She had nowhere else to go.

Claire stepped into the room.

She heard floorboards creak. Then a muffled noise, like someone catching a breath or suppressing a sob.

Claire followed the sound to the far corner, where a wall curved into the room, enclosing a set of tightly spiraled wooden stairs. Looking up, she saw they led to the witch's-hat tower. A slice of the moon shone through a window high above.

The muffled sob again. Definitely real, not a hallucination. It came from somewhere nearby in this darkened room.

"Hello?" Claire called softly. "Where are you?"

No reply, but she heard someone breathing.

"Are you okay?"

Footsteps clattered in the hall. A bass voice boomed from the doorway, making Claire jump.

"Who's in here? What's going on?"

Heart in her throat, Claire turned to see a group of men silhouetted by the hallway light. As she walked toward them, they took on identities. Simon, the Burnham brothers, Peter, a couple of others.

"It's me, Claire Scanlan. I was just ..." She could think of no good excuse for being there.

Simon frowned. "The third story is closed tonight."

"I know. I'm on my way downstairs."

"Look at that window," one of the Burnhams said. "It shouldn't be open."

"Did you open it, Claire?" Peter demanded.

"No. It was that way when I got here."

"I'll close it." Simon started to cross the room.

Claire edged past the others, head lowered, avoiding their eyes. She felt embarrassed and vaguely guilty, like a child caught misbehaving.

She didn't risk looking at Simon.

Now she had to face Tess, who was waiting in her Mercedes, wondering where the hell Claire was and getting angrier by the minute.

Claire had messed up everything. And she hadn't even managed to talk to the elusive Amethyst Girl.

———◆———

Deep in the night, Roxane huddled in her secret niche, the wedge of space behind the curved wall that enclosed the spiral staircase. She'd been curled in this tight spot for what seemed like hours. She fingered the necklace she had borrowed from Lady Celeste. Thank heaven it hadn't been broken or stolen in tonight's melee.

She was wrong to have stayed here in the Future House this evening, no matter how enticing the music and laughter. She should have returned quickly to Chez Celeste, even if Lady Celeste did order her to offer her favors to that loathsome pig, Thaddeus Burnham. Everyone would have been better off.

Particularly the man lying bloody and broken on the pinewood floor.

She still wasn't certain what had happened. The man had spotted her in the shadows of the storage room and spoken to her. She'd been frightened—no one in the Future House had ever been able to see her, except her dear friend Granny Jo. Now tonight there were two more—this man and the woman wearing the necklace like Lady Celeste's. Granny Jo had been gentle, sweet, and too frail to do harm, but who knew what powers these others might have to use against her.

Yet this man seemed kindly, talking as if he thought she were one of the party guests. She made the mistake of letting down her guard. Just as she began to feel at ease, someone grabbed her roughly from behind. Brutal hands shook her and flung her against the wall. She'd crawled into the hiding place and cowered there as the man fought her attacker.

She would never cease hearing the thuds of the man being beaten or the rasping of his last breaths. The stench of his blood and his sweaty fear would remain in her nostrils, and the pulse of energy she felt as his soul left his body would forever tingle along her nerves.

Now the air, stirred into turmoil, had settled, and her tears had drained away. The house had long since grown quiet. It felt empty of any living soul but herself, but she couldn't be sure. What if the attacker was concealed somewhere, waiting for her to emerge?

She didn't dare stay here any longer. Roxane uncoiled herself from her hideaway, stretched her knotted muscles, and crept to the foot of the spiral stairs. There she hesitated, her foot in its kidskin slipper resting on the bottom step. She would doubtless be in trouble when she went back to Chez Celeste, since she'd been gone for so long and had no good explanation for her absence.

But she didn't understand this strange future world, didn't belong here. Staying would surely be worse.

CHAPTER

5

Never do I intend to leave this house. It is too much a part of me, and I of it. These planes and curves and angles shaped the very geometry of my existence. To separate myself from the house would be to destroy my soul.

I was born here more than one hundred years ago, in the same bed where I was conceived. The same bed where my father died, and then my mother, and finally myself.

The bed is gone now. Except for the huge dining table, the rooms have been emptied of their furnishings. I wept to see them leave. I miss having my familiar possessions around me, but even without them I manage to be comfortable here. I've made a high-backed rocking chair; instead of wood and fabric, I fashioned it out of my memories and habits and desires. I lean into its plump cushions and I can pretend that the present is the past—when I was alive, when I was young, when passion heated my blood.

Sometimes I have visitors—my father, my mother, my son, my sweetheart. They come as emissaries from the Place Called Forever, trying to lure me to cross over. But why should I go there? I remember nothing about it, though they tell me I dwelled there before I was born. They say that when I pass through those portals made of light, I will feel like I've come home.

Well, this is my home. This house. I am the grain in the wood panels that line the walls. I am the ray of sunshine that penetrates the *stained glass in the windows. So long as this house remains standing, I will not leave.*

But now I wonder—after what has transpired here tonight, how long can the house and I endure?

Ellie lit the last of a dozen candles she'd arranged around her living room. The flames gave the space a warm, romantic glow. Soft music crooned from her speakers. On the coffee table, the champagne was chilling in an ice bucket. She brought a pair of crystal wineglasses from the kitchen and set them beside it.

Passing a gilt-framed mirror, she frowned and pushed a strand of short blond hair into place. She'd changed from the flapper dress into a filmy robe that flowed to the floor. Now she tightened the sash and adjusted the folds of fabric, hoping to create the illusion of curving hips and full breasts. She wore nothing underneath.

Everything was ready. Where was Peter?

She glanced at the ormolu clock on the antique desk in the corner. Almost one a.m. The gilded cherubs surrounding the clockface seemed to mock her. Peter had put her in the taxi three hours ago, saying he'd be along shortly.

The clock, the desk, the wineglasses, the mirror—many of the objects stuffed into Ellie's small rooms had belonged to Granny Jo. Treasures, family heirlooms. Her brother Richard had insisted on emptying their grandmother's house, auctioning the choice items on eBay and selling the rest to a dealer. Maximize the cash, that was his motto. Ellie had rescued as much as she could. Never mind how out of place the antiques looked in this shoebox apartment.

She worried about what to do with that huge old white

elephant of a house. It was the place of many of her happiest memories. As a child she'd loved the times when Granny Jo invited her to visit—just Ellie, not her brothers. They had tea parties with cakes and cucumber sandwiches; Ellie was allowed to sip tea from one of her grandmother's delicate gold-rimmed cups. At night Granny Jo tucked her into bed under an embroidered coverlet. The china tea set now lived in Ellie's kitchen and the coverlet was spread over her bed.

Which was where she'd expected to be by now, nestled in Peter's arms.

Ellie sank onto the sofa but couldn't relax, couldn't soothe the butterflies in her stomach. She jumped up, paced the room, looked at the clock. Five past one.

Peter had been the one good thing to come out of Granny Jo's death. Ellie knew her grandmother couldn't live forever, had in fact lived far longer than most people have a right to expect. Yet Ellie missed her. Though Granny Jo's body grew frail, her mind had stayed sharp and she'd been good company right to the end. Marc saw little of her in recent years, and Richard even less, but Ellie had been a faithful visitor.

Granny Jo had left her estate to them as equal heirs. For the last six months they'd been haggling and arguing. Then there was the army of attorneys and financial advisors pushing them to sell this, buy that, donate something else. Everyone made different recommendations, and she was sure they all, her brothers included, had their hidden agendas. Trying to figure out what would be in her own best interest was driving her crazy.

Then one afternoon a few weeks ago, Richard dragged her to the office of yet another lawyer, who represented some development firm that wanted to buy Granny Jo's house. Ellie fought going until the moment she was introduced to Peter Mortensen. He was attractive—tall and trim, thick hair the color of wheat. But it was more than that. His smile was so genuine, his hazel eyes so warm.

The day grew late and Peter suggested that they adjourn to Ciboulette, a hot new restaurant near his office, to continue their conversation. Ellie gladly agreed. Even better, Richard couldn't go. Over candlelight and wine she and Peter set aside any thought of business and talked about themselves. He was such a good listener, and Ellie opened up in a way she rarely did. When they came outside into the cold foggy evening, he flagged a cab for her. She was thrilled when he kissed her cheek and asked to see her again.

Since then they'd been together every moment they could, though not nearly as much as she wanted. His law practice demanded incredibly long hours. Too often, he worked late at night and on weekends; they were lucky to be together one or two evenings a week. Tonight was a first—never before had he stayed with her the entire night.

Footsteps! And the lilt of someone whistling a tune outside in the hall. She tensed, waiting for Peter's knock. He must have followed someone into the building; that was why he hadn't buzzed her from the main entrance.

The footsteps passed her door and faded away. A neighbor returning home.

Tears sprang to her eyes. What if he didn't come? What if she'd just been dumped? God, she was so stupid for thinking that Peter might be different, that he might offer a true chance for happiness.

No, it was too soon to give up hope. Maybe his talk with Simon Thatcher had gone longer than he anticipated. Or he'd gotten trapped in some other conversation before he could leave. Or—she had a flash of a car accident, a drunk driver smashing into Peter's BMW, Peter lying dazed and bleeding in the street.

Then another image snuck into her imagination. Peter and that woman Claire laughing as they left the fundraiser arm in arm.

The ormolu clock said one-fifteen.

A tear slid down her cheek and she brushed it away. Allowing herself one long, deep sigh, she began to blow out the candles.

She'd extinguished three of the flames when the intercom sounded, signaling a visitor at the building's entrance. She ran to push the answering button.

"Peter?" she said into the speaker.

"Yeah, Ellie, it's me." His voice crackled with static.

"Thank God! I'll buzz you in."

She ran to the apartment door, had it open before he could knock. He'd removed his bowtie and unbuttoned the top of his shirt. His eyes seemed tired and his hair appeared to have been whipped by wind.

He looked wonderful.

"What took you so long?" She grabbed his hand, led him inside. "I was worried."

"Sorry. I was … some issues came up while I was talking with Simon, so I stopped at my office to check on a couple of things. Guess I should have called you."

She shut the door, not sure whether to feel relieved or angry. "That would have been nice."

"Ah, sweet Ellie, forgive me." He gave her that smile that would melt stone and untied the sash of her silk robe. "You're so beautiful tonight."

Then he pulled her close and kissed her, and the world was perfect again.

———•———

At the top of the spiral stairs, Roxane stopped to collect her wits before returning to Chez Celeste. Up here the reek of the dead man's blood was diminished, and she took huge gulps of air. Hiding in the storage room, she had scarcely dared to breathe for fear the stench of death would make her retch, revealing her whereabouts to the villain who might be lurking close by.

She felt relieved to be in the tower. Of all the rooms in the mansion this was the one she liked best, though it hardly counted as a room because it was so small. If she lay on the floor with her toes to the wall, she could stretch her arms above her head and touch the curve of the wall opposite. She knew this because she'd tried it once out of curiosity, only to have Lady Celeste berate her later for the dust that clung to her dress from collar to hem.

The opening in the floor for the spiral stairs made the room smaller still. Another peculiarity was that it had but a single wall, which encircled the space and met itself again at the beginning. Every other room she'd known in her eighteen years had four walls, but this one had nothing that could be called a corner.

Best of all were the four large curved windows, which gave views all around. Up here, higher than the trees, she could see so far in every direction that the entire world seemed to be spread out before her, waiting for her to discover its wonders and delights.

Looking out now, Roxane let herself be dazzled by the multitude of lights. Not stars—these lights glowed from nearby windows and tall poles that stood along the curbstones. The metal conveyances that moved without the benefit of horses had white lights in the front and red ones in the rear, which made beautiful patterns on distant roads.

Even before coming to the Future House, she'd seen a newfangled electric lamp or two, and last fall a gentleman at Chez Celeste had spent hours marveling about the Great Electric

Carnival he'd attended in Sacramento. But nothing had prepared her for the way the nights of the future blazed with light.

Granny Jo had explained to her how electricity worked, but Roxane could tell it was one of those things a person needed schooling to understand. As a little girl she'd loved school, but she had no more than learned to read and write and do sums when Mama died and Roxane had to stay home to take care of Pa.

Besides, she knew what really made the lights glow—magic. Just like magic made it possible for her to slip from Chez Celeste into the Future House and back again.

She was feeling calmer now. It was time to return to where she belonged.

Despite the lights shining beyond the windows, the tower was so dark that she couldn't see the one black rose among the red ones that patterned the wallpaper. But she had touched it so many times that when she stood in the right place, the angle of her arm and the height of her hand told her where it was.

She pressed on the rose and for a moment, no longer than it took to blink an eye, a golden haze shimmered and sparkled in the air. When it cleared, the tower was dark, because no electric lights gleamed outside. The moon was bright, though, letting Roxane see the gables and turrets of nearby roofs. She was back in Chez Celeste.

The Future House had been her retreat, her sanctuary. She wondered if, after tonight, she would ever dare go there again.

She crept down the spiral stairs and felt her way through the storage room, trying not to stumble against all of the obstacles. In the Future House this space was empty; here in Chez Celeste it was filled with crates and trunks. Finally she reached the hall. She was exhausted, wanted nothing more than to sleep for hours and hours. But Lady Celeste would expect her at the breakfast table first thing in the morning. Then would come church, and in the afternoon she'd have to join the other girls in parlor, groomed and perfumed and ready to work her charms on the visiting gentlemen.

Her fingers against the wall guided her down the hall until she felt the second door on the left, the door to her own chamber. She opened it, ready to collapse upon the bed.

She drew back in shock when she saw that a candle was burning on the wash stand and the bed was already occupied.

"Darling Roxane." Thaddeus Burnham rose to his feet and twisted the end of his handlebar mustache. His voice was an iron file rasping her nerves. "I was wondering when you would return."

His shirt was unbuttoned and his feet were in stockings. Roxane saw his polished boots neatly aligned at the foot of the bed. His vest and his swallowtail coat hung on the back of her chair; his top hat and tall stiff collar had been placed on the seat.

"What are you doing here?" she demanded. He had never been in her room before. A gentleman of stature and means, he had always taken his entertainment in the elegance of the Gold Room or Green Room on the second floor.

"I've been pining for your company. You disappeared from Lady Celeste's birthday celebration. I offered her a generous sum as a gift for the occasion, and in gratitude she has permitted me to wait for you here."

"But—it's past midnight. No men are allowed at this hour. You can't—" She stepped back toward the door. But she couldn't run from him. There was nowhere to go.

"Oh, I most assuredly can, my dear Roxane." He grabbed her wrists and pulled her onto the bed.

———◆———

A woman in a dress made of amethysts embraces a tuxedo-clad man. Together they dance on a staircase whose steps are made of songs. It spirals upward and disappears into a silver cloud.

Suddenly the cloud turns black. A storm rages—lightning, thunder, bitter wind.

An abyss opens and the man tumbles in. The gemstones dissolve and the woman, naked and abandoned, weeps until her tears turn to blood.

Claire woke up screaming.

CHAPTER

6

Claire carried her phone and a mug of coffee to the balcony of the apartment she shared with her best friend, Lindsay. Her sleep last night had been haunted and restless. As dawn broke she jolted awake, panicky, gasping for air. The nightmare left behind a sticky residue of pain and fear.

She sank onto one of the wicker chairs and took a deep swallow of the coffee. Stretching out her legs, she rested her bare feet on the railing and waited for caffeine and fresh air to work their magic.

Such a relief to be wearing jeans and a T-shirt after serving time in that torture chamber of a dress. To be sitting outside on a Sunday morning, looking at early-autumn flowers blooming in the sunny courtyard between the apartment buildings, and not prowling through that dark, spooky house.

Beautiful, yes. A historic treasure for sure. But definitely unsettling. That icy front bedroom, the vanishing rocking chair, the whispers when no one was there …

She wished she'd never seen the Amethyst Girl. No one else paid attention to the mysterious young woman on the staircase above the crowd. Yet when Claire locked eyes with her, she fled.

Why had being seen by Claire distressed her? That question had sent Claire upstairs.

Big mistake.

For one thing, she'd annoyed Tess, something she couldn't afford to do. When Claire finally got into the Mercedes and apologized, Tess had nodded but said little. Driving home, she'd seemed preoccupied. Claire worried that her boss was looking for words to break the bad news: now that Claire's trial period was ending, BayCrest Properties no longer needed her services. At Claire's apartment, Tess said good night and drove away. The promised chat still loomed in the future, and Claire dreaded it. She'd invested so much effort and hope in her new career; what would she do if suddenly it was over?

Not only that, she'd probably ruined her chances with Simon. Assuming she'd a chance to begin with. It was silly to weave fantasies from a few friendly words, a couple of smiles, and the promise of a dance someday. But such magical smiles. And those warm gray eyes. Just thinking about him made her heart beat faster. If only she hadn't been such an idiot, getting caught in a part of the mansion where she didn't belong. She'd brought her phone out on the balcony so she wouldn't miss the call he'd promised, but she didn't have much hope.

Worst of all, by chasing the Amethyst Girl upstairs Claire had run into—what, exactly? Josephine, the Burnham family matri-arch? After living in the mansion for more than a century, that ancient lady might well be reluctant to move on to wherever people went when they died. Or did something more sinister lurk in the house, beyond the boundary of most people's perception?

Most people's. Not Claire's. That was the problem.

Sipping more coffee, she watched a pair of sparrows pecking for seeds in the courtyard grass while she considered what to do.

She'd tried to convince herself that nothing had really happened. The creaky old house, the empty and silent upper floors—in a setting like that, anyone's imagination would work overtime. And Claire had been accused often enough of letting hers run wild.

She knew better, though. The signs were all there. The familiar, unwanted pattern was back.

As a small child, Claire would sometimes walk into a building, a room, a garden—and find the air fizzing with energy. Or she'd become aware of something hovering behind her, only to have it vanish when she twisted around to catch it in the act.

Whenever she told her grandmother and sister what had happened, Gram would shush her and Cassandra would laugh. Friends didn't believe her and teachers chided her for making up stories or telling lies. So she learned very young to keep silent and pretend nothing had happened. Gradually she lost the ability to perceive the strangeness.

But not entirely. When the power, whatever it was, couldn't break through to her conscious mind, it grabbed hold of her unconscious and pushed itself out in the form of nightmares. Cassandra, who hated being awakened by Claire's shrieking, called them scream-dreams. Claire considered an occasional bad dream a small price to pay for being normal.

This summer, to her dismay, her waking self's ability to detect strange energies and haunting presences had come creeping back. When she was selling the house on the coast, this dubious talent had saved her from danger, so it wasn't always a negative. She'd even thought that she'd come to accept it. But last night had reminded her that her power carried the potential for trouble, and she longed to be able to shut it off. Old Josephine might be harmless, but suppose next time she encountered something evil?

If only Lindsay were home. Her best friend, levelheaded and practical, was always good for a reality check. Lately, though, Claire usually had the apartment to herself. A few months ago Lindsay had come home raving about a hot stockbroker named

Brad, and now she was investing most of her time in him. She'd spent last night at his apartment. No telling what time today she would reappear. Claire liked Brad and she was happy for Lindsay, but their romance made it harder to ignore her own loneliness.

A little girl ran into the courtyard. The sparrows took flight.

Okay, no reality check. Claire would have to sort out last night's events on her own. Step one—find out more about the house. Picking up her phone, she did an internet search for the Burnham Mansion.

BAPA's website topped the list of results. Someone had already posted photos of last night's fundraiser on the home page. Smack in the middle was a shot of her brother-in-law and Mirabelle Burnham, standing way too close together. He was grinning at the camera; her attention was focused adoringly on him.

Rage, white and hot, flared up, surprising Claire by its intensity. If Peter was cheating on her sister, she was going to kill him.

She'd suffered that same life-wrenching insult from her own husband, Zach. Last year the house of cards that was her marriage had tumbled down around her. It had taken many bruising and painful months to crawl out of the wreckage. She didn't want her sister to go through that kind of devastation.

Maybe she should call Cassandra and—tell her what? She'd seen Peter hand a woman a glass of champagne? The same woman later asked him to dance?

So what? Claire had danced with Peter, too. It meant nothing. Mirabelle was involved in a matter being handled by Peter's law firm. It made sense that they knew each other, that they'd show up at the same event.

Then how to explain the look of alarm on Peter's face when he realized his wife's sister was present? Or the blond flapper's possessive grip on his arm?

Okay, there was a zing of attraction between them, some flirting going on. But beyond that, Claire knew nothing. She certainly had no proof. Why upset her sister, maybe disrupt her marriage, over a vague suspicion?

Claire's stomach tightened as a picture came into her mind: Arriving at a professor's home where a graduation party for Zach's Harvard Law School class was in full swing. Knowing she'd have to work late, she'd told Zach she'd meet him there, but he was nowhere to be seen—until she opened a door on the second floor, mistakenly thinking it was a bathroom.

She'd screamed, and so had the naked woman in the bed with Zach. He scrambled to his feet, grabbed his pants, and ran after Claire as she fled from the house.

Later he tried to convince her it was a drunken mistake, a one-time error in judgment. But soon she discovered he and Little Ms. Law School had been sleeping together for six months.

If only someone had given her a heads-up early on. Maybe she could have salvaged her marriage. Or spared herself from, if not pain, at least a large measure of shock and humiliation.

Forewarned is forearmed, Gram always told her grand-daughters. *Knowledge is power.*

She found Cassandra's number on the phone's contacts list. The two of them were cordial but they'd never been close. Her sister would be surprised to get an out-of-the-blue call. How would she react if Claire said, *I think Peter may be cheating on you?*

In her head Claire heard Cassandra's snotty teenage voice: *Mind your own beeswax.*

Good advice—maybe. But maybe not. She'd call her sister and see where the conversation led.

CHAPTER

7

The fragrance of coffee and bacon greeted Roxane as she came into the dining room. The four other girls were already gathered around the large oval table with its crisp white cloth, in the midst of eating their breakfast. Lady Celeste sat at the head of the table, presiding over the meal. Roxane slipped into her chair and stared at her silverware, trying to escape being noticed.

Of course the effort was for naught.

"Ma chère Roxane," Lady Celeste purred, her tone a perfect blend of honey and vinegar. "How lovely that you could join us this morning."

Aurélie and Fleur put their hands to their mouths to hide their titters. Véronique gave a derisive snort. Only Yvette, the sole one amongst them whom Roxane considered to have good sense and a level head, kept a sympathetic silence.

The heat of Lady Celeste's intense blue eyes burned Roxane's cheeks. She ventured a quick look at the ormolu clock on the sideboard. Ten minutes past eight o'clock, the appointed breakfast hour. "Good morning, Lady Celeste. I'm sorry I'm late to the table."

Lady Celeste did not release her gaze. She was wearing a daytime dress in her favorite color, which she called celestial blue. The hue brightened her eyes and flattered her upswept blond curls, just as the rosettes on the bodice enhanced her bosom. Lady

Celeste was a small woman—petite, she called herself, liking to show off by using French words whenever possible. But she was as formidable as any man Roxane had encountered.

"We'd hoped for the pleasure of your company at our soirée last evening."

It was bad enough that Roxane had disappeared from the party, but last night had been a special occasion—a celebration of Lady Celeste's birthday. She was coy about her age, but Roxane guessed her to be twenty-five or twenty-six.

"Yes, where did you go?" Fleur asked. "You missed out on the cake."

"Thaddeus Burnham looked for you everywhere," Aurélie added with a giggle.

Véronique tossed back her lustrous black hair. "Don't worry, Roxane. I kept him from becoming too lonely in your absence."

Roxane gave Véronique a dark scowl, then cast her eyes down and kept her tone demure. There would be no advantage to mentioning her shock at returning to her chamber after midnight and finding Thaddeus in her bed. "I regret having to depart early last night. I was feeling … indisposed."

After a tense moment a smile touched Lady Celeste's lips. Roxane took this as a signal that her apology was accepted.

"Bid a proper good morning to Roxane, mes filles," Lady Celeste commanded. Roxane disliked the way she always referred to them as *my* girls, as if she owned them.

"Bonjour, Roxane," the four voices chorused.

"No, no, Fleur, it's not *bonjer*. Say *bon-zhou-our*. Draw it out. When you reach the end of the word, your lips should be pursed, as if you are offering a kiss to your favorite gentleman. Now try again—bonjour, Roxane."

Fleur squeezed her eyes shut and knotted her fingers in her bright red curls. "Bon-joo, Roxane."

Lady Celeste sighed. Roxane expected her to correct Fleur again, but she said, "Très bien. Very good. Better than before at any rate. Now, Roxane, your reply?"

Roxane was fighting not to yawn. She didn't dare commit such a breach of etiquette at the table. After her sleepless and difficult night, this attention was the last thing she needed. The wretched Thaddeus had refused to depart from her bed until dawn. When he left her at last, she'd tried to slumber, but her eyes had refused to close. Now they wanted to do nothing else.

Lady Celeste tapped the end of her silver teaspoon against the table. "Your reply, Roxane," she said in a sterner voice.

Roxane finally managed to come up with the words. "Uh, bonjour, tout le monde. Good morning, everyone."

She was too exhausted to muster the wit it took to shine when Lady Celeste decided to drill her girls on French vocabulary. None of them was French, not even Lady Celeste herself. But she was convinced that the French culture and language represented the epitome of class and elegance, and that was exactly the high tone she wished to create for Chez Celeste. French girls were in great demand and commanded the highest prices. So all of her *jeunes filles,* her young ladies, were expected to convince the gentlemen who sought their favors that they'd come to San Francisco straight from Paris.

Nodding her approval of Roxane's response, Lady Celeste picked up a small brass bell by her plate and rang it. Louise, the housekeeper, bustled out from the kitchen carrying a silver tray. Roxane thought it ridiculous that Louise had been given a French name like the rest of them. One look at her shining black skin and anyone could tell she wasn't French.

"Here you go, mademoiselle." Louise set Roxane's breakfast in front of her. On the gold-rimmed plate were a rasher of bacon, a thick slice of bread, and an egg sitting upright in a delicate porcelain cup. "I'll pour you some coffee and you'll be all set."

Roxane had no appetite, but she dutifully picked up her spoon and tapped the eggshell open. Some of the yellow yolk seeped out. The cracked shell and oozing liquid made her think of the man lying dead in the storage room of the Future House, his head broken and bleeding. She had no idea who he was, but his death saddened her.

Too bad the dead man wasn't Thaddeus Burnham.

But Thaddeus belonged to the present—right now, in 1896. This morning, before coming downstairs, Roxane had tiptoed into Chez Celeste's storage room and was relieved, though not surprised, to see no body there. So long as she didn't visit the Future House again, it would be as though the dreadful murder had never happened. All she had to do was blank the violent deed from her thoughts and memory. But every time she closed her eyes, the awful sight of the dead man floated in front of her.

When Louise returned to the kitchen, Lady Celeste clapped her hands to turn everyone's eyes to her. "Mes filles, let me have your attention. We are expecting a visit today from a very special gentleman—Mr. Isaac Burnham."

Oh, God, no, Roxane thought. Not another one. Two Burnhams were two too many.

Lady Celeste continued, "Isaac Burnham is the father of Thaddeus Burnham, with whom some of you are acquainted. The elder Mr. Burnham has been living away from San Francisco for the past half dozen years, but his son informed me yesterday evening that he has returned and has a particular interest in seeing this house. When he arrives, you must treat him with extra kindness. Should he take a fancy to any of you, I expect you to be especially gracious."

"Why does he merit such generous treatment?" Véronique asked, her tone bordering on the insolent. She was older than the others, and a favorite among certain gentlemen who were drawn to such attributes as raven hair, sultry eyes, and an overbearing manner. If only Thaddeus Burnham were one of them, Roxane thought. Then he might leave her alone.

"Because it is thanks to Isaac Burnham that I own Chez Celeste."

Fleur's eyes widened. "He bought it for you? What a bighearted gift. He must've truly loved you." She was the youngest of the *jeunes filles,* a good-natured girl if a little silly.

Lady Celeste laughed. "Not at all. I earned this house, every board and shingle."

"How did you do that?" Yvette asked.

"It must have cost so much money," said Aurélie, adding, "Beaucoup d'argent," just to show off.

The girls all leaned forward in rapt attention, even Roxane. Here was a story she'd never heard. Lady Celeste kept quiet about the life she'd led before opening one of San Francisco's best parlor houses. Roxane often wondered how she'd come to be the mistress of such a grand mansion, but she'd never felt it proper to inquire. She simply counted her blessings that Lady Celeste had rescued her from a rude cribhouse in the Barbary Coast and given her the chance to live and work in these luxurious surroundings.

Lady Celeste smoothed back a golden ringlet that had strayed from its place. She smiled at her audience, enjoying, as always, being at the center of everyone's interest.

Roxane raised her coffee cup to her lips and drank. Normally she would stir in sugar and cream, but this morning she preferred to taste the dark, bitter brew and feel it coursing through her veins.

"It was a stormy night in the winter of 1890, six years ago," Lady Celeste began. "I was much younger then—"

Véronique interrupted. "Six years younger, in fact."

Fleur counted it out on her fingers. "That's right."

Lady Celeste paid them no heed. "A gentleman friend had escorted me to the Old Poodle Dog for dinner. It is, as you know, the finest French restaurant in the city. We dined in one of the private rooms upstairs. I expected to finish the evening in his amatory embrace—those rooms are comfortably appointed for that activity."

"Amatory—is that a French word?" Aurélie asked with a puzzled frown.

Yvette responded, "Think of amour, meaning love. It comes from the same Latin root."

Lady Celeste nodded approvingly. "So it does. But to my surprise, amour was not on the schedule. When we completed our meal, several other gentlemen arrived bearing decks of cards. It turned out that my escort's lust for gambling was even greater than his lust for women, which I knew to be considerable."

"Are we acquainted with this gentleman, Lady Celeste?" Roxane asked. It could be handy to know who might yield to the temptation of a wager.

Lady Celeste waved away the inquiry with a graceful hand. "Who he was doesn't matter. What's important is that he and his friends were among the city's wealthiest and most prominent citizens. They played cards for hours, while I watched—hand after hand of poker, winning and losing great amounts of money, and drinking great quantities of whiskey."

"Why did you stay, if your friend didn't require your services?" Véronique demanded. "I would have left immediately."

"The rain and wind were fierce, and I had no better place to go," Lady Celeste explained. "Besides, the gentlemen were quite entertaining. And educational, too. I learned a great deal that night. Finally, as the storm ended and the sky began to lighten, I asked to join the game."

"What! You gambled with cards? But you're a woman." Little Fleur appeared shocked at this breach of propriety.

Lady Celeste looked amused. "So I am. But the circumstances made me bold. You see, the gentlemen forgot about me as their game grew intense. Sitting off to the side, I was able to assess their strong points and weaknesses. I studied their faces until I could tell when they were bluffing and when they were hiding a good hand."

"What does all this have to do with Isaac Burnham?" Véronique asked.

"Ah, yes. That brings me to the climax of my story. Mr. Burnham was the best of the players, the biggest winner by far. By dawn he'd driven several of the men from the game without a cent in their pockets. But he was still eager to play, so I gave him the opportunity."

Louise returned with the tall silver coffee pot and refilled everyone's cup. Lady Celeste took a dainty sip before she continued.

"I had little money with me, so my first wager was a promise of hours that the winner of the hand could spend in my company. The other players eagerly raised the stakes. I won that pot and used the cash to stake me for the next hand. I won again, and then again, until I had amassed a veritable fortune and most of the men had passed out drunk. Mr. Burnham was quite inebriated, too, and his pride was wounded at losing to a woman. He had no cash left in his wallet, so he placed a string of purple jewels on the table—in fact, the same necklace that I let Mademoiselle Roxane wear last night—and bet it against all of my winnings."

"You took the bet," Véronique said, a glint of avarice in her eye. "That must mean it's very valuable."

"Why was Roxane the one who got to wear it?" Aurélie pouted, twisting one of her sausage curls.

"Because it was becoming with the color of her gown," Yvette explained.

"I'm grateful for the honor, Lady Celeste," Roxane said quickly.

"So you won the necklace," Fleur prompted. "What happened next?"

Lady Celeste smiled with the memory. "By then I'd won everything of value in the room. Mr. Burnham left, bidding me to wait there at the Old Poodle Dog until he returned."

"And you did that, in a room full of drunken men? How foolish." Véronique didn't bother to hide her derision. "I would have grabbed the money and run."

"The cash was tempting," Lady Celeste admitted. "But Mr. Burnham intrigued me. I thought I might do better to wait. He went to his bank, which was just opening for the day, and returned with the deed to this house. He'd had it built for his family, but his wife died before they could move in. When he offered to wager the house against my winnings, I figured, why not? No matter what happened, I wouldn't leave the Old Poodle Dog with less than I'd brought in."

She grinned wickedly as she added, "We dealt the cards and played the hand. He was confident in his full house, three kings and two queens. What could beat it? Imagine his surprise when I revealed my cards. All I had were deuces. But there were four of them."

Fleur clapped her hands. "Hurray! You beat him fair and square."

"Ah, ma belle Fleur, my beautiful flower. Did I say anything about playing fair?"

Louise entered the dining room once more, this time without a tray. "My lady," she said, "it's time to leave for church."

"Merci, Louise." Lady Celeste patted her lips with her lace-edged napkin and stood, clapping her hands for attention. "Let's go, mes filles."

The *jeunes filles* hastened to drink the last of their coffee and scramble to their feet. Roxane remained in her chair.

"Beg pardon, Lady Celeste," she said, "but I'm still unwell. May I be excused from church today?"

The others turned to stare at her, eyes wide at her audacity. Lady Celeste required them to attend church faithfully every Sunday, in an attempt to establish their good reputation in the minds of her neighbors. She'd taken great care to spread the fiction that she was the landlady of a boardinghouse for girls from respectable families. Such living arrangements would have once been unthinkable, but hard times had beset the country. More and more women from small towns were responding to economic necessity by coming to big cities to find work. Roxane hoped their luck was better than her own.

Lady Celeste took her time to consider Roxane's request. "All right. You may skip church this once. You do look peaked, so please get some rest. I expect you—all of you—to be in the front parlor at three o'clock, when Louise will place the potted palm in the bay window to signal that we are ready to receive visitors. Including our special guests."

Roxane stood. "Thank you, Lady Celeste. Will you permit me another question? How did Isaac Burnham earn the fortune to build this house?"

Lady Celeste gave the matter thought while Louise adjusted a blue cloak around her shoulders. "Hmm, I don't rightly know. I've heard talk about speculation in silver, and even smuggling. And he's rumored to be a magician, though I can't imagine how one would earn money by performing parlor stunts."

"Oh, I love magic tricks," Fleur said. "Can he pull a rabbit from a hat?"

Lady Celeste patted Fleur's red curls. "Perhaps he can show you. Be assured, Isaac Burnham is a wealthy and interesting man." Her voice lingered over his name, as though she were tasting sugar. "We'll want to give him a warm welcome. His son also, and the friend who will accompany them."

Roxane's stomach clenched. "Thaddeus is coming too? He was just here last night."

"That's true," Lady Celeste agreed. "But of course we put no limits on how often a gentleman may visit us. We're always happy to have Thaddeus here."

"Of course." Roxane wiped her eyes, hoping no one would notice the tears glistening there.

A magician. Perhaps she should make a friend of Isaac Burnham. Wouldn't it be wonderful if he had the skill to make Thaddeus disappear.

8

Claire scrolled to her sister's phone number. Before she could make the call, she was startled to hear the door sliding open. Lindsay stepped onto the balcony, mug in hand.

Claire's mood instantly brightened. Maybe she'd get her reality check after all.

"Good morning!" Lindsay raised the mug in a salute. "Thanks for making coffee."

"You're welcome. What brings you here?"

Lindsay laughed. "I live here, remember?"

"Just barely," Claire teased.

"It's such a beautiful day, Brad and I decided to hike up Mount Tam with a picnic. We popped in to pick up my daypack."

"Speak of the devil," Claire said as Brad came through the door. He and Lindsay made a handsome pair, both of them tall and athletic, Brad's dark hair complementing Lindsay's reddish tresses.

"Hey, Claire." Brad slid the door shut. "Who's that passed out on the sofa—Scarlett O'Hara?"

Claire laughed. The knotted tension inside her began to ease. "Just her dress. You can't imagine what a project it was to get out of that thing last night."

"I'll take it back tomorrow," Lindsay said. She and Claire had been theater majors, but while Claire had let that interest go dormant, Lindsay kept her hand in by designing sets for a community theater group. She had arranged for Claire and Tess to borrow their dresses from the costume department.

"I have to get it dry cleaned and mended first."

"Mended? Uh-oh. Is it damaged? What happened?"

"Rhett Butler came along and tried to rip it off you," Brad guessed. "Look, I'm right, you're blushing."

"Who was it? 'Fess up," Lindsay said.

"No one." Claire brushed aside the X-rated image of Simon Thatcher that had popped into her mind. "Don't worry about the dress. The train just has a minor stain and a tiny tear. I had trouble keeping it out from under people's feet."

"Aside from getting stepped on, how did the big bash go?"

Claire entertained them with tales of music and lemon tarts and George's ridiculous effort to play Prince Charming. She kept her account light, bringing up only one of her unsettling experiences in the Burnham Mansion. "You know what was odd? A girl there was wearing my necklace."

"Your strand of lucky amethysts? I thought you were going to wear it yourself."

"I did. I mean hers was similar to mine. The strange thing was, when I tried to ask her about it she ran away, as if I frightened her."

"It wasn't you," Brad said. "She was scared of that dress."

"You're probably right." Talking about the necklace gave Claire an idea, a way to explain to Cassandra why she was calling.

Brad turned to Lindsay. "We'd better get started, hon. Miles to go and all that. And we still have to stop at the market for picnic food."

"I'll go grab my daypack. Hey, Claire, why don't you come along?"

"Wish I could. But I'm handling an open house this

afternoon." She loved the real estate business, but working on Sundays was one of the downsides.

"You got a new listing? Yay!" Lindsay offered a high-five. "Congratulations!"

Claire shook her head. "I'm doing a favor for one of the agents in my office."

"Not George, I hope."

"No—Jeff, the nice one."

"Good luck. Wish you could join us." Turning toward the door, Lindsay added, "Don't wait up."

"Have a good time."

Brad winked. "Oh, don't worry about that."

———◆———

Chez Celeste was blissfully quiet as Roxane went upstairs. She intended to follow Lady Celeste's instructions and take a nap. She sorely needed some rest after her tribulations of the night before.

Though she dared not try it often, she was grateful whenever she found a reason to be excused from church. God had lost favor with her on a winter night six years ago. Her mother fell ill with childbed fever after giving birth to a second daughter. Twelve-year-old Roxane had prayed through the dark hours until morning, begging God to make her mother well. She tried to seal the bargain with promises of good behavior and perpetual devotion. But as the sunrise cast a pinkish glow over the snowy fields outside, Mama breathed her final breath. Soon afterward the newborn child followed her to heaven—to keep Mama company, Pa explained. Roxane, though Roxane had not been her name then, had refused to be comforted. If God was truly loving and merciful, why would He take Mama away? Why would He leave her alone with a father who cared for her only as a target for lashes from his belt? Then she began to blossom into womanhood, and Pa found another use for her. That's when God abandoned her altogether.

Arriving on the third floor, she started toward her chamber. Instead, her feet carried her into the storage room, as if of their own will. Gathering her wide skirt close to her legs, she picked her way along the narrow aisles between trunks and boxes and dusty old furniture, until she reached the spiral steps that curved up into the tower.

There she hesitated. Upon leaving the Future House last night, she'd sworn she would never return. But now, though ashamed to harbor such a macabre desire, she felt compelled to look at the man who had died. She needed to assure herself that there was nothing she could have done to prevent his death, no way she could have helped him.

"What are you doing in there, Roxane?"

The high, girlish voice made Roxane jump. She turned and saw little Fleur standing in the storage room doorway.

"Fleur! You gave me such a start."

Fleur cast her gaze down at her black buttoned shoes. "I'm sorry. I didn't mean to."

"That's all right." In Roxane's opinion, Fleur was always too quick to offer an apology, even when she was not at fault. She was perhaps the sweetest of Lady Celeste's *jeunes filles,* but she seemed to have little sense and less gumption. The only fire the girl possessed was the flame-red color of her curly hair. Her skin was pale, except for the freckles dusted across her nose, and she looked as delicate as a flower. That was probably why Lady Celeste had named her Fleur. "I thought you went to church with the others."

"We're about to leave, but I forgot my hat. I came up to get it." Fleur turned her straw hat round and round in her hands, which set its ribbons twirling. She showed no sign of moving on.

"What are you doing?" she repeated.

"I'm, uh, looking for something." Roxane hoped Fleur wouldn't inquire about the object of her search.

But of course she did. "Looking for what?"

Why wouldn't the annoying girl go away?

Glancing about, Roxane spotted a bookcase filled with dusty leather-bound tomes.

"A book. It was a gift from my mother. It's in a trunk here somewhere with the rest of my belongings." Why had she made up such a lie? She had no trunk and few belongings. When she arrived at Chez Celeste she owned little more than the rags she'd been wearing. Her only memento of Mama was a cheap heart-shaped locket containing a faded photograph of a thin, haggard woman with wispy hair.

Fleur's eyes grew wide. "A book! Do you mean you can read?"

"A little bit," Roxane said. "Not as well as I'd like."

"I never learnt." Fleur sounded wistful. "Could you teach me sometime?"

"Yes, certainly, sometime," Roxane agreed. Anything to get rid of the girl. "Fleur, are you going to church or not? Lady Celeste doesn't like to be kept waiting."

"Ooh, I'd better run. I don't want to make her mad." Fleur whirled away. A moment later Roxane heard her footsteps clattering down the stairs.

Roxane watched from the window until she saw Fleur run out of the house and join the others in the waiting carriage. The driver snapped his whip and the pair of horses pulled the conveyance away from the house. Roxane waited, listening. The house should be truly empty now, but she didn't want someone else to surprise her.

Nothing stirred. She climbed the spiral stairs.

By the time she reached the top she was out of breath and her body was trembling. Maybe she would just stay in the tower for a few minutes. From here she could glimpse the bay. A tall-masted ship was heading toward the Golden Gate, and Roxane wished she were on board, sailing toward some exotic destination. China, perhaps, or Paris. Someday, she thought. Someday I'll find a way to have a grand adventure.

She yawned. Best go to her chamber and sleep. Soon enough the gentlemen would arrive and she'd have to be lively and cheerful. As she started down the stairs, she placed a hand on the wall to brace herself, careful to avoid the black rose imprinted in the wallpaper.

Her fingers twitched. Her hand inched toward the black rose, until she couldn't resist pressing it.

The air began to glow, as if sunlight from the windows had turned floating dust motes into stars. The sparkling particles swirled down the stairs, opening the way into the Future House.

Roxane crept forward, afraid of what awaited her yet impelled to go on.

———◆———

A rank odor greeted her nostrils when she reached the Future House. It conjured a memory of slaughter days on Pa's farm, when he would butcher a pig or two in the hope that the meat would last the family through the winter.

To her surprise, tears stung her eyes at the thought of the farm. Surely she wasn't grieving for the pigs. She'd eaten the salt pork and bacon without one bit of regret for the animals' fate. Butchering was a necessary and natural part of the order of things.

No, what made her sad was thinking of Mama when she had no desire to do so. Her mother was gone—nothing Roxane could do would change that. As Pa had told her repeatedly, there warn't no use wailin' about it.

She wiped the tears with her sleeve and looked around the vast, bare storage room.

Roxane had hoped the murder would prove to be an illusion or nightmare, something that happened only in her head. But no—there was the body, the sole object in the room. Although object seemed a cruel word to describe what had once been a living person.

The dead man was crumpled on the floor beneath the front window, his limbs sticking out at awkward angles. He looked like he'd been a proper gentleman. His black shoes were polished to a high shine, and he was wearing one of the newly fashionable tuxedo dinner suits favored by certain of Chez Celeste's visitors. The whiteness of his ruffled shirt was ruined by rust-colored patches of dried blood. More blood matted his fair hair. A pair of eyeglasses lay near the body, one of its lenses broken.

Her stomach churned, making her wish she hadn't eaten her breakfast. It wasn't that she'd never seen a dead person. Her mother, her father, her newborn sister—she had witnessed them all in their final repose, and wept for them, though her tears for Pa had been scanty. She had been sitting with Granny Jo in her bedroom when the old lady took her last breath. This man was a stranger; Roxane had no reason to mourn him. Yet she felt strangely affected by his death.

The killer, whoever it was, had attacked her first. This man had died a hero, trying to protect her. She wished she knew his name.

She'd never seen him before last night. In fact she'd never seen any man in the Future House. It was a house of women—Granny Jo and the nurses who cared for her and the granddaughter who visited. Granny Jo had spoken of grandsons, too, but they'd never come to see her when Roxane was present.

She sank to her knees beside the body. She didn't believe God would listen, but it would do no harm to offer a prayer for the man, whoever he was.

"How terrible to have such a brutal act take place in this house."

Not God's voice, but her friend Granny Jo's. Sometimes when Roxane visited the Future House, she heard the old lady speak, even though Granny Jo was now in her grave. The first time it happened she'd been frightened, but she'd come to look forward to hearing the whispered words.

"Yes, terrible," Roxane said aloud. "It makes me so sad. I wish you were here, Granny Jo."

"Why do you believe I'm not?"

She could think of no reply.

"Look there. By his hand. What do you see?"

Roxane looked where she was directed, and spotted something small and shiny on the floor by the man's outstretched fingers. She crawled over and picked it up.

A pearl. Rather, a small pearl-like button, the size of the buttons on the dead man's shirt. But his were black.

This one must have come from the killer's shirt.

As her hand closed around it, the tears that had been threatening started to spill. Roxane turned and ran up the spiral stairs. She pushed her fist against the black rose so she could go back home.

No, not home. Chez Celeste wasn't any sort of home. It had been a long time since she'd felt at home anywhere. She wondered if she'd know that feeling of comfort and belonging ever again.

CHAPTER

9

Ellie's coffee was cold. Getting off her sofa to pour another cup felt like too much effort, but sitting here and moping about Peter wouldn't do any good. She went into the kitchen, grabbing the empty champagne bottle from the coffee table on the way. She tossed the bottle into her recycling bin. It landed with a crash.

The perfect sound to go with how she was feeling.

Last night had begun with such promise. When Peter finally arrived at her apartment, they popped open the champagne to celebrate their first full night together. As they drank it, he kissed away all her concerns. In her bedroom, too eager to bother with sliding between the sheets, they made love on top of Granny Jo's coverlet. Peter had never been more intense and passionate. He even whispered, "I love you"—the first time he'd spoken the words she'd longed to hear. Ellie fell into a fevered sleep, warmed by the heat of his body, drunk with wine and joy.

A few hours later she woke up shivering. Peter was gone.

She sat up in a panic.

There he was—standing naked by the window, silhouetted by the glow of city lights.

"Darling? Are you all right?" she asked. The room felt unbearably cold.

"What?" As if coming out of a trance, he turned to face her. "I, uh—I'm fine."

"Come back to bed. Please?" She hated her begging tone.

He did, and they made love again, but couldn't rekindle that blazing heat. Peter went through the right motions, but he seemed preoccupied. His attention wasn't on Ellie but on something deep in his inner world.

Claire. He had to be thinking about Claire.

Eventually he fell asleep, but Ellie's eyes wouldn't close. What was going on? It was as if she'd been with two different men in the same night.

Which one was the real Peter?

In the morning his strange mood was gone. He wrapped his arms around her and pulled her on top of him. "Ah, sweet Ellie," he murmured into the tender spot at the base of her throat. "I love waking up with you." His kiss was as fervent as she could ever hope for.

Later, while she fixed coffee, she tried to probe gently about what had happened during the night. He brushed aside her questions with a joke and a wave of his hand.

He gulped his coffee and set down the empty mug. "I wish I could stay, sweetheart. But there's a ton of work I need to do before tomorrow."

"On Sunday? I was hoping—"

"So was I. But tomorrow's the deadline for filing a motion on a big case. See you soon, I promise." He bent to kiss her. "Hey, why the sad look?"

"I … oh, it's nothing. Call me tonight, okay?" Claire's name was on the tip of her tongue but she couldn't bring herself to say it out loud, to ask Peter about her. She was too afraid of the answer.

After he left, the thought of Claire festered in her brain, like a splinter too deep in her skin to pull out. And as with a splinter, she couldn't resist touching the painful spot over and over.

If she couldn't make herself ask Peter what was going on, maybe the way to stop the hurt was to go to Claire directly.

Claire worked at BayCrest Properties with Tess from the BAPA board—that's all Ellie knew. Well, it was a place to start. Real estate companies were open on Sunday. She got out her phone and found BayCrest's number.

Coming down Chez Celeste's front steps, Roxane settled her flower-adorned chip hat atop her head and patted her neat twist of pinned-up hair. She'd tried to nap, but had only tossed and turned on her narrow bed. Her mind was tormented by the murdered stranger in the Future House. Whether her eyes were open or shut, all she could see was blood.

The breeze was warm and the sky was blue. Roxane unbuttoned the cuffs of her leg-o'-mutton sleeves and pushed them up so she could savor the sun's touch on a bit of bare skin. The summer had been foggy and cold, weather that Roxane wasn't accustomed to at that season. She relished any chance to get the chill out of her bones, as Mama would have put it, though Roxane feared that the chill she felt today was too deep for the sun to reach.

As she walked down Octavia Street, gazing at the splendid houses, she reminded herself to be grateful for living amidst such magnificence. Chez Celeste was grander than many of its neighbors, but the simplest house in this neighborhood was a palace compared to anyplace Roxane had lived before. The farmhouse in Missouri had been small, plain and bare, while the Barbary Coast cribhouses where she'd landed when she arrived in San Francisco were too sordid to bear thinking about. When Lady Celeste took her in, she might well have saved Roxane's life.

It saddened her to know that one day all of these lovely houses except Chez Celeste would disappear. Their porches and gables and towers would vanish, to be replaced by the ugly flat-faced boxes that surrounded the Future House.

"Good morning, miss." A lady strolling by broke into Roxane's dark thoughts. The gentleman beside her tipped his hat.

She made a polite reply and exchanged similar greetings with other passersby. Some of them gave her stern looks because she was a young woman out walking unescorted. But Roxane looked as respectable as any of them. Lady Celeste made sure her *jeunes filles* had the attire and comportment to fit in with the best of society. She took care to keep the neighbors oblivious to the true nature of her establishment, although certain of the gentlemen were well aware of the services to be obtained at Chez Celeste.

Roxane crossed Sacramento Street and entered Lafayette Park. A green expanse that occupied four blocks, this was her favorite place in San Francisco. The land sloped upward on all sides. At the top stood a large house screened by trees, owned by an old codger who claimed the land. The city fathers were suing to get rid of him, contending he was squatting on civic property. Because the place was officially designated as a park, Roxane felt little compunction about climbing the hill to take in the views.

From the summit, she saw a cable car traveling west along Sacramento Street. At the end of the line the passengers would transfer to a steam train that would carry them to see two amazing attractions at the edge of the ocean—the brand-new Sutro Baths with its seven swimming pools and the Cliff House, newly reopened after being destroyed by a fire. It had been rebuilt as a glorious gingerbread chateau, or so Roxane had heard. She'd never been to either place, but a gentleman who patronized Chez Celeste had told her about their wonders. Would a trip to see them constitute a grand adventure?

Finding a patch of soft grass, she sat, spreading her skirt around her. Soon her fatigue overtook her, and she couldn't resist lying down. No doubt a proper young lady would never yield to the temptation to nap on the grass, but sometimes, Roxane thought as her eyes closed, maintaining the illusion of propriety took more effort than it was worth.

CHAPTER

10

Claire carried the velvet box to the balcony. Talking with Lindsay and Brad about her necklace had given her an idea—an excuse for calling Cassandra.

She took out the string of amethyst beads and held it against the sky. So beautiful. The crystals sparkled in the sunlight. The center stone was shaped like a teardrop that she thought of as a tear of joy.

Or a drop of blood.

No. She refused to let an image from her nightmare spoil her cherished necklace. Putting it on for good luck, she settled into the wicker chair and punched in her sister's number. If Peter came up in the conversation, well, she'd figure out what to say.

"Oh. Claire. What can I do for you?" Cassandra's voice sounded tense.

"Is this a bad time?"

"No, no, it's fine. I'm just—Willow, I told you, don't do that."

Claire heard laughter and shrieks in the background. What was her seven-year-old niece up to?

Cassandra's voice rose. "Outside, you two. Right now. Go." Then quieted again. "Sorry, Claire. Willow has a friend over and they're driving me crazy."

"I can call back later."

"Actually, it's good to hear a grownup voice." Cassandra sighed. "How's everything? We haven't talked in a while."

That was true, now that Claire thought about it. "Fine. No big excitement to report, but no complaints either."

"Still seeing that guy you met when you sold the house?"

"Ben? No, he moved to Boston last month. That's where he was from originally. He's the guardian of a little girl who recently lost her family and he thought she'd do better in a new environment."

"He didn't invite you to go with him?"

"I didn't really give him a chance. I spent five years with Zach in the Boston area. The place doesn't hold good memories."

"No, I guess not, after what Zach did to you. And you're probably smart not to tie yourself down to another man so soon. You're building a good life here, a good job, lots of freedom." Did Cassandra sound wistful?

"Actually, I met someone—" Claire broke off. She didn't know Simon; foolish to use him as a blank slate on which to sketch romantic fantasies.

"You have a new boyfriend?"

"It's nothing. I called with a question. Do you remember my amethyst necklace, the one that was Mom's?"

"What about it?"

"I wore it to a party last night and saw a girl with a similar one. It made me wonder about the story behind mine. Where Mom got it and when. I thought you might know."

"I barely remember Mom, you know that. I didn't know that necklace existed until Gram gave it to you." Now her voice held a tinge of resentment, or was it jealousy?

"Okay, it was a long shot. Just thought I'd ask."

"Hold on, Claire. I hear Peter arriving. About time he got home. Let me chase him into the backyard to keep an eye on those little hellions."

"Peter? Arriving from where?"

"Oh, he had to go to some stupid client thing last night. Can you believe their nerve, scheduling a business event on a weekend? It ran really late, so instead of making the long drive home, he stayed over in the apartment his firm keeps in the city. But I thought he'd get here before now."

Claire had a sinking feeling she knew where Peter had spent the night. But this was obviously the wrong time to share her suspicions. "Well, I'd better let you go, Cassandra."

"I'm glad you called. When you moved back to California, I was looking forward to keeping in closer touch. But we're both so busy—say, why don't you come over for dinner?"

"I'd love to. When?"

"I'm checking my calendar now. We're booked next weekend, and the one after that. Tell you what, let's seize the moment. Can you come tomorrow night?"

"Tomorrow? That would be great. I'll see you then."

When they'd said their goodbyes, Claire stood at the balcony railing, staring at the courtyard. In her mind's eye, she saw her brother-in-law and Mirabelle Burnham dancing across the sunny lawn.

She hoped that tomorrow she could look Cassandra in the eye.

———•———

A ruffle of breeze across Roxane's face woke her. Shivering, she reached to pull up her blanket, then realized she wasn't in her bed. The sun had shifted, and her resting place was deep in the shade cast by the old codger's trees.

What time was it? Roxane jerked upright. Long shadows suggested the day was growing late. Dear heaven, could it be after three o'clock? Lady Celeste would be displeased if Roxane wasn't present and presentable when the house opened to gentlemen. Especially today, with Thaddeus Burnham's father arriving as an honored guest.

If only Thaddeus weren't coming with him.

She scrambled to her feet and brushed off her skirt. The grass had made green stains on the fabric. Neither Lady Celeste nor Louise, who did the laundry, would be happy about that.

She dashed down the hill, not caring if running was unseemly behavior. Pins fell from her hair, sending wisps flying around her face. When she reached Sacramento Street, she realized she'd left her hat behind and lost precious minutes retrieving it.

Roxane's breath was puffing and her legs aching by the time she drew close to Chez Celeste. She saw with dismay that the Boston fern in its brass pot was in place on the table in the parlor's window bay. Behind it, the velvet curtains were drawn tight to hide the room from the neighbors' curious eyes. Gentlemen who knew the code would understand that the parlor house was now open for business.

Lady Celeste was going to have her hide for dinner.

Rushing toward the house, she nearly collided with two women approaching from the other direction.

"Oh! I beg your pardon, good ladies."

"You should watch where you're going, miss," scolded one, a middle-aged dowager. Her younger companion nodded in agreement.

From their fashionable attire, Roxane guessed they were women of means. The older lady displayed jeweled buttons on a gray dress that matched her coils of hair. The younger one wore a short blue cape and carried a parasol to protect her pale skin.

"You're entirely right, madam. Again, I ask your pardon." Roxane waited for them to stroll on so she could go inside.

"May I inquire, miss," said the gray-haired lady, "whether you reside in this house?"

Oh dear. How should she respond? "Why do you wish to know where I live?"

"I've been told this is a boardinghouse for respectable young ladies. Is that correct?"

"Yes indeed," Roxane replied.

"And I understand that some of those young ladies might be amenable to finding employment if a suitable situation were to arise."

"You are correct again, madam."

"If you please, I am Mrs. Sedgwick." The woman paused as if expecting Roxane to recognize the name.

Roxane did not, for which she was grateful. As far as she knew, Mr. Sedgwick was not a patron of Chez Celeste. She'd never had to deal with meeting any of the gentlemen's wives, although she knew quite a few were married.

Mrs. Sedgwick added, "And this is my daughter, Mrs. Bisbee."

The younger woman dipped her parasol. "Hello."

Another unfamiliar name. Roxane decided a smile would be fitting. "I'm pleased to make your acquaintance."

Mrs. Sedgwick said, "My house is in the next block, the large yellow one—"

"Oh, that's a lovely house."

"My daughter and her husband and babies live with me. Mrs. Bisbee joins me in doing good works around the city, and we'd like to find a proper girl to mind the house and the children while we are away. The girl would receive room and board, of course, in addition to her wages. Do you suppose any of the residents here would be interested in such a position?"

"If you wish, I'll be happy to let them know of the opportunity."

"That would be appreciated. I had thought to simply knock on the door and inquire—"

"Oh, no need for that," Roxane said hastily. She could imagine Lady Celeste's reaction if the good women of the neighborhood came calling. "Let me tell the girls. If one of them is interested in such employment, may she call upon you?"

"Yes, indeed. Here is my card." Mrs. Sedgwick handed Roxane a calling card. The heavy ivory-colored paper was neatly engraved with a name: MRS. JULIUS SEDGWICK.

"And here is mine." The daughter handed her a similar card, though the paper was whiter. MRS. LEANDER BISBEE. "It's a pleasure to meet you meet you, Miss—I'm sorry, what did you say your name is?"

"I'm Millicent. Millicent Brown."

"Good afternoon, Miss Brown," Mrs. Sedgwick said. "Thank you for your help."

Roxane watched the pair proceed down the street. Whatever had possessed her to tell them her real name? She'd become so accustomed to her French identity that poor Millicent still existed only in the deepest recesses of her mind and memory.

She glanced at the calling cards. What would life be like in one of the other grand homes in the neighborhood, one that housed a real family? Well, that was something she'd never know. They would never hire the likes of her.

She was fortunate indeed to have the shelter and comforts that Chez Celeste afforded her. So why had the encounter with these ladies left her with a lump in her throat and an ache in her heart?

With a deep sigh, Roxane looked up at the fern in the parlor window. Given her state of *déshabillé,* her best plan would be to avoid going in the front door. Instead she went down the narrow walkway that ran between Chez Celeste and the tall fence that screened it from the house next door. She passed the ballroom door, where the visiting gentlemen were admitted discreetly, and let herself in the kitchen entrance, hoping Louise would be elsewhere and the room would be empty. If she sneaked up the servants' stairs, perhaps she could come back down the main staircase and pretend she had been in the house all along.

But Louise was in the kitchen, stirring a pot on the wood-fired stove. "Mademoiselle!" She wagged the dripping spoon. "Where have you been? Everyone's been searching for you. Lady Celeste was sore distressed when you couldn't be found."

"I went for a walk. It's such a fine afternoon—"

"You were supposed to be resting upstairs, and only until three o'clock. You know when the gentlemen are invited to arrive. The bells to open the house have already rung. Hurry—into the parlor with you."

"I must go to my chamber first, to freshen myself."

"Ah, but Thaddeus Burnham is here, and you know what a favorite he is with Lady Celeste. He brought his father with him, and they've requested your company especially." Louise smiled wickedly. "You better hustle out there right now."

Roxane sighed. She took off her hat and set it on the kitchen table, the two calling cards stuck inside.

"I guess I have no choice. Louise, will you help me unpin my hair?"

11

Claire paced yet again through the vacant rooms, her footsteps echoing. In the kitchen she glanced at the clock on the stove. Twenty more minutes until the open house ended.

The only visitors had been lookie-loos—curious neighbors and voyeurs who made a hobby of seeing how other people lived. Claire had dreamed of scoring an offer on the house. Even better, several offers. Or at least encountering a serious buyer or two, leads she could follow up on.

No such luck.

Her colleague Jeff Ortega, whose listing this was, had done his best to write an enthusiastic description of this dreary house for the website and sales flyer, but to be honest, this place was a boring example of forty-year-old tract housing at its worst. Three bedrooms, two baths, no character.

It did have one good thing going for it. No ghosts. No strange, whispered voices or icy rooms or perfume floating in the air. But suppose she'd had one of her strange encounters? What would Jeff say if she told him to add *haunted* to the flyer?

The house was empty except for a card table and a pair of folding chairs that Jeff had set up in the living room. The owners had moved out, and they hadn't been willing to spring for the expense of staging the place. A mistake, Claire thought, dropping onto one of the hard seats. Carefully chosen furnishings helped buyers see a house as a comfortable, happy home. Empty, the house looked barren and cold.

She was tempted to lock up early and go home. But what if a prospective buyer found the place shut and complained to Tess? Better stick it out to the bitter end and not risk tilting Tess's opinion toward letting her go. Strictly speaking, real estate agents were in business for themselves, and Marin County had several big, multi-office companies where she could probably hang her license. But she didn't want to leave BayCrest Properties. Tess had an outstanding reputation as a broker and mentor, and Claire liked BayCrest's intimate atmosphere and her fellow agents. Well, except for George.

To pass the time, she took out her phone and Googled Simon Thatcher. A surprising number of hits came up. Social media sites, news articles. BAPA's website topped the list.

Before she could click on any of the links, a noise made her jump. A ghost, after all?

No, the front door opening. The buyer she'd been waiting for? She stood up and assumed her best professional persona.

A woman came in, raking fingers through silky blond bangs and biting her lips. She glanced up, as if inspecting the ceiling for cobwebs, but avoided looking at Claire.

"Hi, I'm Claire Scanlan. Welcome to 128 Beluga Drive—oh! You're Mirabelle Burnham. I didn't recognize you at first."

Mirabelle looked down, as if surprised to find herself wearing jeans and a sweater instead of a flapper dress. "I guess I look different from last night."

"I liked your dress. It really flattered you." It was true. Peter had certainly found her attractive in that short skirt and silver fringe. He danced with her, brought her champagne—

"It flappered me, you mean." Mirabelle giggled, but it sounded forced.

Claire laughed with her. Whatever the blonde had on her mind, they might as well start on a cordial footing. Maybe she could turn the conversation toward Peter, find out what was going on between them.

"Are you in the market for a new home, Mirabelle? What a coincidence that you happened into my open house."

"Call me Ellie. Everyone does. Mirabelle sounds so pretentious, don't you think? My Granny Jo chose it."

"Granny Jo? You mean Josephine Burnham, whose house we were in?"

"That's right. French names are a family tradition. Granny Jo was named for Napoleon's empress. My father was Edouard, after my grandfather. My brother Marc is Jean-Marc on his birth certificate, and Richard—well, Granny Jo insisted on pronouncing it Ree-shar. He hates it when you say it that way."

"Mirabelle's pretty," Claire said. "So what brings you here? You didn't really come to look at this house."

"Oh, God, I've been rambling, haven't I? I do that when I get nervous." Ellie drifted farther into the living room. She picked up a sales flyer from the stack on the card table and pretended to read it, then looked at Claire. "You're right. I mean, the house looks nice and all, but—I came here to ask you something."

"About Peter Mortensen," Claire guessed.

Ellie's face flushed bright red. An admission of guilt?

"Yes." Ellie crumpled the flyer into a ball. "About you and Peter. Last night—it was obvious he knew you. A family friend, he said, but the way he was acting ... it's more than friendship, isn't it? Is it over between you? I need to know."

"You're right, Ellie. There is something you need to know. Peter—"

The front door flew open. Damn, what a bad time for

another lookie-loo to wander in. Claire turned to greet the newcomer.

An attractive dark-haired man. He seemed familiar, but she couldn't place him. Then she realized who it was.

"You're Daniel Harding. The developer." The man who wanted to wreck the Burnham Mansion, but she didn't add that. Was everyone from the BAPA party about to show up? She fervently hoped the next to arrive would be Simon.

"Hello, Claire." Daniel looked more at home in his khakis and blue sport shirt than he had last night in his tux. "And Ellie! What an unexpected pleasure." His smile brightened.

"Hi, Daniel. I—I was just leaving." Ellie ducked her head. "We'll talk later, Claire."

"Don't rush off," he said, but she pushed past him and scurried out, dropping the wadded flyer in the doorway.

He looked disappointed as he watched her go. To Claire he said, "I hope I didn't interrupt something important."

"Not at all. What can I do for you?"

"I called your office and they told me you'd be here." He picked up the ball of paper and presented it to Claire. "I want to renew my offer to take care of mending that dress I damaged with my clumsy feet."

"Not necessary. I told you that."

"I want to, really. You shouldn't have to bear the expense when it was my fault. I figured you'd be about done for the day. If you're not going somewhere else from here, I can follow you home and pick up the dress."

Claire started to protest again but changed her mind. If she was going to be on Simon's team, it couldn't hurt to know more about the opposition.

"That's kind of you. Let me close up here and we'll be on our way."

Roxane paused outside Chez Celeste's kitchen door to smooth her skirt and undo the top three buttons of her bodice. She shook out her hair, hoping it would fall over her shoulders in alluring waves.

From the parlor she heard laughter and the tinkling of the piano. Yvette, entertaining the visiting gentlemen with the lively new number everyone was singing that summer: "There'll Be a Hot Time in the Old Town Tonight." Yvette was the only *jeune fille* who could play a note of music. The piano had rolls of music and a mechanism that allowed it to play itself when Yvette was occupied otherwise.

Roxane's feet felt planted in place. The last thing she wanted to do was to go into the parlor and see Thaddeus Burnham's leering face. She had spent such a pleasant afternoon, and being in his company would spoil it completely. But of course she had no choice. Not if she wanted to continue residing in the comfort and protection of Chez Celeste.

And today Thaddeus had brought his father with him. What would he be like, a man who had reared such a son? Thaddeus had plenty of money and conveyed an illusion of good breeding, but in his heart he was as coarse and vulgar as any man she had known. She did not have high hopes for the senior Mr. Burnham.

An appalling thought occurred to her. What if they intended to share her company, not just in the parlor but in one of the chambers above? She'd heard of such arrangements; in fact, Véronique had once set the other *jeunes filles* to giggling with a tale of a gentleman with political affiliations who'd invited her to accompany him to Sacramento. He smuggled her in through a side door of the ornate domed capitol, where she entertained an entire committee of the legislature in a single afternoon. Or so she claimed—Véronique was fond of embroidering the truth. Roxane had never been subjected to a situation in which she was expected to provide her favors to more than one gentleman at a time, and she had no desire for such an experience. Especially not if the gentlemen were named Burnham.

She forced her feet forward. Stalling would only worsen Lady Celeste's displeasure. Taking a deep breath, she squared her shoulders and stepped into the parlor.

To her surprise, it was not Yvette at the piano. The musician was a man she'd never seen before, a small fellow with wild white hair and a velvet coat the color of a dove's wing. His hands moved up and down the ivory keys so quickly that Roxane could have sworn she saw sparks fly from his fingertips. As if feeling her startled gaze, he glanced at her, and smiled and winked without missing a note.

Roxane smiled back. The *jeunes filles* were under orders always to smile at visiting gentlemen, and something about this little man made it easy to obey that command.

When he turned his attention back to the piano, she looked around. The parlor was dim. The red flocked wallpaper and dark woodwork absorbed much of the light, and the velvet curtains had been drawn tight to shield the *jeunes filles* and their guests from curious eyes of passersby. Yvette, half clothed, was in the fat armchair, curled up in a gentleman's lap. Fleur and Aurélie, wearing frocks so filmy one could see through them, lounged on the sofa, giggling with a fair-haired young man who visited Chez Celeste every Sunday between the morning and evening services at his church. And on the settee by the fireplace …

"Mamzelle Roxane!" brayed a deep masculine voice. "Where have you been?"

She shuddered at the sound but gave the required smile to the man who'd made it, careful not to show her distaste. "Why, Mr. Burnham, I've been in my chamber dreaming of you."

Thaddeus Burnham slapped his knee and roared with laughter. "I bet you have, darling. And I intend to make all your dreams come true. Come here, sit by me."

"Oh, I would do so willingly, sir, but there doesn't seem to be any room." And thank goodness for that, Roxane thought. Thaddeus was sprawled at one end of the settee. At the other end sat a gray-haired gentleman who could have been Thaddeus's twin had their ages not differed by at least two decades. They both sported handlebar mustaches under sharp noses, and the heavy brows over their eyes were identical. So this was Isaac Burnham, the man who'd lost the house to Lady Celeste in a hand of poker.

Squeezed between father and son was Véronique, clad only in a corset and gartered stockings. She had one arm draped over each man's shoulders, but she was leaning heavily against Thaddeus, apparently unmindful that the older man's hand was resting on her thigh.

"We'll make room." Thaddeus nudged Véronique. "Get up, mamzelle, and bring me another whiskey, there's a good girl."

Véronique untangled herself from the gentlemen, rose from the settee, and took Thaddeus's empty glass, glaring at Roxane all the while. With a languid roll of her hips she crossed the room to the table that held a pair of crystal decanters and filled the glass with liquor.

Lady Celeste, sitting nearby on a throne-like chair, noted the purchase in her record book. She would present a tally to Thaddeus when he was ready to leave. Roxane knew the sale of beverages added quite a bit to the profit Lady Celeste earned from her establishment, the more so because the whiskey was watered down but priced as if it were served at full strength.

Lady Celeste finished writing and looked up. "Ah, ma chère, there you are." Roxane knew better than to be fooled by the sugar in her voice. "We were wondering when you would join us. Mr. Burnham has made a special request for your company."

"Yes, I—I am surely honored."

"Though why he should have any interest when you're in such dull attire, I cannot imagine. You look as if you just came in off the street."

"So I did, Lady Celeste. You see—"

Lady Celeste's ice-blue eyes narrowed even as the smile on her rouged lips grew wide. "I should think that a string of purple beads would brighten your costume."

The amethyst necklace! Roxane's fingers flew to her throat as if she were wearing it. She had intended to return it to its place right after breakfast, but she'd been distracted by thoughts of the man who lay murdered in the Future House. By the time she returned from checking if he was really there, she'd forgotten all about the necklace.

She dropped into a curtsy. "Oh! I'm sorry, Lady Celeste. Let me run up and get it right now. I'll put it in your room."

"In good time, mademoiselle. Right now you have guests to attend to." Lady Celeste beamed a smile at Thaddeus Burnham and a bigger one at his father.

The piano player launched into a spirited rendition of "Love Makes the World Go Round."

"That's right, mamzelle," boomed Thaddeus. "Come attend to your guests."

There was nothing else to be done. Roxane went over and stood before him, making another curtsy. "I'm at your service, monsieur."

Véronique perched on the arm of the settee and handed Thaddeus his whiskey. "You're better off with me, monsieur. I'm far more skilled in the ways of love. Let me show you how good I can make you feel." She ran her practiced fingers across his chest.

Thaddeus brushed her away. "You're a wondrous delight, to be sure, but my heart is set on Mamzelle Roxane."

He grabbed Roxane's wrist so tightly that she squealed in pain. She fell across his lap, and the glass went flying.

Véronique let out a curse. Her corset was soaked with whiskey.

Thaddeus planted a slobbering kiss on Roxane's neck. "Lady Celeste, I've selected my companion for this evening. I want the use of your finest chamber."

"The Rose Room," Lady Celeste said. "Be aware, monsieur, it comes at an extra cost."

"Of course, my lady. And Mamzelle Roxane will entertain me in a style worth the high price. Won't you, my sweet?" He twisted Roxane's wrist until tears sprang to her eyes.

"Yes," she gasped. "Yes, I will."

"Let's go then." Thaddeus pushed her to her feet. Her wrist throbbed. She dreaded to think what he might have in mind to do to her in the Rose Room.

The piano music stopped. The man with the wild white hair walked over to Lady Celeste's table. "Excuse me, signora. The Rose Room—you say it is your finest chamber?"

"That's correct, monsieur."

Thaddeus, hands clutching Roxane, paused to watch their exchange.

"And it comes at a high price?" the pianist said.

"Correct again." Lady Celeste seemed uncertain whether to be puzzled or amused.

He placed a pouch of supple leather on the table in front of her. Closed by a drawstring, it was heavy and bulging, as if filled with coins. "Would this amount be sufficient to purchase the use of it for the night?"

She opened the pouch and Roxane saw her eyes grow large.

The coins must be gold. "Oh! Why, yes, monsieur. More than ample. Oh my!"

Thaddeus tightened his grip. "I've already claimed the Rose Room." His face was behind her, but Roxane could sense his scowl.

Lady Celeste lifted her hands as if she were helpless. "Monsieur Burnham, you see my dilemma. I'm sure the Gold Room will suit you. Unless you care to outbid this gentleman." She turned to the odd little man. "Now, monsieur, which of these lovely jeunes filles would you like to have entertain you? They're all French, you know, and well versed in the art of—"

The man held out his hand to Roxane. "This young lady right here, of course."

"Now, wait a minute," Thaddeus snarled. "This one's mine."

"Unless you are married to her, I do not see how you can claim that. We shall let her decide. Signorina, whom would you prefer to accompany, him or me?"

"Signo—do you mean me?" Roxane wasn't sure, but she might have just been insulted.

"It is Italian," the small man said. "It means the same as mademoiselle. The choice is yours. This gentleman or me."

One of Thaddeus's hands was knotted in her hair. The other gripped her neck. It didn't seem to Roxane that she had any choice at all.

Clutching the leather pouch, Lady Celeste stood up. "Let him have her, Monsieur Burnham. I'll come with you myself, to the Blue Room." She offered him her hand.

Thaddeus squeezed Roxane's throat, then abruptly released her. "As you wish," he grumbled. "But next time she's mine." Roxane was bewildered, but more than that, relieved.

Isaac Burnham grabbed the hand that Lady Celeste had extended to his son. "If you're offering your own company, madam, allow me to take advantage of that opportunity. It's the least you can do after I so graciously let you win that fateful hand of poker."

Lady Celeste laughed. "Only in your fantasies did you let me win. But, yes, come with me. I'll find it amusing to play with you again."

"Poker isn't what I had in mind, madam," Isaac said.

"Nor I, monsieur."

Véronique sidled up to Thaddeus and cooed, "Come along, monsieur. I'll show you more pleasure than the rest of these silly girls could do if they all serviced you together."

Glaring at them all, Thaddeus pulled Véronique close. Once they'd gone upstairs, the white-haired man stepped before Roxane and bowed deep at the waist. "Signorina, I am Alberto Stregoni. I am most pleased to make your acquaintance."

"Likewise, I'm sure, monsieur." Grateful for his rescue, she gave him her most winsome smile. Whatever he was like, he couldn't be worse than Thaddeus.

CHAPTER

12

Claire unlocked the apartment door and beckoned Daniel in.

"Lindsay!" she called, not surprised to get no answer. Lindsay and Brad had probably gone his place after their hike.

Claire waved toward the dress that had taken over the sofa. "There she is—Scarlett O'Hara. Swooning over Ashley Wilkes."

"I thought she loved Rhett Butler."

"She should have. But she pined away for the unavailable Ashley for the entire book."

Daniel Harding swooped the gown into his arms. "Come with me, Scarlett. Let me show you a good time. I'll make you forget Rhett and Ashley both."

"Thanks for doing this," Claire said as he walked to the door, mauve pleats and ruffles spilling over his arms.

"I had a good time," he said.

"So did I." When they left the open house, he'd invited her to grab a bite with him at nearby seafood place. She'd enjoyed his company as well as the linguini with prawns. He talked about a couple of award-winning projects his company had done—saving a historic school in San Jose by converting it to office space, transforming a defunct Oakland factory into a popular retail complex. Apparently he hoped to persuade her that he'd be similarly thoughtful when turning the Burnham Mansion into

85

condos, though he didn't press that point. Maybe he didn't know she was on Simon's team.

Under different circumstances a spark might have ignited between her and Daniel. He was certainly attractive. But through the whole meal she found herself wishing the man across the table was Simon Thatcher. Her mind kept imposing Simon's gray-blond hair over Daniel's neatly clipped brown hair, setting Simon's glasses in front of Daniel's eyes.

"Don't worry about Scarlett," Daniel said now. "I'll take good care of her."

As soon as he was out the door, she checked her phone. No messages, no texts. No call from Simon, despite his promise.

She punched in BAPA's number. A voicemail message. No surprise; why would he be at the office on a Sunday night? Her internet search hadn't turned up his home number. All she could do was sit on the sofa, newly emptied of ruffles, and wait.

She was surprised at how intensely she was wanted to talk to him. Evidently she was on Simon's team in more ways than one.

———◆———

"So this is the Rose Room," Mr. Stregoni said.

"Oui, monsieur." Roxane lit the candle on the table by the bed and replaced the glass chimney to shelter the flame.

The gentleman stepped into the middle of the room and gazed upon its accoutrements.

"It certainly is … rose."

Roxane laughed. She couldn't help it. "Indeed it is, monsieur."

The room was done up entirely in pink. Not a baby's pink, but one that was rich and sensuous. The wall coverings, the damask draperies in the window bay, the pattern of the Persian rug—all shared the voluptuous hue. Several gilt-framed mirrors hung on the walls, along with Lady Celeste's special collection of Parisian prints, which showed lusty French women in a variety of bawdy poses.

Roxane had never entertained a gentleman in the Rose Room. In Chez Celeste's most splendid chamber, an hour came at premium cost. She'd been surprised when Thaddeus Burnham announced his intention to bring her here; he must have been showing off for his father. She was even more astonished when Mr. Stregoni had outbid him.

She saw that Louise had been diligent in performing her duties. Fallen petals had been cleared away from under the vase of roses on the dresser. The water pitcher on the washstand was filled to brimming. A decanter of whiskey and two glasses stood beside the candle lamp on the bedside table. Lady Celeste expected her *jeunes filles* to urge their gentlemen to drink as much as possible and keep track of how much they consumed. The amount would be added to their tab.

For discretion's sake, the Chinese screen had been carefully placed across the window bay. The last of the day's sunlight hit the stained-glass panels at the tops of the windows, creating tiny rainbows on the opposite walls.

Louise had laid the bed with fresh satin sheets, smoothed a pink velvet coverlet over the top, and made a high pile of soft pillows by the carved headboard. The bed had to be four times as wide as the cot in Roxane's chamber; in fact, it looked twice as wide as the chamber itself.

Mr. Stregoni was still standing in the middle of the room. Roxane almost laughed again, but suppressed the urge. It would never do to make a gentleman think she found the sight of him amusing. But he did look comical with his white hair sticking out in all directions and his mustache drooping on either side of his mouth. And his eyes—there was something odd about them.

"Well, monsieur, shall we begin?"

She began to undo her bodice, her fingers fumbling the tiny buttons through the holes. This was the price she paid for coming back late and not having time to change from her street clothes. Instead of wearing a costume that could be easily slipped off her body, she had to work through layers of garments with all of their buttons and hooks and laces. And she had to do it in a flirtatious manner, so that this man's interest would remain high and his money would remain in Lady Celeste's pocket. Roxane was not in the mood.

She had unbuttoned her dress to the waist when Mr. Stregoni said, "Stop, signorina. You need not disrobe."

Her hands fell to her sides. "What do you mean?" He had made no move to take off any article of his own clothing. They didn't need to be naked to do what he'd paid for, but she didn't see how they could accomplish any version of the act if both of them were fully clothed.

Mr. Stregoni patted her shoulder. "I did not bring you up here to assault your virtue."

He settled himself into the rocking chair in the corner of the room.

"My virtue? Are you mocking me, monsieur?" No one had been concerned about her virtue for a long time. Not since Mama died.

"Not at all. I would never make fun of such a charming young lady."

"But don't you want to—? I'm very good at what I do, monsieur. I can offer you a great deal of pleasure."

His mustache twitched as he smiled. "I am sure you can. But the only pleasure I want from you is the honor of your company and the delight of a little conversation."

Emotions swirled through her, making her feel faint. It would not do to swoon, and as a precaution she perched herself at the end of the enormous bed. She wasn't sure if what she felt was relief or disappointment, but she knew there was confusion in the mix.

"But why me, monsieur?"

He drew the rocker closer to where she was sitting. "Because you were the most beautiful young lady in the room. And you looked frightened."

"Frightened!" She jumped to her feet. "Monsieur, I assure you, I am afraid of nothing."

"No doubt you are very brave. But I saw fear in your eyes when you looked at Thaddeus Burnham."

"That wasn't fear. That was …" She fell silent. She couldn't come up with a word for the repugnance she felt for Thaddeus. Besides, it would be wrong to discuss one of Chez Celeste's visitors with another. In her experience, gentlemen always preferred to believe they had a woman's sole and sincere devotion, even when the woman worked in a parlor house.

"Isaac Burnham is an old friend," Mr. Stregoni said. "We met when I was newly arrived from Italy and he from Germany, before he changed his name from Birnbaum. I have known Thaddeus since he was a boy. The father is a good man, but I detect a streak of cruelty running through the son. If Thaddeus fancies you, signorina, it is wise to feel a bit of fear."

Thaddeus Burnham's face hovered in front of her, as if she were seeing a ghost—Pa's ghost. It was odd that she had never noticed how much Thaddeus resembled her father.

Roxane burst into tears.

Mr. Stregoni stood and took her hands in his. She pulled them away and balled them into fists, which she pressed against her eyes as she struggled to regain her composure.

"F-forgive me, monsieur. I d-don't know what has come over me."

"I apologize if my comment upset you. Here, use this." He sat with her on the bed and urged her to take his handkerchief. She dabbed her face with the square of fine white linen, then twisted it with her fingers.

"I'm quite all right," she insisted, and repeated, "Forgive me."

"Let us see if I can cheer you up. Do you enjoy magic tricks?"

"Magic tricks?"

"Like this." He held out his hand. "See here, my palm is empty. Do you agree?"

Roxane nodded, unsure what this strange man had in mind to do. She was further bewildered when he reached up and brushed her hair behind her ear.

"Why, what have we here?" he exclaimed. "Look at what is hiding in these lovely tresses."

He opened his hand again. Resting on the flat of his palm was a gleaming yellow coin.

"Oh my! Is that gold?"

"It is." He gave her the coin. "A golden eagle, worth ten U.S. dollars."

"Ten dollars!" Roxane had rarely held ten whole dollars at once. She turned the coin over and over. On one side there was indeed an eagle, its wings spread wide. The other side showed a woman wearing a crown that bore the word LIBERTY; she was surrounded by stars. "Where did it come from?"

Mr. Stregoni chuckled. "I told you, I found it amongst the glorious locks of your hair."

"That can't be." She ran her fingers through her hair. It was impossible that a coin could have been there without her feeling it, yet she was slightly disappointed not to find another one.

Reluctantly she held out the gold piece to him. Instead of taking it, he closed her fingers around it.

"Keep it, signorina. A little gift."

"Really?" She smiled at the thought of having such a treasure, then wondered what she would have to do to earn it. She'd never known a gentleman to give a genuine gift; every offering came with some sort of price attached. She put her arms around Mr. Stregoni and kissed his cheek, which tasted oddly like cinnamon. "How may I show you my appreciation for such generosity?"

He disengaged himself from her embrace and returned to the rocking chair. Roxane was surprised to feel let down.

"At least let me pour you some whiskey," she said.

"I told you, all I ask of you is to let me spend time in your charming company. Put your gold piece in a safe place, and don't tell Lady Celeste that you have it. If she knows, she will be tempted to claim it for herself."

"Thank you, monsieur. You're most kind." Roxane tucked the coin into the little pocket she'd sewn inside her corset, next to the dead man's pearl button. "May I ask you a question?"

"Of course you may."

"I don't mean to be impudent. But why did you come here? Were you not aware of what sort of establishment this is?"

"Isaac Burnham invited me to accompany him. He owned this house originally, you know. One night he lost his head and his heart to Lady Celeste and risked the house on an ill-advised turn of the cards. Afterward, Isaac left town in humiliation, and who could blame him. Now that he has rebuilt his fortune, he has returned to San Francisco."

"Lady Celeste told us that story this morning. She said Isaac Burnham is a talented magician."

Mr. Stregoni laughed as he rocked back and forth. "Did she now? Do you believe in magic, signorina?"

"Well, I ..." Before she came to Chez Celeste her answer would have been a definite no. Then she stumbled upon the secret that granted her entrance into the Future House. If being able to move back and forth in time wasn't magic, she didn't know what to call it. And now here was this strange little man making money appear in her hair. "I don't understand how magic works, monsieur, so I don't know what to believe. But if Isaac Burnham was truly a magician, then couldn't he have made the cards do as he wished, and not lost his house?"

Mr. Stregoni laughed again. He had quite a jovial disposition. Roxane realized she was enjoying herself.

"An excellent point. Isaac is no magician, though he likes to show off with a few little tricks that I taught him. Now that he is back in town, he was curious to see the house again, and so was I. When Thaddeus told us he planned to visit Chez Celeste this afternoon, we decided to join him."

"If you're a friend of the family, you must have known the house when Mr. Burnham owned it."

"I knew it well. As a matter of fact, I built it for him. I was the architect and the chief of construction."

"Oh! Then you know about the black rose in the tower." The words just jumped out. Roxane clapped her hands over her mouth.

Mr. Stregoni gave her a piercing look. "What did you say?"

She jumped up and moved to the bedside table. "Are you sure you won't have some whiskey?"

He followed her there. "You have found the black rose, signorina?"

Roxane unstoppered the decanter and splashed whiskey into a glass. He took the glass when she held it toward him but set it down without taking a sip.

"Tell me—how did you find it?" His tone was urgent.

She crossed to the Chinese screen in the window bay. "I–I was running from Thaddeus. We were upstairs in my chamber and he wanted to—well, I couldn't, I wouldn't, I don't care how much money he gave Lady Celeste. I fled into the storage room but he followed me. There was nowhere to go, nowhere I could hide, so I ran up the spiral stairs." She looked at the ceiling. The spiral stairs were directly above her and she imagined she could see up into the tower.

"A foolish move," she said, "because in the tower I was trapped. I turned around, intending to kick Thaddeus in the face as he charged up the stairs after me. I braced my hand against the wall to steady myself for the kick. And then …"

Mr. Stregoni came to her side. He slid his hands around her waist, but in a way that was gentle, not lustful. "What happened?"

A tear slid down her cheek, and she realized she'd left his handkerchief on the bed. "You'll never believe me."

"Yes, I will." He kissed away her tear with a fleeting brush of his lips.

She said in a small voice, "All at once Thaddeus vanished. There was nothing on the stairs but a swirl of stardust."

"Go on. Do not be afraid."

"I went down the stairs. I didn't know what else to do. The house was the same, yet it was completely different. The storage room was empty, and so was my chamber. I went down to the second floor and came into this very room. The wallpaper was faded, and the furniture had been changed. The same bed was there, though, right where it is now, and an old woman was lying in it, asleep. I tried to tiptoe out, but she woke up. She called me to the bedside and said—this is the part you won't believe …"

"She said you had found your way into the future."

Roxane snapped up her head. "How did you know!"

"I designed and built this house, remember. Were you frightened?"

"A little bit," she admitted. "But the lady was kind and sweet. She told me to call her Granny Jo. She invited me to stay with her, but I don't know how the future works. I wouldn't know what to do if I were there forever. I had to return to Chez Celeste. I'd be in trouble if I was away too long."

He nodded knowingly. "What did you do?"

"When Granny Jo fell asleep I went into the tower, because that's where I was when time stood on its head. I searched and searched for the way to go back. I ran my hands all over the walls and stepped on every part of the floor. I was afraid I was trapped. At last I discovered the black rose in the wallpaper pattern. When I pressed it, the stardust appeared and led me back into Chez Celeste."

Mr. Stregoni smiled broadly, as if she had delighted him, though she'd done nothing but tell a strange story. "You have the gift of sight, signorina. It is very rare. Most people would see that rose as unremarkable, another red rose slightly darker than the others."

"You mean I can see things that others can't? What a peculiar notion."

"Yes. And when someone travels across time that way, they cannot be seen except by others who share the gift of sight. It is a protection. To most people, visitors from another century seem strange, and those who are strange are not always welcome."

"Is that why no one in Granny Jo's house ever saw me but her?"

"She must have the gift of sight also. Did you visit her again?"

"Many times. At first I went only when I needed to get away from Thaddeus. Then I found I enjoyed her companionship, and she liked mine. It's funny, her name was Burnham too. But she died, and now there's a murdered man in the storage room, and I intend never to go into the Future House again."

"A murdered man?" Mr. Stregoni said sharply.

"Yes, a man from the future. Someone killed him last night while I was there. When I checked this morning, his body was still on the floor." She took the pearl button from her corset pocket. "Look, I found this. I think it belongs to the killer."

Mr. Stregoni reached inside his jacket and pulled out an eyepiece; Roxane had once seen a jeweler use one like it. He examined the button, holding it close to the lens. Then he stared at the Chinese screen for several moments, his eyes fixed on the figure of a dragon.

"A murdered man needs justice, no matter in what century he was killed," he said finally. "Perhaps you had best show me this body. I am sorry if it will distress you. But I assure you, I will keep you safe."

He turned to face her, and Roxane realized what had seemed peculiar about his eyes. They were of two different colors, one gray, the other a yellow-brown. No, that didn't quite describe them. Silver and golden, those were better words.

"I know you will, monsieur. Come, follow me."

CHAPTER

13

The earth shook on the day I was born.

I entered the world at a few minutes past midnight on April 18, 1906. My mother, who was French and beautiful, named me Josephine, after Napoleon's empress. Our servant, Louise, bathed me and wrapped me and laid me in my mother's arms in my parents' wide, soft bed. My father welcomed me with kisses. "Petite bébé," they whispered, "may you never know anything but happiness."

Five hours later, before the sun had a chance to rise and touch me for the first time, the city was wrenched by a massive earthquake. It ripped the land apart and set loose monstrous flames that consumed all of the downtown. Maman was propped up in her bed, in pain and exhausted, and I was suckling at her breast. She heard a rumbling sound. Then the house rocked so severely that we were pitched onto the floor. I wailed, and nothing would soothe me.

Three hours after that, the earth shook again, and Maman joined me in my wailing.

Papa, already an old man who leaned on a cane, went out to see what damage had occurred. He climbed the hill in Lafayette Park, near our home. When he finally pulled his way to the top, he found many of our neighbors there, staring in awe at the Great Fire raging only a mile away. They prayed for a miracle that would spare their homes, but the flames marched closer and closer.

The next day Papa tried to send my mother and me out of the

city. He would remain behind to protect our house and property. Maman refused to leave. Traveling was too big a risk with a newborn child, she said, especially one who was sickly because in her two short days of life she had breathed nothing but smoke.

Even if Maman had been willing, we had no place to go and no way to get there. The boats sailing to Oakland were so crammed with passengers they could barely keep from sinking, and the price of passage was high. The roads were crowded with refugees. Some walked or rode on horseback, bearing no more than the clothes they wore. Others drove wagons loaded with whatever possessions they'd managed to salvage. Families were camping all over the western side of the city. Our side garden was filled with makeshift tents, and Maman's prized rosebushes got trampled.

For three days the sky was black except for the perpetual sunrise engendered by the furious flames to the east.

On the evening of my third day on earth, my parents swaddled me in a blanket and carried me to the top of the Lafayette Park hill. They shielded my tiny face with a wet cloth. The Great Fire had reached Van Ness Avenue, just three blocks away. Van Ness was a grand boulevard lined by some of the city's largest, most elegant homes. The neighbors gathered on the hill watched fearfully as the flames leaped high from burning mansions. San Francisco had turned into hell, and nothing would appease the devils that controlled this fire until it laid waste to the entire city.

All at once, boom! An explosion ripped the air. Then another. Then another. The crowd on the hill panicked. Was this another earthquake? Were we all doomed?

A rumor quickly spread through the crowd: the army was attempting to save our neighborhood, not by dousing the flames with water but by using dynamite. They were blowing up the ill-fated mansions on Van Ness to create a firebreak, a space so wide that even these ferocious flames could not jump over it.

This tale proved true. Over the next few days, brave firefighters finally brought the Great Fire under control. But the smell of smoke and ash hovered in the air for weeks, and it was a long time before life returned to normal. Our family was fortunate, but so many others had lost their homes. Villages of canvas tents sprouted like mushrooms in the parks, on the sand dunes near the ocean, and in any empty lot that wasn't full of charred debris or fallen rubble.

My father's place of business was in ruins. My mother's spirits were slow to recover. She wept for the slightest reason, or no reason at all.

Is it any wonder I distrusted the world that gave me such a cataclysmic welcome? The world struck me as unstable; the fate it offered anyone was capricious at best. My home had been spared, so I decided the wisest course was to stick close to it.

Which is what I did for more than a century. I lived in this house all of my life. Even now I'm reluctant to leave it, though my visitors from the Place Called Forever say the time has come for me to move on. The house is empty now, they tell me, but they're wrong. My memories still reside here. People I care about come and go—my granddaughter Ellie, my little friend Roxane who lived here before I was born.

And now there is the dead man. He hovers near his crumpled body, feeling lost and anguished in a way I have never known. He died too soon, his life stolen away from him by someone evil, whereas I lived for a great many years and expired in peace. I must watch over him until he leaves for the comfort of his final resting place.

———◆———

Curled on her sofa, Ellie stared at the silent phone in her hand. Peter had promised to call her tonight. But the phone refused to ring.

She glanced at the ormolu clock on Granny Jo's antique desk. Nine o'clock. On the evenings when they weren't together, he usually called around eight-thirty. What was delaying him?

Ellie took another sip of her wine and tried to focus on the anatomy textbook on her lap. Peter had inspired her to sign up for the class. When her mother became ill, Ellie had willingly left college to help with her care, setting aside her childhood dream of becoming a doctor. The money her parents had put into her education fund went to medical bills instead.

Shortly after Mom lost her battle with cancer, Ellie's father succumbed to a heart attack. She always pictured his heart breaking cleanly in two.

She'd gone back to school, pushed herself through another couple of semesters. But studying, working full time, juggling student loans—she was grieving and exhausted, and it got to be too much. She'd taken her job with the medical supply firm thinking she might learn something that could help her in her studies. What a joke that turned out to be.

It felt good to be getting her life back on track. *Mirabelle Burnham, MD*. Okay, that was probably out of reach, but with Peter beside her anything seemed possible.

So why hadn't he called?

He'd probably gotten caught up in researching case law or writing a brief. He habitually worked on Sundays, often late into the night, taking advantage of the quiet in the empty office, so that on Monday he could hit the ground running, prepared for the hectic week. That's why they so rarely spent Sundays together.

At least that's what he'd told her. What if he was lying?

The thought hovered over her like a dark cloud. Until this weekend Peter had never given her any reason to doubt him. Now she didn't know what to think. First, his odd behavior last night.

Then Claire's statement: *There's something about Peter you need to know.* Ellie was burning to know what Claire wanted to tell her, yet scared to death to find out.

Everything had been perfect until Claire showed up.

The phone chirped, startling her. She almost spilled her wine. Peter!

"Hello, sweetheart," she purred into the phone.

"Christ, Ellie, don't you even check your caller ID?"

Gloom settled back in. "Hello, Richard. Make it quick. I'm expecting an important call."

"How's this for quick. We're meeting at Granny Jo's house tomorrow at eleven. You, me, and Marc. We're going to make a decision once and for all."

"Tomorrow? I'll be at work."

"Take a sick day."

"I can't. My boss'd kill me. We're really busy—"

"It's a dead-end job, Ellie. Executive assistant." He snorted. "A fancy way to say secretary. So what if you're fired? Once you have Harding and Boyer's money you'll kiss that job goodbye anyway."

"Can't you even have the courtesy to ask me when would be a good time to meet? Why do we always have to do things on your schedule?"

"Don't whine at me. We're not kids any more. Even when we were, your whining wasn't cute."

She refused to burst into tears. Richard had a gift for provoking her. It was a game to him, making her cry.

"For Chrissake," he went on, "for one day they can sell crutches and bedpans without you."

"Easy for you to say. You got to achieve your dream. Marc too."

"What are you talking about?"

"When Mom got sick, you'd already received your MBA and started your company. Marc was nearly finished with his PhD. I'm the one who—"

"Ancient history, Ellie. Just be there. Tomorrow, eleven, Granny Jo's."

"Come on, Richard. All I'm asking is that you respect—"

"You need money, right? So the sensible thing is to sell to Harding and Boyer. We'll tell Marc and make it official."

"You don't know what I need!"

"Oh, please." A dismissal, not a request.

He hung up. Ellie threw the phone across the room. It skittered under the antique desk.

She wondered if he took that same belittling tone with his staff at the home security company he owned. Poor them, if so. Even more infuriating, he was right. She did need money. Peter offered encouragement, but she couldn't expect him to pay her way. Even if they got married, and she desperately hoped they would, she'd want to pay for school on her own and not have him think she loved him because of his wealth.

The phone rang again. She had to get on her hands and knees to pull it from under the desk. Please, this time let it be Peter.

Disappointed again.

"Hey, sis," Marc said, "I'm giving you a heads-up. Richard wants us to meet tomorrow morning at Granny Jo's."

"He already called me. Made it a command performance." She pushed herself to her feet.

"Yeah, he's antsy to sell, and for the highest price possible."

"What else is new?"

"More than money is at stake, you know. The Burnham family made important contributions to this city's history. The house represents that. Our heritage, our legacy—it's worth preserving."

"Sounds like the college professor talking." Though Marc's field was economics, not history.

"You're with me on this, aren't you, Ellie?"

"I understand what you're saying. But Richard makes good arguments."

"Not as good as mine. What can I say to persuade you?"

"Look, Marc, I can't talk right now. I've got a call coming in."

She hit the end button and set the phone on the desk beside a pair of photos in a gold frame. She kept most of the family photos in her bedroom, but for as long as she could remember Granny Jo had displayed these on her desk. It felt right to keep them there.

Both pictures showed a youthful Granny Jo. In one she held a baby—Ellie's father—in her arms. In the other she was smiling at a handsome man in a French army uniform. He and Granny Jo fell in love while he was on leave in San Francisco on the eve of World War Two. When Germany invaded France, he rushed back to his homeland, leaving Josephine with a souvenir of his devotion growing in her womb. Many times her grandmother had told her how he died a hero's death in battle soon afterward, not knowing he'd soon have a son. Ellie had never heard another story so tragically romantic.

Granny Jo had often counseled her, "If you want it and it's good for you, go for it." Now she wondered if this bit of wisdom had been acquired in the romance with the French soldier.

Nothing had ever been as good for Ellie as Peter, and never had she wanted anything as much. It made sense to follow her grandmother's sage advice. Ellie picked up the phone, punched in Peter's number, and held her breath while it rang.

His voicemail answered. Ellie felt a stab of hurt. She didn't leave a message.

———•———

"Yes, this man is most assuredly dead," Mr. Stregoni said. "And he died by a violent hand."

He was kneeling beside the body, examining it by the light of a candle he held.

Roxane hadn't been able to persuade herself to move closer than the bottom of the spiral stairs. She watched Mr. Stregoni slowly rise and dust his knees with his free hand. She couldn't see his face, but his voice was solemn.

"Should we tell the police?" she asked. "Lady Celeste will be most unhappy if they come here in their official capacity." Several officers of law regularly visited Chez Celeste when not on duty; Roxane had entertained some of them herself. The *jeunes filles* were instructed to give them a warm welcome and free whiskey.

"She need not worry. This man belongs to the future. His murder must be investigated by the police in his own time, not ours. But if we step outside to summon them, I fear we will find ourselves in a place far stranger and more dangerous than any foreign land, and with no knowledge of how to navigate our way."

"What shall we do then?"

"Let me think." Mr. Stregoni closed his eyes and tapped his chin. For an instant Roxane thought she saw a star dance away from his fingertip. A trick of the candlelight. Beyond its yellow circle, the storage room of the Future House was filled with gloom. Night had arrived, and all of the electric lights outside couldn't dispel the darkness.

"I have an idea," he said. "We will make a sign and hang it in a window. Someone will notice it and take the proper action. Come, let us get to work. You may precede me up the stairs, signorina. I will catch you if you fall."

Once they were back in the Rose Room, Mr. Stregoni had Roxane use the bell pull to summon Louise. When the servant arrived, he asked her to bring them a light supper, a large sheet of thick paper, and a pen with a fat nib. Louise looked at Roxane, one eyebrow lifted in a question. Roxane smiled and shrugged. Louise had certainly accommodated far more peculiar requests.

Roxane sat in the rocking chair, daintily eating bread and cheese while Mr. Stregoni labored over the sign. Finally he held it up so she could admire his handiwork. He had drawn three words in large black letters.

HELP. SEND POLICE.

"This should do the trick."

"It's a handsome sign," she agreed.

"I will take it to the Future House. Wait here. There is no need to distress yourself again."

"Oui, monsieur. I'll gladly spare myself that gruesome sight."

"I will put the button you found back beside the body. The police will want it. It seems to be the only clue to the murderer's identity."

He left the room, closing the door behind him. Roxane sat and rocked, enjoying the sensation of luxury that the Rose Room afforded her. She felt a level of comfort and contentment she'd not known for a very long time—now that she thought about it, she hadn't felt so good since before her mother died. Funny that a room could make her feel this way, especially since it was not like any room she'd spent time in with Mama. The farmhouse in Missouri had been rude and rough. In fact, Roxane would have bet that Mama had never in her entire life been in a room so grand.

Then a thought occurred to her—what if it wasn't the room that made her feel good, but the company she was keeping in it?

She laughed out loud at the silly notion. When did a man ever make a woman feel happy? Especially such an odd man as Mr. Stregoni.

She heard the tall clock downstairs chime the hour. Nine o'clock! She had been with this gentleman far longer than usual allotted time. She was astounded that Lady Celeste had not sent Louise up to pound on the door and roust them out of there.

Mr. Stregoni returned to the room and said, "The task is done."

"I hope it will prove helpful to that poor man. Now, monsieur, I should say goodbye to you. We are way past the hour. Someone must be waiting for this room, and Lady Celeste will be expecting me downstairs."

He took her hands. "No need to rush. The sum I gave the lady was sufficient to purchase the use of this room and the honor of your company for the entire night. You look tired, although beautiful just the same. Surely you would enjoy sleeping for the night in this soft and lovely bed."

Roxane's first reaction was surprise. Her second was fear. Gentlemen were required to be gone from the house by midnight; neighborhood tongues would wag if they were seen tiptoeing out in the morning. No man but Thaddeus Burnham had ever bought a whole night with her, and she hoped never again to endure what Thaddeus made her do to earn the money.

But if this gentleman had paid for her favors, she was obliged to provide them. And in doing so, she would see what he was really like. Nowhere else did a man reveal his true character as he did in a woman's bed.

She lowered her eyes and looked up at him through her lashes in her most flirtatious way. "Indeed, monsieur. If that is your wish, and you made such an arrangement with Lady Celeste, I'll be delighted to spend the night in this bed with you."

This time he did not stop her as she removed her clothing. As she folded her dress and her undergarments neatly onto the rocking chair, she waited for him to touch her, but he busied himself with pulling down the bedcovers. She laid herself down and posed her nude body enticingly.

Then she waited.

Mr. Stregoni stripped to his undergarments and extinguished the gaslight in the overhead fixture. He blew out the candle by the bed. Finally he bent to kiss her lightly on the forehead.

Her body tensed, anticipating more.

"Sleep well, cara mia—my dear," he said.

She heard the shuffle of his steps as he walked around the bed and the creak of the bed frame as he got in on the other side. A few moments later he was lightly snoring.

What was this? A gentleman who did not want the pleasures she was offering? The favors he'd paid an apparent fortune for? The bed was so large that even if she extended her arm she couldn't reach him.

She tossed and turned, but slumber eluded her. The bed was too soft, the bedclothes too smooth, the pillows too fluffy and abundant. In the middle of the night, she rolled toward Mr. Stregoni. She found his hand and clasped it in her own, and finally fell asleep.

14

Claire was the first to arrive in the BayCrest Properties conference room for the staff's regular Monday Meeting. She sank into one of the black leather chairs, set her coffee mug and elbows on the rosewood table, and put her head in her hands. The sharp edges of last night's scream-dream jabbed at the inside of her skull. It was the same nightmare she'd had the night before—the couple dancing on the steps of song, the fierce storm, the dissolving amethysts, the tears of blood. But this time the vision was more vivid, more distressing.

The man in the tuxedo must be Peter, since she'd danced with him at the BAPA party. What had sent him tumbling into an abyss? And why had he left her naked and crying?

"Hey there, dancing queen."

Claire winced at the voice. She looked up and saw George Pugh leering at her, which made her wince again.

"Had fun Saturday night, didn't you." George was juggling a mug, a napkin, and three powdered-sugar doughnuts. "In fact, from the look of you, the fun lasted long past Saturday."

"Leave me alone, George."

"A weekend of bed and booze. You can't deny it—it's written all over you. I know a first-class hangover when I see one." As he slid his corpulent body into the chair next to hers, coffee slopped from the mug. Splotches landed on Claire's pale blue shirt. "Oops."

She'd danced with George at the party, too. But he couldn't be the man in her nightmare. If he fell into an abyss, she wouldn't shed a tear.

"I have a headache, that's all. Left over from a bad dream." Claire pulled the napkin from his hand and dabbed at the stains. "Not that I owe you any explanation."

BayCrest's three other associates filed into the room.

"Explanation of what?" asked Marlene Murphy, the receptionist.

"Shut up, George," Claire muttered.

Silence from George was too much to hope for. "Did you guys see Claire on Saturday night? Belle of the ball. I only got one dance out of her before some blond hunk whisked her away. I was just, you know, speculating about how they spent the rest of the weekend." George chomped into a doughnut, scattering powdered sugar down his front.

Delia Chan, BayCrest's star agent, gave her a look of mock horror. Or maybe it was real. "Please, Claire, tell me you didn't actually dance with George."

"I saw the hunk." Marlene sat on the other side of Claire. Today her hair was magenta, gelled into spikes. "Yummy! I may model the hero of my book on him." It was an open secret that Marlene used slack times at her desk to work on a seemingly endless romance novel. Tess was probably the only person in the office who didn't know.

"I know how Claire spent the weekend," Jeff Ortega said. "Or at least how she spent yesterday afternoon. She held an open house at my Beluga Drive listing." He smiled at her. "Thanks for doing that, Claire."

Jeff had taken her under his wing when she joined BayCrest at the start of the summer, and was her best friend and staunchest ally in the firm. He embodied the cliché *tall, dark, and handsome,* and she'd briefly flirted with the notion of pursuing a romance with him. That is, until she ran into him at the movies one evening and was introduced to his date, the equally tall, dark, and handsome Anthony.

"Wish I could have brought you a contract," she said. "Or at least some encouraging news."

"That's okay." Jeff gave a can't-win-'em-all shrug.

Marlene reached across Claire and snagged one of George's doughnuts.

"Hey," George protested. "You owe me a buck for that."

"Oh really? I thought you were following the office tradition, bringing doughnuts for everyone when a house you've sold closes escrow." Marlene took a bite. "Mmmm. Delicious."

"Bitch. You know I haven't sold a house lately."

"You haven't sold one ever."

"Hey, I'll have you know—"

"Shush," Claire warned. "Here's Tess."

They all turned their attention to the owner of BayCrest Properties as she hurried into the conference room.

"Morning, everyone." Tess flung a yellow legal pad onto the table but remained standing. Her gaze swept the room. She avoided looking at Claire, or did Claire imagine that?

Tess looked as cool and professional as always in tan slacks and an ivory jacket, but her usual perfection was somehow off. Her hair, Claire decided. The champagne-colored tresses looked as if she'd been running nervous fingers through them.

The group chorused, "Good morning, Tess."

"I want to thank you all for coming out Saturday night and supporting the BAPA fundraiser."

"Great party," Jeff said. "Loved that band."

"It looked like a huge success," Delia said.

George gave Claire a nudge. "It was sure a success for some people. Our dancing queen here managed to—ow!"

Tess's gaze landed on George, then shifted to Claire, who did her best to look innocent, not like someone who'd just stomped on a colleague's toe.

Marlene whispered, "Good work."

"How much money did BAPA raise?" asked Delia, always the practical one.

"I don't know." A frown creased Tess's polished brow. "Simon Thatcher was going to call me yesterday with the figures, but he never did."

Claire felt a shiver pass through her. "He said he'd fill me in on BAPA's campaign to buy the mansion, but I didn't hear from him either."

"I just phoned the BAPA office. He's not in and hasn't been in touch. Strange—he's so reliable." Tess tapped her fingers on the tabletop. "Claire, what are you doing after this meeting?"

An alarm bell clanged in Claire's mind. "Nothing I can't rearrange. Why?"

"The caterer left some things at the Burnham house. Simon and I were both given keys so we could manage the party setup. Since he's not available, I arranged to meet the caterer there and let her in. Come with me, and I'll bring you up to speed on BAPA while we drive."

"Happy to," Claire said, though her stomach had tightened. What if Tess really wanted to talk about Claire's future, or lack of one, at BayCrest?

"Good. Now let's get the meeting started. Reports on last week's activities—who wants to go first?"

———•———

A sharp rapping on the door startled Roxane awake. For a moment she was confused—where was she? Never before had she awakened in such a wide, white, soft bed. Sunshine coming through the window suffused the room with a rosy glow. Had she died in the night and, against all odds, gone to heaven?

Then she heard a snuffle and a snort from the lump of blankets and remembered. She was in the Rose Room with the odd but sweet Mr. Stregoni. This was a new experience too, finding a man still in bed with her in the morning. Chez Celeste's visitors had to depart by midnight, and the louts who had bought her favors when she worked in the wretched Barbary Coast cribhouse—she couldn't call them gentlemen—always left as soon as they got what they'd paid for. Even Pa, back at the farm in Missouri, came and went from her bed in the darkest hours of the night, as if not having daylight shine on his deeds let him pretend he'd never done them.

"Time's up." Louise's drawl came from the other side of the door, followed by more knocking. "I know you had a gentleman in there all night. Lady Celeste says he's got to be out of the house before breakfast. Which is in ten minutes."

Roxane sat up, rubbed the sleep from her eyes. "Another moment, Louise—"

"Ten minutes! And tell him to be discreet about going."

She hadn't been aware of movement from Mr. Stregoni, but all at once he was sitting beside her, his gentle arms around her shoulders. She found it comfortable to lean into him. To her surprise, she didn't want him to leave.

"Never fear," he called out to Louise. "I shall be on my way posthaste."

"You better," Louise replied through the door. "Or Lady Celeste will be very angry. And you, sir, will be charged double the rate."

Neither of them spoke while Louise's stout shoes thumped away down the hall. Roxane savored the warmth of Mr. Stregoni's bare chest against her back, the gentle rise and fall of his breathing. She was disappointed when he let her go and slipped out of the bed.

Using the bedcovers to shield her nakedness, she watched as he donned his striped trousers, his frilled shirt, and his gray velvet coat. Standing before one of the gilt-framed mirrors, he smoothed his mustache and tried to tame his wild white hair. The strands seemed ready to fly from his scalp, each going off in a different direction. Before she could stop herself, Roxane giggled.

Quickly she clapped her hand over her mouth as he turned to face her.

"Do you find me amusing, signorina?" He was smiling.

"Oh, not at all, monsieur. Forgive me. I wasn't laughing at you. I was—I remembered an entertaining story. Please, I'm sorry."

"That is too bad. I daresay many people think me comical. When they laugh, I feel as if I have given them a gift. I would take great pleasure in giving such a gift to you. I sense you have too few occasions for laughter."

Extending his hand, he guided her out of the huge bed.

"You are kind, monsieur. I don't know what to say."

That was certainly true—never had a gentleman spoken to her in such a way. She was at a loss as to how to respond. She tried lowering her eyes and batting her lashes, then gazing up with her most coquettish smile. It was a routine she'd perfected, designed to couple the suggestion of innocence with the promise of worldly pleasures. Gentlemen sometimes rewarded this playacting by giving her a coin or two beyond what they paid to Lady Celeste. Mr. Stregoni had already been more than generous—imagine, ten dollars in gold! She certainly didn't expect more. But a kiss might be nice.

To her shock, he turned away. "Say whatever you wish. But make the words express what is in your heart. You need not employ falsely flirtatious ways with me."

He picked up her folded dress and undergarments from the rocking chair and handed them to her. "You had best go down to your breakfast. And I must be true to my word and leave."

Roxane hugged her clothes to her bosom. "I don't want you to go. That's not being flirtatious. It's what I feel in my heart."

He put his hands on her shoulders and kissed her forehead ever so lightly. "And I would love to stay. But I do not wish to get you into trouble with Lady Celeste."

"Will you come back?" This was a new idea to her, that one might care about seeing a gentleman a second time. She would prefer never again to lay eyes on most of the men she'd met, with her father and Thaddeus Burnham at the top of that list.

Thinking of her father reminded her of the dead man on the floor of the Future House, and she shuddered.

"Signorina, what is the matter?"

"I was remembering that man—the one who was murdered. Do you think your sign will work? Will the police come and bring the killer to justice?"

Mr. Stregoni sighed. "Ah, justice. He deserves justice, whatever that might mean. I confess I am curious to know what will happen with regard to the poor fellow. Perhaps I should go to the Future House and wait there. If the sign does not cause anyone to summon the police, additional measures should be taken."

She reached up to touch his cheek. "If you go there, I could come after breakfast and join you. My time will be my own until the house opens to gentlemen this afternoon."

"An excellent plan." He pulled Roxane closer to him, wedging her bundle of clothing between their bodies. For the first time his lips touched hers. He tasted of cinnamon and honey.

A knock on the door. The sudden sound made them fly apart.

"Mademoiselle! You're late to breakfast. If you're not out of there in one minute, I'm coming in and that gentleman better be gone."

"No, don't come in, Louise! I'm on my way." Roxane flung her dress over her head, and Mr. Stregoni helped her tug it into place. No time to deal with all of her undergarments and their buttons, hooks, and laces. She prayed Lady Celeste would not notice.

Mr. Stegoni gave her a wink and gathered up her leftover clothing. "Do not worry about leaving these here. I shall take them with me and return them to you in the Future House."

He ducked down on the far side of the bed, where he wouldn't be seen from the doorway.

Roxane opened the door and stepped into the hall. "Good morning, Louise. Isn't it a lovely day?"

CHAPTER
15

Tess's Mercedes sailed along the freeway like a big boat, leaving other cars in its wake. Claire figured Tess must subscribe to her ex-husband Zach's motto: *Speed limits are for sissies.*

They crossed the Golden Gate Bridge, zipped through the Presidio, and slowed as they reached Lombard Street. They would arrive at the Burnham Mansion in a few minutes. If Claire was going to bring up what was on her mind, it was now or never.

She took a deep breath. "Tess …"

Tess changed lanes to get around a double-parked truck, then swerved to avoid a family of jaywalking tourists.

"Tess, I was wondering … Saturday on the way to the fundraiser on Saturday, you said you were planning to talk to me about something—"

"Right. The Burnham Mansion. I wanted to recruit you to BAPA's campaign."

"Really? But I thought …"

"You saw what a splendid treasure it is. As we left that night, Simon told me you were on board. I'm so glad. It's a win-win. Your energy will help BAPA and the contacts you make will help you succeed in your career."

Claire laughed with relief. "I was afraid you were going to tell me I didn't survive the three-month trial period and my days with BayCrest were numbered."

"Where did you get that idea?"

"Not sure. But I'm happy I was wrong."

———◆———

Roxane felt odd sitting at the breakfast table without her undergarments.

She tugged at her neckline to make sure she was properly covered, then adjusted her leg-o'-mutton sleeves. She couldn't wait for the meal to be over so she could go to the Future House and reclaim her clothes. And see Mr. Stregoni.

To her relief, no one was paying attention to her state of impropriety. The other girls were busy chattering and chewing, while Lady Celeste, who normally was aware of everything, sat silent at the head of the table, gazing at the coffee going cold in her gold-rimmed cup. She appeared to be lost in a dream.

Roxane dipped her spoon into her oatmeal, wondering what could be on her employer's mind. But it really didn't matter, as long as Lady Celeste didn't notice what was not on Roxane's body.

It wasn't as if Roxane was unaccustomed to going without her corset, chemise, and petticoats. She'd never had occasion to wear a lady's many layers of clothing when she was working on the Barbary Coast. All she'd needed during those two dreadful years was a simple frock that a crude, drunken customer could easily peel away from her.

Even here at Chez Celeste, when the *jeunes filles* entertained gentlemen they wore clothes that hid little, the better to entice the visitors to partake of the goods on offer. But that kind of déshabillé was permitted only when the house was open for business. At other times Lady Celeste insisted her girls be properly attired when they descended to the first floor. Roxane understood why this was necessary when they ventured out-of-doors; they were expected to keep up the fiction that Chez Celeste was a boardinghouse for chaste and respectable young ladies. But she wasn't sure why the rule had to be enforced when they were inside. It wasn't as if the neighbors came calling.

Even as she had this thought, Roxane remembered her encounter yesterday with Mrs. Sedgwick and her daughter, Mrs. Bisbee. They'd said they planned to inquire whether one of the young ladies in residence might be interested in a situation as housekeeper and governess. Perhaps she should alert Lady Celeste to the possibility that the pair could come knocking on the door.

She still had their calling cards tucked into her hat. What would it be like to live in a fine house where she could earn her keep with her hands and her head rather than other parts of her body?

Yvette passed her a plate stacked with toasted bread. Roxane handed it along to Fleur without taking a slice. Thank goodness today was Monday. On Sundays their breakfasts were lavish, but during the week the menu was limited to cereal, toast with jelly, and coffee. The less food they had to eat, the more quickly the meal would be over.

"So, Roxane." Véronique leaned back in her chair and swept her lush black tresses away from her shoulders. "How was your night in the Rose Room with that silly little man?"

Roxane felt herself redden. She made it a rule never to describe the time she spent with gentlemen to the other *jeunes filles*. She certainly didn't intend to tell anyone that she'd felt more peaceful and comfortable with the "silly little man" than with anyone in her life—except Mama, and Mama had passed to her reward so long ago that Roxane's memory of her was becoming frayed and faded.

"He was a gentleman," she replied. Since they referred to all of their visitors as gentlemen, this was a safe statement, revealing nothing. "And the bed was exceedingly soft and fine."

Véronique lifted the lid from the crystal jam pot and heaped currant jelly onto her plate.

"I hope you didn't miss Thaddeus Burnham too much." She dipped her fork into the jelly and lifted it to her lips.

Hearing the name, Roxane shuddered. The movement slipped her bodice askew.

"Not too much," she agreed, making her voice nonchalant as she pulled the fabric straight.

"I'm glad. Because I showed him a very good time." Véronique demonstrated by slowly licking the sweet red substance from the tines.

"I'm sure you did," Roxane said. "I understand you have many skills that are admired by gentlemen." Véronique looked none the worse for her evening with Thaddeus, but that didn't surprise her. He took care not inflict marks or bruises where they would be visible.

"I hope you won't hate me for it, but I suspect you're no longer his favorite."

"If Thaddeus is pleased by you, you're more than welcome to him. I don't know that I have ever been any favorite of his."

"Oh, but you are," piped up Aurélie. "He asked for you specially yesterday, and you saw how distressed he was when the other gentleman claimed your company."

"I'm sure he quickly got over any disappointment. Especially with Véronique to console him. Now, if you'll excuse me, I'd like to finish my breakfast."

Roxane ate a spoonful of her oatmeal, quickly followed by

another, though she knew she would not be dismissed until everyone was done with the meal.

"You shouldn't eat so fast," Aurélie scolded, wagging a finger. "It's not ladylike." She tried to catch Lady Celeste's eye and call attention to Roxane's infraction. Roxane was glad to see that the lady was still absorbed in her own thoughts. Perhaps she could excuse herself and slip away without Lady Celeste's noticing.

She scraped the last of her oatmeal out of the bowl. Véronique set her jellied fork on her plate. Yvette placed her empty cup on her saucer. Only Fleur was still eating. Her red curls bounced as she crunched into a piece of toast.

"You know what was interesting about yesterday?" Fleur said, crumbs flying from her lips. "Meeting Isaac Burnham, after we heard the story about how Lady Celeste won this house."

"Don't speak with your mouth full," Aurélie admonished. She looked at Lady Celeste again and heaved a loud sigh, no doubt frustrated that her efforts to make the rest of them mind their manners were going unobserved. "Anyway, Isaac Burnham is just a sad old man who lost his house and his money. What's interesting about that?"

"He isn't nearly so interesting as his son," Véronique added.

"Indeed," Aurélie said with a pretty pout. "I have to say—"

"Aurélie, hush," Yvette warned, nodding toward Lady Celeste.

"—that I'm glad I wasn't the one who had to entertain him."

"That's enough, Aurélie," snapped Lady Celeste. The mention of Isaac Burnham apparently had roused her from wherever her mind had been drifting. Her bright blue eyes flashed with anger, and Roxane was glad they were aimed at Aurélie, not at her. "You know the rules. We do not disparage our guests. It's because of them that we're able to maintain ourselves in this house, and that's true of no one more than Isaac Burnham."

Aurélie's cheeks flamed red. "I … but … oh dear. I meant no harm, Lady Celeste."

"I believe an apology is in order."

"Oh yes. Of course. I'm sorry for my unkind remarks." She bowed her head toward her empty bowl.

"It appears that everyone has finished with le petit déjeuner," Lady Celeste said, though she'd eaten hardly a bite of her own breakfast. "You're excused from the table."

Roxane couldn't get out of her chair fast enough. First, she would fetch Lady Celeste's amethyst necklace from her room and return it to the lady's chamber. She had it too long and she didn't want Lady Celeste to think she intended to steal it. Next she would freshen her face and comb her hair, perhaps splash on a bit of lavender water. Then she would find Mr. Stregoni.

A horrible thought struck her—what if he wasn't waiting in the Future House as he'd promised? Suppose he'd gone elsewhere, disappeared, taking her undergarments with him? He wouldn't be the first man to lie about his intentions. She might arrive to find herself alone with the murdered body—unless the sign they'd posted had worked, and the police had come.

No, he would be there, true to his word. Something about him made her feel he might be worthy of trust.

As she started up the staircase she was stopped by Fleur's tremulous voice behind her. "Roxane? Can you spare a minute?"

Roxane sighed and turned around. "Yes, Fleur, what is it?"

The girl's red curls were tumbling across her forehead. She was clutching something to her bosom. "Remember yesterday in the storage room? You were looking for a book."

Roxane vaguely remembered telling Fleur something of the sort to get rid of her.

"You said you'd show me how to read. And look, I found this

up there. Is it an easy one to begin learning with? There are lots of pictures and not too many words."

She handed Roxane her treasure—a slim, square, dusty volume.

"An ABC book." Roxane opened the stiff cover and began turning the yellowed pages. The first picture showed a fruit-laden tree. On the opposite page a boy, arms full of the fruit, was running from an angry farmer. She read aloud: " 'A is for Apple, red, round and sweet. B is for Boy, swift on his feet.' You can learn your letters from this book."

"I already know the letter S," Fleur said proudly. "It's in my name."

Roxane said the name slowly to herself, trying to hear its letters. "I don't think there's any S in Fleur."

"Not Fleur. Sadie. My name from before I was a French girl."

"Really? That's a nice name. Where did you live when you were Sadie?"

"In Sacramento." Tears sprang to Fleur's eyes. "It was nice there, before my papa had his accident."

Roxane put her arm around Fleur and led her into the parlor. They sat together on the sofa, the book beside them on a plump cushion. "What happened to him? How did you end up here?"

"He was a railroad man, and doing real well for us. Then one day the train went off the rails and all his bones got broke, and he couldn't work anymore. We lost our house and never had enough to eat. My brothers were too young to go to work, and Ma had her hands full, taking care of Papa and all the little ones. I'm the eldest, so I had to find a way to bring some money in. The preacher told us he knew someone in San Francisco who would give me a position as a pretty waiter girl in an eating establishment. So I came to the city. But that job sure wasn't what I expected."

Fleur's tears flowed freely for a moment, then she wiped them from her freckled cheeks with her sleeve.

"We have similar stories," Roxane confided. "Only when my pa had his accident he got killed. So I came to San Francisco, and I was a pretty waiter girl too. Except there was nothing pretty about it."

"Nothing," Fleur agreed, shaking her coppery head. "I thought I was going to die in that awful place. But the Lord was watching over me. On my third day there a gentleman took kindly to me and brought me to Lady Celeste. It's nicer here, and I earn more than she charges me for the room and board, so I can send money to my family."

"That's good." Roxane patted Fleur's hand. She was glad she didn't have to help out a family with her own meager share of the dollars she earned for Lady Celeste. She kept her money in her leather treasure pouch, which was stuffed inside her mattress; she had pulled stitches from a seam to create the hiding place. She didn't want her money to turn up missing. Paltry sum though it was, she intended to keep every cent of it.

Fleur said, "I'm sorry about your pa. At least mine is still alive. What caused his accident?"

"I don't like to think about it." Roxane stood and set the ABC book onto Fleur's lap. "Here, see if you can figure out some more letters. Later I'll help you. Right now I have things to do."

Ignoring Fleur's protest, she left the parlor. Bunching her long skirt in her hands so she wouldn't trip, she dashed up the stairs in a most unladylike fashion.

CHAPTER

16

Now that she had the answer to the question that had been stressing her, Claire's step was light as she headed up the sidewalk toward Octavia Street. But not light enough to let keep up with Tess, who stayed two paces ahead.

"Richard is the big obstacle." Tess tossed the words over her shoulder. "Marc's on our side. He understands why this house is important to San Francisco, and why making it a museum would honor his family's legacy. But Richard's set to sell out to the highest bidder."

"Does he need the money?" Claire jogged a few steps and drew up next to her boss. How could Tess be so swift in high heels?

"Not unless he has a gambling problem or a high-maintenance mistress. He's just greedy."

"What does he do? I don't know much about the Burnhams."

Tess's steady stride left Claire in the dust again.

"Richard owns his own company, specializing in home security systems. He has a huge house in Mill Valley with a view of the bay from the front windows and a view of Mount Tam from the rear. His wife is high up in a big corporation. They're definitely not hurting. Anyway, it's not like BAPA wants the Burnhams to donate the house. We're offering to buy it. But unfortunately our pockets aren't as deep as that damn development firm's."

"Harding and Boyer." Claire quickened her pace.

"Right, Hardsell and Destroyer."

"They aren't really going to destroy the house, are they? My brother-in-law said they'll turn it into condos and make the original architectural details part of the design."

Tess stopped in her tracks and turned to stare at Claire. "You think that wouldn't destroy it? Taking a gorgeous example of late nineteenth century residential architecture and chopping it into teensy cramped apartments, tarted up with a few Victorian furbelows? Claire, maybe I haven't explained fully what's at stake here, but—"

"Whoa, I didn't say I favor the idea. It's just what Peter—"

"Is it going to be a problem for you, working with BAPA when your brother-in-law is in the enemy camp?"

"No, really. I'm on your side. BAPA's side." Simon's side.

"Good." Tess took off again, and Claire ran to catch up.

"I'm having dinner at my sister's house tonight," Claire said. "Maybe I can talk sense into Peter."

"A waste of breath. He's a lawyer. They don't deal in sense."

Claire started to reply, then realized she couldn't think of a good opposing argument.

"The one we need to persuade is Mirabelle. She's the deciding vote," Tess said, adding, "Oh damn."

"Damn Mirabelle?"

"We missed the light."

They had reached the corner across from the Burnham Mansion just as the traffic light turned red. The don't-walk signal held up its steady orange hand.

"What's your take on her?" Claire asked. "Mirabelle, I mean."

"My impression? She's torn between her brothers and wants to please them both." Tess scowled at the cars blocking their path, then at Claire. "Saturday night it looked like she wanted to please your brother-in-law too. What's going on there?"

"Wish I knew." Even though Tess's disapproval was aimed at Peter, Claire felt discomfited. She avoided her boss's gaze by studying the house—the corner tower with the witch's-hat roof, the bay windows with their stained-glass panels, the shingled surfaces, the spindles and gables. Which details would the developer keep, and which would be sacrificed?

"Well," Tess said, "make it your business to find out."

Uh-oh. "What do you mean?"

The late-morning sun glinted on a windowpane, and for a second Claire thought she saw a face peering out. The third floor—wasn't that the window Simon Thatcher had found open on Saturday night?

Claire blinked and the face was gone. If it had been there at all.

Tess said, "If Mirabelle's ga-ga over your brother-in-law, she'll vote the way he wants. Which is to go with Hardsell, since that's who he represents. We need you to win her to our side."

"How can I do that?"

"Whatever way works. Come on." Tess stepped off the curb and began hurrying across the street.

"The light hasn't changed," Claire pointed out as she followed.

"No cars," Tess said, and it was true that the intersection was clear of traffic.

Arriving in front of the mansion, Claire noticed something odd about one of the first-floor windows. A small square sign hung behind the glass. Tess paid no attention to it as she rushed, key in hand, up the steps to the front door, but Claire paused to see what it said.

HELP. SEND POLICE.

"Tess! Tess, wait!" Claire called, but her boss had already opened the door and gone inside.

———————

Men! Life would be so much easier if they'd all disappear.

Ellie tightened her hands on the steering wheel. She was driving past Granny Jo's house for the third time as she searched for a parking place, a rare prize in the Pacific Heights neighborhood.

Men meant her boss, who'd acted annoyed and suspicious when she called in sick. And to Richard, who, just because he was the eldest, assumed Marc and especially Ellie, the baby, should do his bidding without question. Like rearrange their schedules to show up at their grandmother's house for another bitter, fruitless argument about what to do with the property.

Most of all, men referred to Peter, who'd never called last night, never even texted.

Though, to be honest, if he disappeared it would break her heart.

The person she really needed to make vanish was Claire Scanlan.

Until Claire came along, Ellie's romance with Peter was perfect. Or so she'd believed. Had he been two-timing her all along?

If only Daniel Harding hadn't walked into the open house yesterday just as Claire had been about to confess to—what? Ellie didn't know. That was the problem.

A man stepped into the crosswalk right in front of her car. Ellie slammed on her brakes. Only then did she see that the stoplight had turned red.

No way could she win against Claire. Claire was attractive and poised, and she had a successful career—Ellie could claim none of that. Sure, Peter paid her compliments, called her pretty and smart, but really, what did she have to offer him? How could she compete?

An image rose unbidden in her mind: Claire and Peter in bed, bodies entwined. Peter's lips kissing Claire's, his hands caressing her hips, her breasts. Ellie felt heat rise within her, anger mixed with desire. Peter had such passion, could give such pleasure—and she wanted him to be hers.

Beeep!

A horn blared behind her. The light had turned green. Ellie circled the block again. She was arriving early so she'd have time alone before her brothers arrived. Being in Granny Jo's house always calmed her. She wished her grandmother were still around to give her warm hugs and wise advice.

Ellie made a decision. She would call Peter and insist they meet. She'd look in his eyes so she could see if he was lying, and demand to know the truth.

Finally—a car down the block was pulling away from the curb. Ellie zipped forward to claim the space before another driver grabbed it.

———◆———

Crossing the threshold into the Burnham Mansion, Claire felt like she'd stepped into a freezer. The air was icy. Tess was nowhere in sight.

"Tess!" Claire called. Leaving the front door open, she came into the entry hall, rubbing her goosebumped arms. She'd expected the house to feel cool, but not a chill so deep.

The house was a different place from the festive setting of Saturday night's fundraiser. Sunshine made the stained-glass panels at the tops of the windows glow like jewels, but little light penetrated the gloom. Instead of music, laughter, conversation, there was deep silence. Yet Claire thought she heard a slight hum, like the faint echo of a scream.

She went into the parlor. No Tess. The sign she'd seen dangled from a window latch by a length of string. Claire took it down.

HELP. SEND POLICE.

Thick black letters, hand-drawn on heavy white paper. Who had put the sign there, and why? Probably a party guest, tipsy from too much champagne, had hung it as a joke. Maybe lots of passersby had seen it and decided not to get involved.

But suppose it wasn't a joke. She didn't like the prickling sensation on her skin.

"Tess!" Claire called again.

This time she got a reply: "I'm in the kitchen."

She went back into the entry hall just as Tess walked from the rear of the house, high heels clicking on the hardwood floor. She carried a stack of silver platters, which she set on the bottom step of the grand staircase.

"There. The caterer will be here in a few minutes and we can get on with our day."

"Tess, look at this." Claire held up the sign.

"What?" Tapping her foot impatiently, Tess glanced at her watch and then at the front door.

"This sign was hanging in the window. Maybe it's a prank but—"

"Oh, good, here comes the caterer."

But the person who peered cautiously through the open door wasn't from the catering service.

"Mirabelle!" Tess said. "What are you doing here?"

"Oh!" The new arrival looked startled. "It's you, Tess. Thank goodness. I was worried when I saw the door wide open."

"Good morning, Ellie," Claire said.

"Claire. You're here too." Ellie flashed her a tiny smile, then let her gaze slide back to Tess. "Did Marc or Richard call you? I thought our meeting was going to be just my brothers and me."

As Tess explained their mission, Claire's attention was distracted by another voice, coming from above her: "Ah, good, I thought I heard someone down there."

She looked up to see an odd-looking little man trotting down the grand staircase. The tails of his old-fashioned gray velvet coat flew out behind him. His mustache and his unkempt white hair reminded her of pictures she'd seen of Albert Einstein.

Halfway down the stairs he stopped. "Oh dear. I was hoping you were polizia—police officers—but you are all women."

"Who are you?" Claire asked.

"Alberto Stregoni, at your service." He made a courtly bow and came down to the lowest landing, two steps above the entry hall. "Prego, I pray you, signora, can you summon the police?"

Claire couldn't help staring. His eyes were round as coins, one gold, one silver. "Did you hang this sign in the window?"

"Yes. The police are needed urgently. There has been a great tragedy. The man on the third floor—" As he gestured up the stairs, sparks seemed to fly from his fingertips.

She shook her head in disbelief. Tess and Ellie were looking at her as if she'd lost her mind.

"Claire, are you all right?" Tess said. Claire couldn't be sure if she was concerned or annoyed.

"Who are you talking to?" Ellie asked.

What was wrong with them? Didn't they see him? "This gentleman, Mr., um ..." In her astonishment, she'd already forgotten his name.

"Mr. Stregoni. Oh dear," he said. "Perhaps you had better come upstairs and see for yourself. Prego, follow me." He trotted back up to the second floor.

Still carrying the sign, Claire stepped over the silver platters to the landing, then hesitated. Mr. Stregoni leaned over the balustrade and beckoned her forward.

"Claire, where are you going?" Tess demanded. "The caterer's arrived. We need to give her the platters and get on our way."

"I think we'd better check this out," Claire called back.

At the top of the stairs, she shivered. The second floor was even frostier than the one below. The undertone of the scream rang louder in her ears. A mixture of odors assaulted her nose—the flowers-and-spice scent of a French perfume mixed with the stench of rot and decay.

Something in this house was seriously wrong.

Feeling dizzy, she gazed at the women below her. The caterer looked puzzled, Ellie frightened, Tess angry. The best thing would be to get out of this place and do as the sign instructed: Call the police.

But what would she tell them? The house was cold? She saw a strange man who seemed to be invisible to her companions?

As she turned to go downstairs, Stregoni touched her sleeve. "Prego, signora."

A crystalline tear slipped from his eye.

The floral scent grew stronger and she heard a new voice, a woman's this time, though she saw no one else nearby. It whispered to her, a soft breath against her ear.

"Help us. We need you."

A force tugged at her, pulling her up the stairs like a magnet draws an iron filing. She would see what the strange man wanted to show her, then leave quickly so she wouldn't delay Tess any longer.

"I'll be right back," she called to the others.

"Grazie. Thank you," Stregoni said. "Come this way."

He guided her up the narrow servants' stairway to the third floor. The screaming noise grew louder with each upward step. When they reached the hallway, the odor of rot nearly overpowered her.

"I am sorry to distress you, signora," Stregoni said. "I do not know of any other way to do what needs to be done. Oh, cara mia, here you are."

The last sentence was not addressed to Claire. A young woman stood in the doorway to the big storage room. She held an armload of white fabric—clothing of some sort. Claire recognized the stays and laces of a corset on top of the pile.

"Oh, monsieur," the girl said. "Thank heaven! I was worried when I found you gone and my undergarments in a heap on the floor. I thought you'd disappeared forever."

Mr. Stregoni kissed her lightly on the forehead. "They were not heaped. I folded them neatly. Here, I have brought someone to help us."

The girl looked at Claire for the first time, and her eyes went wide with surprise. With a shock, Claire recognized her too.

"You're the Amethyst Girl! You were here Saturday night, wearing a necklace like mine."

The girl's hand flew to her bare throat. "I didn't steal it. Lady Celeste let me borrow it. I meant to return it this morning—"

"I wasn't accusing you of anything. What's going on? What's that screaming sound? And that terrible smell."

Stregoni put his hand at the small of her back. "Steady, signora. I am sorry to subject you to the sight you are about to see. Dearest Roxane, stand away from the door so we may enter."

The girl stepped aside. Claire clamped her hand to her nose against the stench and followed Stregoni into the room. On the far side of the empty space, she saw the object of his concern—a man lying on the floor beneath an open window.

"Oh, no!" She dropped the sign that said to call the police. "He looks badly hurt. We have to get help."

"I fear, signora, that the poor man's soul has passed on to heaven."

Claire could hardly breathe. She made herself step closer. The man was dressed in a tuxedo. The body was crumpled and the face distorted, but she recognized the glasses and the gray-blond hair, now matted with blood.

"Oh my God! Simon!"

The room whirled around her. The scream grew high and shrill, and Claire realized it was coming from her.

CHAPTER

17

As the room lurched and spun, Claire's knees gave way. She sat down hard on the pine floorboards.

Her heart was pounding in her throat; she had to force herself to breathe.

At the edge of her awareness she heard footsteps rushing up the stairs from the floor below.

She fumbled in her purse, pulled out her cell phone, punched 911.

"Police!" she gasped to the dispatcher. "Send the police. The Burnham Mansion, on Octavia Street. A man is—oh God, he's been murdered."

A voice called, "Claire! Are you all right?"

Tears welled in Claire's eyes as she stared at the body. "Oh, Simon," she whispered.

The man with the Einstein hair crouched beside her. "Do you know him, signora? I am sorry for your loss."

"Claire?" The voice again. Tess's voice. "Where are you?"

The Amethyst Girl came and stood beside the strange fellow. Black buttoned shoes peeked from under her floor-length hem. What had Stregoni called her? Rosalind? Rosina? Roxane, that was it.

What were they doing here? The house was locked when she and Tess arrived. They couldn't have been hiding in here since

Saturday night. Roxane was wearing a different dress and no necklace.

Had they killed Simon?

Roxane searched through her armload of old-fashioned underwear and pulled out a swatch of cloth. Reaching down, she offered it to Claire.

"Here, ma'am, use this."

A handkerchief, fine linen edged with lace. Claire took it and dabbed her eyes.

Tess burst into the room, Ellie at her heels.

"Claire?" Tess stopped short. "Oh! Oh my God!"

Ellie let out a shriek and retreated to the doorway.

"Oh dear." Stregoni gave a comforting pat to Claire's fist, still curled tight around her phone. "What is this?"

Sparks flew from his fingertips as he poked at the device. The phone vibrated and buzzed, and something like an electric current surged through her hand, making it tingle. She gave a startled cry, and the phone clattered to the floor.

"My cell phone." She scooted away from him. "Please, I—"

"Did I shock you, signora? I apologize. That was not my intent." He picked up the phone and turned it around in his hand. "I did not expect this little box to have some sort of power inside it. What does that mean, cell phone?"

Could he really not know what a cell phone was? "It's a telephone. A small wireless phone. I called the police—"

"Claire? Who are you talking to?" Tess demanded. Her face had gone pale.

"No one, Tess. I mean, you. I said I called 911."

Stregoni jabbed at the screen. "A telephone? So tiny! Where are the wires?" He held the device to his ear. "A marvel, to be sure."

Ellie ventured a few steps into the room. "What happened? Who is it? Is he ... dead?"

Tess put out an arm to stop Ellie from moving forward. "Don't touch him. Don't touch anything."

Stregoni stood and helped Claire to her feet. "You say you summoned the police?"

Claire nodded as she brushed off the seat of her pants.

"Good." He held out the phone. To Claire's astonishment, it jumped from his hand to hers.

Roxane pressed close to his side. "We should leave, monsieur."

"Indeed we should." He took her bundle of clothing and nodded at Claire. "May your friend rest in peace, signora."

But rather than head to the door, they started to climb the spiral staircase.

"Wait," Claire called after them. "Where are you going?"

More footsteps in the hall, more shouting voices.

Two men rushed in. Ellie's brothers.

Ellie ran to them. "I'm so glad you're here. Something terrible's happened!"

Everyone was talking at once. Claire stood apart, watching Roxane and Stregoni disappear into the tower.

Were they trying to hide? That made no sense. There couldn't be anywhere up there to go, unless they flung themselves from the tower windows. Besides, they'd already been seen by a room full of people.

Or had they? Nobody but Claire seemed to have noticed the strange pair. Tess had asked who she was talking to.

She hurried to the stairs and climbed high enough to peer into the tower room.

No one there.

"Claire, what are you doing?" Tess demanded.

The windows were shut tight. A cloud of golden particles swirled and sparkled in the space, as if Stregoni and Roxane had vanished in a burst of stardust.

Roxane clutched her skirt to keep from tripping as she followed Mr. Stregoni down the twisting stairs, away from the Future House. She was relieved to see the storage room filled with jumbled boxes and furniture, for that meant they'd safely returned to Chez Celeste. The Future House was no longer a haven. She intended never to go there again.

Cradling the undergarments in one arm, Mr. Stregoni took her hand to help her descend the last steps.

"Merci, monsieur," Roxane said, grateful for this small courtesy. She heard her voice quaver.

She sank onto a nearby trunk and buried her face in her hands.

Mr. Stregoni sat beside her, his lap filled with muslin and lace. He put his arm around her shoulders. She let herself lean into the solace and warmth that his body offered.

"There, there, signorina," he said. "It is natural that you would be upset. The sight of a dead body is bound to be disconcerting."

Roxane sat up straight again. It would never do to appear weak to a gentleman, not even a kind one. "I'm all right, monsieur. I've seen dead people before. My mama and my baby sister, bless their souls. And my father …"

For a second she heard Pa's scream and saw the spurting red fountain of his blood. Despite her resolve to show strength, she couldn't keep from shuddering.

Mr. Stregoni's arm tightened around her. "That is a great many losses to endure. What happened to them?"

Squeezing her eyes shut, she pushed the vision of Pa from her mind. "Do you know what I find so strange to think about? Now that we're back in our own time, the man we just saw dead hasn't yet even been born."

"A paradox to ponder, to be sure."

Roxane stood up, breaking his hold on her. "I beg your pardon, monsieur. I should go downstairs now."

He rose to his feet also, which sent her undergarments tumbling to the floor. "But you are at liberty until three o'clock when the house opens to gentlemen. You promised me your company until then."

"Yes, but we were going to pass the time in the Future House. That's impossible now—it's full of people, and the police will come."

He plucked up a petticoat and shook it free of dust. "Perhaps we could go to your bedchamber. Do you have private quarters, or would other young ladies be present?"

"Gentlemen can't be in my room unless they pay Lady Celeste for that privilege." She felt her face grow hot with anger as she thought of her chamber's most recent visitor. Paid for or not, no woman should have to endure the kind of torment that Thaddeus Burnham enjoyed putting her through.

She took the petticoat from Mr. Stregoni and concentrated on folding it just so.

He said, "Then let us go and find Lady Celeste."

"No!" She dropped the petticoat. "You're not allowed to be in the house at this hour. I dare not be caught disobeying her rules. She'll turn me out, and I have nowhere to go."

Except back to the Barbary Coast. She knew she could find employment again as a pretty waiter girl. She was still young and fair enough that the owner of Bassity's Bar or the Red Cat would hire her on the spot. She would go back to entertaining the rowdy drunkards who frequented such dives, giving them beer on the main floor and then accompanying them upstairs to the rude cribs where they would use her body to satisfy their more carnal appetites. Each day she would serve customer upon customer, many of whom had a taste for entertainments so depraved as to make Thaddeus Burnham appear saintly.

The thought of going back to that life tied her belly into a knot so tight that she almost retched.

"Oh, cara mia, please calm yourself." Mr. Stregoni patted her back and right away she felt soothed. "I promise you will not lose favor with Lady Celeste on my account. I will hide myself, and when the clock chimes three, I shall reappear and reclaim your attention."

Roxane smiled at him. "I'm already looking forward to that moment, monsieur."

He took both her hands in his.

"Until then, I will think of nothing but your sweetness and beauty. Will you favor me with a kiss before you take your leave of me?"

"Willingly, monsieur."

She moved her mouth toward his, intending the kiss to be quick, a simple promise, nothing more. But as soon as their lips touched, a strange and pleasurable heat prickled her. She had never felt such a sensation before, and she couldn't break away. Mr. Stregoni pulled her closer, or she pulled him, she wasn't sure. Their bodies seemed to melt together. She wanted this kiss to last forever.

"Oh my goodness." The voice came from the doorway, cleaving them apart like an axe splitting cordwood.

Fleur was standing there, holding her ABC book in front of her.

"Roxane?" Fleur said in a tremulous voice. "I was looking all over for you. What are you doing?"

Roxane brushed a strand of hair out of her face. Her forehead felt damp. She took a deep breath to calm the racing of her heart.

"I—that is, we—I mean—"

"I thought I heard another voice. Is someone else here?"

Roxane looked around. Mr. Stregoni was nowhere in sight. Her relief was mingled with dismay.

"No, I'm alone. Until you came, that is. Sometimes I talk to myself. Out loud. I babble. A silly habit."

Where had he gone? He must have ducked behind a trunk. It was the only sensible explanation.

"What's this on the floor?" Fleur touched the heap of clothing with the toe of her shoe.

"It's—well, it's—I was gathering my laundry to take to Louise. You startled me and I dropped it." Roxane hastily gathered up the clothing and headed toward her chamber.

Fleur trotted behind her. "It's Monday. Laundry day isn't until Thursday."

"You're right." Roxane gave up on thinking of a good explanation. She opened the chamber door and tossed the white bundle onto the narrow bed. "Shall I read to you? Would you like to learn more letters?"

A smile brightened Fleur's face as she held out the book. "Oh, please, would you? That's why I was trying to find you."

"I'll make you a bargain. I'll read to you if you won't tell a soul what you saw me doing in the storage room just now."

"You mean talking to yourself and dropping your laundry?"

"Yes, exactly. I don't want anyone to think I might be taking leave of my senses." Roxane took the book. "You must cross your heart."

Fleur's finger drew an X across her chest.

"All right then. Let's go down to the parlor, shall we? We'll be more comfortable there."

Fleur clapped her hands. "Yes, let's. Oh, thank you."

Roxane closed the door behind them, hiding her undergarments from view.

Thank goodness it was Fleur who interrupted the kiss. She hated to think what Aurélie or Véronique would have demanded as a price for keeping silent.

CHAPTER

18

"Come on, Claire," Tess said from the storage room doorway. She looked eager to follow Ellie and her brothers, who had retreated downstairs.

"Go ahead," Claire said. "I'll just be a minute."

Tess, usually so calm and regal, seemed flustered. She was probably wondering why any fool would want to remain behind with a corpse.

But it seemed rude to abandon Simon without taking a moment to pay respect. Once Tess was gone, Claire whispered, "Goodbye, Simon. I wish I'd had the chance to get to know you. I think I might have fallen in love."

She didn't really expect an answer but listened anyway, half hoping, half fearing she'd hear a whispered word. Nothing broke the silence except the hum of traffic out on the street. Good. She hoped Simon's spirit had moved on to wherever souls go, and had found peace.

She spotted a tiny object near Simon's outstretched hand. Taking care not to touch it, she crouched down to peer at it more closely.

A pearl stud from a tuxedo shirt. Not Simon's, though. The stones in his were black, probably onyx.

Had the murderer left the stud behind? If he'd been wearing a tux, he must have been one of the men at the fundraising party.

141

But who? And why did he want to kill Simon? She blinked back tears as she left the room.

Reaching the second-floor hall, she heard a commotion in the foyer below. Two paramedics carting a gurney rushed up the grand staircase. She ducked out of their way as they wrestled their equipment up to the storage room, and moved aside again for a heavyset uniformed cop hurrying behind them.

Her 911 call had brought results.

Continuing downstairs, she saw another cop, a young guy with a shaved head, blocking the front door.

"What do you mean, we can't leave?" Richard Burnham had his fist half raised. Marc and Ellie stood next to him, Ellie clutching Marc's sleeve. Tess was several paces away, keeping her distance.

"Sorry, sir," the cop said. "When the detectives get here, they'll need to talk to you."

Richard pushed forward. "I can't wait. I have an important meeting this afternoon."

The cop spread his arms, widening the barrier he made. "We all have important things to do, sir. Why don't you people wait in there?" He herded them into the parlor. "How come there's no furniture in this place?"

"There are chairs in the kitchen," Tess said. "The ones we rented for the fundraiser. Simon was supposed to return—" Her voice caught, and she turned her head away.

"I'll get some." Claire headed to the kitchen before anyone could stop her. She came back lugging five wooden folding chairs and helped the cop set them up around the parlor at widely spaced intervals—too far apart for anyone to whisper with others and conspire on a story.

"Everybody take a seat," the cop said. "The detectives from Homicide will be here soon."

Richard Burnham grabbed the chair closest to the front door.

Claire claimed the one in the window bay. Gazing out at the garden, where a few late roses bloomed amidst the weeds and overgrown grass, might keep her mind from dwelling on the tragedy upstairs.

"What are we supposed to do?" Ellie asked in a tremulous voice.

"For now, ma'am, you wait."

Ellie squirmed in her seat. It felt like they'd been trapped in the parlor all day, though it had been only an hour. So far. She couldn't bear being in this house much longer.

A man murdered in Granny Jo's home—the one place where she'd always belonged, the location of some of her happiest memories. It was too horrible to think about. Yet she was stuck on this chair with nothing to do but think—and try to keep from screaming or breaking down in tears.

If only she could talk to someone. Not Richard—she could tell from his scowl and the way he kept looking at his watch that he was in no mood to be consoling. Not that he was ever in that mood. She got along better with Marc, but right now he was slumped on a chair across the room, elbows on his knees, face in his hands.

The paramedics had left; there was no one to save. Simon's body would wait for the medical examiner. The chubby cop had come downstairs and was moving around the parlor, asking each person the same questions in stiff, formal tones. Name, address, reason for being at the house, relationship to the deceased. The other cop, the bald one, carefully wrote the replies on a clipboard.

They came to Ellie last. When she tried to speak, her throat closed, and she stumbled through her replies. She didn't know why—the questions were easy enough, though she wasn't sure how answer to the last one.

"Relationship? I didn't know Simon, not really. We only met a few times."

The cops glanced at each other and nodded. Did they think she sounded suspicious?

She twisted her fingers in her lap. "That's all I can tell you, honest."

"Thanks for your cooperation, Ms., uh, Burnham," the bald cop said, consulting his clipboard for her name.

A noise at the front door. Ellie looked up. Two people came in: a dark-haired man wearing a business suit and a grim expression and a blond woman in crisp black slacks and a camelhair blazer. The homicide detectives. They conferred with the uniformed cops in voices too low to overhear. After a few moments all but the bald one went upstairs.

Three more people entered, lugging heavy black cases. Crime scene technicians, Ellie guessed. Carrying fingerprint powder and chemicals for identifying bloodstains and who knew what. She'd watched lots of crime shows but they'd taught her nothing about dealing with a real murder.

Murder. The dreadful word—the reality of what had happened upstairs—made her shudder.

If only Peter were here to hold her, soothe her, make things right.

She looked at Claire sitting in the window bay. The sunlight behind her made her a silhouette, her expression invisible. Was she thinking the same thing, longing to be in Peter's arms?

The minute Ellie got out of here, she was going to call him. If he loved her as much as he claimed, he'd understand how much she needed to be with him on this awful day. It had been such bliss on Saturday, having him in her bed the whole night. If only he could be there tonight, not for sex but for solace.

Then she remembered—Peter hadn't been with her for all of Saturday night. After sending her home from the party, he hadn't shown up at her apartment for hours. When he finally arrived he seemed nervous, distracted. Why was he so late? Because, he told her, he had to cool down after an argument with Simon Thatcher.

Was it possible Peter had—no. Ridiculous. She shoved the stupid thought out of her head.

The chubby cop came downstairs, heavy shoes thumping on the uncarpeted treads. He looked at Claire, then at Ellie.

What now? Ellie's pulse began to race.

"Claire Scanlan?" the cop said.

"That's me." Claire stood, ran a hand through her brown hair. She looked anxious.

"Follow me. The detectives want to speak to you."

Ellie sighed with relief. But her turn would come, and the cops' next questions were sure to be harder to answer.

———◆———

The detectives had set up shop in Josephine Burnham's bedroom.

"Come in, Ms. Scanlan. I'm Inspector Vargas." The man wagged a beckoning finger as Claire hesitated in the doorway. He made his words sound like an invitation, not an order, but Claire knew better.

If he smiled, he might be attractive. Tall, wide in the shoulders, black hair turning silver at the temples. But he didn't look like he kept a smile in his arsenal of facial expressions.

He nodded to the slender fair-haired woman beside him. "My partner, Inspector Flaherty."

Flaherty had warm gray eyes and a reassuring smile. She held up a sheaf of notes. "Take a seat, please. We'd like to go over a couple of points."

They had brought up three of the folding chairs and a small table they'd unearthed somewhere. Trying to push away her nervousness, Claire perched on the empty chair across from them. The hot seat.

Bumping and scraping noises came from overhead—the crime scene team going about its work.

She rubbed her hands along her thighs, smoothing nonexistent wrinkles in her skirt. Her mouth felt dry, and her heart was pounding.

There was so much she couldn't explain.

Okay, Claire, focus. Justice for Simon—that's what matters.

Simon. Murdered. Tears sprang to her eyes, and she fought them back.

"Don't be upset, dear."

She jerked up her head. Who'd said that? Maybe she was babbling out loud. She hoped the detectives hadn't heard.

She glanced around the room. Saturday night it had been dark; all she'd seen was the vague impression of a rocking chair, her imagination working overtime. Now she noticed elaborate woodwork, high ceilings, tall windows in the rounded alcove that was part of the Queen Anne tower. Vivid pink rectangles and ovals in the faded wallpaper revealed where pictures had hung, perhaps for decades. This must have been a splendid room in its heyday.

She took a deep breath, inhaling a scent of flowers and spice.

"Ms. Scanlan." Vargas's voice was a deep bass rumble.

Claire snapped to attention. "Sorry."

"We're told you discovered the body." Vargas's forehead was shiny with perspiration. Didn't he notice the room was freezing?

"Yes, I—I did."

"Why don't you tell us what happened," Flaherty said gently.

Claire described the fundraiser and explained how she and Tess had come to the house to let the caterer retrieve the platters that had been left behind.

"What made you go up to the storage room?" Vargas asked.

The question she'd been dreading.

Claire shifted uncomfortably under their gaze. Did she dare mention strange Mr. Stregoni or Roxane in her old-fashioned dress? As far as she could tell, she was the only person who'd seen them, even though they'd been moving around right in front of everyone.

Bad enough that she sometimes perceived wisps of sound or scent that others couldn't. But seeing flesh-and-blood people that no one else knew were there—that took her unwanted talents to a new and terrible level.

Honest, Inspector, there were a strange man and woman, invisible to everyone but me. They lured me to the third floor. When I saw Simon's body, they rushed up the spiral stairs into the tower. And vanished.

Right. That would establish her credibility.

If she mentioned the peculiar pair and no one backed her up, the police were sure to think she was lying.

Or crazy.

Or both.

But what if she was wrong? Suppose someone had seen Roxane and Stregoni and told the detectives. She'd look equally bad if she failed to mention them.

When Claire was growing up, Gram had been firm in her insistence that she and Cassandra tell the truth. *Remember, girls—honesty is always the best policy.* Gram never told her what do if the truth she experienced was at odds with what everyone else understood to be real.

"Ms. Scanlan, please answer the question," Flaherty said.

"Sorry," Claire said again. She knew she looked fidgety. "What was—?"

"What made you go upstairs?" Vargas repeated.

"There was a sign in the window—HELP. SEND POLICE. Tess thought it was a prank, but I decided to look around to make sure."

"A sign. What happened to it?"

"I dropped it on the floor when I saw Simon … lying there." The horrible sight rose again in her mind's eye. Claire shivered.

Vargas and Flaherty exchanged glances, which told her they'd found the sign.

"Who put it in the window?" Flaherty asked.

Claire shrugged. "No idea."

Flaherty slipped on a pair of glasses and ran her finger down her page of notes. "You said you also went upstairs on Saturday night. Why?"

I was chasing an invisible girl with an amethyst necklace.

"I was curious … to see the rest of the house."

"And that was the last time you saw Simon Thatcher alive?"

"Yes. He came into the storage room with several other people."

"What happened then?"

"Nothing. I went downstairs and Simon went to close an open window. He was in charge of the party, so he probably stayed after everyone left to make sure things were in order. Maybe an intruder broke in—"

"The 'several other people.' Who were they?"

"Um, I'm not sure. I wasn't paying close attention." Which was true. When Simon ordered her downstairs, her focus had been solely on the bad impression she'd made, being caught where she didn't belong.

"You didn't recognize any of them?"

"Well, the Burnham brothers. Both of them, or at least one." Claire's mouth was dry.

Vargas jotted a note. "Anyone else?"

"Peter. Peter Mortensen." The name slipped out. She hadn't intended to say it.

"And Mortensen is … ?"

"He's my, uh—a lawyer for the developer who wants to purchase the property." Better leave out the fact that Peter was her brother-in-law, as well as her suspicions about Peter's involvement with Ellie Burnham. Their relationship, whatever it was, surely had nothing to do with Simon's murder. Having cops pester her with questions wouldn't be a good way for Cassandra to learn her husband might be cheating.

She'd nearly forgotten she was going to her sister's for dinner tonight. What would she say to Cassandra? Or to Peter?

"Poor Mirabelle. So unlucky in love. Like me."

That voice again, a soft whisper. Claire sat up straighter.

Vargas cleared his throat. "Ms. Scanlan."

"Excuse me, what did you say? My mind is—all this has been very upsetting."

"Was there any trouble at the party? Any fights or arguments?"

"If there was, I didn't see it." Then she remembered: she'd been in the dining room eating lemon tarts when Peter and Simon came out of the library, hurling angry words.

"It's almost as if our family were cursed."

A puff of warm breath tickled Claire's cheek. The floral scent grew stronger.

"Ms. Scanlan?" Flaherty said. "You look as if you have something more to tell us."

"No, really, I don't know anything."

"I know my Edouard loved me. My tragedy came from the cruelty of war. But Mirabelle's heartbreaks are dark gifts bestowed by the cruelty of her men."

She turned toward the whisper. No one there, but the rocking chair had appeared beside her—empty, yet moving slowly back and forth.

"Josephine?" Claire reached out to touch the needlepoint cushion, but her fingers felt only air.

"What did you say?" Vargas demanded. "We couldn't hear that."

"I know my Edouard was true to me."

"Nothing. Just a sigh."

The next questions were a blur. Claire stumbled through vague answers until finally Flaherty said, "Okay, I think we're done. For now."

Vargas gave a confirming nod. "You can go, Ms. Scanlan—"

"Thank you." Claire leaped from her seat. She couldn't wait to get out of this house.

"—and rejoin the others downstairs. After we've spoken to everyone, you'll all be free to leave."

At the doorway something brushed Claire's shoulder.

"Thank you for helping that poor dead man. May he rest in peace."

She ran downstairs as fast as she could.

CHAPTER

19

The dead man is gone. The jagged shards of energy that burst through the air when violence exploded have settled to the floorboards, like dust. The house is quiet again.

His body has been carted away and his spirit has moved on to find peace in the Place Called Forever. I was surprised that he crossed the threshold so quickly, so easily. He offered to take me with him, reached for my hand. But I've never let any man touch me except my true love.

Oh, my dearest! Just thinking about you always made my body tremble and my blood heat up as it coursed through my veins. If I still had breath, it would catch at the sound of your name.

Edouard Trevillon.

Given my family's background, perhaps it was no coincidence that I fell in love with a Frenchman. Until I met him, I despaired of ever loving anyone. I'd had beaus on occasion, but no one who kindled enough sparks in my heart that I wanted him for a husband.

"Marry for love," my mother told me. "Don't marry out of loneliness or boredom or a need for money. A single woman who has beauty, wit, and cunning, all of which you've inherited from me, can always make her way in the world. If the world glances at her with its eyes askance and tsks its tongue, well, that just makes life more interesting."

When I asked her what she meant, she only shook her head and added, "And certainly never marry because you're afraid."

The day I met Edouard is engraved in my memory: July 14, 1939. An organization of French expatriates was holding a Bastille Day picnic in Aquatic Park. Maman was ill and insisted I go alone.

I was standing at the edge of the crowd and had just sipped the last of my champagne when a man came up to me with a full bottle.

"I see your glass is empty, madame," he said. "May I refill it for you?"

He wore a French soldier's brown uniform and stood tall and straight.

"Non, merci," I said. "One drink is enough for me."

"Is that true even if a gentleman buys it for you, or are you steadfast in your devotion to abstemiousness?"

I laughed. "You have a delightful way of expressing yourself, monsieur."

"I'm just practicing my English, madame." He smiled, and my heart melted into a puddle around our feet.

That made me bold enough to say, "In my case, it's mademoiselle."

He bowed to me. "I beg your pardon."

"I must say, your English is excellent."

"Thank you. I studied English in Paris for a long time, but here in America I'm aware of my awkwardness."

"You don't seem awkward to me," I assured him. Then I surprised myself by adding, "Perhaps I'll have more champagne after all."

He filled my glass and his own. "I am Edouard Trevillon."

"Pleased to meet you. I'm Josephine Burnham."

"Burnham—that's not a French name. I thought this party was for French people."

"My mother is French. She named me for Emperor Napoleon's wife. And you—do you live here in San Francisco?"

"I'm on leave from in the French army, visiting my cousin. Will you join me to watch the fireworks, Mademoiselle Burnham?"

"Of course." My spirit soared. "And please call me Josephine."

The fireworks were to be set off from a barge on the bay. All of the seats in the viewing stand were taken, so I settled with Edouard on the grass nearby. He poured more champagne, emptying the bottle.

As dusk turned into night, the sky lit up with exploding flowers and pinwheels and showers of sparks. Halfway through the spectacle Edouard took my hand. His felt warm and strong. I didn't pull away.

Afterward he walked me home. I felt dizzy in his presence, and I knew the sensation had nothing to do with drinking champagne, not even three glasses of it.

I was thirty-three years old, and that was the day my life truly began.

———— ◆ ————

Roxane settled onto the velvet upholstery of the sofa in the parlor and opened the ABC book. "All right, where were we?"

"Here." Fleur turned the page and pointed. The two facing pictures showed a kitten and a pup staring at each other, mouths open. They looked like they were about to fight.

Roxane began reading. " 'C is for Cat, who says meow. D is for Dog, who goes bow-wow.' "

She flipped to the next page as Fleur curled up beside her and rested her head on Roxane's shoulder.

" 'E is for Elephant, with a long, funny nose. F is for Flower—in the garden it grows.' " In the drawing an elephant pranced through a field of daisies, one of which was almost as large as the magnificent beast.

"E-e-e." Fleur breathed out the letter as a sigh. "Ef-f-f. F stands for Fleur."

"You're right. In fact, Fleur means flower, just like the picture."

Roxane was having a hard time concentrating. All she could

think about was her undergarments. Could Fleur, pressed so close to her side, tell she was wearing nothing beneath her dress? Funny—Roxane could display her naked body without embarrassment to gentlemen visiting Chez Celeste. Yet she felt uncomfortably immodest in her ordinary daytime dress without the usual layers of white linen underneath.

"Have you ever seen an elephant?" Fleur asked. She ran a finger along the animal's upraised trunk.

"Never," Roxane said. "I don't think they really exist. They're probably a myth, like dragons and unicorns."

"Oh, they're real, all right." Fleur nodded sagely. "When the circus came to Sacramento, it had an elephant."

"And you got to see it?" Roxane felt a small stab of envy.

"Well, not the real elephant. We didn't have any money for circus tickets. But its picture was on posters all over town. The preacher went and told us all about it. The elephant was as big as our house, and his ears were like the sails on a boat and his nose was longer than I am tall." Fleur's arms flew out in extravagant gestures as she described the wondrous creature.

Louise bustled into the room. "What are you all doing down here? It's almost opening time. You should be upstairs getting ready for the gentlemen." With strong black arms she lifted the potted fern from the floor and set it on the table in the window bay.

Fleur scrambled to her feet. "Oh dear, I didn't know it was so late. Come on, Roxane, we must hurry."

"It's Monday. Maybe there won't be any gentlemen today," Roxane muttered. She knew better—there had never been a day when Chez Celeste had no visitors. But the house usually enjoyed less trade early in the week, and she could hope. "Or better, just one," she added, thinking of Mr. Stregoni.

"Don't say that." Louise drew the draperies to keep passersby from seeing past the fern and into the room. "You want plenty of gentlemen. Running this house costs a pretty penny. Last week Lady Celeste had to pay off a judge to keep him from shutting us down, and judges don't come cheap."

"She should have just offered him the opportunity to visit us for free," Roxane said. "Like the newspaper editor and the chief of police."

"Not him. He's one of those judges who's pledged to cleanse San Francisco of vice and sin."

Roxane stood and gathered her skirts about her, preparing to go upstairs. "If he's after vice and sin, he should go to Maiden Lane and the Barbary Coast. I could give him quite a few addresses."

Louise made a dismissive wave. "Nobody cares about those places. They've been sinful forever. It's expected that low men will wallow in that filth. But a parlor house in a respectable neighborhood—lots of folks object to us being here."

Roxane thought of prim Mrs. Sedgwick and her timid daughter Mrs. Bisbee, seeking a proper girl to mind their house and children. If they knew the truth about Chez Celeste, they would probably lead the campaign to shut it down.

"Only our gentlemen know what kind of establishment this is," Fleur objected. "And they come in the side door so they won't be noticed. The neighbors think we're a boardinghouse for young ladies."

Louise shook her head. "You can only pull wool over people's eyes for so long. I'm afraid our days in this house are numbered."

"Oh no," Fleur said in a small frightened voice. "Where would we go?"

An icy hand gripped Roxane's heart. She would die if she had to be a pretty waiter girl again.

If Chez Celeste were to close, how would she survive?

CHAPTER

20

When the police finally said they could leave, Ellie bolted out the door. She paused beneath the filigreed scrollwork of the porch, gulping in fresh air and blinking in surprise at the sunlight. After being trapped for hours in gloom and darkness, she'd half expected to step outside and discover it was midnight.

Claire and Tess hurried down the front steps without a parting word. She didn't blame them; she was in no mood for meaningless niceties either.

Then her brothers emerged. Marc slipped an arm around her, asking, "Hey, Ell, you okay?"

Her first impulse was to lean against him and release the tears that had been threatening to spill all afternoon. But not with Richard watching. She pulled herself tall and lifted her chin.

"I'm fine. Let's get out of here."

She led the way to the street but the men's long strides quickly left her behind. Running after them, she ran her fingers along the arrow-tipped iron spikes that fenced the side garden. The metal was pocked and rusty. When she was a child the fence was always shiny and black, the yard lush with green grass and fragrant roses. She and Granny Jo made a game of searching for elves under the glossy leaves of the shrubbery. It broke her heart to see the garden now, weedy and forlorn.

"Christ, what a terrible situation," Richard was saying when she caught up.

Ellie nodded. "It's tragic. Poor Simon."

"We wouldn't be in this fix if you two hadn't dragged your feet."

"What fix?" Ellie asked. She realized they were walking away from where her car was parked. Like when they were kids, she'd blindly trailed in her brothers' wake like a duckling.

"Whoa," Marc said. "You make it sound like Ellie and I killed Simon ourselves."

"Don't be an ass," Richard said. "I'm only saying if we'd already inked our deal with Harding and Boyer like I wanted, we'd be counting our money now and they'd be the ones stuck with a worthless property."

"Worthless?" Ellie echoed. "What do you mean?"

Halting abruptly, Richard turned to face her. "Grow a brain, Ellie. Harding and Boyer plan to turn the house into condos. Who wants to live in a place where someone's been murdered? The deal's as dead as that guy in the attic."

"Richard!" Ellie cried. "How can you be so disrespectful?"

Marc said, "You're forgetting there's already been a death in the house. Granny Jo died right there in the rose bedroom—"

"Not the same thing," Richard said. "The natural death of a very old woman. But a murder—just watch, Harding and Boyer will pull their offer off the table so fast it'll make our heads spin."

Marc said, "That's why BAPA's offer is better. If the house becomes a museum—"

"You'd love that, wouldn't you? You've been pushing for it all along. As if you've got tons of money and can afford to sell out to the lowest bidder. Cut Ellie and me out of what's rightfully ours."

"It's not like you need money, Mr. Hotshot CEO. You think I'm just an underpaid college professor, but I know what has real value."

"What's that crack supposed to mean?"

"Stop it, you two." Ellie put a placating hand on Marc's arm. "The idea behind meeting here was to talk calmly and sensibly about what to do. That coffee shop Granny Jo liked is only a couple of blocks away. Let's go there and—"

Richard shot back his jacket sleeve and tapped his Rolex. "Can't. I've missed one important appointment and I'm late for the next one." He jabbed a finger at Ellie's face. "Dinner. Ciboulette at seven. Be there. You too, Marc."

Ciboulette. The restaurant where her relationship with Peter began. Ellie sighed.

"What?" Richard barked. "Don't tell me you've got something better to do on a Monday night."

She had planned to spend the evening studying. But she'd never be able to concentrate. What she wanted to do was call Peter, convince him that tonight of all nights she needed his company ...

"I don't know, Richard. Ciboulette's so expens—"

"Don't worry about that. Just be there."

Richard never took no for an answer. And for once he was right—it was time to resolve the question of the house.

"Okay, I'll 'just be there.' What about you, Marc?"

"I'll come," Marc said, though he didn't look happy.

Richard pulled a key remote from his pocket. Lights flashed on a silver BMW parked nearby. Ellie didn't recognize it, but she could never keep track of his cars; he had a new one every year or two.

Richard opened the driver's door. "Seven o'clock. I'll make the reservation in my name. Don't be late."

She watched him drive off. Then Marc said, "I'll walk you to your car, Ell. Where is it?"

"Back there, past the house." She pointed. "I'm a big girl now, Marc. I can walk to my car on my own."

"I didn't mean—never mind. See you later."

"Ciboulette at seven." Her purse slipped from her shoulder and she hitched it higher. "I don't know, it seems thoughtless somehow. Indulging in a fancy dinner right after finding that poor man …"

"I'm really sorry about what happened to Simon Thatcher. But this could be our chance to bring Richard around to our side."

"Your side, you mean."

"What are you saying. Ellie? I thought you were with me on this. Don't tell me you're standing with Richard."

"I'm not standing with anybody. It's just—Harding and Boyer are offering a lot more money …"

"This isn't about money. It's about preserving the Burnham legacy, our family's place in history. Richard's a selfish bastard, so he doesn't get it, but I know you do. It's what Granny Jo would have wanted."

Ellie glanced at the house, half a block away. The cops had strung yellow tape across the front, declaring it a crime scene.

"It would honor the murdered man too," she said. "We'd be carrying out the good work Simon was doing."

"Exactly."

"Who do you think could have killed him?"

"No idea. But I hope they catch the creep soon." Marc hugged her. "See you tonight, Ell."

She started hiking to her car. Fog was rolling in, ghostly gray wisps floating across the sky from the direction of the ocean. The breeze had turned cold and biting. Walking past the house, she shivered. The wind, she told herself, just the wind. But even after she was safely sheltered inside the car, she couldn't stop shaking.

———•———

"What an awful thing to happen!" Tess slammed her hand on the steering wheel.

They were crossing the Golden Gate Bridge, heading back to Marin. Mist blew past the windshield and obscured the bridge towers, but sunlight still shone on the hills across the bay. In the middle of the choppy waters Claire saw the rocky crags and the high gray walls of Alcatraz. Too bad the infamous prison was closed and turned into a tourist attraction. Whoever had killed Simon deserved to rot in one of its frigid, barred cells.

Simon—how could she feel such a sense of loss for someone she didn't really know?

Tess sighed. "I'd better call the BAPA board members. Tell them about—" Her voice broke, and her eyes glistened with tears. "I'm going to miss him so much."

So am I, Claire thought. So am I. "I'm sorry, Tess. It's hard, losing people."

"He was a good man. A good friend."

"I wish I'd had the chance to get to know him."

"I wish that too," Tess said. "You would have liked him."

They left the bridge and passed the vista point. Its parking lot was full of cars, tourists marveling at the view of the city across the Golden Gate, half in sun, half shrouded in fog.

"Claire, I have to ask. What made you go upstairs and find him? You were acting a little, well, strangely back there."

That proved it. Tess might have been too preoccupied to notice the hand-lettered sign, but she couldn't have missed Stregoni with his crazy hair or Roxane with her armload of corsets and lace. If she'd seen them, she'd never have asked that question.

Claire rubbed her temples; she felt a headache coming on. Why could she see people who were invisible to everyone else? What kind of freak was she, anyway?

"I can't explain why. I just had a feeling that something was wrong."

When they were kids, Cassandra taunted Claire for seeing ghosts. Some of her strange experiences did seem to connect her to people who were no longer alive. That voice she'd heard in Josephine Burnham's pink bedroom—it must belong to the ancient lady herself, some sort of echo that lingered in the room where she'd slept for many decades.

But how could she explain Stregoni and Roxane? They couldn't be ghosts—they were too solid, too real. Yet apparently no one else could see them.

That made no sense.

Maybe she was going crazy after all.

She didn't dare say any of this. Her status at BayCrest still felt too precarious—she didn't want to give Tess a reason to change her mind.

As they left the freeway, the emotions of the day caught up with her. Tears pricking her eyes, she searched in her purse for a tissue. She didn't want Tess to catch her crying.

Tess asked, "Are you all right?"

"I'm fine. I mean, under the circumstances …"

"Would you like to spend the evening with my husband and me? It's hard to be alone at a time like this."

"Thank you, that's really kind, but I'm having dinner at my sister's." Though she didn't expect to find much comfort there.

Damn, she didn't have any tissues. But what was this bit of cloth? She pulled it out and unfolded it.

The lace-edged handkerchief Roxane had given her. She'd forgotten about it.

That proved it. She hadn't imagined those people. They were real.

———◆———

Behind the closed door of her chamber Roxane peeled off her dress and tossed it on top of the undergarments on her narrow bed. At any moment the evening's first visitors would arrive. She had to make herself ready, and do it quickly. Lady Celeste insisted that when the gentlemen came in, they would find the *jeunes filles* waiting in alluring attire and with smiles full of charm.

Naked now, she shivered. Outside the window, fog had grayed the sky. Yesterday morning, after Thaddeus Burnham finally departed from the room, she had opened the window in the hope of clearing away the lingering stink of him. It hadn't been shut since, and a chilly draft whistled in. She jerked the sash closed with a thud.

She dreaded going downstairs and finding Thaddeus there. He had promised to return this evening to take his pleasure from her in the Rose Room. Last night he'd been infuriated to lose her company to Mr. Stregoni, and he would be eager to make her suffer the consequences of his rage. If only that bodacious strumpet Véronique had truly done as she'd boasted and given Thaddeus a night of such exotic pleasure that any thought of Roxane was wiped from his mind.

All she could do was pray for someone else to claim her before Thaddeus arrived. If fortune were smiling, Mr. Stregoni would be waiting as promised when she came downstairs. But fortune was much too fickle to let her to count on such a happy circumstance.

She stuffed the clothing from the bed into the wooden wardrobe. The chamber was so small that she could move from the bed to the wardrobe without taking a step.

Then she checked the pitcher on her wash table. Louise had done her duty and filled it with perfumed water. As Roxane poured an inch or two into her basin, the fragrance of violets surrounded her. She splashed the water on her face, under her arms, on her breasts, between her legs.

Using the thin white towel Louise had left for her, she slowly rubbed her body dry.

She found a box of scented powder and a rabbit's-fur puff and patted herself all over, sneezing as the fine dust touched her nose.

Her chemise for this week was hanging from a hook; she took it down and pulled it over her head. This was a garment that every woman wore, yet no respectable woman would allow hers to be seen; it would be hidden from view by her corset and several petticoats. Roxane had observed that gentlemen found the sight of one very enticing.

Hers was made of the thinnest cotton. It had no sleeves, merely ribboned straps that tied at the top of each shoulder, where a gentleman could easily reach the tail of the bow and undo it. The lace-trimmed hem fell only halfway to her knees. More lace decorated the neckline, which was not placed at her neck at all but cut so low that most of her bosom was exposed to the gentleman's scrutiny.

All too soon some man, sweaty and eager, would be in this room or a chamber downstairs, pulling the garment away from her. He would grab her close and make her lie with him on the bed. He would caress her skin, kiss her most private parts, thrust his manhood into her again and again until he exploded with satisfaction.

If that man was Thaddeus, he would make sure she felt pain.

She shivered again, but not because she was cold.

One more thing to do before she went downstairs. She opened her pot of lip rouge, touched her finger to the color, and rubbed it along the contours of her mouth. Touching her lips brought back the memory of Mr. Stregoni's kiss—the honey-and-cinnamon taste of his mouth, the tickle of his mustache, the magnetic pull of his body drawing her close. A wave of heat surged through her veins and took her breath away.

Could this peculiar feeling be what the other girls called love?

Impossible. Mr. Stregoni wasn't handsome, which seemed to be one of the requirements. On the contrary, he looked rather funny. All he had to recommend him was kindness and gentleness and a certain talent for magic.

Maybe that was it—he had woven a spell like a spider's web, seeking to entrap her. Though for what purpose, she wasn't certain. If he wanted her, all he had to do was pay the price to Lady Celeste.

Roxane knew love could exist between a mother and child. Her own dear mama had shown her that. But she'd learned from Pa and so many others after him that a man's whispered words of affection were hollow and false. A man and woman loving each other? That was a fool's notion.

If she were allowed her preference, no man would touch her ever again, not her body and certainly not her heart.

A brass bell jingled for the second time. The first had summoned the *jeunes filles* to the parlor; this one signaled that the house was now open to gentlemen. Roxane would be making a tardy entrance for the second day in a row, which was certain to displease Lady Celeste.

She hurried out of her chamber but paused in the hallway to steady her breath. There was no telling who might claim her tonight. Hope and terror were battling within her, and before she went downstairs she needed to subdue the pounding of her heart.

CHAPTER

21

Claire drove her lime-green jellybean up the lane to her sister's mini-chateau in the East Bay town of Lafayette. The house sat high on a hillside overlooking Mount Diablo and the surrounding countryside. She figured the sweeping vista would boost the home's value by at least ten percent.

She pulled to a stop on the guest parking pad beside the three-car garage and gazed at the house—Cassandra's reward for marrying a lawyer. Maybe Claire had missed out by divorcing Zach. After all, he was an attorney now. For an instant she wondered where he lived now and whether he'd married Little Ms. Lawyer, the classmate she'd caught him sleeping with. Then she decided she didn't care.

Now Cassandra might be facing the same kind of betrayal. Claire hoped this evening would convince her that her suspicions were baseless.

She turned off the engine and tried to pull herself together. The slog through rush-hour traffic had further frayed the nerves rubbed raw by the shock of Simon's murder. She'd nearly phoned Cassandra to cancel, but they got together so rarely. And Tess was right—better not to be alone on a night of sorrow.

A tap on the driver's door made Claire jump. The door was flung open and Willow, her seven-year-old niece, reached in to tug her hand. Wisps of blond hair haloed the little girl's face.

"Why're you still out here, Aunt Claire? C'mon, let's go."

Claire got out of the car and gave Willow a hug. "Hello, sweetie. Wow, you're getting so tall. How's my favorite niece?"

Willow laughed. "I'm your only niece, right?"

"But you're the best niece any aunt could have."

Willow nodded as if she knew this already.

Claire grabbed the bottle of zinfandel she'd brought and closed the car door. Willow led her around the garage to the broad flagstone terrace behind the house, where white wicker chairs and lounges were arranged to take advantage of the view. Fog might be blanketing San Francisco, but here the evening was clear and balmy. The setting sun had burnished the mountain slopes to a deep gold, and the air smelled of dry grasses and Cassandra's herb garden.

Willow ran to the French doors and poked her head inside, calling, "Mommy! She's here, she's here!"

Claire set her bottle on a glass-topped table where a bottle of cabernet sauvignon and three wineglasses were waiting. Bringing a red wine had been a good guess.

Willow came skipping back. "She says she'll be out in a minute and make yourself at home. Hey, I like your necklace."

"Thank you. So do I. It used to belong to your grandmother." Claire had worn her mother's heirloom necklace. After the day she'd been through, she needed its good cheer and good luck.

"Purple's my favorite color."

"One of mine too. These stones are amethysts."

"Amefizz," Willow repeated, stumbling over the sibilant sounds. She raised her arms and twirled on her toes like a ballerina, her sun-struck hair floating out around her head. "When I grow up I'm gonna be a dancer and wear amefizz all the time."

"Good plan," Claire said.

The French doors opened and Willow's brother, Jake, came out carrying a stack of cocktail napkins and a basket of baguette slices nestled in a gingham napkin. "Hi, Aunt Claire," he said with a grin.

"Hey, Jake." She swept him into a hug, pleased that he didn't pull away. He was nine, and before long he would consider himself too old for displays of auntly affection. Both kids were growing up way too fast. She vowed to make a point of seeing them more often.

A moment later Cassandra appeared, bearing a tray of cheeses. "Claire! Welcome!"

"Thanks for inviting me," Claire said. "You're looking great." In truth, Cassandra looked tired, and tight lines of tension bracketed her eyes. "I like the new hairdo."

"This?" Cassandra set down the cheese and ran her hand through her locks. They'd been trimmed short and highlighted with blond streaks since Claire saw her last. "I had it done months ago. Has it been that long since we've been together?"

"Easter, I think."

"Impossible. Surely you've been here more recently than that." Cassandra shook her head, then smiled. "Well, tonight we'll make up for lost time."

"Sit here, Aunt Claire. Next to me." Willow settled onto the wicker loveseat and patted the cushion beside her.

Cassandra picked up the wine Claire had brought. "Oh, this looks good." She reached for the corkscrew. "Might as well get started. Help yourself to the hors d'oeuvres."

Claire spread herbed chevre cheese onto a baguette slice and sat beside Willow.

"Where's Peter? Isn't he joining us?"

"He should be home any minute." Cassandra poured wine

into two of the glasses and handed one to Claire. "He probably ran into extra-heavy traffic."

"He thaid he'th gonna be laid." Jake's mouth was stuffed with bread.

"Jake! Don't talk with your mouth full," Cassandra scolded. "How many times do I have to tell you? Now swallow, and repeat what you said so that people can understand you."

Jake made exaggerated motions of guiding the bread down his throat. "I said, he's gonna be late. Didn't you hear the message? I played it while you were putting the groceries away."

"You mean he called while we were at the supermarket?"

"That's what I'm telling you. He's meeting a client or something. It came up at the last minute."

"What? He can't do that. He knew your Aunt Claire would be here tonight." Cassandra took a quick gulp of wine and set down her glass. "Excuse me, I'd better go listen to the voicemail. Why couldn't he call my cell phone? He knew I'd be out shopping this afternoon."

Perhaps that's why, Claire thought as her sister hurried across the terrace. Easier to leave a message than listen to someone get upset with you.

———◆———

Pushing open the door to Ciboulette, Ellie glanced at her watch. Seven-twelve. She was late. Richard was going to be angry.

The entry area was crowded with diners waiting to be seated. She threaded through the pack to the sleek blond desk, where an equally sleek blond maitre d' was holding court. Ellie tapped her fingers on the wooden surface, trying to get his attention. Someone tried to elbow her aside, and to her surprise she elbowed him back. "Sorry, I was here first."

"Good evening, madam." The maitre d' barely glanced at her. His mustache had turned-up ends that twitched as he spoke. "Do you have a reservation?"

Madam? Not miss? Suddenly Ellie felt old and dowdy. She'd worn her black dress, which seemed right for both a day spent at a tragic murder scene and an evening at one of the city's trendiest and priciest restaurants. Trying for an elegant touch, she'd thrown a paisley scarf over her shoulders. Maybe the scarf was a mistake.

"I'm with the Burnham party."

"Ah, yes. The gentlemen are expecting you." He swooped up a leather-bound menu and handed it to a tuxedoed waiter hovering at his elbow. "Please show the lady to table thirty-six."

The waiter made a slight bow. "Right this way, madam."

Madam again. Clutching the scarf to keep it from slipping, Ellie looked around as she followed him through the restaurant. It was a place for romance. Low lights, soft music, sweet and spicy smells. Crisp white linens on the tables. Silverware gleamed, crystal glasses sparkled, candles in small globes gave each table a warm glow. She'd been here only once before, the night she fell in love with Peter.

"Here we are, madam."

Ellie stopped short. The gentlemen were there, all right. Only there were four of them, not two. Marc and Richard. Daniel Harding from the development company.

And Peter.

Her heart jumped. For an instant she thought he was a phantom, a mixture of longing and memory. Then he grinned and she knew he was real.

All except Richard rose to greet her. Daniel smiled a welcome.

Ellie was happy to see that her chair was next to Peter's. The waiter pulled it out and gestured for her to sit. He took the snowy napkin at her place and snapped it across her lap.

"What's this? I thought it was going to be just the three of us." She aimed the question at Richard, making her tone light to show Peter and Daniel she intended no offense.

"He's ganged up on us," Marc grumbled.

"Not at all." Richard put up his hands in denial. "I happened to talk to Daniel this afternoon, and mentioned our get-together. He suggested that he and Peter tag along, in case they can answer any questions. Right, Dan?"

Daniel nodded. "That's the truth."

The way he said it made Ellie certain Richard had phoned him specifically to issue the invitation. No matter. The unexpected joy of seeing Peter at the end of this awful day made up for Richard's sneakiness.

"I'm glad you're here," she whispered to Peter.

"You look lovely." His finger traced a paisley curve on her shoulder, sending a shiver through her.

A waiter arrived with drinks. Richard had ordered his usual martini. The others received glasses full of amber liquid over ice. Single-malt Scotch, probably. Peter was fond of it.

"Would you care for a beverage, madam?" the waiter asked.

"Um, sure." What should she order? She didn't like whiskey or gin. "A glass of white wine?"

"Certainly, madam. Chardonnay, sauvignon blanc, pinot grigio?"

"So many choices." She didn't want to have to make another decision. Why couldn't anything today be easy?

"Shall I bring the wine list?"

Richard snorted with impatience.

Peter came to her rescue. "Bring the lady a glass of champagne."

"Perfect," Ellie said gratefully.

"What, you have something to celebrate?" Richard said.

Peter smiled. "She can celebrate being the loveliest woman in the place."

"Here's to that." Daniel lifted his Scotch in a toast.

Ellie felt the warmth of Peter's thigh pressing against hers beneath the table, and her mood lightened. Maybe her worries were foolish. He seemed genuinely glad to see her. After dinner she'd take him back to her apartment and they'd rekindle the intense flame from Saturday night. Even better, maybe he'd invite her to his place for the first time. Maybe he'd say those wonderful words: I love you, Ellie.

He rested a hand on her knee, and she put hers on top of his. Yes, everything was fine now.

A fanfare of trumpets blared. She was startled until Peter reached into his pocket for his phone. He scowled at the caller ID and pressed the phone to his ear.

"Hey … Dinner with a client, where did you think … I left you a message … what? Claire? Damn, that's tonight?" He pushed back his chair. "Hold on. Let me go outside." To the group at the table he said, "Back in a minute."

"Who is it?" Ellie immediately wished she could bite back the words.

"Nobody you know."

Claire—he'd said Claire. She'd been right to worry. She watched him walk away.

"Well," she said, keeping her voice bright, "as long as we have this interruption, I think I'll go freshen up."

She trailed Peter at a discreet distance to the front of the restaurant. Glancing back to make sure the others weren't watching, she followed him outside.

Ciboulette was downtown, near Union Square. Pedestrians jostled past her, their faces made garish by neon lights. Peter was leaning against the building's wall, facing away from her. She crept as close as she dared, pulling the scarf tight around her shoulders to protect her from the fog and cold wind.

"Look," Peter was saying into the phone, "I can't come now, I'm in a meeting … of course it's important, a major client … yes, it is an unreasonable request. Tell Claire I'm sorry … oh damn it, sweetheart, stop that … all right, for Chrissake. Quit yelling. I'll be home in time for dessert."

Sweetheart. The word hit her like a punch to the stomach. She doubled over, let out a moan. He was going home to someone he called sweetheart.

She tried to slip inside before he noticed her, but she'd taken only a step or two when his hand landed on her shoulder. "Ellie! What are you doing out here?"

She almost couldn't see him through a red haze of grief and anger. "Who were you talking to?"

"You're shivering. Let's go inside." He urged her forward.

She pulled away. "Sweetheart. You called her sweetheart. You're going home to her."

"This isn't a good time, Ellie."

"Who is she? Not Claire, you weren't talking to Claire, you were talking about her."

"Ellie, darling, it's not what you think—"

"How do you know what I think? Have you ever cared what I think?"

"What do you mean? Of course I care." He bent to kiss her forehead, a gesture she'd always loved from him. Now it felt demeaning. He was just like Richard, treating her like a child.

"Is she your wife? That's it, isn't it? You're married."

"Please, Ellie. Go finish your dinner. I'll call tomorrow and explain—"

"Oh, God, I'm so stupid."

She took off at a run. The light at the corner was green, and she dashed across the street to the edge of Union Square. She looked back but couldn't see Peter. Maybe he'd gone back inside; maybe she'd simply lost sight of him in the crowd.

One thing was certain—he wasn't coming after her.

"Stupid, stupid, stupid!"

So many warning signs she'd been careful to overlook. So many red flags she'd refused to heed. Ignorance was bliss, people said—well, the bliss Peter brought into her life depended on her ignorance.

Claire was a friend of the family, he'd said. He meant a friend of his wife's.

She sat on one of the hard metal benches in the square, put her head in her hands, and began to cry.

Traffic hummed on the streets. Horns blared. People shuffled by her bench, all of them ignoring her except for one whisker-stubbled man in dirty jeans and cracked shoes. His words floated toward her on boozy fumes: "You okay, lady?" She told him to go away.

She'd never been through a more terrible day. It had started with murder and was ending with betrayal, humiliation, dashed dreams. What was she going to do? Peter had ruined her life and didn't even care.

She shivered. She was so cold, but she couldn't go back to the restaurant and face the men's laughter or, worse, their pity.

Gradually an idea took form. She told herself no, then gave in. Pawing through her purse, she found her phone and the business card that the homicide detectives had given her. As she punched in the number she rehearsed the message she would leave.

To her surprise a real person answered.

"Vargas here."

"Inspector Vargas, this is Ellie Burnham. You interviewed me today—the Simon Thatcher murder? You said to call if I remembered anything that might be helpful. Well, I thought of something. Rather, someone."

"Yes, Ms. Burnham. Who is it?"

"This man argued with Simon that night. Then after the party he was missing for several hours. He refused to say where he was. You should talk to him."

"Who?" Vargas repeated.

Ellie took a deep breath. "Peter Mortensen."

"I've heard the name. Tell me more."

When Cassandra returned to the terrace, her face was shadowed with pain. She brushed at her eyes with her hands, and Claire was sure she'd been crying.

"Are you all right?" Claire asked. "Did you reach Peter?"

"He's at a dinner meeting. It came up at the last minute. An important client." Cassandra wiggled her fingers, making quote marks around the adjective. "So much more important than his own family. The bastard."

Willow, who'd been leaning against Claire in the wicker loveseat, sat up straight. "Mommy! You said a bad word."

"Where's our drinks, Mom?" Jake asked. "You were gonna bring out drinks for Willow and me."

"Oh, damn, I forgot."

Hearing the second bad word, Willow put her hands to her mouth and giggled.

"Go inside, Jake, and pour yourself a glass of—something. One for your sister, too."

"Anything I want? A Coke?"

"Milk or juice, or—oh, hell, go ahead, have a Coke."

"Yes!" Jake pumped his fist and loped toward the French doors. Willow ran at his heels.

The doors slammed behind them. Cassandra picked up her wineglass and carried it to the edge of the terrace. She stared out at Mount Diablo, the devil mountain. Its slopes were dark, no longer gilded by the sinking sun.

Claire walked over to stand beside her. Did Cassandra know what Peter was up to? Did she imagine someone like Ellie hovering at the boundary of her marriage, haunting it like a ghost?

Maybe Claire was wrong. She didn't really know if her suspicions had any basis. But after such a traumatic afternoon, it made sense that Ellie might call the man she loved and beg for his company and comfort. And if that man was Peter …

"Who's the client?" she asked. "The one Peter's having dinner with?"

"I don't know, some developer. Easy guess—all his clients are developers. It doesn't matter, really."

Cicadas in the grassy meadow were tuning up their music.

A breeze quickened, making Claire shiver. A star—well, a planet probably—winked on in the indigo sky. She made a wish that she and her sister could be closer, that she'd know the right words to say.

"Is that the necklace you asked about when you called yesterday?" Cassandra asked.

Claire realized she was fidgeting with the amethyst crystals. She let her hand drop. "I thought if you saw it you might remember the story behind it."

"I told you, I didn't know it existed until Gram gave it to you." Cassandra aimed her gaze at the star and Claire wondered if she was making her own wish. "None of Mom's things that I got were anywhere near that nice."

"I'm sorry," Claire said, though she wasn't exactly sure what she was sorry for.

"Don't be. I have plenty of nice things now." The sweep of Cassandra's arm took in the big house, the terrace, the mountain.

She raised her wineglass as if toasting it all. "But everything comes at a price, doesn't it."

"What do you mean?"

"Do you ever wonder what our lives might have been like if Mom and Daddy hadn't died so young?"

"Sometimes. But I was a baby when the accident happened. I have no memories of them, just Gram's stories. You and she are the only family I've known."

"Ah, Claire, count your blessings." Cassandra lifted her glass to her lips and seemed surprised to find it empty. "We should go inside," she said. "It's getting dark."

———◆———

After her call to Inspector Vargas ended, Ellie sat slumped on the bench. She had no more tears, only a hollowness where her heart used to be. She couldn't make herself move. Time passed in a blur.

She was startled when someone sat down beside her. A man's voice—not Peter's—said, "Mirabelle."

She lifted her head to see who it was.

Daniel Harding, holding out a handkerchief. "Here, use this."

She took it, wiped her eyes, blew her nose. "Thank you."

"Peter said you ran off, upset. He had to leave, so Marc and I went looking for you. Richard stayed at the table in case you showed up there."

"Peter's married. Did you know that?"

"Is that what this is about?" He stood and extended his hand to her. "Come on, I'll take you home. Where's your car?"

"I took a taxi." She stood too, and looked around in a daze. "What about the dinner?"

"Dinner's not happening. If you're hungry we can order something. Pizza or Chinese."

"That's kind of you." She was drained of energy. It was all she could do to put one foot in front of the other.

"I'll call your brothers, tell them I found you. Come on. My car's in the garage in the next block. Ready?"

She nodded. "Yes. Thank you."

"You're shivering. Here, put this on."

Daniel took off his suit jacket and eased her arms into its sleeves. When her scarf got in the way, he took it from her shoulders and flung it around his own. He put his arm around her waist to guide her and left it there until they reached his car.

———◆———

"Roxane," purred Lady Celeste, seated by the drinks table in her throne-like chair. "Do come in and join us."

"Yes, of course, Lady Celeste." Roxane stepped forward into the parlor. No gentlemen were present, not yet. The other *jeunes filles* sat at the games table playing with a deck of cards.

"What am I to do with you, mademoiselle? You were late yesterday, and today you're late again. I'm beginning to believe that you no longer appreciate your accommodation here."

Roxane heard the veiled threat. She curtsied to her employer, although it was difficult to make a proper curtsy in her skimpy chemise. "I apologize. I lost track of the time. It won't happen again."

"It's impossible to lose track of the time in this house. Do you see that clock?" Lady Celeste pointed to the tall floor clock in the corner of the room. "It's there so we all can be punctual for our obligations. And no doubt you heard the bell summoning you to the parlor, and the second bell indicating that the house is open to gentlemen."

"Oui, madame," Roxane said, hoping that the French words might appease the lady. "I'm not so late this time, only a few minutes. And it's not as if my services are needed right now."

"We anticipate guests at any moment," Lady Celeste said. Indeed, she was acting as if she expected someone. Though her gaze was aimed in Roxane's direction, it was focused beyond her, at the top of the stairs from the ballroom. The lady bit her lip and drummed her fingers on the drinks table, making the glasses rattle.

Except for her anxious expression, Lady Celeste looked especially beautiful tonight. She had painted her face to put roses in her cheeks and rubies on her lips. Her golden hair was pinned up in an elaborate arrangement that left delicate curls falling in front of her ears. Her blue dress was surprisingly fancy for a Monday.

As if she had conjured it, the ballroom bell chimed, signaling the arrival of gentlemen.

Please, Roxane prayed, though she doubted that any deity ever listened, please let it be Mr. Stregoni. Let it *not* be Thaddeus Burnham.

23

Expecting a casual supper in the family room, Claire was surprised to see that Cassandra had turned her visit into a special occasion. She'd spread a white damask cloth over the table in the formal dining room and set five places with gleaming sterling silverware. A crystal bowl filled with roses from the garden graced the center of table. Willow was proud and eager when Cassandra let her light the tall candles that flanked the flowers.

Yet it was not a festive meal, though Cassandra's rosemary-scented pork was delicious. Claire struggled to find things to say to her sister, who seemed preoccupied and distracted. Fortunately the kids' chatter about school and soccer practice created an illusion of lively conversation.

The specters of two absent men—Simon Thatcher and Peter Mortensen—seemed to float in the room, though there were none of the signs Claire was learning to associate with having spirits close by. No whispered voice, no faint and fleeting smell, no knot of charged energy.

Peter was almost as a strong a presence as if he were sitting at his vacant place. And Simon—every time her eyes blinked shut, she saw him. Sometimes he was the warm, energetic man she'd fallen for on Saturday night, sometimes the cold corpse she had discovered this afternoon. One image filled her with longing and regret, the other with grief and horror.

She hadn't found the right moment to talk about either man.

Finally Jake pushed aside his plate. "Is it time for dessert yet?"

"Wait 'til you see what we're having, Aunt Claire," Willow said excitedly. "I helped make it."

"If you two clear the table, we'll serve dessert," Cassandra told them, and they scrambled out of their seats. "More wine, Claire?"

Claire placed her hand over the top of her glass. "No, thanks. I have a long drive home."

"I might as well polish this off then." Cassandra drained the bottle into her glass and took a long drink. Claire had no idea how much her sister had consumed, but it was a good thing Cassandra didn't have to get behind a wheel.

Willow came back from the kitchen with a stack of dessert plates. She set one at her father's empty place. "Mommy, when's Daddy coming home?"

Cassandra glanced toward the hallway, as if expecting Peter to come in and sit down. "I don't know, sweetheart. He said he's on his way, but it takes awhile to get here from the city."

"He'll be sorry if he misses our special dessert."

"Don't worry. I'll make sure he gets a piece."

And a piece of her mind, too, Claire thought.

Jake came in proudly bearing a huge chocolate cake, its glossy frosting dotted with sprinkles. As he set it on the table Claire heard the muffled rumbling of the garage door.

"There he is!" Willow cried. She ran to greet her father.

Cassandra shook her head and lifted her wineglass to her lips again.

Willow returned a moment later, her small hand in Peter's large one, tugging him into the room.

"Claire!" he boomed. "Great to see you. Sorry I had to miss so much of the evening."

Peter brushed her cheek with a brotherly kiss, then went to

Cassandra and did the same. He looked surprised when she turned her face away and didn't speak. Taking his seat at the head of the table, he gestured toward the wine bottle. "I'll have a glass of that."

"It's empty," Cassandra said curtly.

Frowning, he went to select another bottle from a rack in the corner. If he didn't find one there that suited him, Claire knew there were plenty more in the temperature-controlled wine cellar that was his pride and joy.

He set a bottle on the mahogany sideboard and picked up the corkscrew.

Jake was wriggling in his seat. "When're we gonna cut the cake?"

"Go for it," his father said as the cork popped.

"Me?" Jake squeaked. "I get to cut it?"

"Why not?" Peter sent wine burbling into his glass. "Get the cake knife out of the silver chest."

As Jake made the first cut, the doorbell rang.

Everyone froze at the unexpected sound. Then Cassandra got up, dropping her napkin onto her seat. "Who the hell could that be?"

"Mommy!" Willow scolded. "You said another one."

But Cassandra was already in the foyer, opening the door. "Yes?" she said to whoever was there. Apparently a stranger.

Claire was surprised to recognize the bass voice that answered. "Sorry to disturb you. We're looking for Peter Mortensen. I understand this is his residence."

Inspector Vargas.

Cassandra's voice rose. "You're police?" Vargas must have shown her his badge.

"If we could speak to Mr. Mortensen, ma'am."

"Yes, of course." She appeared again in the dining room, her raised eyebrows turning her face into a question. "Peter? These people want to see you."

Vargas, wearing the same dark suit and somber tie as earlier, stepped around her into the room. Inspector Flaherty came up beside him. They both looked tired.

"Ms. Scanlan," Flaherty said. "We weren't expecting to see you here."

Claire felt awkward, slightly guilty, as if caught doing something wrong. "I was invited for dinner."

Vargas frowned. "You didn't mention that you and the Mortensens are friends."

Cassandra turned to Claire. "You know these people?"

Peter stood up. "I'm Peter Mortensen. What can I do for you?"

Flaherty introduced herself and her partner. "We have some questions to ask you about a homicide investigation."

"Homicide!" Cassandra's shocked voice set the word humming in the air.

Peter opened his arms in a way that suggested his innocence. "I don't know how I can help you."

"Who got killed?" Cassandra demanded.

"Someone got killed?" Jake echoed, waving the cake knife. He looked frightened. Willow had slid out of her seat and was clinging to her mother's side.

Peter hadn't asked the same question, Claire noted. How had he learned about Simon's death? Easy: Ellie had told him. The "client" he'd met with tonight.

"Just a few questions, Mr. Mortensen," Flaherty said. "We understand you were at a fundraiser in the city on Saturday night. For the Bay Area Preservation Alliance."

Peter frowned. "Look, we're in the middle of dinner. Come to my office tomorrow. My assistant can set up an appointment."

Vargas shook his head. "Perhaps there's another room where we could talk privately?"

"Tomorrow," Peter said firmly. "I don't want you disrupting my family."

Flaherty's fair hair had drifted over her brow, and she brushed it away. "What did you wear to this event, Mr. Mortensen?"

"What did I wear? What's that got to do with—?"

"His tux," Cassandra blurted out. She tightened her arm around Willow, who began to whimper.

The cops exchanged glances. Vargas said, "Your tux? Not a rental, you own it?"

Flaherty said, "We need to see it."

Claire recalled the pearl stud she'd seen on the floor near Simon's body. Could it be Peter's? He'd worn a tux on Saturday, but so had most of the men.

"It's at the cleaners," Peter said. "Right, darling?"

Cassandra bit her lips. "Well, I …"

Willow piped up with, "No, Daddy, it's upstairs. Mom putit in the car when we went to run errands, but we ran out of time so she brought it home." Apparently Cassandra was passing on Gram's honesty-is-the-best-policy dictum to the next generation.

"Seriously, Cass?" Peter said.

Cassandra sank onto her chair. "I had so much to do today. It's in the master bedroom closet."

Vargas said, "Please show us, Mr. Mortensen."

Peter shrugged elaborately for Cassandra's benefit. "Come with me."

He left with the two detectives. Claire heard their footsteps thumping up the stairs.

Cassandra put her head in her hands. "What the hell is happening? A murder? And Peter's mixed up in it?" She looked up and glared at her sister. "You better tell me everything, Claire. How do those cops know you?"

"Should we talk in front of them?" Claire nodded toward the kids, who were listening avidly. "That's why I didn't say anything earlier."

Jake brandished the cake knife, its broad blade smudged with frosting. "What about the cake?"

"Cake! Now is no time for—okay, you can each have one piece. Go eat it in the family room. Then it's bedtime."

When they'd disappeared with their dessert, Claire told the story of the murder, carefully weighing what to include, what to leave out, how to balance facts and suspicions and reassurances. As she talked, she imagined Simon's specter pushing in close.

She decided not to mention Peter and Ellie; Cassandra was dealing with enough.

While Cassandra refilled her wineglass, Claire asked, "What sort of studs does Peter wear with his tux?"

"Studs? He has these old pearl buttons he found in an antique store. Why?"

"Is one of them missing?" She described the one she'd seen near Simon's body.

"Oh my God," Cassandra said. "I have no idea. But they can't seriously suspect Peter of kill—of being involved."

Reaching across the table, Claire laid her hand on her sister's. "I'm sure it's just a routine inquiry. The cops must be talking to everyone who was there Saturday night."

Peter and the detectives came back downstairs. Vargas carried a large garment bag, Flaherty a tiny paper one. The tux in one and the pearl studs in the other, Claire guessed.

"Please note that I've been cooperative," Peter said to the cops. "If you want anything further, call my office." He moved toward the door, clearly ready to usher the cops out of the house.

"Better idea," Vargas said. "You come with us now to the Hall of Justice."

"Now? Didn't I just say—"

"It's not a request, Mr. Mortensen."

"Wait!" Cassandra jumped up. "Are you arresting him? For murder? Peter, what's going on? Should we call a lawyer?"

"No one's under arrest, ma'am." Vargas's tone was not reassuring. "Some questions, that's all."

Peter raised his hands again, this time in surrender. "Look, I'll come with you. Answer what I can. But I'll tell you now, I don't know anything that will help."

"Good," Vargas said. "Let's go."

"Peter, don't—" Cassandra protested.

He came over and hugged her. "It's okay. I'll be back as soon as I get this straightened out. Call Frank Jesperson. He handles criminal matters for my firm."

"Criminal," Cassandra whispered.

Peter and the cops departed. The heavy oak door slammed behind them.

Cassandra brushed tears from her eyes. Claire understood that she didn't want her little sister to see her crying. Claire was near tears herself.

"You'd better go," Cassandra said.

"Sure you don't want me to stay? I could—"

"Just leave."

When her sister wanted to exile her, it was useless to protest, much less offer help.

As Cassandra sat there motionless, Claire blew out the candles. They had burned down to stubs, leaving drips of hot wax on the tablecloth.

Then she went into the family room, where she found two empty plates on the coffee table and two kids asleep at opposite ends of the sofa. She kissed each child on a chocolate-smeared cheek.

She left through the French doors. A brisk breeze blew, and a half moon sent shadows creeping across the terrace. In the distance an owl hooted.

In her car, she rested her forehead on the top of the steering wheel, trying to gather her energy. Then she turned the key in the ignition and began the long drive home.

CHAPTER
24

At the sound of the ballroom bell, Lady Celeste looked up eagerly and put on a radiant smile. She twisted a strand of her yellow hair into a fetching curl and pinched her cheeks to brighten their rosy color. How strange, Roxane thought. While Lady Celeste always welcomed gentlemen with the utmost in graciousness and courtesy, she maintained a cool reserve befitting a woman of business. Today she was barely concealing her excitement. Whom could she possibly be waiting for?

Whoever it might be, she could not be as eager to see him as Roxane was to greet Mr. Stregoni.

They both were disappointed when the new arrival appeared in the hall. Two new arrivals, in fact. Both were strangers.

Rising to greet them, Lady Celeste extended her hand to the elder one. He removed his hat, revealing a mane of silver hair, and lifted her hand to his lips, bestowing a courtly kiss in the continental fashion. The lady batted her long eyelashes in appreciation.

"Bienvenue, messieurs. Welcome to Chez Celeste," she cooed. "I am Lady Celeste. Whatever your pleasure may be, you've come to the right place."

"Thank you, madam." The man made a bow. "We're happy to make your acquaintance. I am Mr., uh, Smith, and this is my friend, Mr. Jones."

Mr. Smith seemed at ease in his present surroundings, but the younger Mr. Jones, a tall, skinny man, looked decidedly less comfortable. His hair, drooping from a center part, was the color of a ripe pumpkin, and his face was turning a bright tomato red.

"Oh my," Mr. Jones said as he gaped at the *jeunes filles*. "Oh my, oh my. You're right, Julius. This is no boardinghouse."

"Oh, but it is, monsieur," Lady Celeste assured him. "These charming girls reside here, having arrived from the finest neighborhoods of Paris. At certain hours we open our house to special guests and provide the sort of entertainment that the women of France are well known for. May I inquire who recommended our establishment?"

"Several friends have told me about this place," Mr. Smith said. "Your fine reputation is spreading throughout the city."

Lady Celeste nodded. "Come into the parlor and enjoy a glass of whiskey while you meet our jeunes filles."

"Whiskey—a fine idea. What is the cost for two glasses?"

Lady Celeste told him the price and he set the money on the drinks table. She poured two generous measures of the watered-down liquor.

Mr. Smith drank a large gulp. "Now, what is the cost for other services that may be on offer?"

Lady Celeste explained the hourly charges for each of the chambers. "When you select a jeune fille to accompany you for a private conversation, her time is at your disposal for as long as you have reserved the room. The payment is made in advance. If you make a special request of her, she'll be happy to explain the necessary terms and conditions, and you will make that payment when you leave. Now, allow me to introduce you."

She beckoned the *jeunes filles* to come together. Roxane hated these moments when they lined up in a row so that the gentlemen could make their leering inspection, as if they were prize pigs at the fair. Lady Celeste named each girl in turn and described the special attributes that would make her an appealing selection.

"So difficult to choose," Mr. Smith murmured, gazing upon one bosom after another. His large white teeth and the glint in his dark eyes made Roxane think of a wolf. "They are très belles, every one."

Mr. Jones hadn't moved from the hallway. His whiskey glass sat ignored on the drinks table. But now he sidled up to his companion.

"Psst," he said, his voice low and urgent. "Julius, we must leave. You cannot mean to stay here. This place is filled with—fancy women!"

Mr. Smith laughed. "Of course it is. That's why we're here, Leander. Whatever were you expecting?"

"I thought … I expected … well, not this!"

The older man clapped his hand on his young friend's shoulder. "Well, now that you're here, be sure to enjoy yourself. It's my treat—a gift to you, my boy."

"I cannot—a generous offer, I'm sure, but … I've never been in a place like this. Look at them, Julius. They're hardly wearing any clothes!"

"Don't be so shocked. You're a married man," Mr. Smith said. "Surely you've seen at least one naked woman before."

"No, of course not," Mr. Jones replied. "Martha is a decent woman. She would never allow me in the room while she dresses or, uh, disrobes. Whenever I'm with her, she's fully attired or else in her nightdress. She'd be mortified if I were ever to see her nak—I mean, without her clothes."

"Then I raised her badly," Mr. Smith said. "However did you manage to have three children?"

Roxane wouldn't have thought that Mr. Jones's face could grow redder, but it did. "Well, I … we … you know, it is always dark when we …"

"Well, then," Mr. Smith said, "which of you lovely ladies would like to explain a few things to Mr. Jones about the pleasures of the flesh?"

Véronique strolled languidly to Mr. Jones and ran her hand along the young man's crimson cheek. Roxane saw him shiver. "Let me do it. I can teach you so much, monsieur, and you'll be thrilled to learn it all."

"I cannot … I dare not … I … oh dear!"

Véronique slipped her arm around Mr. Jones's skinny waist. "Come along, you handsome devil. I'll show you how to have a good time."

Mr. Smith beamed with satisfaction as Véronique led the timid young man up the stairs. He gave Lady Celeste the necessary money and took Roxane's hand. "Lady Celeste, I'd be pleased to get to know this little dove. Not only is she beautiful but she has a hot spark of intelligence in her eyes. I imagine an hour with her will be very rewarding. Tell me your name again, sweetheart."

"I'm … Je m'appelle Mademoiselle Roxane," she said, remembering at the last minute to speak French. That earned her a nod of approval from Lady Celeste. "I'm pleased to meet you, monsieur. Would you care to come with me to my chamber?"

Mr. Smith gave her his wolfish smile as he draped his arm around her shoulders.

Before they could move, the bell at the gentlemen's entrance rang again and footsteps thudded up from the ballroom entrance.

"Oh, there you are at last!" Lady Celeste cried out when the latest visitors appeared in the hallway. She hurried to greet them.

The Burnhams, father and son.

Roxane moaned. What terrible timing. Another minute and she would have been safely upstairs with Mr. Smith, and Thaddeus Burnham would have had to settle for one of the others. Not that she would have wished him on Yvette or even Aurélie. And certainly not Fleur.

"What's this?" Thaddeus's voice boomed. "My girl in the arms of another man?"

He crossed into the parlor and wrenched Roxane from Mr. Smith's side, sending her spinning across the room. She nearly tumbled to the floor but caught herself in time to avoid that embarrassment.

Mr. Smith stared in wide-eyed astonishment as Thaddeus came at him, fist clenched. He raised his open hands and backed away. "Beg pardon, sir. I didn't realize she was spoken for."

Roxane straightened herself and smoothed her chemise over her hips. "I am not spoken for, monsieur, not by him. You have the claim on the next hour of my time. Let's go upstairs."

It was Thaddeus's turn to look amazed. "You know better than to cross me, mamzelle."

She looked around at the others. Aurélie and Fleur appeared frightened, but Yvette gave her a smile of encouragement. And Lady Celeste …

Clearly Lady Celeste wasn't going to come to her rescue. She was paying no attention to the drama in the parlor. She and old Isaac Burnham were still in the hallway, he with his hands on her waist, and she gazing stupidly into his eyes.

Roxane sighed as she turned to Thaddeus. "It's not my intention to cross you, monsieur. I'm merely asking you to wait for your turn. This gentleman has already paid for his time. If no one else suits you, you'll have to be patient. An hour will pass quickly enough."

"Very well then," Thaddeus grumbled. "But the wait entitles me to a whiskey on the house."

There was no such rule, but Roxane didn't point that out. Let him drink all the whiskey he wanted. He was no meaner when drunk than when sober. If she was very lucky, he'd pass out before the hour was up. But she didn't expect such good fortune.

To her surprise Lady Celeste made no protest as he went to the drinks table and filled a glass to the brim. She was still caught up in the charms of the senior Mr. Burnham, although Roxane couldn't imagine what those charms might be.

She went back to Mr. Smith's side. "Are you ready, monsieur?"

He glanced at Thaddeus, who was slugging down the whiskey, and offered Roxane his arm. "I shall be most pleased, mademoiselle."

"Yes, you shall. I promise you the most wonderful hour of your life."

She wondered what sorts of pleasure this gentleman most enjoyed.

And what sorts of pain.

As they climbed the stairs, Roxane couldn't help but recall that just last night she had gone up the same stairs to the Rose Room with Mr. Stregoni. He had promised to arrive at three o'clock—why wasn't he here? Would she ever see him again?

Her heart had rarely felt so heavy.

CHAPTER

25

Daniel set two bags on Ellie's kitchen counter. They'd stopped on the way to her apartment to pick up Chinese food and a bottle of chardonnay. "Let's see," he said, "we need plates and glasses and a corkscrew. And silverware? I got chopsticks …"

Ellie wished he would leave but it didn't seem fair to make him go after he'd bought the dinner. She pointed vaguely at cabinets and drawers, which began to spin around her. "Find what you need. Excuse me, I—I'll be back in a minute."

She went into the bathroom and shut the door. The mirror showed her short blond hair spiking out at odd angles from combing it with frantic fingers. Tears had left salt tracks on her cheeks and a network of red lines in her eyes, a map of her pain. A rhythm beat in her head: stupid, stupid, stupid.

She ran water into the sink and when it was too hot to bear, she soaked a washcloth and pushed it against her face, letting it burn, breathing the steam.

When she returned to the kitchen she felt slightly better. At least enough so that she could remain upright.

Daniel was spooning food onto the plates. Kung pao chicken, sweet-and-sour pork, potstickers, fluffy white rice.

"Quite a feast. Thank you." Ellie forced herself to sound enthusiastic.

He poured the chardonnay into a pair of Granny Jo's wineglasses and handed one to her. She gratefully took a sip.

"Where shall we eat?" Daniel asked.

"I usually sit on the sofa." She couldn't remember the last time she'd had a guest to dinner. She didn't even own a dining table or chairs.

He carried the plates into the living room and set them on the coffee table. She caught him looking around, giving her home a developer's professional assessment. She followed his gaze, trying to see what he saw. Small, cramped rooms. Low popcorn ceilings. Boring white walls. Granny Jo's possessions stuffed everywhere.

When Harding & Boyer Associates made their bid to buy Granny Jo's house, she'd checked the portfolio of projects on their website. Elegant, upscale, expensive.

Well, she had nothing to apologize for. This place was what she could afford, and she was living within her means. Okay, not really. No matter how careful she was with her money, every month she came up short.

At least the apartment was neat. She'd spent all of Saturday cleaning and polishing, making it as perfect as possible for Peter. The candles were still arrayed around the room—and her silky robe was in the middle of the floor, where it had fallen when Peter pulled it off her body. She snatched it up and tossed it into the bedroom.

"Nice place," Daniel said. "You've made it homey."

"I think I'll light a couple of these candles." Maybe that would dispel the gloom that was settling into the corners.

"Let me." He took a lighter from his pocket and touched the flame to every wick. The candles gave the room a romantic glow. Too bad her visitor was the wrong man.

But Peter, damn him, was the wrong man too. Why had she been too blind to see that? *Stupid, stupid, stupid.*

She and Daniel settled at opposite ends of the sofa. Ellie could think of nothing to say. No way could she ask him the questions pushing at the edges of her brain. He was being nice, but he was Peter's client, and in the end he'd be on Peter's side. Men were their own tribe. They stuck up for one another, condoned each other's bad behavior. Not that they considered it bad behavior to break a woman's heart.

She picked up the TV remote and pushed the button. A stadium appeared on the screen. Monday night football. Some team wearing red versus one wearing white, playing somewhere in pouring rain.

"More wine?" Daniel asked.

Ellie was surprised to see that although her plate was still full, her glass was empty. He poured more chardonnay. She sipped it in silence. Finally she said, "What is she like?"

Startled, Daniel set down his chopsticks. "What? Who?"

"Peter's wife."

"I've never met her."

"But you knew he was married."

"I guess I did. He doesn't talk about her much."

"That figures."

"It's not like we're friends. It's a business relationship. Lawyer and client."

Ellie sighed and nibbled on a potsticker. "At first I thought the problem was Claire."

"Claire Scanlan? You thought she was married to Peter?"

"An ex-wife, maybe. Ex-girlfriend. They obviously have some kind of history. He said she's a family friend."

"Maybe she is."

"There's more to it, I can tell. That's why I went to the open house in San Rafael yesterday, to find out what the story is. Claire was about to tell me when you showed up."

He reached over and squeezed her hand. "I'm sorry. I didn't mean to interrupt something important."

"God, married. I still can't believe it." The wine felt soothing as it slid down her throat. "He was talking about her on the phone."

"Talking about who?"

"Claire. Outside the restaurant, talking to his wife. He said, 'Claire? That was tonight?' Like he blew off plans with her to come to Ciboulette and help Richard work on Marc and me."

Daniel frowned. "What does that mean, work on?"

"Tonight was supposed to be just my brothers and me. I couldn't believe it when I got there and saw you and Peter."

"You looked pleased enough to see Peter, if not me."

"That's not the point. Inviting outsiders was unfair."

"Richard says you're the swing vote. He wants to sell the house to my firm. Marc wants it to go to BAPA. So you have the power—you get to decide."

"Power?" She hadn't thought of it that way. Powerful Ellie. The idea made her smile, just a little.

"So which way are you leaning?"

"Well, selling to you is a better deal financially—"

He nodded. "We're offering an excellent price."

"—and like Richard says, we can't stay stuck in the past. It's important to move forward." She took another sip of wine. "But Granny Jo would love BAPA's museum idea. Once the house is torn down, there's no way ever to bring it back."

"No one's tearing it down. We'll keep the basic structure intact. Our project will be a sensitive repurposing of the property—"

"Repurposing?"

"Oops, there I go, lapsing into jargon. It means converting a valuable old building to modern use while honoring its past."

"What are you going to do, exactly?"

His eyes lit up with excitement. "I'll show you. Do you have a paper and pencil?"

"Over there." Ellie pointed. Daniel jumped up went to the desk.

"That's Granny Jo in the photos. The baby she's holding is my father."

He picked up the gold frame holding two photos side by side. "The soldier? Is that your dad too?"

"My grandfather. Edouard Trevillon. He died in World War Two, a hero of the French resistance."

"How come your name's not Trevillon?"

"That was Granny Jo's idea. Burnham's a grand old San Francisco names. With Grandfather gone, she thought using her name would open doors for her son."

He brought a pad and pen back to the sofa. "Does it work? Does the name Burnham open doors for you?"

Right this minute she felt as if every door in her life was slammed shut. "Show me your plans for Granny Jo's house."

He sat much closer to her this time. She could sense his body's heat and energy. Two nights ago she and Peter had sat here, drinking champagne and kissing until the fire inside them drove them to her bed. *I love you,* Peter had whispered. *Oh, Ellie, I love you so much.*

And she, stupid fool, had believed him.

"Are you okay, Ellie?" Daniel asked.

"I'm fine." She poured more wine.

He made the pencil dance over the paper. A rough outline of the house's footprint emerged. "We're calling it Burnham Gardens to honor your family. We'll keep the Victorian character. From the street the house will look almost the same, but instead of a single-family home it will have multiple units."

It was hard not to be buoyed by his excitement.

"You mean a separate apartment on each floor?"

"Two, actually. Six condos. They'll be beautiful—up to date but full of historic charm." He added more lines with a flourish. "And six more in the new structure. Twelve in all."

"What new structure?"

"The one we'll build on the vacant lot." He drew another irregular shape next to the first.

"Vacant lot?" Ellie was puzzled. "There are big houses on both sides."

"Your grandmother's property consists of two lots, you know. The house fills one, but the other is empty. That's one reason this property is so amazing. Do you know how hard it is to find vacant land in that part of the city?"

"Wait, you mean the big side yard? Granny Jo's rose garden?"

"It's mostly weeds. The parcel is too valuable not to put it to good use."

"Granny Jo loved her roses. Her mother planted the first ones. Roses have grown there for over a century."

"Life means change, Ellie." Daniel's voice was soft, sympathetic. "And this is a positive change for you. It will make you wealthy." He touched her hand to reassure her. His fingers were gone in an instant but her skin kept tingling. "We'll keep the Burnham memory alive while letting other families make new memories there."

She sighed. "Everything comes down to money, doesn't it?"

But he was right. She was tired of living at the edge of poverty. She closed her eyes and saw herself on a stage in a cap and gown, a university diploma in her hand. She hated siding with Richard, but maybe he was right. It was time to get unstuck, to move forward with her life. Granny Jo was gone. Clinging to her house made no sense. If she voted to spite Richard by selling to BAPA, she would be spiting herself as well.

Her cell phone rang. Peter? She couldn't wait to hear what that bastard had to say for himself. Heart pounding, she ran into the kitchen to retrieve the phone from her purse.

Richard's name showed on the screen.

"What the hell's going on, Ellie?" he demanded.

She tightened her grip on the phone. "What do you mean?"

"That little stunt you pulled. Running out of the restaurant like that."

"I didn't plan it. I—something happened."

"The whole evening was a waste, thanks to you."

"It was a waste anyway. You said it would be the three of us, but you brought in reinforcements for your side. Totally unfair!"

"You don't get it. BAPA's guy getting killed in our house—that changes things. Unless we handle it carefully, it will create all kinds of complications for the deal we're trying to work out."

"How can you talk like that? A man's life ended and you don't even care."

"Of course I care. But—"

"The only person you care about is Richard. You've always been that way."

"Stop it, Ellie. I didn't call to argue. We have to get the papers signed before this murder gives Harding and Boyer cold feet. I talked to Marc. We're meeting tomorrow night."

"I'm busy tomorrow night." She had no plans but refused to give him the satisfaction of bossing her around.

"Breakfast then. Eight a.m. at that café near Granny Jo's. We can't go to the house, it's sealed off as a crime scene."

"I have to be at work at eight-thirty."

"So be late."

"I can't." Pushing the END button was the only good thing that had happened all day.

When she came back to the living room Daniel was gazing out the window, hands thrust into in his pockets. She moved to his side, expecting to see the city's lights beyond the glass. Instead she saw her own reflection. The image looked dark, hazy, sad. It was like seeing her own ghost. A thought came: *I don't want to be that person.*

"I'm sorry," she said. "For messing up everyone's evening."

"Not your fault." He rested a hand on her shoulder, gentle, undemanding. "I'm really sorry Peter was such a jerk to you."

Peter. Hearing Daniel say his name made her heart feel tight, as if a fist had clenched around it.

She wondered what Inspector Vargas was doing in response to her phone call.

Turning back to the coffee table, she picked up the sketch. "About Granny Jo's house," she said. "I'd better tell you about the murder."

26

"For you, Roxie." Mr. Smith reached into the pocket of the pants he had just put on and pulled out a shiny quarter-dollar. "Our, uh, meeting this evening has been most satisfactory."

"Merci, monsieur." Roxane took the coin and bobbed an awkward curtsy.

Though his dark eyes and large teeth made him look like a wolf, Mr. Smith had turned out to be neither wild nor vicious. In fact, he was a man of simple and straightforward appetites, and Roxane had been able to satisfy him quickly and with little exertion. Now that his allotted hour was over, he seemed grateful to her and very pleased with himself.

As he turned his attention to tying his cravat, she slipped the coin into her leather treasure pouch, hidden inside the ripped seam at the corner of her mattress. Unlike the proprietors of other establishments where Roxane had worked, Lady Celeste allowed the *jeunes filles* to keep the occasional small tip that a gentleman might offer them. Roxane dreamed of saving enough money that she would have no further need of gentlemen, but deep in her heart she knew better than to think she could ever amass such a grand sum, even adding in Mr. Stregoni's gold coin.

She dipped her head and looked up at Mr. Smith through fluttering eyelashes. "I hope I will see you again soon, monsieur."

"Count on it, Roxie. If you cheer me up next time as well as you did tonight, you'll be seeing me often."

She winced each time he called her Roxie. The nickname grated on her ears, but she didn't feel she could insist on being called Roxane when it wasn't her true name to begin with. She covered her reaction by offering her sweetest smile.

"I'll look forward to the next occasion, monsieur. Now it's time to return to the parlor, though I wish we could linger here."

That last statement was only thing she had said to him all night that was true. She dreaded going downstairs, where Thaddeus Burnham was waiting.

Then she felt a sparkle of hope—perhaps Mr. Stregoni had arrived.

"Come here, Roxie, be a good girl and kiss me goodbye."

Mr. Smith pulled her against him and she let him have a last moment of fun with his eager lips and hands. Then she drew away and opened the door.

She accompanied him down the two flights of stairs, following Lady Celeste's instruction never to permit a gentleman the opportunity to wander in the house alone. With every step, her heart beat faster. By the time they reached the foyer, she found it hard to breathe, as if her heart had risen into her throat and was choking her.

She stole a peek into the parlor. Louise was at the post by the drinks table. Three youthful gentlemen, hardly more than boys, were gathered around the piano, plunking out tunes and singing lustily as they waved glasses of whiskey about. Mr. Smith's young friend, the pumpkin-haired Mr. Jones, was perched on the edge of the settee, his bowler hat on his knee. He was tapping his foot, which made the hat bounce up and down as if impatient to be on its way.

Thaddeus Burnham wasn't there.

Roxane was so dizzy with relief that she had to catch herself on the doorframe to keep her knees from buckling.

But Mr. Stregoni was not there either.

Fine. What had she really expected? It was folly to pin her hopes and desires on any man, to believe she could count on a single one of them.

She let go of the support and made herself stand straight.

Mr. Smith clapped his friend on the shoulder. "So, Leander, did you enjoy yourself?"

Mr. Jones's face turned so red that Roxane feared he might explode. He leapt up, exclaiming, "There you are, Julius. At last. Let us be gone from this sinful place."

Louise drummed on the drinks table with her fingers. "Please settle up before you depart, gentlemen. Mademoiselle, did you make Mr. Smith happy?"

"I do believe so," Roxane replied—the code phrase that indicated she'd performed no service requiring an extra payment. There were other possible answers to the question, each of them signaling a particular amount that the gentleman should be charged.

"Then we thank you for visiting us, good sirs," Louise said. "We hope you'll come again."

"Most certainly," said Mr. Smith. At the same instant Mr. Jones muttered, "Never."

"Please leave by the same door where you entered." Louise smiled at them, her white teeth gleaming in her dark face as she waved toward the ballroom stairs.

As soon as they had departed, Roxane asked her, "What happened to Mr. Burnham?"

"Which one?" Louise picked up a crystal decanter, the one containing whiskey for the *jeunes filles*. Theirs was even more watered down than the spirits sold to the gentlemen. She poured a small measure into a tumbler and handed it to Roxane. "Lady Celeste is entertaining Mr. Isaac in the Rose Room. Mr. Thaddeus has gone upstairs with Véronique."

Thank heaven! Roxane sighed with gratitude and sipped her drink. "I thought Véronique spent the last hour with Mr. Jones."

Louise laughed. "She and that redhead came downstairs so quick that I felt like offering him a refund."

"A refund? Surely you didn't."

"Of course not. House rules are, you pay for at least an hour. If you want to spend the hour sitting in the parlor with a nervous twitch, that's up to you. And speaking of nervous"—she pointed toward the piano—"come with me."

Watching them approach, the three young men, barely old enough to grow whiskers, poked each other with their elbows and tried to stifle their giggles.

"Gentlemen, may I present Mademoiselle Roxane, one of the most beautiful young ladies ever to come from gay Paree. Would one of you care to go upstairs with her for an hour of intimate conversation?"

"You go, Ralph." One of the lads shoved his friend forward.

"Maybe just another glass of whiskey will do for me," Ralph said, beating a retreat to the drinks table.

The first boy followed him, demanding, "What about our bet?"

Louise shook her head. "You all paid for your hour. We can't give you back your money."

The third boy, a gangling fellow with a faint shadow of a mustache adorning his upper lip, stared at Roxane with wide eyes and open mouth.

"I'll go," he said. "Can you take me upstairs and, uh, show me—well, whatever it is you do?"

She made herself smile as she took his hand. "Avec plaisir,

monsieur." He looked puzzled so she repeated her words in English. "With pleasure. Come with me."

———◆———

Exhausted. Bone tired. Claire had never felt so weary.

As she drove across the bay on the five-mile span of the Richmond–San Rafael bridge, gusts of strong wind pushed at her car. Fog swirled across the lanes, obscuring her vision.

The emotions of this horrid day pressed in on her. Rage at Peter for betraying her sister. Helplessness in the face of Cassandra's stiff-upper-lip attitude, a mask to hide her anguish. The shock of finding Simon's body, followed by deep grief.

The cops had dragged Peter to police headquarters. What if they arrested him?

What if he was guilty?

A hollow place opened up in her at that thought.

No, it couldn't be true. Peter was a total jerk, but surely not a murderer.

Tears welled up. Trying to focus on the taillights of the car in front of her, Claire slipped her hand into her purse and felt around until she found the small square of cloth, soft as a cloud. The lace handkerchief.

In her memory she heard a whispered voice: *Did you know him, signora? I am sorry for your loss.* And another: *Here, ma'am, use this,* as a girl's hand reached down to offer her the hankie.

The odd pair who'd led her to Simon's body. Stregoni, the man with the Einstein hair, and the Amethyst Girl, Roxane, with her Victorian dress and her armful of laundry.

They knew something about the murder. They had put the sign in the window asking passersby to summon the police. Yet when the police arrived, they'd rushed up the spiral stairs to hide in the tower. Roxane and Stregoni had been right there in the middle of things, but in all the confusion no one but Claire had seen them.

They weren't ghosts. Ghosts didn't put up signs and hand out hankies.

So how had they managed to make themselves invisible to almost everyone? And why was she the exception?

She should go to the police, tell them about Roxane and Stregoni. But then she'd have to justify why she didn't mention them earlier, and she had no satisfactory explanation. The detectives would suspect her hiding guilty secrets, or else they'd decide she was crazy. Even if they took her seriously, how would they find and question two people they couldn't even see?

Stregoni and Roxane held the key. If Simon's murder was going to be solved, she'd have to find them herself and discover what they knew.

The place to begin looking was the Burnham Mansion. So what if it was closed off as a crime scene.

A horn blared. Claire's head jerked up, and she saw she was drifting into the next lane. She twisted the wheel to set the lime-green jellybean back on course. A car shot past her and vanished into the mist.

Her heart took a long time to stop pounding.

CHAPTER

27

"Well, good night, Ellie." Daniel stood half in and half out of her apartment doorway.

"Thanks for all your help." Even to her own ears Ellie's voice sounded flat and unenthusiastic.

"I'm glad you told me about the murder. I'm sure it would have come up at the restaurant if we'd stayed, but —"

"Is it going to make a difference? With your plans to buy the house and build those condos?"

"Too early too tell." Daniel shook his head. "Poor man. I didn't know him really, and I guess we were on opposite sides when it came to your grandmother's house. But I liked him. He didn't deserve what happened."

"No one deserves to be murdered." She squeezed her eyes shut, trying to erase the image of Simon's twisted body on the pine floorboards of the storage room.

Until today she'd seen dead people only at funerals, after they'd been fussed over by the mortician. Granny Jo had been laid out neatly in a satin-lined coffin with brass fittings. She looked so serene, so peaceful, her wisps of white hair framing her delicate face. She was wearing her favorite dress, a concoction of silk and lace that she'd told Ellie was her wedding gown.

Simon had looked anything but peaceful.

Murdered.

208

What had she been thinking, phoning the police about Peter? She'd practically accused him of being the killer. Yet that couldn't be true; she would never have fallen in love with someone capable of such horror. She'd made the call out of anger, to pay Peter back for breaking her heart.

And yet—Simon had been killed Saturday night, apparently between the time when Peter sent her home from the party and when he showed up at her apartment making lame excuses for being late.

Ellie shuddered.

"Sure you're all right?" Daniel's voice cut through the murk in her mind.

"I'm fine. Really." She tightened her grip on the doorknob. Why wouldn't he just go? She needed to be alone.

He leaned forward, and for a second she feared he was thinking about kissing her good night. She tensed up, ready to push him away, but then he stepped into the hall.

"I'll call you tomorrow. Make sure you're okay."

"You don't have to—"

"I know. I want to."

"That's … kind of you."

"Good night," he said again, and headed toward the elevator.

She had what she wanted—he was gone. So why did she feel disappointed?

Tears pooled in her eyes as she shut the door. She leaned her back against it and slid down its smooth surface until she was sitting on the floor. By the time she landed, she was sobbing.

———◆———

Roxane lay in her narrow bed, her body curled into a tight ball. As soon as the last of the gentlemen was gone from her room, she had cracked open the window, hoping to banish the stench they left behind, but that meant letting in cold, foggy air. Her thin chemise and skimpy blanket did little to warm her, and she couldn't stop shivering.

Alone in the dark she could drop the pretense of being Roxane. She became Millicent again, little Millie on the Missouri farm, longing for her mother's comfort and protection.

"Mama!" A whimper, lost in the darkness.

She had entertained only four gentlemen tonight, which would have made for a tolerable evening had it not been for the last man.

Mr. Smith had been easy to please and grateful for her favors. The same was true of the gangling boy with the faint mustache, so astonished by the delights her body presented to him that he could scarcely contain himself.

When she and the boy came downstairs, Sergeant Crowley of the San Francisco police was waiting, and the boy stumbled over his own feet in his haste to flee.

The sergeant often ended his patrol of the neighborhood with a visit to Chez Celeste. The first time Roxane had seen him in the parlor, standing tall in his blue uniform with a seven-pointed silver star pinned to his chest, she'd been terrified. Surely he was going to drag them all to jail. When he grabbed her hand she nearly fainted. But instead of arresting her, he'd led her up to her chamber. To her surprise he was gentle and shy. After that he chose her frequently. While she couldn't say she enjoyed his company, she minded him less than most. Still, she always kept cautious around him. She didn't dare let a policeman discover the secret buried in her heart.

Tonight the sergeant had made her laugh, and she was in good spirits when she brought him back downstairs.

Louise was still sitting at the drinks table. It was odd not to see Lady Celeste there. Could she still be with that old goat, Isaac Burnham? Roxane had been surprised at how pleased the lady had looked when he arrived.

"Mademoiselle, did you make this gentleman happy?" Louise asked.

"I do believe so."

"You bet she did," the sergeant added.

"Please come back to see us again, Monsieur Sergeant," Louise said. He tipped his hat to them and headed for the ballroom door.

"Now, mademoiselle," Louise said, "there's another gentleman who's waiting for you most anxiously."

Mr. Stregoni! He'd come back. Roxane's feet and her heart both skipped with delight.

She looked around but couldn't see him. The parlor and hall were empty except for herself and Louise. "Where is he, Louise?"

"Right here, mamzelle," boomed a deep voice, and Thaddeus Burnham emerged from the shadows of the dining room, a space normally off limits to gentlemen.

"Mr. Burnham!" Roxane gasped. Her hands flew up, crossing themselves across her breasts as if the gesture could protect her. "I thought you went with Véronique tonight."

"Oh, I did." His mouth twisted in a smirk beneath his dark mustache. "For an hour or so. Véronique is fun to play with. But you know full well, mamzelle, that it's your company I crave."

Roxane backed away. "Please, no. Not tonight—"

"The gentleman has already paid for your company," Louise said in a warning tone. "Are you refusing to go with him?"

Thaddeus seized her wrists, pulled her arms out to her sides. His eyes raked over her, up and down, and her skin burned from the heat of his gaze.

She had never noticed before how much he looked like Pa.

He tightened his grip. "What's your answer, mamzelle? Are you refusing me?"

"No, monsieur. I wouldn't dare—" She could barely force the words past the hard lump in her throat.

"Then let's go and enjoy each other." He grabbed her waist and half carried, half dragged her up the stairs.

In her chamber he threw her on the bed and began taking the liberties he'd paid for.

She knew she was supposed to accommodate his passions, but no one else ever asked of her what Thaddeus did—although he didn't ask; he imposed his twisted desires against her will. He apparently treated Véronique and the other *jeunes filles* more kindly, for they spoke well of him. Roxane had no idea why he reserved his most brutal attentions for her.

She could never understand how he found pleasure in the things he did to her, but in the course of his many visits she'd learned how fond he was of doing them. He relished the pain he inflicted. Yet he was careful never to leave any mark on her. No telltale bruise would back up her story if she ever tried to accuse him. Not that anyone would listen to a girl like her.

Tonight, as his body descended on hers, she closed her eyes and pretended she was not with him on this cramped bed in this tiny chamber at Chez Celeste. She traveled through the clouds to the farmhouse kitchen in Missouri, where she helped Mama roll out a piecrust and nibbled on bits of sweet dough. Then they transported her to a strange foreign land where she strolled down a village street wearing an amethyst necklace, with Mr. Stregoni at her side.

Beautiful clouds. Drifting, drifting, drifting …

A sharp blow stung her cheek.

"Wake up, you slut," Thaddeus muttered. He hit her again. "Don't you dare drop dead on me."

She tried to roll away but was pinned beneath his heavy body. "Please—I beg you, stop."

She squeezed out a tear and hoped it would be enough. He liked begging, but she could never be sure how he would react to it. Sometimes it encouraged him to ease away, but on other occasions it made him redouble his efforts to hurt her.

From far away came the chime of the floor clock in the vestibule. Midnight.

Thaddeus knew the rules of the house. He rose from the bed and put on his clothes. Thank heaven he hadn't bribed Lady Celeste with an extra payment to stay the night.

Her pain was so intense that she was bent double as she went down the stairs to report to Louise and make sure Thaddeus left the house with the other departing gentlemen. The *jeunes filles* gathered round the drinks table so Louise could dismiss them for the night.

Lady Celeste was not there.

As the other *jeunes filles* returned to their chambers to sleep, Roxane slipped into the kitchen. She felt around in the darkness, exploring the stove and the sink and the work table until she found a boning knife. She slipped it inside her chemise and carried it up the back stairs to her chamber.

Now, in bed, curled in a ball, she shivered. "Mama!" Her cry this time was louder. She reached to touch the knife wedged between her mattress and the wall. Feeling the edge slice across her fingertips, she withdrew her hand and put her fingers in her mouth.

She tasted blood. Good. That meant the blade was sharp enough to do the job.

———✦———

A woman in a dress made of amethysts embraces a tuxedo-clad man. They dance on a staircase that spirals upward into a storm-ravaged cloud. Lightning flashes, thunder cracks.

A dark shape appears and shoves the man into an abyss. The gemstones dissolve and the woman is naked.

The shadowed figure seizes her, twists her body, almost breaks it in two. Yet he forces her to continue the dance. She weeps until her tears turn to blood.

Claire woke up screaming.

CHAPTER

28

The morning sun is touching the parlor windows. The stained glass above the clear panes glows like rubies and sapphires. And diamonds, making me think of the ring Edouard gave me along with his precious promise.

A new day. A fresh beginning. Maybe today is the day he will come at last to take me with him to the Place Called Forever.

The evening after we met at that fateful picnic, Edouard invited me to dinner. The next night we went to the theater. Every day for three weeks we kept company, and we fell deeply in love. And then he asked me to marry him.

"What shall I do?" I asked Maman. "It's so sudden. A month ago I didn't even know him."

She was sitting in her rocking chair in the window bay, watching the world go by.

"He seems like a nice man," she said. By now she'd met him several times.

"And he's French, like you. A point in his favor, don't you think?"

She laughed. "Quite a bit more French than me, I daresay."

"What do you mean?"

Her hand, thin and shaky, waved away the question. "Where will you live? In Paris? Or will he be posted to some remote place like Morocco?"

"He's going to resign his army commission. I want us to live here. I mean, in this house. It's big enough for all of us."

"Your Edouard may have other plans."

"He loves this house. He told me so."

Maman sighed. "The house has been quiet for too many years. Sometimes I miss the laughter, the music, the sounds of ... merry-making. There was a time, you know, when this house knew a certain glory." A gleam appeared in her blue eyes, then faded.

"Are you talking about when you ran the boardinghouse for young ladies?" I knew she'd done this before I was born.

"Never mind. It was long ago." She rocked in silence, then asked, "Does he love you?"

"He says he loves me more than anything on earth."

"Do you believe him?"

"Of course. He's a man of honor. He wouldn't say he loves me if he doesn't."

"He's a man—reason enough to take anything he says with a grain of salt. Even if he's telling the truth, a man's definition of love is quite different from a woman's."

"How can you say that? You know Papa loved you truly."

She smiled at the memory of him. "Yes, he did. But I have more knowledge of men than you realize. I hope your Edouard lives up to the best of them, not the worst."

"What sort of knowledge?" The way she said the word puzzled me.

Instead of answering, Maman turned to stare at the windows. Night was falling and blackness pushed at the glass. I drew the curtains but her gaze didn't waver. I had the notion that she was looking at something far away from this room.

Eventually she sighed and said, "There's only one bit of advice I can give you. Listen to your heart, but listen to your head also. If they tell you the same thing, that's the course you should follow. If either one expresses doubts, then tell your Edouard no."

I jumped up. "What wonderful advice. Merci, Maman!" I kissed her on the forehead.

That night I told Edouard yes, I would marry him.

We celebrated our engagement at the new cocktail lounge everyone was talking about, the Top of the Mark on the nineteenth floor of the Mark Hopkins Hotel, high on Nob Hill. Glass walls on every side let us see the entire city. It was as if we were seated in the sky.

I was happier than I'd ever been in my life.

The full skirt of my scarlet dress swirled when we danced to the band's swing music. At our table we drank champagne and planned our future.

A spring wedding at Notre Dame des Victoires, the church where the French in San Francisco had worshiped since the Gold Rush. A honeymoon in Paris. A beautiful life in the house on Octavia Street, which we'd fill with children.

At the end of the evening he gave me a small velvet box. I opened it and gasped at the sight of the world's most beautiful diamond ring.

As August drifted toward September, I was giddy with bliss. I shopped for a wedding dress, and we reserved our wedding date at the church. Every evening we went to the movies or a café or a nightclub. When we got home, Maman would tactfully retreat to her bedroom while Edouard and I sat on the parlor sofa and talked about—well, everything. Our hopes, our dreams, our future.

And we kissed, long lingering kisses that left me gasping, trembling, hungry for more.

I couldn't wait to be married.

———◆———

Yesterday had been the worst day of Ellie's life.

First, finding Simon Thatcher's body in Granny Jo's house. Then discovering Peter's treachery.

The murder had shaken her to her core. But Peter's betrayal had shattered her heart.

He was married. That blow had left her body stiff and sore, as if he'd pummeled her with his fists. The passion they'd shared, the loving words he'd whispered, the promises he'd made—all lies.

She had cried all night. Her mind replayed every moment she'd spent with Peter, every phone conversation, searching for warning signs she'd missed. This morning she'd opened her eyes and realized she'd made a decision.

Maybe he hadn't lied about loving her. What did she know about his marriage? Men fell out of love with their wives all the time. If he had to choose, who was to say he wouldn't pick Ellie? Last night, in shock, she'd run away. She hadn't given him a chance to explain.

It was only fair to hear his side of the story. Until she did, she wouldn't be able to think about anything else.

That was why at nine a.m. she was walking along a crowded sidewalk in the Financial District. She'd angered Richard by skipping his command-performance breakfast meeting and annoyed her boss by calling in sick for the second day in a row. She was on her way to Peter's office, to confront him once and for all.

What was she going to say? All morning she'd been rehearsing her words, but the thought of the coming confrontation made her stomach clench. Excitement? Anger? Fear? She wasn't sure.

A don't-walk sign stopped her at a corner, and the building across the street caught her eye. Short compared to its neighbors, though probably the tallest around when it was built. The top rose to an elegant peak, where an American flag flapped in the breeze. Above the first-floor windows stretched a terra cotta frieze. She could make out a pattern of twining leaves and lions' faces.

Granny Jo would have loved the lions.

When Ellie was little, the city had seemed full of magic. She and Granny Jo had a game they played on shopping trips downtown. Granny Jo challenged her to seek out the animals and mythical beings that adorned the older buildings—granite bears, terra cotta eagles, goddesses carved from sandstone—and gave her a dime for each one she found. At the end of the afternoon, they spent that money and more at the ice cream parlor. As they ate their sundaes, they made up stories about the creatures they'd found.

Tears sprang to her eyes. She missed her grandmother so much. Granny Jo would have had good advice to offer about the mess Ellie had made of her life.

What would that wise old woman have made of the way her grandchildren were fighting about her house? What would she think of a granddaughter who was in love with a conniving, two-timing, self-centered, married pig?

The light changed. Ellie stepped off the curb but jumped back when a siren wailed. A police car zoomed past.

It reminded her of the call she'd made to Inspector Vargas. Had she gotten Peter into trouble? Would he understand she'd acted in the heat of moment? Would he forgive her?

No way was he a murderer. She didn't believe that for a moment. She'd lashed out to pay back the pain he was causing her. She didn't really want to get him trouble.

Okay, maybe she did, a little bit.

Peter's building was a sleek glass tower. No lions, no magic. Squaring her shoulders, she went inside. Riding the elevator to the twenty-seventh floor, she hastily combed her short blond hair and straightened her collar, taking advantage of her reflection in the shine of the chrome-paneled door. Her heart hammered and her stomach tightened.

The elevator opened to reveal a high, curved desk across miles of pale carpet. Taking a deep breath for courage, she covered the distance with careful steps.

The polished young woman behind the desk granted Ellie a smile. It must have cost her a fortune to get her teeth that white. An engraved brass nameplate told Ellie her name was Aubrey.

"Good morning. How may I help you?" She had an accent, British or Australian. The blond highlights in her hair and her blue designer cardigan probably cost more than Ellie earned in a month.

Ellie tried not to hate her.

"I'm here to see Peter Mortensen," Ellie said.

Aubrey gave her a cool stare. "Do you have an appointment?"

"He'll want to see me. Tell him it's Ellie Burnham."

A frown marred the receptionist's perfect face for the briefest instant. Did she recognize the name? Did Peter talk about Ellie at the office? Until yesterday she would have considered that a positive sign. She felt herself flush with embarrassment.

Aubrey pursed her rouged lips. "Are you a client?"

"Not exactly. I'm—uh, the client is Harding and Boyer. The developers who want to buy the Burnham Mansion, my family's house. It's essential that I see Mr. Mortensen."

"I can schedule a time for you." Aubrey tapped a couple of keys on her computer.

"He's here, right? Can't you let him know I'm—"

"He's not available. That's all I can tell you." She gave Ellie a look of sympathy, or was it pity?

Ellie felt as if the air had been sucked out of her. "I'll wait."

"As you wish." Aubrey gestured toward an alcove where a leather sofa and several armchairs where arranged around a low glass-topped table. "Would you like coffee?"

"No, thank you." Ellie didn't need caffeine. She was already too keyed up and jittery. She sank into a chair's butter-soft cushions and thumbed through the stack of magazines on the table. *The American Lawyer. The National Jurist. Harvard Business Review.*

It might be a long wait. And definitely a boring one. But she had the whole day.

Sooner or later Peter had to come through this room. And she was going to be ready for him.

29

"Good morning," Claire said as she came into the BayCrest office, though she wasn't sure what was good about it.

Marlene Murphy, at the rosewood reception counter, looked up from her keyboard and took off her reading glasses. She was forty-ish, but her spikes of magenta hair made her look younger. From a distance, anyway.

"Hey, early bird."

Early? It was midmorning. Claire glanced past Marlene to the open bullpen where the sales agents worked. All six desks were empty.

Marlene followed Claire's gaze. "They waited for you, but it got late so they left." Before Claire could ask, she added, "The agents tour."

"Oh, right. It's Tuesday." Claire shook her head. Yesterday had been such a catastrophe, so out of synch with her normal life, that she'd forgotten there was such a thing as a usual routine. Tuesday was the day when Marin real estate companies showed off their new listings to each other's agents.

"Everyone went except you and George," Marlene said. "No idea where he is."

"Working with a client, maybe."

"Ha! In your dreams." Then her forehead wrinkled with concern. "Are you okay, Claire?"

"I'm fine, why?"

"You look like you're not feeling well."

"Headache, that's all." To change the subject, Claire nodded toward Marlene's computer screen. "How's the romance novel coming?"

"Wrapping up chapter fourteen."

Claire gave a thumbs-up. "Can't wait to read it."

Marlene nodded, then leaned forward. "Sure you're all right? It must have been awful, finding that body in the Burnham Mansion."

"Much more awful for Simon than for me."

"Do the cops have any idea who did it?"

A picture flitted through Claire's mind—Peter being escorted from his house by the homicide detectives.

"I don't know what the cops are thinking."

"Any guesses? It was someone at the BAPA party, that's certain. Just think, we were rubbing elbows with a killer." Marlene gave an exaggerated shudder. "But I didn't see anyone who looked, you know, suspicious."

"Neither did I." Claire had nothing to gain by mentioning the Amethyst Girl or the man who looked like Albert Einstein—unseen by everyone but her. She could hear Marlene now: *Tess, I'm worried. Claire's acting unhinged.*

The phone rang on Marlene's desk. "Probably another reporter," she said as she reached for it. "We've had seven or eight so far this morning. Tess said to tell them no comment."

"Wise idea. Good luck with the writing."

Claire got coffee from the office kitchen and took the mug to her desk. Broken images from her scream-dream swirled in her brain. She'd had the same nightmare for three nights running, but the latest one had a twist—the shadow of evil, pushing the tuxedoed man into the abyss.

The man in the dream wasn't Peter, as she'd thought. He was Simon, dancing with her as he'd promised. Her dream-self had witnessed his murder but failed to grasp the most crucial detail—the killer's identity.

She took a long swallow, hoping the heat and the jolt of caffeine would help bring the dark figure into focus. But it remained elusive, out of reach. Giving up, she turned to her computer to check the internet for news of the murder.

Marlene's phone rang again, reminding Claire that her own phone had rung while she was driving. Pulling it out of her purse she saw that the message was from Cassandra. "Claire, I—everything is so crazy … Willow, stop that! Sorry, Claire, the kids are upset and … Jake, you behave yourself … I let them stay home from school, but maybe that was a mistake … It's awful. Peter never came home last night. The police … Call me as soon as you can."

Claire did but got voicemail. She left a message, struggling to make herself sound calm and reassuring.

———◆———

" 'G is for Girl, pretty and sweet … ' "

Roxane ran her finger over the picture on the left-hand page. A girl in a calico dress was walking down a road, carrying a basket of flowers. Orange curls peeked out from under her straw hat.

"See here?" she said to Fleur, snuggled beside her on the parlor sofa. "This girl looks like you."

Fleur wrinkled her nose in disgust. "I'm not pretty. Or sweet either."

"Sure you are. Of all the jeunes filles, you're the prettiest." Roxane thought for a moment and came up with: "La plus jolie."

"No, I'm not," Fleur insisted. "Please, read some more."

Usually this was Roxane's favorite time of day. Breakfast, with everyone squabbling and sniping, was over. The house wasn't yet open to gentlemen. The hours between were a quiet time when Roxane could collect her thoughts and enjoy simple pleasures, like the sweet sound of Yvette practicing the piano and the warm sun coming through the bay windows and turning the Persian rug into a carpet of rubies and sapphires. It was a time when Roxane could pretend she lived a different life—the only problem being that she couldn't imagine what that other life might be or how she could possibly achieve it.

Today, though, she felt restless, out of sorts. She longed to see Mr. Stregoni, though she wasn't sure why. He was neither handsome nor young, and some of his behavior was decidedly peculiar. Yet she felt a steadying comfort in his presence.

Why hadn't he returned last night as he promised?

"Roxane." Fleur tugged her sleeve, drawing her attention back to the book. "What's the next letter?"

"It's an H. 'H is for Houses that line the street.' "

The girl with the flower basket was walking toward a row of houses on the right-hand page. A white farmhouse with a big front porch stood next door to a redbrick cottage. The third house was yellow with blue scrollwork trim.

Fleur sighed. "Do you think that girl is going home?"

"I don't know. Maybe."

"I hope so." Another sigh. "I hope she lives in this house." She tapped her finger on the yellow one. "Mine looks like that."

"No, it doesn't. This place is gray. And it's much bigger."

"I don't mean Chez Celeste. I'm talking about my house in Sacramento, where I lived when I was Sadie."

"Oh. Well, my house looked like this one." Roxane pointed to the farmhouse. She remembered sitting on the big porch with

Mama in the summertime, listening to her tell stories as they shelled peas for dinner. "That was in Missouri."

"Is Missouri far away?"

"Very far."

"As far as Sacramento?"

"Even farther, I think. It took a whole week on the train to get to San Francisco."

"A week on a train, oh my!" In a wistful voice Fleur asked, "Do you ever wish you could go back there?"

"No, never!" As terrible as San Francisco could be, Roxane had no desire to return to the little town she'd come from. Nothing awaited her there but trouble.

Her fierce tone made Fleur look up from the page. Tears welled in her eyes. "Well, I do. Every day I dream about going home. I miss them so much—my ma and my papa, my little brothers. Only I bet they're not so little anymore."

"Maybe you could go for a visit," Roxane said. "Ask Lady Celeste if you—"

"No! I can't go back—I can't let them find out what happened to me. They'd be so ashamed."

Roxane patted Fleur's hand. She often wondered if Mama despaired as she looked down on her wayward daughter from heaven.

"They listen to the preacher," Fleur went on. "You should have heard Papa carry on after the preacher gave a sermon about women who ... with men ... he called them soiled doves."

Roxane nodded. "I've heard men say that."

"The preacher said girls like us—we're evil."

"But wasn't it your preacher who brought you here to be a pretty waiter girl?"

Fleur burst into sobs.

Roxane put her arms around the younger girl. Yvette abandoned the piano to come and kneel in front of the sofa. She dabbed at Fleur's wet cheeks with a linen handkerchief.

Véronique picked that moment to saunter into the parlor. As always, Aurélie trotted at her heels.

"What have we here?" Véronique said with a smirk. "Did someone break your heart last night?"

Fleur cried harder.

Yvette rose to her feet. "I believe Fleur is weary of gentlemen altogether," she said. "Who can blame her?"

It struck Roxane that this was a peculiar word—*gentlemen.* Because really there was nothing gentle about any man she'd ever met, up until Mr. Stregoni. And even he had broken his promise to her, failing to return to Chez Celeste last night.

Véronique laughed. "In that case, why don't we let Fleur entertain that silly Mr. Jones the next time he's here? He was too afraid of his shadow to make any demands on me at all. In fact, he fled the chamber before his time was up. No man has ever done that to me before. Usually they beg to stay longer."

Yvette said, "Lady Celeste should have returned his money, since he didn't receive the services he paid for."

"You know better than that," Véronique replied.

Aurélie said in a pious tone, "It's better to be paid for what's not provided than the other way around." With an arch look, she added, "Isn't that right, Roxane?"

This turn in the conversation took Roxane by surprise. "What do you mean?"

"Oh, nothing. Merely that I've been told we're never to offer our affections for free."

A sudden fear clutched Roxane's heart. "Yes, that's the rule."

"And we're never to have gentlemen in the house when it's not officially open for business."

Roxane felt her face go red. Fleur must have tattled about seeing her kiss Mr. Stregoni right before he disappeared. Yet she'd been so sure that Fleur hadn't noticed a thing.

Could Aurélie, the little sneak, have been hiding in the shadows of the hallway, peering into the storage room?

"In fact"—Aurélie fixed her dark eyes on Roxane—"Lady Celeste has said that any jeune fille who does such a thing will be dismissed from the house."

Véronique was regarding Aurélie with great interest. "It sounds like you're talking about something in particular. What happened?"

"Oh, nothing. Your remarks about Mr. Jones set me to thinking, that's all. I wanted to remind everyone of the rules." Aurélie's smile reminded Roxane of a cat that had cornered a mouse. "I'm sure Lady Celeste would welcome being informed of any transgressions."

"Please don't," Roxane whispered.

Fleur had stopped crying and was staring at her. They all were staring.

Roxane jumped to her feet. The book slid off her lap and landed with a thud on the floor. She dipped down in her most ladylike fashion to retrieve it. When she gave it to Fleur, her hands trembled.

"Fleur, why don't you study the letters I've shown you?" she said. "I feel a bit faint. I believe I'll go up and rest."

"Are you ill, Roxane?" Fleur sounded worried.

"No, I'll be fine. Never fear, I'll be downstairs by the time the gentlemen arrive."

"Perhaps Aurélie and I should follow," Véronique said, "to make sure you'll be quite alone up there."

"That's not necessary," Roxane replied over her shoulder as she left the room. "I assure you, I've never been more alone in my life."

30

"Thanks, Daniel." Ellie shifted her position in the law firm's leather chair as she spoke into her phone. "Don't worry. Really, I'm fine. See you tonight."

It was nice of Daniel to call and check on her. He'd invited her out because he felt sorry for her, but so what? Having dinner with him would be much better than throwing a pity party alone.

She ended the call, glancing at the time. Almost noon. All morning people had come and gone, and each time Ellie had looked up hopefully from the magazine on her lap, but it was never Peter. Now and then the receptionist, Aubrey, sleek and smooth and way too smug, looked at Ellie and shook her head or shrugged her shoulders as if offering sympathy. What a faker.

Where the hell was Peter, anyway? On a Tuesday morning wasn't it reasonable to expect him to be at work? Ellie suspected he was hiding in his office, refusing to face her. Aubrey had probably given him some sort of warning signal that there was a pathetic woman in the reception area, lying in wait.

Well, she was sick of waiting. It was almost lunchtime. Sooner or later Aubrey would leave her desk to eat, or at least take a restroom break. The minute she did, Ellie was going to slip into the corridor to the lawyers' offices and hunt Peter down.

Someone coming along that corridor caught her eye. Peter, finally? She sat up straight, ready to intercept him.

But the person who emerged was an older man with look of a senior partner. His silvery gray suit almost matched his carefully combed hair. He stopped to speak to Aubrey, who pointed in Ellie's direction. Pretending to ignore them, Ellie strained to listen. She couldn't hear most of their words, but a few jumped out.

Crisis management … Mortensen … police …

Police? Oh, God. Her call last night to Inspector Vargas …

The senior partner strode toward the elevator lobby. Aubrey came around the desk, heading for Ellie. "Ms. Burnham? Mr. Mortensen won't be in today. You'll have to lea—"

But Ellie was on her feet, hurrying after the man in the silver suit. She caught up as he pushed the elevator button.

"Excuse me. I heard you mention Peter Mortensen. What's happened? Did you say—there's a crisis?"

He narrowed his eyes. "I'm sorry. You are … ?"

She felt herself cringe. "Ellie Burnham. Peter is … a friend of mine. Is he all right?"

A chime signaled the elevator's arrival.

"I have no information to give you, Ms. Burnham."

The door glided open, and he stepped in.

She reached to catch his sleeve. "You have none, or you won't tell me?"

He swatted her away, as if she were a mosquito. The door slid shut with Ellie on the wrong side.

Ellie turned to see Aubrey standing a few feet away, arms folded tightly across her chest.

"He told you something about Peter," Ellie said. "Please, what did he say?"

Aubrey shook her head. "It's best if you leave. I don't want to call security."

Ellie punched the button for the elevator. It took forever to arrive. Aubrey watched her the whole time, and stood in front of the closing door to make sure Ellie didn't get out again.

Ellie kicked the elevator wall in frustration. The past few days had been awful, and now something bad had happened to Peter. How was she going to find out what it was?

———•———

Roxane forced herself not to run up the grand staircase. She needed to get away from Aurélie and Véronique, with their smirks and suspicions, but she took slow, measured steps and trailed her hand along the carved banister. If she was claiming to be ill, she should look the part.

On the second floor she was surprised to hear a murmur of voices. Who could it be? The other *jeunes filles* were all down in the parlor, and Louise was at the market buying provisions for the kitchen. No one would be on this floor except Lady Celeste, and Roxane had never known the lady to talk to herself. Yet the voices came from the Blue Room, the chamber at the rear of the house that Lady Celeste reserved for her own use.

Roxane tiptoed down the hall and put her ear to the door. Yes, voices, two of them. She could make out the rising and falling cadences of a conversation, though not the actual words. One voice was light and musical—Lady Celeste's. The other was a deep rumble.

A man! Roxane stepped back in shock. If there was a gentleman in the room at this hour, Lady Celeste was breaking one of her own strictest rules.

Someone inside the room sighed. Then came a familiar sound: the creaking a bed made when two people settled onto it.

She crept away, careful not to make a sound that might give away her presence. Climbing the stairs to the third floor, she wondered who the man might be and what entitled him to special privileges.

Then she recalled Louise's dire prediction that the days of Chez Celeste were numbered. Perhaps the secret visitor was a judge or city official collecting a bribe for not shutting down the house. Or someone seeking payment of a debt. Lady Celeste appeared to be making a huge income, but Roxane knew nothing of money except the meager dollars hidden in her mattress. For all she knew, Chez Celeste was teetering on the brink of ruin. Lady Celeste had won the house in a hand of poker; perhaps she'd gambled it away again and the man in her chamber had come to claim his prize.

Thoughts all a-jumble, Roxane wandered into the storage room. She plopped down on the trunk where she'd sat yesterday with Mr. Stregoni, his arm around her offering comfort, his body giving her warmth. And a few minutes later, that magical kiss …

All at once she was flooded with such a longing for his presence that her body felt like it would burst. Her heart thudded like a drum in her chest, and she could scarcely draw in a breath. Perhaps she was truly ill, after all.

She had never yearned for anyone before, certainly never a man. The only exception was Mama, but she'd quickly learned it was a waste of time to wish her mother were still alive. After she went to heaven, Pa couldn't bear hearing her name; any mention of Mama earned Roxane another thrashing with his belt, so she cloaked her grief in silence. First Pa, and then every man she'd met since leaving Missouri, had convinced her that her life would be better if she never saw a man again.

Yet here she was, pining for Mr. Stregoni. She wanted him to kiss her again, to enfold her in his embrace. As these thoughts filled her mind, her skin grew hot and a peculiar tingling settled in the place between her legs. She felt flushed and fevered. It made no sense.

Yes, it was definitely some form of illness. She needed to lie down and hope she felt better before it was time to entertain today's gentlemen.

She stood up and shook herself like a wet puppy, trying to force the odd sensations out of her body. It would do her no good to think of Mr. Stregoni. So what if he'd been kind to her for a night. He had broken his promise to come back; most likely he would never return. Even if he did, he was bound to disappoint her. After all, he was a man.

Best to put him out of her mind and give thought to what she would do if Chez Celeste were to shut down.

That idea made her feel even more faint. She sat again on the trunk lid and lowered her head to her hands.

What would she do? Where would she go? Her paltry sum of money was far from enough to let her make her way in the world. Mr. Stregoni's gold coin had raised the total, as had the twenty-five cents she'd received last night from the grateful Mr. Smith. On Friday Lady Celeste was due to pay the *jeunes filles* their small share of Chez Celeste's earnings, but what if the house closed before then?

She had better go fetch her treasure pouch, so she could count what money she had and make some computations. The locket with Mama's portrait was in the pouch too. And the amethyst necklace—she really must put it back in Lady Celeste's room, but she didn't dare do that right now. Not with a gentleman there.

She pushed herself up from the trunk, determined to make some sort of plan for her future, as bleak a prospect as it might be.

In her chamber she went straight to her bed. She found the opening in the mattress seam and thrust her hand into the batting.

Nothing there.

The hiding place was empty.

With a cold hand clutching her heart, she wriggled beneath her bed, and felt around, hoping her precious treasure had fallen to the floor.

Nothing there but dust.

Her pouch was gone.

31

Claire's breath caught at the sight of Simon's face on her office computer. The photo looked like a detail cropped from a candid shot taken somewhere outdoors. Simon's hair was tousled by a breeze, and he was laughing.

Such a tragic loss.

She scrolled down, reading the coverage of Simon's murder on the *San Francisco Chronicle* website. The article described the fundraiser at the Burnham Mansion and BAPA's plans for the historic house. It had little of substance to say about the murder itself. The autopsy results weren't in, and the police were keeping tightlipped about their investigation.

Peter's name wasn't mentioned.

An obituary accompanied the story, giving Claire details about Simon's life that she'd hoped to learn directly from him as they got to know each other. He had a sister, an elderly mother, an ex-wife. No children, but he was a devoted uncle to his nieces and nephew. He held a graduate degree in urban planning and historic preservation. He loved sailing—perhaps the laughing photo had been taken during a day on the bay.

Given all of her strange experiences in the Burnham Mansion, she was surprised she'd sensed nothing yesterday from Simon. She'd been right there, kneeling beside his body, yet his spirit had kept silent. There wasn't the slightest vibration to suggest he was hovering nearby, even though the violence had left the energy in the storage room highly charged. If only he'd lingered long enough to give some sign of his killer's identity.

Who killed him? Not Peter. Vargas and Flaherty might suspect him, but they had to be wrong. Other men had been on the third floor when Simon chased her downstairs. The killer could be any of them.

Stregoni and Roxane had answers. They'd found the body and hung the sign asking for help in summoning the police. One of them might even be the murderer. But how could the detectives find and question people they couldn't see?

Claire would have to do that herself. Which meant she had to get inside the Burnham Mansion.

"Hey, dancing queen, what'll you give me if I get you in there?"

Oh, God, she must have been muttering aloud. She snapped her head up to see George coming into the bullpen. He flicked a pudgy hand in a wave.

When had he come in? Just her bad luck that he had overheard her.

"What are you talking about, George?"

"The Burnham Mansion. You want to get in, I could give you the key."

"You have a key?"

"Not me, sweetheart. Tess. She's chair of that BAPA group's board. She had to get her committee in to set up for the fundraising bash." George came over to her desk.

"Oh, right." How had she forgotten? Yesterday when they went to meet the caterer she'd watched Tess unlock the door.

"You gonna investigate the murder?"

"Go away, George. I'm busy."

"You heard about it, didn't you?" George sounded excited, as if talking about a thrilling TV show. "Saturday night after the party was over. That save-the-house guy got whacked. Can you believe it? I mean, one minute I'm shaking the guy's hand and the next minute—kaboom!"

"What? You saw Simon right before he was killed?"

"Well, not exactly. Early on, when I first got there. I came up right behind you, remember? But still, the same night and all—it's weird."

"More than weird. It's—" Claire didn't know how to end the sentence. Tragic … frightening … heartbreaking? All of the above.

She had to get away. Grabbing her phone and her coffee mug, she got up and tried to push past him.

His hand landed on her shoulder. "Hey, you want that key or not?"

It was tempting. With the key she could get in easily. But she hated to think of what price he'd demand for fetching it for her.

The key must be in Tess's office, and Tess wasn't in. Perhaps Claire could find it before Tess returned. Right, that would be easy. More likely Tess catch Claire going through her desk and fire her on the spot.

"I'll come with you." George grinned. "Protect you from any murderers lurking around."

Ugh. "No way, George."

When she reached the kitchen she let out a long breath, as if she'd had a narrow escape.

Marlene had made a fresh pot of coffee. Claire poured herself some and listened again to Cassandra's message: *It's awful, Claire. Peter never came home last night.*

Had the police held him all night? Or had he left the detectives and spent the rest of the night with Ellie?

She tried to return the call. Again, she reached Cassandra's voicemail.

How could she get Tess's key without incurring a disastrous debt to George? If the cops showed up while she was at the Burnham Mansion, how would she explain why she was there? What was she going to do about Cassandra and Peter and Ellie? Was Peter involved with Simon's death?

Too many questions. Too many emotions.

As she came out of the kitchen, Marlene beckoned to her. "Claire! You have a visitor."

At first Claire saw no one. Then a woman with short blond hair rose from one of the armchairs in the reception area.

"Ellie! What brings you here?"

Ellie clutched her purse in front of her. "Hello, Claire. I—I didn't know who else to talk to. I'm worried about Peter Mortensen, and since you know him—he said you're a family friend …"

It was time to be blunt. "He's my brother-in-law. My sister's husband."

"Oh! So that's it." Ellie cast her eyes down. "I didn't know he was married. Not until last night. When I saw how he acted around you at the BAPA party—well, never mind what I thought."

Claire noticed that Marlene had stopped working on chapter fourteen and was listening avidly. "Come on, Ellie, we can talk in the conference room."

Ellie stood rooted in place. "Has Peter been arrested? I heard something about the police … I called Inspector Vargas, but he brushed me off."

"I haven't heard about that," Claire said. But it would explain the panicked voice in Cassandra's phone message.

"They can't think he killed Simon Thatcher. Peter would never—he's a scumbag, I hate him, but I can't believe … I wish I could see him, talk to him, find out what's going on."

Ellie sank back into the armchair and dropped her head in her hands. Marlene gave her a Kleenex.

George picked that moment to stroll up from the direction of Tess's office, fists buried in his pockets. "Well, Claire, ready to go?"

Claire restrained from pushing him away. "I'm busy here, George."

He pulled out a brass key on a little chain and dangled it in front of her eyes. "The key to the Burnham Mansion."

Ellie looked up with a startled expression.

"Not now, George," Claire pleaded.

"Say the word and we'll be on our way."

"Why are you going to my grandmother's house?" Ellie asked.

"I'm not," Claire said. "Not with him."

"If you want to go there, I'll take you," Ellie said.

George tossed the key from one hand to the other. "I'm coming too. Since I've got the key."

"We don't need it," Ellie said. "I have my own."

"Hey, I recognize you," George said. "We met at the shindig on Saturday. You're one of those Burnhams. Myrtle, Marie, don't tell me, I'll get it." He thrust out his keyless hand for her to shake.

"Mirabelle," she said stiffly, touching his fingers just long enough to avoid being rude.

"Let's go, Ellie," Claire said, feeling caught between the rock that was George and the hard place that was Ellie. "We can talk on the way. Let's take my car. It only seats two."

CHAPTER

32

Ellie stared out the windshield of Claire's VW as they headed down the grade to the Golden Gate Bridge. To their left was the vista point, and she imagined the tourists gathered at the rail to admire the bay and the city beyond it. She saw a ferry crossing the water and a container ship chugging toward a pier. The afternoon sun struck the downtown towers, making them as bright as diamonds.

The view to the right better suited her mood. The high Marin headlands, wild and windblown, met the Pacific at what seemed like the edge of the world. The ocean stretched out, disappearing into a fog bank that blurred the horizon between sea and sky.

She sneaked a look at Claire negotiating through the traffic. Silence hung between them like a curtain. Despite Claire's promise that they would talk on their way to Granny Jo's house, neither of them had said a word since the car doors slammed shut.

She's pretty, Ellie thought, noting the tendrils of brown hair framing Claire's face, her smooth skin, good cheekbones, hazel eyes. So much prettier than me.

Did her sister look like her? If so, there was no way Ellie could compete. Not that she wanted to. She had no desire to break up a marriage, maybe tear a family into shreds. An image swam into her mind: Peter reaching for a woman who looked like Claire,

240

gathering her into his embrace. Peter and his wife. She leaned forward in her seat, clutching her stomach.

She thought she'd known him so well, but really all he'd shared was the physical aspects of himself. She knew his smile, his scent, the sweet taste of his lips, the heat of his skin. She knew how his muscles tightened as he pulled her close and how his neck met his shoulder in a comfortable curve where she liked to rest her head. She knew that he made her feel complete when they made love.

But his dreams and ambitions? A total blank. How he spent his time when he wasn't with her or at his office? A mystery. His plans for the future, the ones that included her? All lies.

Ellie could no longer stand the silence. "Your sister—what's her name?"

"Cassandra," Claire said.

"How long have they been married?"

"Fifteen years."

"Are there children?"

"Two. Their son is nine, their daughter is seven."

"Where do they live?"

"In the East Bay. Lafayette."

"Does she know … about me?"

Claire shot her a look. "What is there to know, exactly?"

Ellie couldn't think of a good way to respond. She let the question drop, along with so many others she didn't dare ask, even if Claire could answer. Had Peter really loved her, as he'd claimed? Had his passion for her made him break his marriage vows for the first time, or was cheating on his wife a casual habit, with Ellie merely the latest in a series of flings?

Tears welled in her eyes and she rubbed them with balled fists.

Damn him, anyway.

"Are you okay?" Claire asked.

Ellie sat up straighter. "I'm fine," she lied.

"Peter's not worth it, you know. He doesn't deserve your tears."

"I know." After a moment she added, "I'm sorry. I never meant to do anything hurtful. I thought Peter was—well, free."

They came off the bridge and into the Presidio. The road through the historic army post carried them past redbrick buildings and stands of tall eucalyptus trees. They passed the military cemetery, its white grave markers arranged in orderly rows on the hillside.

"Tell me about your grandmother," Claire said, and Ellie accepted the change of subject as a gift.

"She was the sweetest person you could imagine," she said. "I miss her so much."

"And she really lived in that house all her life?"

"More than one hundred years. Can you imagine? She died in the same room where she was born."

"Didn't she ever want to go somewhere else?"

"Well, when she was young her parents thought she should live with them until she got married. After her father died she stayed on to take care of her mother."

"But she got married and had a child. Why didn't she set up her own home with her family?"

They were on Lombard Street now. Restaurants and motels in every block. Red lights, impatient traffic.

"That's the sad part of Granny Jo's story," Ellie said. "My grandfather was from Paris. I think she would have loved to live there with him, but she never got the chance."

"Why not?"

"He was a French soldier visiting cousins in San Francisco right before World War Two. They met at a Bastille Day picnic and fell in love at first sight. But then Germany invaded France, and of course he had to go back to defend his homeland. Before he left they had a hasty wedding. My father was born nine months later. Soon afterward Granny Jo received word that her true love had died a hero's death on the battlefield." Ellie sighed. "When I was little, I thought that was such a romantic story."

"So your father grew up in the house also?"

"Yes, until he went to college. I always wished I could've grown up there too. Now it's probably going to get made into condos."

Claire turned right onto Octavia Street and started up the long hill. "Not if you vote for BAPA's plan."

"Yes, but …" Ellie stopped speaking. No point in telling Claire, practically a stranger, how much the money from the sale of the house would mean to her. The chance to quit her dead-end job, focus on her studies. But if the house became a museum, she could come back whenever she wanted. She wouldn't have to lose her favorite place in the world.

With her brothers split, the fate of the house was hers to choose. The decision was a heavy weight on her heart.

"Your grandmother lived for so long," Claire said. "It's amazing she could manage the house on her own as she got older."

"In the last few years we arranged for people to come in and help her. But really, she was in good shape for her age, though toward the end she spent most of her time drifting through memories. And—this was odd—she developed an imaginary friend, like little kids do."

"An imaginary friend?"

"Yes, a young woman. Granny Jo said she came often to visit, and she always wore Victorian clothes. Granny Jo called her Roxane."

Claire's face went white. She gave Ellie a sharp look.

"Roxane? Are you sure?"

"That's what she said. I guess it's true that elderly people go back to being children in some ways. She really looked forward to those fantasy visits."

"Did you ever see this Roxane?" Claire asked.

"Of course not. Although a couple of times she supposedly appeared while I was there. It was all in Granny Jo's imagination, but if believing in Roxane made her happy, I wasn't going to discourage her. Claire, what's the matter? You look like you've seen a ghost."

Claire laughed, as if Ellie had cracked a joke. "There's the house," she said. "Look, we're in luck. Someone down the block is pulling out of a parking place."

"Oh good." Ellie watched Claire warily. She'd been so eager to take advantage of this chance to find out more about Peter that she hadn't thought to ask why Claire wanted to come to the house. But now she wondered—what were they doing here? And why was Claire suddenly so jumpy?

Her treasure pouch was gone.

Every possession she held dear was missing.

The money that might have bought her a few days of survival if Chez Celeste were to close.

Lady Celeste's necklace, the beautiful strand of purple jewels that would get Roxane into deep trouble if she didn't give it back.

The locket containing Mama's portrait, the only thing Roxane had to connect her to the time when she was Millicent and someone had loved her.

She'd searched her chamber to no avail. The room was so small and barren that tearing it apart took only a couple of minutes. The knife she'd brought into her room last night after all of the gentlemen left the house was still where she'd hidden it, wedged between the wall and the iron bedframe. But the leather pouch was truly gone.

Roxane sat on her bed, elbows on her knees, head in her hands. Tears sprang to her eyes but she squeezed them back. Tears never solved a problem; experience had taught her that. If anyone caught you crying, your troubles got worse.

Be strong, Millicent. She could almost hear Mama's voice speaking: *My sweet girl, be brave.*

Last night when Mr. Smith gave her a quarter-dollar, she'd

put the coin in her pouch. So she'd had it then. It must have been stolen this morning.

Véronique. She was the one. There was no other likely suspect.

If Lady Celeste was anxious to have her necklace back she would have knocked on Roxane's door and demanded its return. She had plenty of ways to enforce her wishes, so no need to resort to theft. Louise, whose job it was to handle the laundry and make up the beds fresh when they needed it, must have known the pouch was there; if she wanted to take it, she'd have done so before now.

So it was one of the *jeunes filles*. Fleur was too innocent, Yvette too honorable. Aurélie took too much pride in sticking to the rules and pointing out everyone else's transgressions. Véronique, sly and spiteful, had to be the thief.

Hoping Véronique was still downstairs, Roxane hurried across the hall to her chamber. She paused to listen, then tapped on the closed door. Hearing nothing, she slipped inside, shutting the door behind her.

Véronique's chamber was nearly identical to her own. The narrow cot. The plain white pitcher and bowl on the washstand. The tall pine wardrobe. But whereas Roxane kept her chamber neat, here the bedclothes were rumpled, a silk stocking drooped from mattress to floor, and one of the wardrobe doors hung ajar.

She searched the room quickly but found nothing until she explored the wardrobe. Sifting through a heap of clothing at the bottom, she uncovered a wooden box with flowers carved into its lid. It was the right size to hold a pair of ladies shoes, though too fancy for that purpose.

She lifted the top and gasped at what she saw. Money—such a lot of money! Several gold pieces glittered amongst the pennies and dimes. The corner of a dollar bill poked up from the coins.

Roxane couldn't resist pulling it out. It was one of the fancy new bills she'd heard about. One side had a picture of a goddess and a young boy sitting by a river and pointing to an open book, while the other bore two portraits, President George Washington along with his wife. So beautiful!

Véronique was fond of boasting about her special skills in giving pleasure to gentlemen. Roxane hadn't believed her, but the wild claims must be true if she earned tips so lavish that she could amass such a fortune.

Roxane suspected her own money was now in this box, but she'd never be able to prove it. She dug through the coins, searching for her leather pouch, and Lady Celeste's necklace, and Mama's locket, but the box held only money. Where could Véronique have hidden what she'd stolen? Under a loose floorboard, perhaps, or in a small hole cut into a wall?

She heard something bump, then felt a blow as the chamber door swung open and smacked her.

"Hey!" Véronique's voice, sharp, accusing. "What are you doing?"

Before Roxane could rise, Véronique grabbed a fistful of her hair and yanked it upward. Yelping from pain, Roxane staggered to her feet.

Véronique slapped her hard across the face. "Stealing my money! How dare you!"

"No! I'm looking for what you stole from me."

"Liar!"

Véronique grabbed Roxane's shoulders, shook her hard.

Roxane pummeled her rival with her fists. "Stop it! Give me my locket!"

"Get out of here, you thieving whore!"

A blow to her temple made Roxane's ears ring and her feet stumble. She landed hard on the floor and Véronique dove on top of her, clawing at her face. They scratched and punched and dug at each other. Roxane couldn't get out from underneath. Véronique straddled her, pinning her in place, closing her hands around Roxane's throat, choking off her scream.

"Heaven almighty!" someone cried.

Muttering a curse, Véronique released her hold and slowly got to her feet. Roxane sat up and pressed a hand against her chest to still her hammering heart.

The other *jeunes filles* crowded the doorway, jostling for the best view. They had all exchanged their morning dresses for their attire for welcoming gentlemen. Fleur looked frightened, Yvette sad.

"You know fighting is against the rules," Aurélie scolded. Though her tone was stern, her eyes sparkled with delight. "Wait until Lady Celeste finds out."

"You'd better not tattle," Véronique warned.

Yvette shook her head. "There will be no need to tell her. Your dispute shows plainly on your faces."

"Roxane is to blame." Véronique rubbed a cut on her mouth. A bruise was purpling on her cheekbone. "I caught her stealing my money."

"That's not true—" Roxane protested, but Yvette cut her off.

"You'd better hurry if you don't want to be late downstairs. The first bell has already rung." Stepping into the chamber, she took Roxane's hand and helped her to her feet.

"Are you badly hurt?" Fleur's voice quavered.

Roxane's face was sore and stinging. Her throat still felt pinched, her shoulders ached, and her knee throbbed. Putting a hand to her forehead, she felt a sticky wetness that meant she was bleeding.

"Not at all." She brushed dust from her clothing. "I'm fine." She had endured worse beatings many times, from Pa, from

Thaddeus, from drunken men in the cribs of the Barbary Coast. More men than she could count. This little spat hardly counted. She'd gain no advantage by letting anyone see her distress.

The brass bell rang a second time, signaling that the house was open to gentlemen. Fleur and Aurélie scurried for the stairs. Yvette patted Roxane's shoulder and left the room. Roxane slipped out behind her, without a backward glance at Véronique.

In her own chamber, she poured water from her pitcher into the basin and splashed her face to remove the blood. She took her looking glass from the wardrobe shelf. Lady Celeste presented a mirror to each new *jeunes filles* when she arrived at Chez Celeste, to help her make sure that she looked her most alluring when it was time to receive gentlemen.

Roxane's reflection told her she was failing that test. Véronique's fingernails had raked tracks across her cheeks, and one side of her mouth was puffing up. The skin below her left eye looked angry and dark. She found her pot of rouge and dabbed some on, but couldn't tell if it made her look better or worse.

She shrugged into her chemise, brushed her hair, and pinned it into an arrangement that hid as much of the damage as possible. The style didn't flatter her, but she couldn't think of a more becoming solution.

No gentleman could possibly desire her when she looked so ugly. What if no one chose her today? To be honest, she'd be happy to forgo the effort of pleasing a man, but that was foolish thinking. Lady Celeste would have no patience if she didn't earn her keep.

With the way her luck was running, Mr. Stregoni would return and be repelled by the sight of her.

The brass bell rang again. It meant trouble when Louise had to sound the signal a third time. This was the third day in a row that Roxane was late to the parlor, so she was already in Lady

Celeste's bad graces. Roxane dreaded to think what the lady would say when she saw her battered face.

Her body, aching and tired, resisted going toward the stairs. Roxane forced it to move. She limped down the steps, slowly, carefully, clinging to the handrail.

You have no choice, Millicent, she told herself. *Be brave. Be strong.*

34

Ellie gazed up at the gables and scrollwork of the house she loved—and at the yellow crime-scene tape across the front. No matter which offer she chose, Granny Jo's home would be changed forever.

Claire stood beside her. "It really is a splendid place."

"When I was little," Ellie said, "I called it the Castle. I thought if my parents would only let me move in here with Granny Jo I'd turn into a fairytale princess."

Claire frowned. "There's a seal across the door. Is there another entrance, where it won't look like someone broke in?"

"Maybe we shouldn't go in. Once the police release the house we can—"

"It needs to be now. Please. It's important."

"Why? What are you looking for?" Ellie asked. Claire still hadn't told her why they were here.

"I … I saw something Saturday night. And again yesterday. I think it may hold some answers to Simon's murder."

"Really? What was it?"

"Well, not *what* exactly. More like *who* …"

"A person? You mean you saw the killer?"

"It's hard to explain." Claire was looking at the sidewalk, not meeting Ellie's eyes.

"Yesterday the house was swarming with detectives and crime

scene people. Any clues that were here, they must have found them."

"And those clues led them to Peter. Look, Ellie, I know he behaved terribly to you. He's been awful to my sister too. But if he's innocent, do you want him rot in jail?"

"Of course not. Let's go this way. Maybe they didn't seal the ballroom door."

Ellie ducked under the yellow tape and led Claire down the skinny concrete path between Granny Jo's house and the apartment building next door.

"People call this level the basement," she said. "But really it's the ground floor, since the main floor is up so many steps. In Victorian times the family had parties down here, and guests came in this way. Easier for the women; they didn't have to worry about tripping over their long skirts on the stairs."

Oh Lord, she was chattering like a magpie—that's how Granny Jo would have put it. She wasn't sure why she was so nervous. Because the police had put the house off limits? Or because Claire was keeping her mission such a mystery?

No seal on the side door. Ellie inserted the old-fashioned brass key in the lock. She and Claire stepped into a large room that was shrouded in shadows.

"This is the ballroom. Well, you know that. You were dancing here the other night. With Peter." Her voice caught on his name. Despite everything that had happened since, the memory of seeing Claire in Peter's arms brought pain to her heart.

Claire walked around the edges of the room, touching the walls. "This may sound odd, but does the house have any kind of secret passage?"

"No. I always wished it did. When I was a kid I went all over the house knocking on every surface, listening for a hollow sound that might reveal a hidden compartment. No such luck."

"Let's go upstairs," Claire said.

This time she led the way and Ellie followed.

On the first floor Claire wandered from room to room with no particular aim that Ellie could see. She peered into the corners and stared at the medallions on the ceilings. From time to time she stopped and tilted her head as if listening for a sound to penetrate the quiet.

Ellie listened too, but heard nothing except the tapping of their footsteps on the bare floors. Everywhere she looked there was another memory. Decorating the Christmas tree in the parlor window bay. Curling up on the velvet-covered sofa in front of the marble fireplace with a storybook and cup of cocoa. Helping Granny Jo in the kitchen as she arranged roses from the garden into tall glass vases or rolled out cookie dough and let Ellie sneak a bite.

But she had a feeling Claire wasn't interested in any of that.

Finally Ellie asked, "Can I help you find whatever it is you're looking for?"

Claire shook her head. "Believe me, I wish you could."

"If you'll tell me what it is …"

"I'm not sure exactly." Claire started to go up the grand staircase.

"I liked playing apartment house on these stairs," Ellie said, trotting behind. "I'd set up doll furniture on each step. Sometimes I pretended the first landing was a church because it has that big stained-glass window."

On the second floor she stayed in the hallway, leaning against a wall, while Claire walked in and out of every room. Granny Jo's bedroom was last. When Claire didn't come out right away, Ellie went in to see what she was doing.

The table and folding chairs that the police detectives had set up for their interviews were still in place. Claire was sitting in a chair right where Granny Jo's rocker used to be. She had one elbow propped on the table and her chin resting in her hand.

"Are you okay?" Ellie asked.

Claire's head jerked up. "Oh! You startled me."

"Sorry, I didn't mean to—"

"Ellie, when you're in this house do you ever hear your grandmother's voice?"

Ellie smiled. "All the time. I see her too."

"Really? You do?" Claire sounded eager. "What's it like?"

"You know how it is. Memories can be so vivid …"

"I don't mean memories. I'm talking about—never mind." She rose from the chair.

Ellie ran her hand along the tabletop, thinking back to yesterday. To Vargas and Flaherty and all of their questions. Questions for which she had no answers. What if they came back to search for more evidence? She didn't want to be caught here. "We should leave. Have you found what you're looking for?"

"Let's check out the third floor."

"But … that's where the … where Simon was." As much as she loved this house, she didn't want to go into the storage room ever again.

"Exactly. That's why they might be up there," Claire said as if that would make everything clear. She walked out of the bedroom.

Ellie trailed her up the narrow stairs to the servants' quarters. "Who's *they?*"

"You said your grandmother had a visitor in her last days. Someone named Roxane."

"You can't be looking for her. She was a figment of Granny Jo's imagination. A nice figment, but still …"

"Did Granny Jo ever mention seeing a man?" Claire asked. They had reached the third floor. "A white-haired man who looked like Albert Einstein?"

"What? No, of course not. What are you talking about?"

Claire paced the hall. "So many doors!"

"My great-grandparents divided up the space so that their servants all had their own bedrooms. It was generous of them, even though the rooms are tiny."

Claire frowned. "They could be hiding anywhere." She went into the storage room. "Let's look in here first. This is where I last saw them."

Suppressed a shudder, Ellie followed.

The body was gone, for which she was grateful. Still, she couldn't take her eyes away from the spot beneath the window where it had lain. Blood had seeped into the old pine floorboards.

She and her brothers would have to arrange to clean that up. Or maybe not—if they sold the house to Daniel's company, he'd rip apart the whole third floor. The storage room and the cubbyhole bedrooms would disappear. New owners would move into modern, polished spaces. The past would be erased, yet they could boast about living in a historic mansion. Assuming she voted to sell. Assuming the murder wouldn't ruin the property's sales appeal, as Richard feared.

A sharp noise from downstairs punctured her turmoil of thoughts. A door slamming? She'd relocked the side door, she was sure.

The cops must have come back.

Feeling panic, Ellie looked around for Claire. She was nowhere to be seen.

"Claire?"

No answer.

"Claire, we need to go. I think the police are here."

Then Ellie spotted her—or rather her shoes, near the top of the spiral stairs.

"Claire, come down. Please!"

"In a minute," Claire called. "Could there be a trapdoor up here that leads somewhere?"

"No! The tower's just for show. There's no place to hide anything."

The clump of footsteps rose from below. Ellie shivered. Could a prowler have broken in?

Had Simon's killer returned?

Claire hadn't come down. Damn it, this was no time to take in the view.

"Claire! We have to get out of here." Ellie hurried up the winding stairs. She would drag Claire down by force if necessary.

But the lookout at the top of the tower was empty.

Claire had vanished.

CHAPTER

35

Daylight is departing. Shadows fill the rooms. Perhaps tonight Edouard will arrive to take me to the Place Called Forever. That would be especially fitting, because this is the anniversary of what was, thanks to him, the happiest and saddest time of my life.

On a September evening like this one he arrived at the door wearing his uniform and carrying an extravagant bouquet of red roses.

"How beautiful!" I exclaimed. "They're like jewels."

"You are the jewel, chérie," Edouard said. "Tonight we'll go back to the Top of the Mark. I have something important to tell you."

"You've already asked me to marry you. What could be more important than that?" I held out my left hand with its sparkling diamond and laughed.

Maman arranged the roses in a vase while Edouard pinned a half-opened bud to my bodice. It matched my scarlet dress perfectly.

"I like the way this man makes you smile," Maman said. "Edouard, be kind to my girl."

"Always, madame," Edouard said. "I give you my word."

"Let's go," I said, eager to hear what he wanted to tell me.

He said little in the taxi to the Mark Hopkins, and stayed quiet on the elevator to the nineteenth floor. I began to worry.

We sat at a table with a fine view of the new bridge over the Golden Gate. City lights glittered at our feet. The band played the summer's hit song, "Moonlight Serenade." I tapped my feet impatiently but Edouard didn't want to dance.

As we sipped martinis I chattered about our wedding plans. He merely nodded his head. Finally I said, "Sweetheart, what's wrong? It's not like you to be so quiet."

He raised his empty glass, signaling for another round. "I've received distressing news. It doesn't lessen my love for you, but it forces us to change our plans."

I felt my heart stop.

"What news? Change our plans how?"

Edouard grasped my hand. "For more than a year my country watched in alarm as Hitler gobbled up territory in Eastern Europe—Austria, Czechoslovakia, the Sudetenland. There has been great concern that Poland would be his next target. France pledged to support Poland's independence."

"Yes, I've read about that." I knew troubles were brewing in Europe, though to be truthful I hadn't followed the news closely. "But what does it have to do with us?"

The waiter set our fresh martinis on the table. Edouard swallowed his in two gulps. My worry increased.

He said, "The invasion we feared has happened. Now France—ma patrie, my country—has declared war on Germany. I must return to Paris."

"Paris? No!"

"It's my duty as a soldier and a citizen. I leave on Friday morning."

"So soon! Just three days away! When will you come back?"

"Once Germany feels the power of the French army, that scoundrel Hitler can't last. If fortune smiles, I may be back in San Francisco in the spring—"

"In time for our wedding."

"But it might be longer. A year, perhaps more. And you must

understand, chérie … in war there's always a risk. Some soldiers achieve their final glory on the battlefield."

"Are you saying you might die? Oh, Edouard—" I burst into tears.

Edouard gripped my hand more tightly. "Forgive me, chérie. I didn't mean to break the news in such a clumsy fashion." He wiped the tears from my cheeks with a cocktail napkin. Then he beckoned to the waiter. "Bring the lady another martini, s'il vous plait. I'll have one too."

Feeling desolate, I looked around. Other couples were gazing into each other's eyes, laughing at each other's jokes, dancing in each other's arms.

"Josephine." Edouard said my name so tenderly. I couldn't bear to look at him. "This isn't the end for us. It's the beginning." His face took on an eager expression. "Chérie, elope with me. Tonight."

"Elope! You mean get married right now?"

He looked down, biting his beautiful lip. "What I mean is, we must make the most of the time we have. The law in France won't let married men serve in the army. Our wedding ceremony must wait until the fighting is over. But what is a ceremony, really? Merely words."

"Not just words. It's the blessing of God."

"Ah, Josephine, God can be found everywhere, in the blooming of a flower, in the rustle of a leaf in a breeze, in the laughter of water rushing over stones. You believe this, yes?"

I nodded. "Yes, but—"

"If God can be found in such things, then surely his blessing is present whenever two people in love come together. Isn't that his commandment, that we should love one another?"

I gasped in shock. I couldn't believe what he was asking me to do. "I can't, Edouard. It's sinful—"

"No, it isn't. We'll pledge our eternal love by offering each other *the greatest gift a man and a woman can give. Whenever love is present, God rejoices."*

He lifted my hand to his lips and kissed it. Even that brief touch took my breath away.

"We have only three nights. Let's spend them together like the husband and wife we'll become one day."

I knew I should say no to this foolish proposition. But the force of our love pulled me to him as irresistibly as a moth to a flame.

He said, "I've taken a room here in the hotel, three nights for Monsieur et Madame Trevillon, as private and comfortable as you could wish."

He smiled, and his eyes gleamed in the candlelight. He paid our bill, then stood and took my hand. "Come with me, my dearest … my bride."

As I stood I felt wobbly. I was amazed at how eager I was to commit this sin.

Edouard put his arm around my waist and I let him lead me toward the consummation of our undying love.

Never, not before nor since, have I known such bliss as I did in those three days. We didn't leave the room, hanging a do-not-disturb sign on the door for the maids. Room service delivered our meals. We spent our time wrapped in each other's arms, enjoying each other's bodies, exploring the endless ways that a man and a woman could express their love. I was astounded by Edouard's inventiveness, and even more by my own.

His departure time came too soon. Fog hung over the bay as we waited at the pier for his long journey to begin—the ferry to Oakland, the train to New York, the ship that would take him to France and to war. Edouard wore his uniform. So handsome, so wise, so loving, so brave.

I did my best not to let my tears spill over. I didn't want him to carry away a memory of my weeping.

"Take this." I pressed a handkerchief into his hand. I had soaked it with Evening in Paris. "Keep it to remind you of me."

He lifted the handkerchief to his nose. "Whenever I smell this lovely scent, I'll dream that you're next to me." He smiled as he tucked it into his breast pocket. "As I go into battle, I'll carry it for good luck."

The ferry whistle gave a long low toot. The people milling around us began to move, almost as one, toward the boat.

"I'll write to you every day, chérie. Never forget that I love you."

He lifted me until my toes no longer touched the dock, and we shared a kiss that stirred my soul but was much too brief.

"I love you too," I called as he headed up the gangplank. "I love you too!"

He waved from the upper deck as the ferry pulled away from the dock. I waved back until he disappeared into the fog and I could no longer hold back my tears.

Oh, Edouard, please come for me tonight!

"You are disgraceful, both of you!"

Hands on her hips, blue eyes flashing, Lady Celeste looked from Roxane's damaged face to Véronique's and back again. Roxane wished she could sink straight down into the parlor's Persian rug and disappear.

"I run a respectable establishment. You know I don't tolerate fighting." Lady Celeste's voice shook with anger. "That sort of behavior belongs in the cribs of the Barbary Coast, where you two came from. Perhaps I should send you back there."

"But, my lady—" Véronique sputtered through split lips. Roxane couldn't suppress a twinge of satisfaction at the fact that Véronique's face had fared worse than her own.

"Mademoiselle Roxane!" Lady Celeste turned to her. "Is that a smile I see? Do you find this situation amusing?"

"No, my lady." Roxane quickly cast her eyes down, lest some twitch of her mouth betray her further. She wanted to give Lady Celeste no excuse to carry out her dire threat.

Behind her she heard the plinking of the piano as Yvette picked out a tune. Thank goodness no gentlemen had yet arrived.

"It wasn't my fault," Véronique said. "She started it. I caught her snooping in my room and then she attacked me—"

"You liar! You thief!" The words jumped out before Roxane could swallow them. Véronique deserved so much more punishment than the scratches Roxane had inflicted.

"Close your mouths." Lady Celeste waved her hand to stop the flow of accusations. "I know full well what happened."

Roxane heard a snuffle. She turned to see Fleur, curled into a corner of the settee, wiping her eyes like she was crying. Aurélie, sitting beside her, giggled and fluffed her sausage curls. Roxane had no doubt who had tattled.

Véronique reached for Lady Celeste's sleeve. "Let me explain—"

Lady Celeste swatted her hand away. "I said, fermez les bouches!"

Véronique's mouth snapped shut.

"You two go to your rooms. We'll have visitors at any moment, and I cannot have you here where the sight of you will disgust them. We'll work out later how you'll repay me."

"What? Repay—?" Véronique's voice squeaked as she said pay.

"Of course. Your childish fight has deprived me of your services for today. You cannot expect me simply to absorb that loss of income. Now go. Allez-vous en." Lady Celeste pointed to the grand staircase.

Roxane's heart sank. With her treasure pouch gone, she had no money at all. How could she possibly pay a debt if she couldn't work? Yet if she could work, she'd have no debt in the first place. She was spinning in a mad circle that she would never escape. She was going to owe money to Lady Celeste forever.

A sudden fatigue overwhelmed her. She turned toward the hallway, intending to obey Lady Celeste's command. It would be a relief to have a night where she need do nothing but sleep. She would worry about the money tomorrow.

Fleur rushed over and flung her arms around Roxane's waist. "Don't go, Roxane!"

Lady Celeste frowned.

"I'm only going upstairs," Roxane said, touching Fleur's flame-red hair. "I'm not wanted down here tonight."

"She said she might send you back to—"

"No! I'm not leaving Chez Celeste." Roxane glanced at the proprietor of the establishment, hoping her words were true.

"I couldn't bear being here if you went away."

Roxane sighed. "I'm not sure I can bear it if I stay. But don't worry. I have no place to go. No place as good as this."

Louise bustled in from the kitchen and set a tray of decanters and glasses on the drinks table. To Roxane's surprise she was followed by Isaac Burnham, a tumbler of whiskey already in his hand. How peculiar. Though the house had opened to gentlemen, she'd not heard the chime that announced someone's arrival.

Then something even odder happened. Lady Celeste gave Isaac her hand and her warmest smile. "There you are, mon cher. I wondered what had become of you."

He planted a kiss on her fingertips. Bright spots of pink bloomed in her cheeks. "I'm always here for you, sweetheart," he said.

A thought occurred to Roxane—could Isaac be the man she'd heard earlier in Lady Celeste's chamber? If the lady of the house was going to bend the rules for a gentleman, it seemed strange that she would choose a gray-haired fellow twice her age, especially when she'd already won his money and his house away from him years ago in that poker game.

The ballroom bell chimed, indicating that a gentleman had come in the side door. Lady Celeste seemed reluctant to turn away from Isaac, but she put on a businesslike air. Tossing her blond curls, she took her seat in her throne-like chair, the vantage point from which she oversaw the hospitality of the house.

Véronique sat in the overstuffed armchair and arranged herself into an inviting pose. Despite her less-than-alluring face, she clearly did not intend to mind Lady Celeste's orders.

Heavy footsteps came up the stairs.

Roxane felt a flutter in her belly. What if the visitor was Mr. Stregoni? She didn't want to be hidden in her room where he couldn't find her. Nor did she want him to see her all scratched and bruised. But maybe this wasn't the mysterious little man. What if it was—

Thaddeus Burnham emerged into the hallway.

She dashed to the grand staircase and up the first two steps. A pair of rough hands yanked her back and spun her around.

Thaddeus leered at her and tightened his grip. "Where were you going, mamzelle? And all alone too."

"Let me go, monsieur. I'm not working this evening. Lady Celeste has forbidden it."

"Really? Why is that?" Without allowing her to answer, he steered her back to the parlor, where Lady Celeste sat making notes in her record book. He nodded to his father, now sitting on the settee. Aurélie was working her wiles on the elder Mr. Burnham, but his gaze was fixed on Lady Celeste.

Thaddeus rapped his knuckles on the table to get the lady's attention. "Madam, I want to spend time tonight with Mamzelle Roxane. But she tells me she's not available."

Lady Celeste set down her pen. "I've instructed her to take the evening off. To heal herself. As you can see, she is ... not so appealing as usual."

"I appreciate your kindness, my lady—" Roxane began.

Thaddeus cut her off. "Oh, I find her very appealing. In fact, I believe I'll purchase her company not just for the usual hour but the whole time until midnight. And in the Rose Room, if you please."

Oh God, save me! Roxane couldn't tell if she was praying or taking the Lord's name in vain. So many hours with this brute would be unbearable. And in the Rose Room—she'd loved her night in that room with Mr. Stregoni. Being there with Thaddeus would only sully that memory. If she must endure him this evening, why could it not be in her own chamber, where she'd hidden the knife? Then at least she'd be able to defend herself if he took his cruelty too far.

She wanted to scream. She wanted to run. She dared not do either.

Lady Celeste's tongue flicked out for a second before she looked up at Thaddeus and smiled. Roxane had frequently noticed that when the lady was about to make a deal involving money, she took on the look of a cat anticipating a taste of cream.

"The Rose Room is not spoken for. So if you'd like to book it for all that time, it is yours, monsieur. But don't expect a discount based on Mademoiselle Roxane's condition."

"I'm prepared to pay the full price, madam. As to her condition ..."

He ran his thick finger along Roxane's cheek, following the line of the deepest, most painful cut. His touch made her flesh sting and her eyes burn with tears, but she refused to give him the satisfaction of seeing her flinch.

" … it makes her that much more attractive to me. She looks so deliciously … vulnerable."

36

Ellie crept down the servants' stairs, listening to the sound of footsteps roaming the first floor. The police. Who else would be in a house sealed off as a crime scene?

Simon's killer, that's who. The thought stole her breath.

If only she could make it to the ballroom and out the side door. She felt terrible about deserting Claire, but she had no idea where Claire was. She'd searched the tower, but it was empty. She'd called Claire's name without response.

She couldn't explain it, but Claire was gone.

No time to search further. Whether the person downstairs was a cop or a killer, Ellie needed to escape.

Reaching the first floor, she peeked around the corner. No one in sight. Good. She had to go into the main hall to reach the steps to the ballroom, and she didn't want to be seen. She tiptoed, pressing close to the wall.

"Hey!"

Ellie jumped. Then froze in place.

"There you are!" The man behind the voice came into view. Not a cop—it was the creepy guy from Claire's office. George. His hand was thrust into an open bag of potato chips.

"What are you doing here?" she demanded.

"You and Claire came to search for clues, right? Didn't want to miss the fun." He stuffed a fistful of chips into his mouth as he glanced around. "Never been to a murder scene before. Where did Simon get whacked?"

Ellie shuddered. "You're not supposed to be here. What did you do, steal your boss's key?"

"Don't worry, I'll put it back." He wiped his greasy fingers on his corduroy pants.

"Didn't you see the crime scene tape, the seal on the door?"

George glanced at the front door and shrugged. "You're here, aren't you? Same tape, same seal."

He held out the chip bag.

She drew herself tall, hoping to gain some appearance of authority. "It's different. It's my house."

"One-third your house. Hey, where's Claire?"

Ellie sagged again. "She's—I don't know, we were upstairs and she kind of ... disappeared."

"Disappeared? You mean hiding?"

"No. Well, yes, maybe."

"Why would she do that?" George ate the last of the chips, crumpled the bag, and stuffed it in his pants pocket.

"I don't know," Ellie said again. "She went up in the tower, but when I followed her, she was gone. I can't imagine where she went."

"Hey, what if the killer got her."

She shivered. "The killer?"

George bounced on his toes and laughed. "The guy who snuffed Simon. Could be he's here in the house. He kidnapped Claire, stashed her in some secret compartment."

That possibility had already occurred to her. Maybe the killer was here in the house.

Maybe he was right in front of her.

George had been at the BAPA party Saturday night. Now here he was again. Hadn't she read that murderers always return to the scene of the crime?

"You have to leave." She hated the quaver in her voice. "Right now."

She fumbled in her pocket for her phone. Could she dial 911 without his noticing?

"What we have to do is find Claire." His voice was eager, his eyes wide with excitement. "Come on."

He grabbed Ellie's hand and pulled her down the hall.

———◆———

Claire's steps faltered as she made her way down the spiral stairs. The air exploded with flashing stars, like hundreds of Fourth of July sparklers bursting around her head.

Claire, we have to get out …

Ellie's voice, faint and echoing, then gone.

When her feet touched the storage-room floor the stars winked out. Feeling woozy, she clung to the railing and blinked her eyes in disbelief.

What the hell was happening?

When she'd climbed into the tower, the storage room had been empty. Now it was crammed with antiques and old-fashioned trunks.

How could that be? She'd been up there for only a couple of minutes.

This house was freaking her out.

"Ellie!"

No answer. Ellie was nowhere in sight.

Where had she gone? And how had she filled the room so quickly with so much stuff?

Or an image of stuff. That had to be it—she was seeing an illusion created with projectors, or lasers. A hologram, something like that. Claire had no idea how the trick might work, but

Richard Burnham's company specialized in home security. He must have set up some sort of high-tech system here.

Ellie had probably flipped a switch that made the room appear to be full of junk, and then laughed as she left the house. A practical joke at Claire's expense.

She poked the nearest trunk, expecting her hand to glide through it as easily as piercing a beam of light. But her fingers bumped against an unyielding surface, its leather covering smooth and cool to the touch. She jerked her hand away, as if the trunk had burst into flames.

"Ellie! Where are you?"

Had she gone downstairs? Disappeared into thin air? Claire shivered.

"Ellie! This isn't funny!"

Still no response.

But now Claire heard a lively piano tune coming from somewhere deep in the house. A familiar, old-time tune. She caught herself humming along—*"Casey would waltz with a strawberry blonde and the band played on."*

Hadn't Ellie once mentioned that Granny Jo played the piano?

"Josephine? Is that you? Are you doing this?"

She waited to feel a breath at her ear, or hear a whisper, or smell the spice-and-flowers fragrance she'd come to associate with the old woman.

If Granny Jo was nearby, she gave no sign.

Claire's muscles tensed. She knew that strange kinks in the energy of a place suggested the presence of spirits, and she was reluctantly becoming familiar with the way they manifested—a scent, a murmur, a wink of light, a glimmer of motion.

But the sudden appearance of a roomful of solid objects? Nothing could explain this.

These things looked like they might be Burnham family belongings from long ago. Trunks, cases, and crates. A dressmaker's dummy in a far corner. Two or three small, ornately carved tables. An easy chair with ripped upholstery. Even a couple of chamber pots.

She glanced at the place beneath the front window where Simon's body had lain. A stack of hatboxes occupied the space.

The dizziness overwhelmed her. Claire pressed her hands to her eyes. Please, she thought, when I open them, let everything be back to normal.

She counted to ten and raised her eyelids. The boxes and trunks were still there.

Whatever was causing this awful hallucination, she had to make it stop.

What could have happened? She'd been in the tower only long enough to make sure it had no place where Roxane and Stregoni could hide. The windows were latched, and sweeping her hands across the floorboards and tapping the walls hadn't revealed a secret compartment.

Now she'd come downstairs into what seemed like a different world.

Or maybe—the thought struck so hard that her knees buckled and she landed on top of a flat-topped trunk—into a different era.

Had she stumbled on their hiding place after all? Could the strange couple have figured out the secret to moving back and forth in time?

No. That made absolutely no sense.

Yet it explained so much—their antique style of dress, their ability to disappear, the way no one could see them.

What if somehow she'd followed them through clock and calendar to an earlier century?

Her stomach coiled into a knot. Bad enough that the dear and not-so-dear departed pestered her while they left other people alone. She had no desire to add time travel to the list of weird things that happened to her and no one else.

Another dreadful thought—had she been given a one-way ticket?

If time had flipped around, how was she supposed to swing it back so she could land at the moment where she'd started?

The magic had happened in the tower. Maybe if she went up there again, everything would be normal when she came back down.

Her heart thudded as she twisted her way up the stairs. Beyond the tower windows the blue sky was deepening as the day waned. She gazed through the curved panes, dismayed at the view—so different from the one she'd seen a few minutes ago.

The towers that defined downtown San Francisco were missing; she could see above the roofs of the houses all the way to the bay. Across the street was a Queen Anne house, a cousin to the Burnham Mansion, instead of the apartment building that should be there. Directly below, a woman in a long dress with leg-o'-mutton sleeves strolled with a man sporting a top hat. A horse-pulled buggy clattered along the paving stones.

A bleak feeling came over her. Never had she wished so hard to see a traffic jam, with cars spewing exhaust and horns honking.

Concentrate, Claire. If she could recreate her movements, maybe she could reverse this eerie spell.

She circled the tower, knocking on the walls, brushing the floorboards, twisting the finial at the top of the stair rail. The view outside didn't change.

Perhaps the trigger was on the spiral stairs. It was impossible to recall exactly where she'd stepped before, so as she corkscrewed down the steps she ran her foot all the way across each tread.

She hoped against hope that when she reached the bottom, the storage room would be empty.

No—the crates, trunks, and boxes were still there.

She was trapped.

She dropped onto the flat-topped trunk, filled with terror and despair.

Again she heard the distant piano. Then, much closer, the light sound of a woman laughing, followed by the rumble of a deep male voice.

Roxane and Stregoni? Please let it be them so they could tell her how to go home to her own time.

Nerves taught as wire, she got up to investigate.

At the storage room doorway she stopped short. In the hall a young woman with sausage curls was locked in a tight embrace with a plump, balding man. The woman wore only a corset. The man had on a dark suit, but just barely. His jacket dangled over one arm, his shirttails flapped free, his cravat hung untied around his neck, and his trousers were making a slow descent toward the floor. With a giggle, the woman reached behind her, opened the door to one of the little bedrooms, and drew her sweetheart inside. The door slammed. They'd paid no attention to Claire.

She stared at the closed door as stillness settled over the hallway. Were the lovers real? Or one more delusion in the nightmare she was trapped in?

Either way, they were unlikely to help her. Claire had to find someone who would.

She crossed the hall to the stairs. Her heart caught in her throat. If the third floor was so unnerving, what was she going to encounter in the rest of the house?

She dreaded finding out.

But, really, what choice did she have? With shaking steps, she headed toward the piano music.

CHAPTER

37

"This is a fine place for love, don't you agree, mamzelle." Thaddeus Burnham closed the door to the Rose Room. The snick of the latch sounded as loud to Roxane as a prison door slamming. "We shall enjoy ourselves this evening."

"If you say so, monsieur." She stared at her feet and traced a curlicue in the pattern of the Persian carpet with her toes. Her body was trembling, but not with desire.

She knew how to act the coquette, smiling and flirting and pretending a gentleman's affection was all she wanted in the world. She was good at the role, but she couldn't summon the strength or the will to play it. Not tonight. Not with Thaddeus.

"Yes indeed." Thaddeus put his top hat on the dresser and sat down heavily on the bed. He patted the pink velvet coverlet. "Come to me, sweet mamzelle."

Roxane didn't move. She could see her reflection, ghostly pale, in the gilt-framed mirrors that adorned the walls along with Lady Celeste's bawdy prints from Paris. Her face was bruised, her eye blackened. Deep gouges on her cheeks were a dark angry red. She was not a pretty sight. Not that she cared to be pretty for this horrid man.

She hated the idea of being in the Rose Room with Thaddeus. Its comforts and luxuries were meaningless in his company. This was the same chamber where two nights ago she'd spent such pleasant hours with Mr. Stregoni. The same bed where, receiving no demands from him, she'd had the best sleep of her life. Whatever Thaddeus planned to do in this room, it would feel like they were desecrating a sacred space, as if she'd come into paradise on the devil's arm.

Thaddeus frowned. He slapped the bed again, harder, then tried to grab her wrist. She stepped back out of reach.

"Wouldn't you like to have a drink before we begin, monsieur? You arranged to have my company for the entire evening. We've plenty of time to … enjoy ourselves, as you put it. We need not rush to get started."

She moved past him, dodging his hands, to the bedside table where the decanter of whiskey and two glasses had been set out. She poured him a full measure and gave him the glass, then tipped a little into the second glass for herself, knowing he would expect her join him. She'd have to start a tally in her head, so Lady Celeste could levy the proper charges when Thaddeus was ready to leave. It was a long time until midnight. If only she could get him drunk enough to pass out and leave her alone.

She raised her glass in a toast. "To your health, monsieur."

He took a long swallow and set his glass down.

"Come here, mamzelle." He seized her arm and yanked her toward him. Her glass flew from her hand, splashing her with whiskey. It hit the baseboard and shattered.

She knelt to gather the shards but Thaddeus pulled her to her feet. "Never mind that," he growled. "Didn't I tell you to come to me?"

Still sitting on the bed, he pinned her legs between his knees. "Your clothes are wet. I shall have to do something about that." He put his mouth to her breast and began sucking on the thin fabric that covered it. "Ah! Never has whiskey been so delicious."

He slid her chemise up over her shoulders, then over her head. His mouth was gone from her breast only for an instant and then he was kissing her bare flesh.

Suddenly he bit down, hard.

Roxane forced herself to not to gasp or flinch. Glancing down, she saw a short, thin line of blood.

Thaddeus grinned to show that he knew he'd hurt her and was pleased to have that power.

She stood unmoving between his knees. Tonight she would pretend her body was made of stone. She would be a column of marble—smooth, cold, hard, unyielding. Incapable of feelings, impervious to pain.

Thaddeus planted his hands under her arms and rose to his feet, lifting her off the floor. He threw her down onto the pink coverlet. She watched warily as he folded his coat and laid it on a pillow. Then he removed his shoes, his cravat, and his shirt, exposing his broad, muscular chest. Finally he climbed onto the bed and straddled her.

"I'll give you the pleasure of removing my trousers, mamzelle."

She was made of stone; her fingers refused to move.

"Right now!" His low, silky whisper was far more menacing than a shout.

"Oui, monsieur." She fumbled with the buttons at his waist and worked her way down as slowly as she dared.

"That's the way. We're going to have fun, you and I." He brushed her hair away from her face and caressed her cheek, rubbing his fingers over the cuts and bruises. "I have exciting plans for us tonight. If you make me happy, I have a gift for you."

"A gift, monsieur?"

"Indeed. A very special surprise."

She knew she should act pleased, excited. If she didn't show him the appreciation he expected, things would not go well for her.

She smiled, fluttered her lashes. Slipped her hand into his open fly. "Being with you for a whole evening in this beautiful room is gift enough. And now another present? You are more than generous."

"Yes. Let me show it to you now, so you can look forward to the reward you'll receive when midnight comes. So long as you have satisfied me, that is."

He stretched out on top of her, pushing her down into the soft mattress. His weight was almost more than she could bear. He kissed her swollen lips, his mouth hard and hungry. She struggled to breathe.

My body is stone, Roxane told herself. She knew he expected an eager response, but for the life of her she couldn't muster the energy to fake one.

I've sinned so much, my soul is condemned anyway. Nothing he does can touch me.

Finally he rolled over, so that he was lying beside her. Exactly as Mr. Stregoni had done on Sunday night. She blinked back tears.

"Is that your gift, monsieur?" She kept her voice light. "It's always a thrill to receive your kisses."

"That's just a taste of what's to come. This is your gift."

He twisted to reach the folded coat on the pillow and took a small bundle from one of the pockets. He held it cupped in his hands so she couldn't see what it was.

"It's something I know you'll cherish. In truth there is more than one gift, all together in a charming package. Take a look."

He moved his hands to reveal a pouch of worn leather, dangling by its drawstrings between his thick thumb and finger.

Her treasure pouch!

"That's mine!" She rose up and lunged for it, but he pulled it away.

"It will be yours later. Assuming you've earned it."

He swung the pouch back and forth from its strings, like a clock's pendulum. Just out of her reach.

"You! You stole it from me! I blamed Véronique—but it was you!" She grabbed for it again, without success. "Thief! Give it back!"

He slapped her hard, knocking her back onto the mattress. Then he calmly got to his feet, pouch still in hand, and picked up his whiskey glass. He took a drink and smacked his lips with satisfaction.

"I stole nothing. I found this old sack last night in your chamber, after you fell asleep on me. It was tucked away and forgotten. I merely rescued it from ending up in the trash."

She scrabbled to her knees on the bed and clasped her hands together as if she were praying. "Please, monsieur—let me have it back."

"Let's see what's in here that's so desirable." He pulled the pouch open and dumped the contents onto the bedside table.

Her coins.

The amethyst necklace.

Her locket with Mama's portrait inside.

Roxane's breath was ragged. She couldn't resist reaching for the locket.

Thaddeus hit her again.

"You may have these when I say so, and not until then. Though what you want with them, I don't know."

She put her hand to her cheek, which throbbed with pain. It felt wet to her touch, and her fingertips came away red with blood. Thaddeus's blow had opened one of the cuts.

"The money is a paltry sum." He swept the coins off the tabletop and they scattered, landing among the bits of broken glass.

Roxane's heart went hollow. She had to get the money back. Without it she had no hope.

"And this." He held up the locket. "It's worth nothing, a piece of junk." He dropped it to the floor and raised his foot, as if he were about to crush it.

"No!" she cried, then bit her lips.

"Is this silly trinket precious to you? Very well. I promised to give it to you at the end of the evening, and so I shall—if you treat me right." He picked it up and slipped it back in the pouch. "If not, well, it's too cheap to worry about. And there's nothing inside but a picture of an ugly whore."

"You … you will be pleased with me tonight, monsieur."

"Yes, I believe I will. Now this"—he held up the amethyst necklace; the purple stones gleamed despite the waning light—"this is an item of beauty and value. But it doesn't belong to you, does it? If there's a thief in this room, it's you, mamzelle. Not me."

"I didn't steal it. Lady Celeste lent it to me for her birthday festivities on Saturday night."

"Yes, I saw you wearing it. You were beautiful; you always are. Even tonight." He stroked one of the gashes on her face. "But it's no longer Saturday, is it? When someone refuses to return a borrowed item, don't you call it theft? A breach of trust? What will Lady Celeste say when she finds out you've squirreled away her jewelry for yourself?"

"I didn't! I never would …"

Thaddeus came around the bed to stand behind her as she knelt on the mattress. He clasped the amethyst necklace around her throat and pointed to her reflection in the mirror opposite.

"The necklace suits you, mamzelle. How sad it would be if Lady Celeste learned you intended to sell it for your own gain."

"You can't mean to tell her such a lie!"

He drew the necklace snug against her throat. "She'll probably turn you out of the house. And where could a girl like you go?" He pulled tighter. "Or perhaps she'll have you sent to prison."

Roxane went utterly still. Did he know he was voicing her deepest fears? Was he planning to make them come true?

"Please, monsieur—you're choking me!"

He released her and dropped the necklace into the pouch with the locket. He put the bundle on the dresser and set his top hat over it so it was out of sight. When he sat beside her, she hadn't moved. She hadn't even breathed.

He maneuvered her onto his lap and kissed her damaged cheek. "You need not worry. If you're forced to leave Chez Celeste, I'll take you in. I'll give you my protection. If you behave yourself, I shall even make you my wife."

She shook her head. Surely she had heard him wrong. "Your—wife?"

"You see, I am in love with you."

Love. The cruelest word in the language. Roxane suppressed a sob. Marrying Thaddeus would be a worse fate, far worse, than going back to being a nickel whore on the Barbary Coast. Even worse than prison.

Thaddeus apparently mistook the strangled sound she'd made for a sigh of happiness. "Yes, sweet mamzelle, I love you. Surely that's no surprise. It can't have escaped your attention that I favor you over all of the other joon fees in this house."

"I'm aware that you frequently seek out my ... companionship. An ... honor, to be sure."

He chuckled. "I'll wager you never thought anyone would make an honest woman of you, did you?"

"No," she whispered. Let him think it was an answer to his question.

"That's assuming, of course, that you're good to me tonight. If we enjoy each other's company, you'll have your foolish locket, as well as my silence. I'll see that Lady Celeste gets her necklace without discovering your thievery."

"And—my money?"

To her surprise he laughed. "After our wedding you'll have no need of money."

He kissed her cheek, his tongue rasping her wounds as if he craved the taste of her blood. Then his mouth attacked her lips, her throat, her breasts. She felt like he was trying to devour her. Her stomach churned and she swallowed hard to prevent herself from becoming ill. She forced herself to embrace him, to stroke his back, to rock her hips against his. To pretend she was in ecstasy.

He let her go long enough to wriggle out of his trousers and leave them in a tangle on the floor. She dared to stand up.

"Now that I've declared myself, sweet mamzelle, you must tell me you love me too."

Her lips were so sore that she couldn't push any words past them.

Thaddeus locked his fingers behind her neck and stroked her throat with his thumbs. "What's the matter, are you so overwhelmed with passion and gratitude that you cannot speak?" He pressed the soft spot at the base of her throat. "Say it!"

"I—I … love you, monsieur." The lie had a bitter taste, like bile.

"That's right. Now prove it." Thaddeus ran his hands down her body, from her shoulders to her breasts to her hips. "You have until midnight to convince me." He thrust a fist between her legs and pushed thick fingers into her very core.

So many men had seen her nakedness, had used her body, had taken pleasure from her and left behind pain. Never had she felt as terrified as she did right now. Never had she been so sure that this was the night she would die.

"I—I do love you. Please believe me." To her distress, she was whimpering. She made her voice stronger. "And if you'll permit me—I know a secret that I do believe will give you the greatest pleasure you've ever known."

She dipped her head and looked at him through her lashes, and forced her swollen lips to form what she hoped was an enticing smile.

"A secret, eh? Show me."

"To do that, I'll need … something from my own chamber. I don't have the proper … supplies in this room. Let me run upstairs to fetch them."

He reached for his trousers. "I'll go with you."

"No! I must go alone. This secret requires certain preparations. The magic will be spoiled if you see them in advance. Please—stay here where it's comfortable. Have more whiskey. I'll return quickly."

She scurried to find her chemise, which lay on the floor with her coins and the broken glass.

He moved to the door and blocked it. "Mamzelle! You owe me your time until midnight. How do I know you'll come back?"

She tried another flirtatious smile but wasn't sure it was convincing. "Why would I not come back when I love you? Besides, I'm eager to have the gifts you promised. My locket—and your silence."

He gave a curt nod. "Go then. If you're not back in quick order, I will find you. And you may be sure you'll regret ever leaving this room."

Roxane pulled the chemise over her head and settled it into

place. She dipped her knees, making an awkward curtsy. "Merci, monsieur. You'll be overjoyed with what I bring you, I promise."

Thaddeus frowned, but he opened the door and let her out. She half ran, half stumbled toward the third-floor stairs.

CHAPTER

38

Claire paused at the top of the grand staircase. Along with the piano music, a buzz of voices rose from the first floor.

What kind of vipers' nest was she about to enter?

She counted out ten deep, slow breaths, the method her grandmother had taught her for dealing with nervousness. Gram also advised thinking soothing thoughts, but right now Claire's brain refused to come up with one.

She started down the stairs, straining to hear what was being said below. At first she couldn't make out any words. Then one voice, a woman's, grew loud and angry.

"It's not fair! You let Roxane go with a gentleman, why not me?"

Roxane! Claire's heart jumped. They knew the Amethyst Girl here in this crazy, flipped-around world. If only she could find her.

Someone murmured a reply, but the angry woman didn't like it. She burst out of the parlor and into Claire's view, yelling, "A pox on all of you!"

She was young, with long dark hair that reached the top of her old-fashioned black corset—her only garment. She might have been pretty if her face weren't scratched and bruised.

"Véronique! Stop!" someone called out.

The woman ignored the command and raced up the stairs,

284

almost colliding with Claire. She rushed past without pause or apology, as if Claire weren't even there.

Claire stared as Véronique turned a corner and disappeared. A cloud of jasmine perfume hung in her wake.

A close call. The corset-clad woman had been too blind with fury to see her. The pair of lovers upstairs hadn't noticed Claire either, but that was because they were so wrapped up in each other. Wasn't it?

She crept down the stairs and stood at the parlor entrance. After the shock of the storage room, she wasn't surprised to see the parlor filled with antiques. No, wait, not antiques. If she'd really been thrust back in time, these Victorian furnishings must be new. The red velvet upholstery wasn't worn, and the mahogany surfaces gleamed with polish. Heavy velvet drapes in front of the window bay blocked the waning daylight, but the room was brightened by gaslight gleaming in the globes of a brass chandelier.

The music came from a piano against the wall, but to Claire's astonishment no one was playing it. The keys rose and fell on their own. She felt a frisson of fear until she realized what was happening. Of course—a player piano.

A man with a bushy brown beard lounged on a settee, between two women in lacy old-style underwear. He had an arm draped around each of them. The brunette on his right was snuggling close, stroking his upper thigh. The little redhead on his left had her hand on his other leg, but she looked stiff and uncomfortable in his embrace.

Neither of them was Roxane.

"Heaven!" the man muttered, but he didn't seem to be praying, unless it was to the bronze statue of a naked Venus on the mantelpiece. "That's right, girls, take me to heaven."

A suspicion had been growing in Claire's mind. Now she was certain—the Burnham Mansion had once been a whorehouse!

Did Ellie know this? Had Josephine been aware of this chapter in her family home's history?

Or was it all a delusion, a drama that Claire's imagination was staging for reasons she couldn't fathom?

Whatever was happening, she longed for things to return to normal, the way they were before the Time Flip. If only she knew how to make it flip back.

"That's enough, monsieur," said a feminine voice, drawing Claire's attention to a stately blond woman in a high-backed chair. An elaborate wooden filigree topped the chair, making it look as if the woman was wearing a crown. Claire guessed her to be in her mid-twenties. Her low-cut dress had puffy sleeves and lots of tucks and ruffles, and its robin's-egg blue color matched her eyes. She was the first woman Claire had seen who was fully clothed.

"Oh, no, ma'am," the bushy-bearded man drawled. "Not nearly enough."

Claire heard a chuckle and realized another man was in the room. A fellow with a gray mustache sat in an armchair, a glass of amber liquid in his hand. A table between them held a pair of crystal decanters and several clean glasses, along with a ledger book, a brass bell, an inkwell, and a jeweled pen.

"In that case, monsieur, it's time for you to pay for your hour and take one of these jeunes filles upstairs." The blonde spoke with brisk efficiency. "Which is your choice?"

"Well, they're both—what's that saying you taught me last time, about the bell?"

The blonde nodded. "Très belles. Oui, monsieur, they are both very beautiful, but you may only have one, unless you're prepared to pay the extra charges."

Mr. Bushy Beard disentangled himself and turned to examine the women. "I've enjoyed the pleasure of this one's company several times—"

He lifted the brunette's hand it to his lips. Smiling, she rose to her feet.

"Mademoiselle Yvette," the blonde said approvingly.

"—so this time I believe I'll make the acquaintance of the other." He dropped the brunette's hand and reached for the little redhead, whose gaze stayed fixed on the floor.

The blonde pursed her lips. "Are you certain, monsieur?"

"Yes, ma'am. This one tickles my fancy."

"Ha!" said Mr. Gray Mustache. "That's the least of what you want tickled, my boy."

The customer took a fat money clip from a pocket and handed some bills to the blonde. Apparently he didn't need to be told the amount due.

She made a note in her ledger. "Mademoiselle Fleur will show you the way, monsieur."

But Mr. Bushy Beard took the lead, pulling the redhead toward the stairs. They passed so close to Claire that the girl's free hand brushed her arm. Neither one paid any heed to her.

Claire shivered. Could they really not see her? Not only had the Time Flip spun her back to an earlier century, it seemed to have made her invisible.

Was that what happened with Roxane and Stregoni? No one besides Claire would admit to seeing them. Except Granny Jo—Ellie had mentioned that her grandmother claimed to have an imaginary friend named Roxane.

If you moved into an era that wasn't your own, did you remain outside the awareness of the people there? And was that a good thing or bad?

Claire drew in a sharp breath. If no one could see her, how could anyone help her get home?

———•———

"Wow, how cool is this!"

George's voice drifted down from the tower.

"You found something?" Ellie rushed up the spiral stairs but stopped two rungs from the top. The platform didn't have enough space for two people, especially when one of them was George.

He grinned at her, seeming to enjoy the advantage he got from the extra height. "Nope. But if you stand right here and look between these buildings"—he pointed out the east-facing window—"you can actually see the bay."

"This isn't a sightseeing expedition." She didn't bother to hide her frustration. "We've got to find Claire."

"Well, she's not up here. Just like the last three times we looked."

He made a shooing motion, and she backed down the stairs. George clambered after her.

"She has to be in the house somewhere," Ellie said. "A person can't just disappear."

George felt around in his pockets and came up with a candy bar. He peeled away the wrapper, dropping shreds of paper and silvery foil.

"Bet you fifty bucks you looked away for a moment and Claire waltzed right past you and out the front door. Want a bite?" He broke off a piece of chocolate and held it out.

"No." She backed away. She had no desire to eat anything his grubby fingers had touched. "You're wrong. She wasn't out of my sight long enough to go anywhere. Besides, why would she leave without telling me?"

He shrugged. "We've searched the place top to bottom. No way she's still here." He popped the chunk of candy in his mouth and walked away.

She knew he was right. If Claire were hiding in the house, they'd have found her. They had scoured every level from ballroom to tower, looked in every closet and cupboard. They'd yelled Claire's name and got no response except echoes. They'd called her cell phone and heard it ringing in her purse, which she'd left with Ellie's in the parlor. Ellie had no idea why Claire had deserted her, or how, but she definitely was gone.

The good thing was, they hadn't found her body either.

They went down to the first floor. Ellie kept her distance, out of George's reach. She couldn't shake the creepy feeling he gave her. The way he'd shown up right when Claire vanished, his lack of concern—Ellie worried he knew more than he was letting on. And that she herself might be in danger.

"What do we do now?" she wondered aloud.

She wasn't really asking his opinion but he gave it anyway. "I say we go find some dinner. Come on, I know a great burger place near here."

"No!" she said, too sharply. "I'm having dinner with a friend," she added, glad for her invitation from Daniel Harding. If she hadn't had plans, she would have lied and claimed she did—anything to keep from going with George. "In fact we're supposed to meet in twenty minutes."

"How? Didn't you come here in Claire's car? Hey, want me to give you a lift?"

The idea made Ellie shudder. "I'll call him. He'll pick me up."

"Oho. It's a guy." George managed to leer with his voice as well as his face. "Lucky man. Hope you, um—have fun."

"It's not like that. He's just a friend."

"With or without benefits?"

She shot him a *stop-being-an-asshole* look. "I can't leave yet anyway. Not until I find Claire."

"Claire's a big girl. She'll turn up." He finished the candy bar and stuffed the wrapper in his pocket with the potato chip bag.

"I hope so, but … I'd better call the police."

"Whoa! That sounds kind of drastic."

"Don't you get it? Someone was murdered in this house. What if the killer somehow got to Claire?"

"Well, no police for me. I'm outa here." George's mood had shifted. Suddenly he was eager to be gone. "Nothing but a big empty house. I thought a crime scene would be more interesting."

He hurried out the front door, leaving it wide open. Ellie watched him duck under the yellow tape. Then she shut and locked the door.

Thank God he was gone.

Suddenly the house was silent. A deep, eerie hush seeped through it, like gas filling the rooms.

Goosebumps rose on her arms. This house had always been a warm and happy place for her. But right now she couldn't wait to get out.

On the parlor hearth, Claire's purse leaned against her own, as if it needed propping up. The sight of it put a catch in Ellie's throat.

"Claire!" she yelled. "I'm leaving. Let's go!"

Her voice echoed against the bare walls.

One last try. "Claire!"

Ellie slung her purse over her shoulder. She started to pick up Claire's too, then changed her mind and left it.

She ran to the ballroom and out the side door, locking it behind her. She didn't look back.

———◆———

Turning the knob to her chamber door, Roxane felt the urge to flee. To dash through the storage room, up the spiral stairs, and into the Future House. Thaddeus would never find her, never again be able to inflict the pain that gave him so much pleasure.

But running away was no solution. She couldn't survive alone in that big empty house, and the world outside its walls seemed even more strange and terrible than this one.

Heaving a sigh of despair, she went into her chamber and closed the door.

The knife from the kitchen was where she'd left it, wedged between her bed and the wall. Good. She balanced it in her palm and ran a finger along the smooth, sharp blade. Then she curled her hand around the handle and plunged the blade into the mattress. She thrust it again, and again, and again, until her hand steadied and the motion felt natural.

Now to get the knife into the Rose Room without its being noticed.

In her wardrobe she found a green ribbon sash that she sometimes wore with her everyday dress. She tied it around her waist, underneath her chemise, and made an extra knot to hold the knife. The blade felt hard and cold against her skin.

Time to go back downstairs.

As she moved toward the door, it opened on its own. Roxane jumped in surprise.

Véronique stood there, her eyes wide, her mouth making a startled O. No, a Q, Roxane thought as her wits returned—the split in Véronique's lower lip formed the crossbar.

"Oh my! Roxane! I didn't expect to see you."

"What are you doing, coming into my room?" Roxane pushed past her rival into the hallway and shut the door with a bang.

Véronique swept her black hair away from her shoulders and put on an innocent air. "I heard a noise, so I thought I'd make sure everything was all right. I wouldn't want anything more to happen to your belongings."

You wanted to find something to steal, Roxane thought. To pay me back for going into your room earlier.

"I appreciate your concern. But if there was any noise, I made it myself." She held herself motionless, resisting the impulse to put her hand against her waist to make sure the knife stayed in place.

"You're supposed to be in the Rose Room," Véronique snapped. "It's not fair. You're allowed to earn money tonight, while I'm forced go deeper in debt to Lady Celeste. She won't let me entertain a gentleman for even an hour, while you get to enjoy the entire evening in the company of the best one of them all—"

"The best! How can you say such a thing?"

"He's kind and gracious and generous and—"

"To you perhaps. To me he's—" Roxane bit her lip. She had nothing to gain by saying insulting words about a gentleman, even if they were true.

"I don't understand why he prefers you. Such a skinny twig"—Véronique thrust out her hip and arched her back to show off her curves—"and ungrateful on top of it."

"Beg pardon," Roxane muttered. She moved toward the stairs, but Véronique blocked her path.

"Here you are, when you should be with him! You have the nerve to cheat Thaddeus out of the time he's paid for. Lady Celeste will be most interested to know you're treating one of our most distinguished visitors so shabbily. Especially when just yesterday you were seen giving away your favors for free."

Roxane's heart stopped. "What! Who saw—what did you see?"

With a mirthless laugh, Véronique turned to leave.

Roxane grabbed her shoulder. The knife shifted but didn't fall.

"Please, say nothing to Lady Celeste. I'm on my way back to Thaddeus right now. I merely came up to fetch something for him, something to add to his pleasure."

"And what is that?" Véronique demanded.

"It's a secret." Roxane put her hand on her waist, reassuring herself with the feel of the blade beneath the thin fabric. "A—a love potion. I don't know if it will work as I intend it to. If you say nothing to anyone now, I'll tell you about it in the morning, and you'll have something new and wonderful with which to please your gentlemen."

Véronique kept silent. Roxane could almost see the calculations she was running in her head as she tried figure out what course of action would work to her best advantage.

"Please!" Roxane begged.

She endured an endless moment before Véronique said, "I'll hold my tongue for now. If the secret you tell me tomorrow is worthwhile, then you've bought my silence."

"Thank you!"

"And if it's not—well, Lady Celeste will appreciate knowing you didn't give a gentleman full value for his money."

Véronique walked down the hall and disappeared into her own chamber.

Roxane's feeling of relief lasted only a second. She'd dealt with Véronique, but Thaddeus was waiting.

The knife's blade pricked her belly as she made her cautious way downstairs to the Rose Room.

If Thaddeus enjoyed pain so much, then by heaven she'd give him some.

CHAPTER

39

"Excuse me," Claire said to the blonde in the high-backed chair. She seemed to be in charge. "I need help."

The woman didn't look up from scribbling in her ledger. No one acknowledged Claire's presence in any way.

The bushy-bearded man and the girl with the red curls—Mademoiselle Fleur, the blonde had called her—were hurrying up the stairs. The others had relaxed, like actors during a play's intermission.

The scantily clad brunette rejected by Mr. Bushy Beard stretched out on the settee and closed her eyes. Mademoiselle Yvette—Claire had noted that name, too.

Mr. Gray Mustache refilled his glass from one of the crystal decanters. Claire wished she had a glass too. Alcohol couldn't solve problems, she knew that, but right now she could use a shot of whiskey.

She sank onto an oval-backed chair. If she paid close attention to what was going on, maybe she could pick up a clue about how to get back to the present-day world. Her own present-day world—everyone else in this room must believe they were in the here and now, even though they were stuck in the late Victorian era.

And she was stuck there with them.

A shudder passed over her. What was she going to do?

Never had she felt so helpless, so frightened.

"Care for some, my dear?" Mr. Gray Mustache held up the decanter. He wasn't addressing Claire; he didn't seem to realize she was there. He gave the blonde a courtly bow.

"Non, merci, mon cher. I'm working, you know." Something about her—the blue eyes, the angle of her chin—reminded Claire of Ellie.

"Ah yes, you're working." Mr. Gray Mustache slid a coin to her across the polished wood of the table.

"Don't be silly." She smiled at him and shoved it back. "I've told you, Isaac, your money is no good here. The whiskey is on the house."

Isaac! Could this man be Isaac Burnham, family patriarch and builder of the house? Claire leaned forward to look more closely.

The blonde gave him a coquettish smile. "In fact, for you, mon cher, all of the services offered here are on the house."

"You're too kind," he said. "But I must tell you, Celeste, I prefer to have them on the bed."

She leaned across the table to plant a kiss on Isaac's lips. "Later," she promised coyly. "After midnight, when the paying guests have departed."

He frowned. "You said you wouldn't take other guests. I don't want to share you, Celeste." He drained his glass, then poured more, emptying the decanter.

"I'm yours alone, Isaac." She ran her fingertips along his whiskered cheek. "But I must manage my business well. I have to make sure the jeunes filles earn their keep and the gentlemen abide by our rules. I worry that we may not be welcome in this neighborhood much longer."

"Nonsense. The men around here are delighted to have such a fine facility close at hand. And the women are convinced you're running a respectable boardinghouse."

"That's the impression I've hoped to convey, but—"

A bell rang down in the ballroom, making everyone jump, including Claire, who'd been avidly eavesdropping.

Its deep tone was echoed by a jingle as Celeste shook the brass bell on her table. A middle-aged woman with ebony skin appeared from the rear of the house. Her dress was plain, not sexy at all. A servant, Claire guessed.

"We need more whiskey, Louise." Celeste told her. "A gentleman is arriving and I expect he'll be thirsty."

"If he's not," Louise said with a chuckle, "you'll persuade him he is." She took the empty decanter and slipped away.

Claire heard the stomping of boots. Two men burst into the hall from the ballroom stairs. Apparently they'd come in through the same door she and Ellie had used earlier today—or had it been today? The way these people would count it, Claire had entered the house many years in the future.

Grappling with the scrambled flow of time made her head throb.

She slumped on her chair and watched Celeste cross the room to the newcomers.

"Welcome to Chez Celeste, gentlemen." The blonde's voice was like sugared tea. "If you've come for a good time, you're in the right place. Have a drink and make the acquaintance of Mademoiselle Yvette. She has just arrived from Gay Paree, where she learned all sorts of ways to give you pleasure."

Claire saw that Yvette had sprung awake. She still lounged on the settee but in a very different pose. She had arranged her negligee to show off maximum cleavage, her legs were spread wide, and a hand rested on the lace at her crotch. She blew the men a kiss.

"Oh, I know Miss Yvette." The taller man winked at his companion. "I know this saucy minx very well." He sat beside her and she took him into her arms as if he were the one person in the world she wanted most to see.

The other man lingered in the foyer. Short and heavyset, he wore a striped vest that strained across his middle.

"Entrez, monsieur. Come in and have a drink." Celeste beckoned the reluctant fellow into the parlor. "You may pay for it now, or we can settle accounts when you leave."

Louise had returned with the decanter, and she filled a glass with whiskey. The man grabbed it and took a swig, then blurted out, "What about a—a girl?"

"One of our jeunes filles should be downstairs presently. Take a seat and enjoy your whiskey and the music," Celeste said. Claire realized the player piano was still pumping out its frisky tune.

"Yes, ma'am." Whiskey in hand, Mr. Striped Vest aimed for Claire's chair. Before she could react, he plopped his full weight on top of her.

She let out a yelp. No one reacted.

The man wriggled around as if he couldn't get comfortable. Squashed beneath him, Claire pushed and pinched, trying to get him to move. Finally he lumbered to his feet. She slid off to the side, landing in a heap on the floor.

"Is something the matter, monsieur?" Celeste asked.

"No, ma'am." He brushed off the red velvet seat. "The cushion felt lumpy, that's all." He sat again and downed more whiskey. "Um, how soon will a girl be ready?"

"Ha," said his friend, who now stood at the table with Yvette pressed to his side. He swatted her on the rear before handing money to Celeste. "This one is very ready."

The happy couple walked toward the grand staircase. Claire scooted aside just in time to avoid being stepped on.

"Look, monsieur," Celeste said. "Here's another jeune fille now."

Another pair had come downstairs—the balding man and the girl with sausage curls whose amorous embrace Claire had witnessed on the third floor. The man's face was flushed bright red and his suit jacket hung askew.

"So, Mademoiselle Aurélie," Celeste said, "did you make this gentleman happy?"

"I do believe so." The girl gave her companion a sly glance. "Right, darling?"

"Oh yes." He broke into a wide grin. "Happy, happy. Yes indeed."

Celeste made a mark in her ledger. "Would you care for another drink before you depart, monsieur?"

"I'm drunk on love," he said. "May I see you tomorrow, sweetheart?"

"Of course you may, darling," Aurélie said, but Claire could see she'd already shifted her attention to the next customer.

The instant the balding man left, Aurélie slithered into Mr. Striped Vest's lap. He was so surprised that he dropped his whiskey glass. With a deft move, she caught it and set it on a nearby table. "Please excuse my bold approach, monsieur. You're so handsome I couldn't resist. I hope you aren't here to see some other girl."

"Um, I—no. I mean—"

She cut him off with an ardent kiss. At least Mr. Striped Vest probably thought it was ardent.

When Aurélie lifted her lips from his mouth, he gasped for air. "You—you'll do just fine."

Aurélie, Yvette, Fleur, Celeste. Funny that the girls all had French names. There was nothing truly French about any of them, other than an occasional phrase spoken with an awkward accent.

Roxane—that was French, too. The Amethyst Girl was

nowhere in evidence, but maybe she was upstairs with some man, doing—well, whatever special French thing these girls did.

The French connection continued with the Burnham family's names—Josephine, Mirabelle, Jean-Marc, Richard with the accent on the second syllable. According to Ellie, Granny Jo's mother came from France and started the tradition.

Could the Burnham lineage really have begun in a bordello?

Claire tried to recall what she'd heard about the origins of Isaac Burnham's wealth—vague references to silver mining and mercantile enterprises. What if those tales were fictions, told to hide the fact that the family patriarch was a Victorian version of a pimp?

The bell from below rang again. Celeste, Isaac, and the servant Louise all came to attention. Mr. Striped Vest tightened his grip on Aurélie.

This time the footsteps on the ballroom stairs were softer. A small man with a dove-gray velvet coat appeared. He looked around, running his hand through a cloud of wild white hair.

Alberto Stregoni! Thank God.

Relief made Claire's heart leap. She could get answers about Simon's death. Even more crucial, he could show her how to go home.

She would plead. Beg. Sob if necessary.

She stepped forward but Stregoni ignored her, hurrying past her toward Celeste's table. Couldn't he see her? Was she as invisible to him on this side of the Time Flip as she was to everyone else?

She felt hurt, disappointment, dismay—as if she'd been spurned by a lover.

Isaac stood and shook Stregoni's hand. "Alberto, my friend! Glad to see you. That girl, what's her name, she must have shown you a good time the other night."

"Signorina Roxane. Yes, she did. This is why I have come back for her."

"My son is fond of her too. I haven't tried her out myself, but he tells me she's something special."

"Very special," Stregoni said, urgency in his voice. "I need to see her."

Celeste tried to dazzle him with a smile. "I'm sorry, monsieur. Mademoiselle Roxane is spoken for tonight. But another jeune fille will be happy for your company. Please enjoy a drink while you're waiting." She poured some whiskey and gave it to him without noting it in her book.

Stregoni took a sip, apparently without thinking, because on tasting the liquor he looked surprised to find a glass in his hand. He set it on the table.

"I do not desire anyone else. I will wait for Signorina Roxane."

"I fear you misunderstood me," Celeste said. "Theodore Burnham has purchased all of Mademoiselle Roxane's time this evening, just as you did two nights ago."

"But I must see her tonight! Where is she?"

Now Celeste frowned. "It's not possible, monsieur. Tomorrow perhaps—"

"Tonight! I will go up and find her!"

He turned toward the stairs, but Isaac grabbed his shoulder.

"That wouldn't be wise, my friend. Sit down and enjoy your drink. One of those other pretty girls will make you forget all about that Roxane."

Stregoni dropped onto the settee and stared at the floor. Seizing the moment, Claire sat beside him. He looked up, startled.

"Signora Claire! What are you doing here?"

"I don't know," she admitted. "I was exploring the house, looking for clues to Simon's murder. Looking for you, because you led me to his body. I went up into the tower and when I came down, I was here. In a different year. A different century!"

To her surprise, he chuckled.

"It's not funny! I'm trapped. You have to help me get home."

He patted her knee. "Never fear. I will show you the secret. I know it well. I designed the portal in the tower myself, when I helped my friend Isaac draw up plans for his house. I thought we might learn things of great value if we could observe the future firsthand."

"Has that proved true?"

Stregoni sighed. "I confess that what I have seen of the future is more frightening than reassuring. Perhaps creating the portal was a mistake. But I was eager to see if I could make it work."

"It works." Claire had to look away. The mismatched eyes, one gold, one gray, were unsettling. "So you're some kind of magician?"

"I prefer to think of myself as a scientist. I merely push the boundaries of what is known, push them ever so slightly. Reality has broader limits than most people realize, signora."

"Yes." Claire said. "I've been learning that myself."

"I never intended for my little experiment to create problems."

Claire noticed that Celeste and Isaac were watching them. Or at least watching Stregoni.

"Monsieur?" the blonde said. "Are you all right?"

Stregoni waved a hand. "Pay me no mind. As my friend Isaac will tell you, I am known for babbling. If you will permit me a favor, dear lady, might I play your piano?"

"Be my guest, monsieur." She raised her eyebrows at Isaac as if asking, Is your friend crazy?

"Come with me, signora Claire," Stregoni whispered. "If I play the piano while we talk, they will think I am merely singing to myself. They will lose interest and be less inclined to throw me out. Because I intend to stay until I see Signorina Roxane."

Claire watched as he removed the piano roll. "They can't see me, can they? Just like most people couldn't see you and Roxane yesterday."

They sat on the bench. Stregoni srtuck up a sprightly melody.

"That is true," he said. "I set up the portal that way for the safety of anyone who crossed the barrier. Strangers are not always welcome in new places, or different times. Now I am not so sure it was a good idea, but it is done. It cannot be changed."

"So everything that goes through the Time Flip is invisible?"

"Objects can be seen. Living creatures cannot. Each of us, while we are alive, is surrounded by an aura of energy. It extends a short way into the space around our bodies, as if we were wrapped in a blanket. When we cross into a time that is not our own, then whatever lies within that aura—a person like you or me, the clothes we are wearing—is invisible to whomever we might encounter there."

She tried to make sense of what he was saying and doing. She could have sworn sparks were flying from his fingertips, as if the musical notes were points of light, like stars.

"But I saw you and Roxane. And Granny Jo, the elderly woman who lived here before … or after … oh, whenever it was. She saw Roxane too, didn't she? Ellie called Roxane an imaginary friend, but she was real to Granny Jo."

Stregoni segued into a slower tune. "A few people, a very few, have the gift of sight so keen that they can perceive what most cannot. I don't know this Ellie, but yes, Roxane told me about her friendship with the old woman in the Future House. She was deeply sad when the lady died."

The Future House. So that's what they called it. And Claire was stuck in the Past House.

"Please—can you get me back there? To the Future House?"

"We must wait until midnight. The men will leave, and the girls will sleep. Then I can sneak upstairs and find Roxane. Before I leave with her, I will show you the secret of the portal."

"Midnight! That's too long."

"It is the best I can do, signora."

"What do I do until then? Can I explore? What happens if I go outside?"

"The neighborhood will seem foreign to you. You will risk becoming lost or running into danger." His fingers picked up their pace. "Did you not have questions to ask me? About your departed friend?"

"Simon. Yes." Saying his name made her voice tighten. "You found his body. What happened? Did you see him—" Her throat closed; she couldn't push out the word die.

"I was not there. Roxane showed me his body afterward. She was in the Future House when it happened, but she was hiding. She saw nothing. Though perhaps she knows more than she realizes."

Claire jumped up. "Then I have to talk her. You can't leave before I get a chance to—"

She was interrupted by the sound of hammering on the front door.

"What's that!" Celeste cried. Her face went white.

Isaac leaped from his chair.

"Open up!" yelled a voice from outside.

No one moved.

The pounding grew more forceful.

"Open up, I say! Open up for the police!"

CHAPTER

40

"That's so weird," Daniel said. "People can't vanish in front of your eyes."

"I know. It's scary." Standing beside him on the sidewalk, Ellie stared at her grandmother's house.

"You think this guy George has something to do with it?"

"I don't know what to think."

By now it was dusk. Lights were coming on in windows up and down the street, but this house was dark and blank. Except—no, it was nothing. For the briefest instant she thought she saw a flicker of movement in Granny Jo's bedroom window, as if someone had brushed aside a curtain to peer out and then let it drop back into place.

"Are you all right?" Daniel slipped his arm around her shoulders. She was surprised by how good it felt. "You jumped as if something startled you."

"I'm fine." A shiver passed through her. "I had the oddest impression that I saw my grandmother looking out the window."

"Could it have been Claire?"

"I wish. But George and I searched that room. We searched every inch of the house. It's so bizarre!"

"Maybe she found a hiding place, or—"

"Why would she hide?"

"Then she must have left."

"She would've taken her purse. And her car is still here." Ellie pointed down the block. "See that green VW under the streetlight?"

"Have you tried phoning her, or texting?"

"Her phone's in her purse. It just kept ringing."

"First the murder, now this," Daniel said. "I wish I had a good explanation, if only to give you peace of mind."

"What if they're related? Do you think Claire's disappearance could be connected to Simon's murder?"

"I heard a news report. The police are talking to—well, a 'person of interest.' "

"Peter?" Saying the name aloud stirred anger and longing within her. "It's okay to mention him, I won't faint." Her voice caught. "He didn't do it, Daniel. He lies and cheats, he's a scumbag—but he'd never kill anyone. The murderer is still out there."

Daniel tightened his arm, pulling her closer. She leaned against him, finding comfort in his solidness, his strength.

"What do you want to do?" he asked.

She lifted her head, looked again at the house. Lights caught the edges of the gingerbread trim and cast crazy shadows across the ornate façade. The windows were black voids, but she had the odd sensation that they were staring at her.

"We should go to the police. Tell them Claire is missing."

"Open up! Police!" The pounding on the bordello's front door didn't let up. "Open the door now or we'll break the glass to get in."

Claire didn't move. The piano fell silent. Everyone seemed to stop breathing.

Then Mr. Striped Vest dumped Aurélie to the floor and bolted for the ballroom stairs. Louise grabbed the whisky decanters and hustled toward the kitchen. Isaac Burnham snatched up the ledger, inkwell, and jeweled pen, and ran after Louise.

Aurélie, whimpering, lay curled in a ball on the carpet. Celeste nudged her with a foot. "Get up, you foolish thing. Go warn everyone. Take the servants' stairs, and tell the gentlemen to sneak down that way."

"Wh-what about us?" Aurélie rose shakily to her feet.

Celeste put her hands on her slim hips and frowned. "You girls know what you're supposed to do. Hurry!"

Stregoni leapt from the piano bench. "I must find Signorina Roxane."

He hastened behind Aurélie toward the back stairs.

Claire hurried after them. Most likely the cops wouldn't see her even if she stood right in front of them, but she'd better not take that chance.

———◆———

Roxane stood outside the Rose Room, her hand on the knife at her waist. All of her breath was balled up in her throat.

She listened to Thaddeus rustling around inside. He was coming toward the door, as if he could tell she was there.

Then she heard a commotion downstairs. Someone shouted: "Open up! Police!"

Oh, dear heaven! She hurried to the grand staircase and peeked over the banister.

Lady Celeste was opening the front door.

"Why, gentlemen," she purred, "whatever is so urgent that you must disturb a quiet household at this hour?"

Two policemen in stiff blue uniforms pushed their way in. The first had a handlebar mustache and a swagger that said he was accustomed to being in charge. He was a stranger, but Roxane knew the other man well. He had frequently enjoyed her company; in fact, she'd entertained him just last night. If she couldn't escape, perhaps he would show her mercy.

"Sergeant Crowley!" Lady Celeste held out her hand. "So good to see you again."

Crowley shuffled his feet and stared at the floor, ignoring her hand and avoiding the other policeman's disapproving look.

More people crowded into the house behind them. First came two gentlemen, one older and one younger, wearing suit coats and bowler hats. They had also visited the house last night: the enthusiastic Mr. Smith, who'd given Roxane a welcome two-bit tip, and his reluctant son-in-law, Mr. Jones.

They were accompanied by two ladies. To her surprise, Roxane recognized them. In fact, their calling cards were tucked in the hat she'd worn for her Sunday walk.

Young Mrs. Bisbee maintained a firm grasp on the arm of Mr. Jones—apparently Jones was not his real name. "I told you, Mother," she said sternly. "This is no boardinghouse."

Mrs. Sedgwick gawped at the wallpaper, carpets, and ceilings as if she expected to see couples fornicating on every surface. "Imagine! A bawdy house in our own neighborhood!"

"Last night when I overheard Leander and Father talking about what went on here, I couldn't believe my ears," Mrs. Bisbee blathered on.

"Sergeant!" snapped the mustached cop. "Go upstairs and bring down everyone you find."

Roxane ducked back in a panic as Crowley trudged up the grand staircase. She had to escape. But where could she go?

The door to the Rose Room burst open. Roxane jumped as

Thaddeus Burnham loomed beside her. He tightened his fist around her arm until she yelped with pain. "I heard you out there, mamzelle. Get in here. How dare you keep me waiting."

He tried to pull her into the chamber. It took all her strength to wrench out of his grip. She dashed toward the back stairs.

Other doors opened—the Green Room, the Gold Room. Fleur and Yvette and their visitors peered into the hall.

"The police are here! Run!" Roxane shouted.

Someone screamed. Doors slammed as the *jeunes filles* and the gentlemen scurried back into the rooms to scramble for their clothes.

Sergeant Crowley, breath puffing, arrived on the second floor. "Everyone here, come out to face the law!"

Roxane reached the back stairs, but heard footsteps coming up. More cops?

She sprinted to the third floor. If she could make it to the tower, she could hide in the Future House until Chez Celeste was closed and empty. Then she'd come back and—

Her mind went blank. She had no idea what she'd do, how she'd survive. But if the police caught her, if they learned of her crime, she'd surely go to prison. Maybe she'd hang.

Someone thundered up the stairs behind her. A voice called her from below.

"Signorina Roxane!"

Mr. Stregoni! He was here—thank heaven!

At the top of the stairs she spun around to greet him.

To her dismay she saw Thaddeus, who had hastily pulled on his clothes. He reached for her. She jerked away and heard her chemise rip. She bunched up a handful of the fabric and pressed it against her belly, trying to hide the knife.

She couldn't stab him, Not here, not now. Too many witnesses, and the policemen were just a few steps away.

Turning from Thaddeus, she collided with Véronique, emerging from her chamber.

"What's happening?" Véronique demanded. "What's all the rowdydow?"

"Police!" Roxane gasped.

She ran into the storage room, Thaddeus on her heels.

"Signorina Roxane!"

But she didn't dare stop. Zigzagging around trunks and boxes, she fled toward the spiral stairs. If only she could make it to the Future House, then maybe, just maybe, she'd be safe.

———◆———

Claire heard the two men yelling.

"Signorina, wait!"

"Stop, mamzelle!"

She kept close behind them as they maneuvered through the maze of the storage room. She felt caught up in the chase, though she wasn't sure what was going on. She knew only that both men were pursuing Roxane.

The taller, younger man, three steps ahead of Stregoni, was gaining on the girl.

"Mamzelle," he roared, "get back here if you know what's good for you!"

Roxane, wearing just a thin slip, hurried up the spiral stairs. She was bending slightly at the waist and had her hands tight against her stomach, as if she felt ill.

As the tall man set his foot on the lowest step, Stregoni pushed forward and yanked him to a stop.

"Thaddeus! Leave her be."

The man—Thaddeus—peeled Stregoni's fingers away, then turned and laughed. The sound, full of malice, made Claire shiver. His hair and mustache were thick and dark, and he might have been handsome if his face weren't twisted with scorn. He glared at Claire, and the force of his gaze made her step back.

Oh God—he could see her.

"Go away, old man," he said. "Mamzelle Roxane is mine. This evening we became engaged to be married."

"No! She would never consent to that. She is coming with me to—"

"Nowhere! She goes nowhere with you."

Claire glanced up. Roxane was at the top of the stairs, watching the men, eyes wide in a face that had gone pale.

"Signorina!" Stregoni called to her. Then, to his rival: "Stand aside, signor."

He tried to push past Thaddeus, but Thaddeus thrust his fist hard into the older man's midsection. Stregoni staggered, fell over a box, and crashed into a small marble-topped table. Both the table and Stregoni toppled over. Claire heard a loud thump as his head hit the floor.

Above them in the tower, Roxane shrieked. Looking up, Claire caught a flash of movement and a flurry of sparks, as if a stick had stirred a dying fire. The girl disappeared.

Before Claire could make sense of what she'd seen, she heard a low moan. She rushed to Stregoni's side and dropped to her knees.

"Mr. Stregoni! Are you all right?"

No answer. Strands of his unruly white hair were streaked red with blood. Taking his wrist in her hand, she tried to find his pulse.

"Please wake up," she whispered, her heart in her throat. She was frightened not only for him but for herself. Without Stregoni's help she couldn't reverse the Time Flip.

Thaddeus bent over them, reeking of whiskey.

"Who the hell are you?" he snarled. "You're not one of the joon fees. I know them all."

"G-go away!" Her voice shook.

Stregoni wasn't moving. Claire leaned closer, tried to detect any flutter of breath.

"Is he dead?" Thaddeus shoved her aside. "Let me make sure."

She jabbed at him with her elbow. "Leave him alone."

He crouched down. His hands circled Stregoni's throat.

Claire pulled herself to her feet, looked frantically for something to use as a weapon. She saw a key protruding from a trunk lock, a pile of blankets on an old chest, the toppled table.

She grabbed the table by two legs and swung the marble top at his head.

Thaddeus must have detected the movement because he rolled away just in time. The momentum of the swing threw Claire off balance.

He stood up, caught her in steel-trap arms. "Now look, you dolly-mop—"

Claire raised her knee, going for his body's most vulnerable part.

"Hey you!" called a voice from the storage room doorway.

Thaddeus dropped her abruptly, spoiling her aim. "What the—"

"Police! You're under arrest."

He spun around and dashed up the stairs to the tower.

"Hey! Stop!" The officer picked his way through the obstacle course as quickly as he could, but not fast enough. By the time he arrived at the spiral stairs, Thaddeus had reached the top.

The sparks Claire saw earlier flared up again. Just like Roxane, Thaddeus vanished.

CHAPTER

41

Inspector Flaherty drummed her fingers on her desk in the homicide squadroom. She focused a laser glare at Ellie over the top of the glasses perched on her nose.

"Let me get this straight. You entered a house that's been cordoned off as a crime scene?"

Ellie, seated next to Daniel on the opposite side of the desk, tried to keep from squirming. The detective's piercing gaze and the hard wooden seat seemed calculated to make whoever sat there feel guilty. How many cases, she wondered, got solved simply because the perpetrator couldn't stand the discomfort any longer and blurted out a confession?

"It's my house—well, partly mine. I have a right to be there."

"Not until we give you the okay."

"No one was there. I figured you must be done with—whatever you do at a crime scene."

Her purse was on her lap, and she didn't realize she was nervously twisting the strap until Daniel reached over and placed his hand on hers. She shot him a quick smile, glad he'd come with her, grateful for his calming presence.

Flaherty tapped a pencil on a manila folder lying on her desktop. The case file for Simon Thatcher's murder? The desk was stacked high with papers, files, and notebooks. Desks nearby looked just as cluttered. Most of them were unoccupied, Ellie noticed. Flaherty's partner, Inspector Vargas, was nowhere in sight.

Tap, tap, tap. "You say Claire Scanlan was with you, and then she disappeared. Tell me what happened exactly."

Ellie went through the story again, trying to be clear and consistent. Flaherty jotted notes and asked questions, most of which Ellie couldn't answer. If she had answers, she wouldn't be here in the first place.

"Maybe it's nothing," she said when she was done. "But what if Claire's trapped somewhere, or she got hurt? I wouldn't be so scared if it wasn't for the mur—what happened to Simon Thatcher." She sighed. "I can't even say the M word. It's a horrible thing to happen anywhere. But in my grandmother's house! A place I love."

Flaherty nodded. "That makes it worse. I understand." She pointed her pencil at Daniel. "What's your involvement, Mr. Harding?"

Daniel leaned forward. "None, really. I came here to support Ellie."

"Do you know Claire Scanlan?"

"Not well. I met her at the BAPA fundraiser. I stepped on the hem of her dress, so I offered to get it cleaned. I picked it up on Sunday, and yesterday I took it to the dry cleaner." He lifted his open palms. "That's the extent of our relationship."

"What about Simon Thatcher? Did you know him?"

Daniel hesitated, as if considering how to reply. "Somewhat. We were on opposite sides, frankly, of the discussions about the Burnham Mansion."

"How so?

"I'm a real estate developer. My firm is proposing to buy the property from Ellie and her brothers. We plan to create an exciting condo project, and—"

Flaherty frowned. "You're going to tear down that gorgeous house?"

"Not tear it down. We're going to reinvigorate it. Repurpose it."

"Isn't it a historic landmark?"

"There's no official landmark designation. It's a fine example of Victorian architecture, and we'll honor that in our design."

"How? You'll put up a plaque?"

"Much more than that. We're keeping the underlying structure intact, and—"

"If you're going to tear down the house, why were you at the fundraiser? Wasn't the idea to raise money to make it a museum?"

Daniel sat up straighter. "I certainly didn't go there to kill anyone, if that's what you're implying."

Flaherty looked at him, saying nothing.

"BAPA does good work, and I liked Simon personally, even if we didn't see eye to eye on this particular project. But what happens to the Burnham Mansion isn't our call. It's up to Ellie and her brothers." He squeezed Ellie's hand.

This time his touch didn't comfort her. She eased her hand away. Was he just being nice so she'd vote his way about the house?

The conversation was getting off track. She wanted to steer it back. "I heard you arrested Simon's killer, is that true? So maybe there's an easy explanation and Claire's not in danger at all."

"Actually, no," Flaherty said. "We've been talking to various people, but we haven't made any arrest."

"Really? You mean Peter's not—I thought he was here." She'd been picturing him in a bleak interrogation room like the ones on TV cop shows. Or a jail cell.

"If you're referring to Peter Mortensen, he came in to answer some questions for us. Inspector Vargas seeing him out now."

They were letting Peter go. Good news, though not for Ellie, not really. She couldn't care less what happened to the jerk.

Flaherty stood up. "Thank you for telling us about Ms. Scanlan. Let us know if you hear anything further."

A polite brush-off. With a sigh Ellie got to her feet.

Daniel put a guiding hand on her back as they headed for the elevator. Ellie hardly noticed. She had too many thoughts tumbling through her brain. Too much turmoil for her emotions to deal with. Claire's disappearance, Simon's murder, Peter's lies, Granny Jo's death, the pressure to decide about the house—it was almost more than she could bear.

———◆———

Roxane pushed open the storage room window and drew a deep breath, hoping the fresh air would calm her. The bareness of the room and the sight of the ugly apartment building across the street told her she was safe in the Future House.

Safe for now.

What would she find when she returned to Chez Celeste? Would the business be running as usual, the policemen happy to accept Lady Celeste's payment for their trouble? Or would he house be closed for good, the *jeunes filles* having fled or, worse, been carried off to jail? Véronique would probably wrap the guards around her finger and think of prison as a great adventure, but what of Fleur with her delicate sensibilities? The thought of Fleur behind bars made Roxane's heart break.

And herself? Would she be sent to prison, locked away forever? Or would she end up back in a rude crib in the Barbary Coast, the plaything of drunken, swinish men? She wasn't sure which fate was worse.

Yet she had no choice but to go back. She could never remain in this strange future time, where women wore trousers, and metal carriages zoomed down the street under their own power, and electric lights made midnight almost as bright as noon. She had never ventured outside the doors of the Future House and knew little of what lay beyond them. But from what she'd seen of Granny Jo and her helpers, the people of the future weren't all that different. Women were just as helpless, men just as cruel.

She was certain of one thing—money was as necessary in this time as in her own, and the ways by which a poor girl might earn it were probably even more wretched and brutal than anything she'd already endured. Now that sweet Granny Jo was dead and buried, there was no one here to help her. Most people couldn't even see her. She could never survive.

In the morning she would return to Chez Celeste. By then the policemen should be gone. The coins that Thaddeus had scattered on the floor of the Rose Room no doubt had disappeared into the policemen's pockets. The amethyst necklace as well. But if fortune had even the smallest regard for her, they'd overlooked her locket, or dismissed it as too cheap and tarnished to be worth their while. Whatever fate befell her, at least she'd have Mama's picture.

Overcome with weariness, she sank down, leaned against the wall beneath the window, and let her eyes drift shut. She wouldn't fool herself into thinking she might sleep, but she needed rest if she were to have her wits about her tomorrow. A pity that Granny Jo's family had removed all of the beds from the Future House. A bed would be so lovely right now, so long as she occupied it alone.

Or with Mr. Stregoni. He was the only man she'd ever been glad to have in a bed with her, even though he had hardly touched her—or perhaps because of that. A wave of yearning swept over her. Never had a man inspired such a feeling in her, a sensation so intense she could scarcely contain it. Mr. Stregoni knew the secret to entering the Future House. If only he would follow her here.

A chilly breeze blew through the window. She shivered in her thin chemise and rubbed her goosebumped arms, longing for a blanket.

Then she sat up with a jolt. Suppose her shivering came from a ghost walking on her grave. She was sitting in the exact spot where the murdered man had lain.

Scrambling to her feet, she ran across the room and flipped the light switch. The brightness from the bulb overhead would send any ghost back where it came from.

Something brushed her shoulder, a touch lighter than a feather. She heard a whisper: *"My little friend. Don't be afraid."*

My little friend. Granny Jo had called her that. Maybe the ghost wasn't the murdered man. She looked in the direction the voice had come from, but saw nothing.

Then she heard a sound even more surprising: the hammering of heavy boots coming down the spiral stairs. With a rush of relief, she turned to greet the only person who could have followed her here—Mr. Stregoni.

But the man confronting her was not the kindly white-haired gentleman she'd pinned her hopes on.

She pressed a fist to her mouth to force back a strangled sob.

"You look surprised to see me, mamzelle." Thaddeus Burnham grinned. "Did you think you were the only one who knows how to push the black rose on the tower wall and come down into an empty house?"

CHAPTER

42

Confused and frightened, Claire knelt beside Stregoni and looked up into the tower. The flying sparks faded and blinked out. The policeman in the old-fashioned uniform clomped back down the spiral stairs, shaking his head.

"Dangedest thing I ever saw," he muttered. "That fellow just up and disappeared. How do you reckon that?"

Claire didn't answer. He was talking to himself, not her. Like most people in this crazy Time-Flipped house, he couldn't even see her.

She turned back to Stregoni, lying pale and still on the floor, and took up his wrist. This time she felt the weak, ragged beat of a pulse. She tried to recall what she'd learned in a long-ago first aid class. Press the chest rhythmically. Start mouth-to-mouth resuscitation. Take care to keep the head aligned with the spine.

The policeman squatted beside Stregoni, knocking Claire aside.

To her relief, Stregoni's eyelids fluttered open. The cop looked startled at the sight of his gold and silver eyes.

"Good, good. You're alive." The cop rose to his feet. "Stay there, sir. I'll get help." He dodged through boxes and trunks to get out of the storage room.

Stregoni gripped Claire's hand. "Signora? Wh-what happened?"

"Are you all right? You bumped your head and passed out." The details could wait, she decided. "You cut your scalp too, but the bleeding has stopped."

He struggled to sit up. "Dio mio!"

She helped him lean his back against a trunk. "How do you feel? Are you woozy?"

"Am I what?"

Was *woozy* a slang term that he, as a foreigner, didn't understand? Or maybe the word didn't exist in the nineteenth century.

"Are you dizzy?" she tried. "Is your vision clear?"

"I am fine. Where is Signorina Roxane?" Leaning heavily on the trunk lid, he pulled himself to his feet.

"She went into the tower. Thaddeus went after her."

"Oh, no! If that lout is after her, she is not safe." He took a shaky step.

Claire put a restraining hand on his arm. "Stay here. You should rest, make sure you haven't suffered serious damage."

"I have a little headache, that is all." He touched his blood-matted hair and winced. "And a small lump."

"I'll go." She couldn't let this chance slide by. It might be her only hope of getting home. "They went through the Time Flip. Tell me how to make that work."

"I must find her. And do it before that policeman returns and hauls me to jail for being caught in a bawdy house." Stregoni staggered to the spiral stairs and gripped the railing. "Come with me, signora. I will take you back to your own time."

Wobbling and swaying, he hauled himself up the steps. Claire followed, ready to catch him if he fell. Her heart beat faster at the thought of learning the house's secret. To her surprise she also felt a pang of regret that her adventure in the past was almost over.

"The mechanism is simple." Stregoni teetered for a moment and braced his hands on a windowsill. "The portal opens with a push on the right spot on the wallpaper. Most people will never discover it. See here? This flower."

"The black one?" Claire reached out to touch it, then quickly drew back her hand. How had she not noticed this distinctive rose? The other all were red.

"It looks black, yes, to those who have the gift of sight—as you do, signora. To everyone who lacks that gift, the rose appears only slightly darker."

"I didn't see it before. Yet I obviously opened the portal, as you call it. Was that just an accident?"

"Perhaps you were guided by the hand of fate."

"The hand of fate—seriously? I don't think—"

"No time for philosophy. We must hurry." He rose to his full height, only an inch or two taller than Claire. "I am ready now. I have balanced my body and collected my wits. Push the rose, signora. We have no time to dawdle."

———◆———

Roxane flinched as Thaddeus's fingers dug into her shoulders. "I beg you, monsieur, go away. You don't belong in the Future House. Leave me alone."

"How can you say that, mamzelle? Do you not desire the company of the man who will soon be your husband?" His voice was soft, crooning, as if he were pleading for her affection. She'd learned he used this tone as a cruel mask for his anger. "Don't forget—I've paid, and quite handsomely too, to have the pleasure of your attentions this evening. Moreover, now that we're engaged to be married, you cannot deny me what I want."

"I—I regret that I cannot marry you. I do not deserve such a husband." She hoped he would take this as a compliment, a suggestion that she was unworthy of a fine gentleman. What she truly meant was that not even a wretch like herself should have to go through the torture he would inflict on her if she became his wife. To enter wedlock with Thaddeus would be to sign her own death warrant.

If she hadn't signed it already.

She looked past his shoulder to the spiral stairs, hoping against hope to see Mr. Stregoni. He'd come tonight to Chez Celeste—she'd heard his voice. Surely he was looking for her. If only he would come now to the Future House and help her escape. Then she wouldn't have to go through with what she'd planned to do to Thaddeus.

She touched her waist, her fingers finding the knife hidden beneath her chemise.

"Look at me!" Thaddeus wrenched up her head so she could do nothing but stare into the black pools of his eyes. They reminded her so much of Pa's, the way no light shined in them. "You were watching for Stregoni, that stupid fool, to come to your rescue—don't deny it! You're sweet on him, aren't you?"

He squeezed her head, as if his hands were the clamps on a vise. She kept her arms at her sides. Touching him would only make things worse. She didn't dare go for the knife. He was standing too close. He would detect her movement and turn the knife against her.

"No! He's nothing to me. Just one of many gentlemen who come to Chez Celeste."

"I heard Stregoni talking to my father about you. He said how much he enjoyed your company the other night. Apparently you showed him an especially good time."

"That's not true! We did nothing. He didn't even get what he paid for—"

"He told my father he's in love with you. He plans to take you with him back to Italy."

"I—I know nothing of that." Could it be true? Did she have a chance to find happiness in—where was Italy?

"I understand what your position in this house has made you do, mamzelle. But now that we're to be wed, that is over. I will not tolerate your loving another man."

"I've never felt love for a man, monsieur. I only—"

"You're lying. I see how your eyes go soft when I say Stregoni's name."

"Please, let go. You're hurting my head."

He squeezed harder, then let up the pressure slightly. "Well, you needn't pine after that old mooncalf any longer. I've taken care of him."

Roxane's blood went cold. "What do you mean?"

"He is dead, mamzelle. He met with a tragic accident."

No! She wanted to scream, but made her voice stay calm. "How did it happen?"

Thaddeus smiled. She had never seen a sight so evil.

"He fell and hit his head. There was much blood. I'm sorry to give you such terrible news."

"You killed him! You wicked man, how could you—"

She pounded her fists against his chest. He didn't even seem to notice. She tried to wrest his hands from her head, which just made him squeeze harder.

"It's not the first time I've killed a man for you, mamzelle."

"I—I don't understand."

"I knew you'd been sneaking off to a secret place, so at Lady Celeste's birthday celebration I watched you closely. Sure enough, you slipped away. I followed you to the tower, but then you disappeared. I guessed it was one of the tricks that the old goat, Stregoni, had built into my father's house. It took awhile, but finally I found the black rose that holds the magic."

"Monsieur, let me go—"

"When I came down the stairs I saw my suspicions had been correct. There you were, consorting with the lover you were trying to hide from me."

"What? I had no lover—"

"Fair-haired, handsome. You were standing by this very window."

"That man Simon? I didn't even know him. We spoke only for a moment. You must believe—"

"When he saw me, he tried to challenge me. I put my hands on his throat, like this …"

Thaddeus slid his hands down until they circled her neck.

Now was the time. She had to act. She had only one chance.

Keeping her movements as small as she could, she raised the hem of her chemise and grasped the handle of the knife.

" … and I tightened my hold, like this …"

"Monsieur—" Roxane gasped for breath. "I beg you."

" … and I slammed his head against the windowsill."

She saw stars dance, pinpoints of light flickering against the growing darkness. She twisted the knife free of the knotted sash.

"Don't worry, mamzelle. Just a little fun. I won't hurt—"

She thrust the blade. Thaddeus screamed as it sliced into his belly and upward behind his ribs.

Blood pumped out of him, red and thick. She was covered with his blood. The same as when Pa had his fatal accident.

Thaddeus's hands released her as he slumped to the floor.

At last she could breathe. She gulped in sweet air, over and over, until the gulps turned to sobs. She sank to her knees and couldn't stop crying.

CHAPTER
43

I never heard from Edouard again. The promised letters didn't arrive.

After a month of wondering and weeping, I went to his cousin's house to find out if he'd had news. To my dismay, the house was empty.

Maman took me to the French consulate to inquire about my beloved husband, which is what I considered him to be. The staff was kind but had no information to help us. One of the clerks promised to check the army records. Weeks later we received a letter informing us that French military officials had no record of a soldier named Edouard Trevillon.

Some dreadful mishap must have befallen him on his journey, before he could report for duty. I came to a devastating conclusion—my darling Edouard was dead. Nothing else could explain his silence.

Maman suggested I take my engagement ring to the jeweler to have it appraised. I was distressed to learn that the glittering stone wasn't a diamond after all, just an artfully cut piece of glass. Whoever sold Edouard the ring had cheated him.

Real or fake, I would cherish it forever, because Edouard gave it to me.

Maman came to despise him. The counterfeit diamond, the lack of any record of his army service, his failure to contact me—all of these things convinced her he'd been a fraud and deceiver from the start. She even began to doubt he was really French.

But she was wrong. I was the one he'd kissed and caressed, the one he'd brought to states of ecstasy, and I knew his feelings were genuine. When he said he loved me he was telling the truth. He couldn't have lied about everything else.

What's more, he'd left me with a gift far more precious than any ring. It was proof for all time of the love we shared.

My son—Edouard's son.

Maman insisted that the baby's last name be listed as Burnham on his birth certificate. Edouard and I had never been legally married, she said, so calling the child Trevillon would be a sham.

I insisted on giving him the same first name as his father. Maman disapproved even though the French name honored her heritage as well. She never called her grandson anything but Eddie.

But to me he was always Edouard. And from the first moment I held him in my arms, I adored him. How could I not? He had his father's beautiful eyes.

His father. My husband in spirit. My true and eternal love.

Soon he'll come back and take me with him to the Place Called Forever. Until then I'll stay in this house, waiting.

———◆———

"Are you okay?" Daniel asked. He and Ellie stood outside of the Hall of Justice, at the top of the wide steps leading down to Bryant Street. Traffic streamed along the one-way thoroughfare, late commuters heading to the Bay Bridge and their homes in the East Bay.

The wind had kicked up, and fog was rolling in. The air was damp. Mist gave the streetlamps a ghostly glow. The neon signs and lighted windows of the bail-bond businesses across the street gleamed in the darkness like beacons of hope. False hope, Ellie thought darkly.

"I'm fine. Why?" Shivering, she turned up the collar of her lightweight jacket. When she got dressed this morning, the day had promised to be warm.

One more promise broken.

"You seem distracted. And a little sad."

"I'm fine," she said again.

"Where would you like to go to dinner?"

She turned to look at him. She'd almost forgotten their original plan for the evening.

"Please don't be offended, Daniel, but can I take a rain check? I need to go home. It's been a long, strange day."

"Come on. You need to eat."

"Really, I'm not hungry. In fact I feel a little queasy."

"Okay." He lifted his arms in defeat. "Another time. I'll take you home."

"May I ask a huge favor? I have to get to Marin. I left my car in front of Claire's real estate office."

"Sure thing. Daniel's Luxury Limo at your service." He didn't sound sarcastic but she couldn't be certain.

"Never mind. I shouldn't impose. I'll get a ride-share."

"No need. It's my pleasure. Anything to keep us together longer."

She shook her head and started down the steps. "You don't have to do that, you know."

He hurried to catch up. "What do you mean?"

"Be nice to me so I'll side with Richard and sell you Granny Jo's house."

"Hey now. That's not—I like you, Ellie. It's that simple. You're an attractive, charming, intriguing woman, and I want to get to know you better. No matter what happens to the house."

"It's not a house to you. It's a development project."

"Sure, I'd like to do the project. But if it doesn't happen, well, another deal will come along. Let's go. The car's this way."

As they turned to the left, Ellie saw a man standing at the curb, beneath one of the trees that lined the sidewalk. Her step faltered. With the scant light and the shadows of leaves, she couldn't see his face clearly. But his height and his build and the slant of his shoulders told her it was Peter.

She shouldn't be surprised. Inspector Flaherty told her Peter was there. So why did the sight of him fold her in two, like a sudden punch in the gut?

"Ellie?" Daniel said. "What is it?"

"I'm fine." If she said it often enough, made it a mantra, maybe she'd start to believe it.

Peter was watching the street, peering toward the string of police cars parked down the block behind her. If his eyes shifted only a fraction he'd see her. She lowered her head, focusing on the cracks in the concrete. Maybe he wouldn't notice them as they went by.

No such luck.

"Ellie!" Peter cried out in surprise. "And Daniel. What are you two doing here?"

Ellie straightened and thrust her trembling hands in her pockets. "We're not here, not really. Pretend you didn't see us."

Daniel's smile looked forced. "We were talking to the police."

"About me?"

Peter was staring at Ellie, and she couldn't stop herself from staring back.

"No," Daniel said. "But I did hear a rumor that they arrested you for murdering Simon Thatcher. Glad they came to their senses."

Peter gave a nervous laugh. "You and me both."

"Can we, uh—" Daniel looked at Ellie as if seeking a cue about what to do next. "Do you need a ride somewhere?"

"Taken care of." Peter tossed the words toward Daniel but Ellie could tell he'd scarcely heard Daniel's offer. He cupped his hands on her cheeks. "Ellie … sweetheart. We need to talk."

She tried to ignore the flutter in her heart. Funny, she'd spent the entire morning in the reception area of his office waiting for exactly this opportunity. Now she didn't want to speak to him at all. Whatever she'd had with Peter, it was over, finished, done.

She stepped back. "There's nothing to talk about."

"Yes, there is. I want to apologize for that little misunderstanding last night. Let's—"

"Little misunderstanding! You're married. That's not a 'misunderstanding,' it's a lie! Everything you ever said to me is a lie."

"I said I love you, and that's God's truth. Ellie, we can work this out."

Even as he said the words, Peter glanced beyond her shoulder, watching something, or someone. She looked back but saw nothing that might have caught his eye.

"Come on, Ellie," Daniel said. "Let's go."

She motioned him away. "It's okay, Daniel. I need to finish this."

"Ellie, look at me." With a gentle touch, Peter lifted her chin until she couldn't help but gaze into his eyes. Her knees buckled.

Leave now, her mind warned. Before she could pull away, their lips met. A lightning bolt zinged along her nerves, and her heart began to race.

Peter drew her closer. His mouth on hers was soft and searching. How could she stand to lose him? Maybe he did love her. Maybe she should fight for him, take a chance on their future together—

No! She was not going to give in. Summoning all of her strength, she broke free.

"That kiss was goodbye, Peter." She tried to force air back into her lungs.

Peter grabbed her shoulders. "Sweetheart! You don't mean that—"

She slapped him as hard as she could. The action surprised her as much as kissing him had.

The blow made her palm sting, and she realized she'd intended it for herself more than him. To shock herself into good sense and reason.

"It's over, Peter. I'm taking my life back. There's no way I'll let you into it ever again."

A car glided to a stop beside them. Ellie glanced at it. A BMW or something like that, similar to Richard's.

She beckoned to Daniel. "I'm ready. Come on, let's get out of here."

The car's horn beeped long and loud.

"Oh God. Not now," Peter muttered.

Ellie took Daniel's arm, turned her back on Peter and the car, and started to walk down the block.

"Ellie!" Peter called after her in a choked voice.

She stopped, turned around. The streetlight lit his blond hair like a halo, if the devil could wear a halo. He was rubbing his cheek as if her slap still stung. Good.

She called, "Goodbye, Peter."

The driver got out of the car and slammed the door. A slender woman, curly hair. She reminded Ellie of Claire.

"Peter!" The woman planted herself in front of him. "What the hell is going on?"

His wife! She had to be Cassandra. Claire's sister. Peter's wife.

Ellie's queasiness grew more intense.

"That's her, isn't it?" The woman glared at her and Ellie suddenly understood the meaning of the phrase *if looks could kill.* "I saw your little lover's quarrel."

Peter kissed her cheek. "Darling. It's not what it looks like—"

"You kissed her!" She pushed him away. "Did you think I wouldn't see? You knew I'd drive up any minute. You wanted me to see—you wanted me to know you're a cheating bastard."

"Let me explain—"

"You can't explain. Not this time. Not ever again."

Cassandra got back in the car, gunned the engine, drove away. Peter stood there looking stunned.

Well, for all Ellie cared he could stand there all night. He could stand there for the rest of his goddamn life.

She turned on her heel and walked away.

"Ellie!" Peter called. "Sweetheart, come back. I love you!"

Hearing his running steps behind her, she quickened her pace. She felt moisture on her cheeks; it had to be the fog, because no way was she going to let herself shed another tear over Peter.

Finally the footsteps stopped. In front of her, the taillights of Cassandra's car receded, became pinpoints, disappeared.

Daniel, walking beside her, slipped his arm around her waist. She let it stay.

CHAPTER

44

Claire jabbed the black rose, half expecting to be jolted with electricity.

Nothing happened.

Beyond the windows the view of Victorian San Francisco didn't change.

Panic rose in her. She might have to spend the rest of her life in a time before she was born, in a place where she'd be devoid of human contact because no one could see her.

She punched the rose again. And again.

"It doesn't work!"

"Press softly," Stregoni told her. "Always be gentle with magic."

Claire followed the instruction and felt a pleasant tingling. Sparks swirled around her in a golden stardust cloud. The earth tilted ever so slightly, then came back to rest.

"Hurry, signora!" Stregoni called. Now his voice sounded far away.

The cloud cleared; the golden sparks settled at her feet and winked out. She was standing in the same place, yet everything had changed. The evening darkness was now brightened by the glow of streetlights below and the yellow gleam from windows of nearby apartments. Car horns blared and traffic buzzed along the street—sounds that often annoyed her but right now made the most beautiful music she'd ever heard.

She was back in her own time. She was home!

Claire's heart soared.

Then a scream from below sent it crashing.

"Hurry!" Stregoni dashed past her to go down the spiral stairs, quick and surefooted despite his injuries. "There is no time to waste. I pray we are not too late."

Suddenly she was terrified.

What was waiting below?

———◆———

She found the storage room empty of boxes and trunks, just as it should be. But something was seriously wrong.

Two people were lying in heaps beneath the front window, in the spot where Simon had died. Both were covered with blood.

Roxane was curled in a fetal position, sobbing as if her life were about to end.

Thaddeus wasn't moving. His hands rested against a wound in his midsection.

On the floor between them lay a knife.

What horror had happened here?

Claire's knees gave out and her stomach heaved. She abruptly sat on the bottom step as Stregoni rushed to Roxane and gathered her into his arms.

After a deep gulp of air, Claire made herself stand. She tiptoed toward Thaddeus, careful not to step in the blood. A wave of nausea threatened to overtake her. Then it passed, and she knelt beside him.

"We have to get help," she said to Stregoni.

"I will help Signorina Roxane." He dabbed the girl's face with a large white handkerchief. "Thank heaven she seems not to be injured. The other one is not worth saving."

Claire felt Thaddeus's neck for a pulse. Nothing. She laid a finger across his black mustache. No breath.

"Too late," she said.

Roxane's sobs began to subside.

"What on earth happened?" Claire asked.

"You need not answer, cara mia," Stregoni instructed in a tender voice. "Come with me. I will take care of you."

He tried to assist Roxane to her feet but she refused to budge. She shook her head, and droplets of blood flew from her hair. "No, monsieur. You d-don't want to get t-tangled up in my wickedness."

"Hush. Do not speak of—"

"He's d-dead … isn't he?" Roxane looked at Claire with pleading eyes. Her tears were no longer falling but they hadn't disappeared from her voice.

"I'm afraid so." Claire stood up, backed away from the body, and put her hand on her heart. She needed to acknowledge the presence of death but wasn't sure what to do. Should she close Thaddeus's eyes? She'd seen people do that in movies but wanted no part of touching the corpse.

Two corpses in two days—she wasn't sure she could stand it.

Roxane said, "I—I thrust the knife. I stabbed him as hard as I could."

"No one will blame you," Stregoni assured her. "You were defending your life."

Roxane relented and let him help her rise. Claire could see goosebumps on the girl's bare skin. Though the room was cold, her shivering seemed to be a reaction to something deep inside her. Even so, Claire closed the window to shut out the chilly breeze.

"He was g-going to—to k-kill me." Roxane touched her throat. "I had no choice. I had to—"

"You are safe now, cara." Stregoni drew her to his side.

Roxane didn't say where the knife came from. Claire hadn't seen it in her hand earlier, and it couldn't have been hidden in those skimpy clothes. She must have wrested it from Thaddeus as he attacked her.

Roxane clung to Stregoni. "He k-killed the other man too."

"What man?" Claire's gaze shot to the corners of the storage room, dreading the sight of another body.

"The man who d-died on Saturday night. Here in this very spot."

"Simon!" Her attention zipped back to Roxane. "You mean Thaddeus killed Simon?"

… a dark shape appears and shoves the man into an abyss …

Roxane gave a small nod. "Yes. Because of me."

Claire's nightmare flashed into her mind, clearer now. The dark shape was Thaddeus. The woman he'd chased into the mist wasn't Claire—she was Roxane.

"Tell us what happened."

"We had a celebration for Lady Celeste's birthday. Thaddeus was drunk. He—disobeyed her rules. I couldn't take him any longer so I escaped to the Future House. It's my refuge when Chez Celeste is too much to bear. A ball was going on here too. You were there, Claire. You followed me to this room."

Claire nodded. "You were wearing a necklace like mine. I wanted to ask you about it."

"You frightened me, so I hid behind the spiral stairs."

"You were scared of me?"

"Most people in the Future House can't see me—I thought Granny Jo was the only one. But you saw me."

"Yes," Claire said. "Mr. Stregoni explained that. But I would never have hurt you."

"When I thought everyone had gone, I left my hiding place. But that man—Simon—was still there. He saw me too. He thought I was a guest at his ball. He asked if I was having a good time and said I should go downstairs. I smiled ... right then someone grabbed me—"

"Thaddeus."

"I didn't see who it was. I never dreamed Thaddeus had discovered the Future House. I thought it was my secret." Roxane's voice broke, and her shivering grew worse. She couldn't take her eyes from Thaddeus's body.

"That villain!" Stregoni growled. "That blackguard!"

"He convinced himself I was meeting a lover. He couldn't stand the idea that I'd give my heart to another man. When I smiled at Simon—Thaddeus is strong and mean. When he's angry, nothing can stop him." She burst into tears. "They fought—over me! Simon's death is my fault."

"No, it's not," Claire said. "Don't blame yourself."

Without letting go of Roxane, Stregoni managed to bow to Claire. "Forgive me, but Signorina Roxane and I must bid you farewell. I need to take her back to our own time."

"No! Not yet!" Roxane pulled away from him. "The policemen—"

"Do not worry. By now they have frightened everyone out of the house or else taken them to jail. Either way, I am sure the policemen are gone. When we are safely back in Chez Celeste, I will show you what I have brought for you. It will make you happy, or so I hope. You will have nothing more to fear."

He guided Roxane toward the spiral stairs. She kept looking back, as if the sight of the dead man held her mesmerized.

"What about Isaac?" she asked. "He'll ask what became of his son."

"We will tell him that when the police arrived, his son ran away. It will astonish no one that Thaddeus would flee rather than face up to being shameful and cowardly. Isaac will assume he has made his way to a new city to begin life again under a different name. Perhaps you can say Thaddeus mentioned such a plan."

Roxane nodded. "That's a lie I'm willing to tell."

"Come now, we must return." Stregoni stepped aside to let Roxane precede him up the stairs. "Arrivederci, signora Claire. Farewell."

"Wait!" Claire said. "You can't just leave me here with the body of a man from another century."

Stregoni ran his fingers through his hair. "We cannot take him with us. He is too heavy and awkward to haul up these twisting stairs."

"How am I going to explain him? Who he is, what he's doing here …"

"It is simple. Tell your police you have found the murderer they are seeking."

"And say, 'Oh, by the way, he's dead'? They'll think I killed him. They might think I murdered Simon too. "

"Your dilemma is indeed difficult, signora."

"Is he invisible?" Claire asked hopefully. Maybe that would take care of the problem. "If the police can't see him—"

Stregoni's hair swirled as he shook his head. "Now that he is deceased, his protective aura is gone. Anyone can see him."

Roxane, halfway up the stairs, offered, "Just go home and let him be. If the police ask you questions, you can make up a story."

A breath of air wisped across Claire's cheek. She heard faint words: "Let the man tell his own story."

She looked around. No one there. But the voice gave her an idea.

"Please, stay a few more minutes and help me. I think I know what to do."

"How can we help?" Stregoni asked. "We cannot speak to your police. We are invisible to them."

"Thaddeus will speak for himself," Claire said. "We'll write a letter, a suicide note. A confession. We'll say he came to the fundraiser, argued with Simon, and killed him by accident. Then, in a fit of remorse, he came back tonight and stabbed himself to death, right here in the same spot."

"Hmm." Stregoni stroked his chin as if it would help him think. "An unusual method of suicide, but the way the knife entered—yes, he could have done it himself."

Roxane took Stregoni's arm. "You can't say Thaddeus killed that man because of me."

"True. That would just raise more questions. What shall we say they argued about?"

"The heirs are quarreling about what to do with the house," Claire said. "Maybe they fought about that."

"I have it." Stregoni was warming to the charade. "We will say he was a distant cousin, come from the Old Country to claim a share of the old woman's estate. When Isaac came to San Francisco from Germany as a young man, he changed his name to sound more American. Birnbaum became Burnham. We can sign the letter Thaddeus Birnbaum."

"That might work." Claire could see plenty of problems with the idea, but she didn't have a better one. With luck the police would accept the letter and close the case, and not chase off to Europe to do genealogical research.

Stregoni rubbed his hands together. "Good. I will go back and fetch some paper and a pen."

"No. We need modern paper and ink. I have a pad and pen in my purse. It's downstairs. I'll get it." She hurried toward the door, then turned. "Mr. Stregoni, you'll need to write the letter. It can't be in my handwriting."

He bowed again, a sweeping, gallant gesture. "I am at your service, signora."

45

Claire slipped through the darkness, feeling for the edges of steps with her feet and running her fingertips along walls and banisters. Reaching the pitch-black hallway on the second floor, she wasn't sure which way to turn. Then a whispered voice told her: "This way, dearie."

She didn't dare turn on a light. That might attract attention, make passersby wonder what was happening inside a house where no one lived and which had been yellow-taped as a crime scene. Bad enough that the glow of the overhead bulb could be seen in the storage room window. With luck, the third floor was high enough that no one outside would notice it.

In the parlor, streetlights beyond the uncurtained windows made it possible to see. She was relieved to find her purse on the fireplace hearth where she'd left it.

No sign of Ellie. She must have given up and found another way home. What had she done when Claire didn't come down from the tower? Made a search? Gone into panic mode?

Claire felt panicky herself. She dreaded going back upstairs. So tempting to keep going down to the ballroom and out the door. To flee the horror in the storage room.

To escape from this lunatic house.

From the blood, brutality, death. Corpses on the floor, two days in row.

From the Time Flip. Visitors from another century who were invisible—except to her.

Why did she have to be one of the few with the gift of sight? Not a gift—a curse. Just like her ability to hear whispered voices, to feel knots in the flow of air in a room, to sense if not see the hovering spirit of someone whose body was gone, whom everyone else assumed was departed.

Why couldn't she be normal?

Her head throbbed, and she was exhausted. She wanted to go home and sleep, though she knew tonight she'd have nightmares.

This fake-cousin thing, the suicide note. What had she been thinking? Ridiculous idea, it would never work.

Somebody touched her hand.

Suppressing a cry, she jerked back. Tried to push away her attacker.

"You can't leave yet."

She smelled a perfume, familiar now, spice mixed with flowers.

"Granny Jo?" Claire said aloud. She rubbed her tingling hand. This was the first time the old woman had touched her.

"Please, we need your help. You must to put an end to this terrible business."

"I can't. It's beyond my power."

"Justice should be served. And only you can serve it."

"Why am I the only one?"

Silence. Maybe she'd imagined the whispers. Maybe every strange thing she'd experienced in this house was a hallucination.

But the voice was right. If Claire left now, the police would be dealing with two unsolved homicides.

Ellie would tell the cops about visiting the house with Claire. When the medical examiner established the time of death for Thaddeus, the two of them would top the list of suspects. They'd been in the right place at the right time to have killed him.

If Claire told the truth about the two deaths, no one would believe her. The cops would assume she was a liar, and a bad one at that. They'd arrest her for murder or dismiss her as one more crackpot with a crazy tale.

Either way, she'd be at risk and Simon would never receive justice.

Tonight was her only chance to create a plausible fiction that could answer even a few of the cops' questions.

"I don't really have a choice, do I?" Her words echoed in the darkness.

"Be brave. You can do it. Come with me."

Claire let the whispering voice lead her back upstairs.

———◆———

Stregoni wrote carefully, making small precise strokes in Claire's notebook.

"Can't you go faster?" Frayed nerves made her tone harsher than she'd intended.

"D-don't snap at him," said Roxane, sitting at the bottom of the spiral stairs. Stregoni's coat was draped over her skimpy bloodstained nightgown.

"It is this peculiar pen, signora. I have never seen one like it." Stregoni shook Claire's ballpoint. "It feels awkward in my hand, so writing is difficult. But I believe I have put down all that needs to be said."

He handed her the notebook so she could read what he'd written—the tale they'd agreed on about the long-lost German cousin who had come to San Francisco to claim his birthright. He showed up as the fundraiser was ending, fell into an argument with Simon, and took Simon's life in a powerful burst of anger. Torn apart by shame and remorse, he returned to the scene and made retribution the only way he could—by killing himself.

The wording was stiff and old-fashioned, but that only made the letter sound more authentic, since English wouldn't have been the German cousin's first language. The handwriting looked foreign too. Stregoni had added an ornate signature. Claire could barely decipher the name: *Thaddeus Birnbaum.*

"Good. This should do."

"Where will you put it?" Stregoni asked. "In his pocket?"

And touch the gruesome corpse? No way.

"I'll just lay it near his hand. The pen too."

He started to give her the pen.

"Wait a minute." Rummaging through her purse, she found the lace-edged handkerchief Roxane had given her. Holding the cloth, she rubbed the pen and ripped the page from the notebook.

"What are you doing?" Roxane asked.

"Removing fingerprints."

"Fingerprints?" Roxane looked puzzled. "What do you mean?"

"Ah, yes, I have heard of this," Stregoni said. "The work of Sir Francis Galton. He claims that no two people have fingerprints that are exactly alike. It is becoming a way to catch criminals. A woman in Argentina was proven to have murdered her sons because she left behind a bloody thumbprint."

"Exactly," Claire said. "Our story has Thaddeus handling the notebook, the pen, and the knife. If the police find other people's prints on them, they won't believe the letter."

"But his fingerprints are not on any of those things," Stregoni pointed out. "Will that not confuse the police?"

"You're right. We need to make sure everything has his prints."

Avoiding the blood, Claire carried the letter and pen to the body. She picked up Thaddeus's cold hand. Her stomach lurched; she willed it to behave. Hurling now would be a disaster. She pressed the dead man's fingers against the pen, then the letter.

Where to put them? She set them near the wall, not far from the body but beyond the reach of spurting blood, hoping the police would believe a suicidal Thaddeus had deliberately placed the items there.

"Where's the knife?" she asked. It was no longer on the floor.

"Here." Roxane drew it from beneath Stregoni's coat. "I stole it from the kitchen. Lady Celeste will be upset if I don't put it back."

"We have to leave it. It's essential to this tableau we're setting up."

Stregoni put his hand on Roxane's shoulder. "It is all right, cara. I will find a way to explain its absence to Lady Celeste."

Claire took the knife and wiped the handle. "I'd better leave the blade bloody. Otherwise the scene won't look natural."

Nausea roiled in her again as she wrapped Thaddeus's fingers around it.

If his stab wounds had been self-inflicted, what would he have done with the weapon? Held onto it, dropped it, flung it across the room? She released his hand and let the knife fall.

She couldn't step away from the corpse fast enough.

"That's the best we can do. The police will have a lot of questions."

"For your sake, signora, I hope they do not look too hard for the answers." Stregoni helped Roxane to her feet. "Now we must go back."

"Goodbye, Claire," Roxane said. "I hope everything goes well for you."

"For you too," Claire said. "I'm glad I met you both."

When they reached the top the spiral stairs, Roxane lifted her hand in a small wave. Stregoni made a courtly bow.

Claire waved back. "Farewell!" Not a word she normally used but it seemed like the right thing to say.

Stregoni touched the black rose. A swirl of stardust enveloped the pair, and they were gone.

Claire felt bereft, as if they had torn away a part of her and taken it with them.

46

Roxane clung to Mr. Stregoni's hand as they crossed the third floor of Chez Celeste.

The big house was silent. No piano music from the parlor, no laughter or moans of pleasure from behind closed doors. The eerie quiet frightened Roxane more than the yelling of the policemen and the screams of the *jeunes filles* as they'd fled. She didn't really count the other girls as friends, but she hated to think of them locked up in jail, or driven to the dives of the Barbary Coast. Especially Fleur—how would such a delicate flower ever survive?

"You will need clothes," Mr. Stregoni said, drawing Roxane's thoughts back to her own predicament. "Which of these rooms is yours?"

"This one." Roxane opened the door to her chamber and gasped in shock. "Oh, dear heaven!"

The thin mattress had been pulled off her bed. The door of the wardrobe gaped open. Her few belongings were scattered around the room.

"Don't worry, cara. It is all right." Mr. Stregoni tugged the mattress back into place. "A greedy policeman searching for something to steal. Is anything missing?"

Tears filled her eyes. "I don't think so." Her only possession of value was her treasure pouch with its precious contents, and

Thaddeus had already stolen that from her. He'd taunted her with it in the Rose Room. Could it possibly still be there?

Mr. Stregoni plucked her plaid everyday dress from the floor. "Put this on. I promise to look away."

"That's not necessary. Men have seen every bit of me." She stripped off his coat and the bloody chemise.

Despite her assurance, he kept his head averted. She was pleased that he thought her modest and deserving of privacy. She found some knickers and put them on, but petticoats were too much of a bother. She pulled the dress over her head.

"You may look now," she said, fastening the long row of tiny buttons.

"Do you have a valise? I will pack your things while you get ready for our journey."

"What journey?"

He took an envelope from his coat pocket. She hadn't noticed it was there. Thick paper the color of cream. Her name on the front, written in an elaborate script.

"Open it and you will see."

She broke the seal on the flap and drew out four pieces of paper.

"What's this?"

"Tickets," he said. "Two of them will take us to New York on the railroad. The next two give us passage on an ocean liner. We will sail to England, and travel from there to Italy. I have a villa in Tuscany that I believe you will find quite comfortable."

Railroad? Ocean liner? The words made Roxane's head spin. Tuscany? She'd never heard of it. Was *villa* a fancy word for a whorehouse?

"I don't understand, monsieur."

He put his arms around her. "I am aware that we have known each other for only a few days. But you have not been out of my mind for a minute since we met. The reason I could not come back to see you before tonight is that it took time to make all of these arrangements."

Pulling free of his embrace, she sat on the bed and buried her face in her hands. "Monsieur, you're the kindest man I've ever met. I'm grateful, truly I am. But I can't go away with you."

He knelt in front of her and took her hands in his. "Look at me, cara. I am asking you to marry me. To be my wife. We can have our wedding along the way. Just pick the place you like best."

"Wedding!" Until today she'd never heard that word from the lips of a man, certainly not one who intended her to be the bride. Now she had heard it twice.

Her head was spinning, her heart beating wildly.

He got up and sat beside her. "This is the right course for both of us, I am certain. I will make you happy, I promise you that."

He drew her close and kissed her, a soft, tender kiss that made her tears flow harder.

"Very happy, I'm sure, monsieur." All of the sorrows she'd ever known were wrapped up in the lump of despair in her heart. "But I can never marry you. You don't want a terrible person like me."

"Don't speak like that. I love you, Roxane."

"You don't know me! You don't know what awful things I've done!"

"You only did what you must, working here. In Italy you will have a fresh start. No one will ever know how you once earned your living."

"I don't mean that. I'm talking about k-killing." She clapped her hands over her mouth. She'd sworn to herself that she would never speak a word about her horrible deed.

"No one can lay fault on you for that. Thaddeus attacked you. You had every right to defend yourself."

"I don't mean Thaddeus. Or rather, not only him."

"Do you mean to say there was another?"

Roxane pushed herself up off the bed. "It's a long story, monsieur. We need to leave, in case the police come back."

Mr. Stregoni pulled her back and settled her onto his lap. "They will not come back. They have had their fun, and satisfied the outraged citizens who sent them. Tell me your story, cara."

"If I do, you will despise me."

"Rest assured, I shall not. Begin at the beginning."

His voice was soothing. She felt as if he had spread a blanket over her. Soft. Warm. For years she had felt herself in the grip of a chill she couldn't shake, and now it was melting away.

"It was in Missouri. I grew up on a farm. A small farm, with poor soil that was stingy when it came to growing things. Pa rented the place. In exchange for living there, we gave a certain portion of the crop to the landlord. In the lean years there was little left for us."

"So you went hungry?"

"It wasn't so bad while Mama was alive. She kept a garden and chickens and was good at cooking. She knew how to stretch a few scraps into a hearty meal. She was the most wonderful woman ever—oh, I miss her so much."

His arms tightened around her. "What happened to her?"

"She kept trying to give my father a son. I was the firstborn, and he was so disappointed that I was a girl. Three times after that she was in the family way, but it always ended badly. A few weeks would go by, and then she would cramp up with terrible pain and lose the child in a rush of blood. She grew weaker, more sickly, each time. And—and then ..."

Oh, Mama! All of her words fled.

"It is all right. I am listening," He drew her closer still. "When we talk about our troubles, they become easier to bear."

Moments passed before she was able to speak. "The fourth time we all were excited. The baby lived long enough to be born. I prayed hard for a brother, because a boy would make Pa happy. Then the baby came, and everything was ruined."

"A baby's birth should be a time for joy. What happened?"

"It was a winter night, bitter cold. A hard wind blew the falling snow. The baby was fat and red, and she bawled right away, so we knew she was fine—"

"She," Mr. Stregoni said.

"Yes, my little sister. Pa was distressed—he wanted a boy so much, a son he could call Frank Junior. He couldn't believe that God had denied him that. He named my sister Frances, and called her Frankie."

"A girl called by a boy's name. What did your mother think about that?"

"She—she ..." Roxane let out a sob. Mr. Stregoni pressed her face against his shoulder and held her there.

"M-mama never woke up," Roxane said. "She'd worked for nearly two days to push the baby out and she was exhausted. She fell into a heavy sleep and soon I saw she was burning with fever. Pa said we couldn't fetch the doctor from town because the snow was too deep. Mama—oh, monsieur, Mama never woke up!"

"Dearest Roxane. I am so deeply sorry."

"And Frankie—she was so hungry. I got milk from our cow and tried to tip it into her mouth with a spoon. But she ate almost nothing, just squalled and squalled all the time. I held her and rocked her, but nothing stopped her crying. Finally Pa took her from me and placed his handkerchief over her face—to comfort her, he said. Sure enough, the noise stopped. She followed Mama to heaven."

"Such a tragedy. Then it was just you and your father?"

"Yes." She didn't want to think about Pa. She didn't want Mr. Stregoni to know the truth.

"Is he still in Missouri, or did he come with you to San Francisco?"

Pa's face, his eyes narrowed in an accusing glare, floated in the dark space of Roxane's mind.

"He's dead." She spat out the words.

"Dead," Mr. Stregoni echoed. "He's the one you—"

"Pa met with a fatal accident. He was carrying an axe in a careless manner, and he tripped and fell. The axe blade pierced his belly."

That was the story she'd told the sheriff. The doctor who examined the body had been kind enough to back her up.

Pa came to her that night, as he had almost every night since Mama was buried. It was her duty, he explained the first time, to take over for her mother. She would leave school behind, become homemaker and helpmeet. She was twelve years old, a sufficient age to cook the meals and clean the house, to take care of everything her father needed now that he no longer had a wife.

The days she could endure. But she learned to dread the nightfall. Four long years proved more than she could bear.

On that fateful night, after she made sure Pa was quite dead, she dragged his body from her bedchamber and out of the house. With much effort she loaded him onto their wagon. She poured what remained in his whiskey bottle over his head so the sheriff would assume, rightly enough, that this misfortune had befallen him while he was drinking. Next to him she placed the axe, which earlier that day she had concealed beneath her mattress, the same way that last night she'd hidden the knife.

She went back into the house and scrubbed the trail of blood from the floorboards. She stuffed the cleaning rags and her nightdress and the bedclothes into the woodstove and watched them burst into flame. Finally she filled the washtub. She scoured every inch of her flesh, again and again, cleansing it not just of Pa's blood but also his smoky, sweaty stench and the feel of his rough skin and the seed he had spilled on her legs and belly. All the while she kept whispering: *Never again. Never again. Never again.*

When she realized that trying to feel clean was hopeless, she went outside and hitched the horse to the wagon. She drove Pa's body into town, arriving as day was breaking.

She talked to the sheriff, and together they talked to the doctor. Leaving the wagon, horse, and corpse in their care, she bought a train ticket with the few dollars she'd found in the coffee canister where Pa hid his drinking money. She didn't dare stay in town in case the sheriff discovered the truth.

She wanted to go to San Francisco, where a cousin of Mama's was supposed to live. Pa's money took her only as far as Omaha, but when she got there a gentleman at the railroad station offered to help her. All she had to do was give him and his friends the same kind of favors that Pa had wrenched from her, and they'd pay the rest of her fare. She felt as much revulsion for herself as for them, but she saw no other choice. When she finally reached San Francisco, the cousin was nowhere to be found. Alone and penniless in a strange city, she had fended for herself as best she could.

"So you see, monsieur," she said, her voice trembling as she finished her story, "I'm most unsuited to be a true companion for any man. Certainly not a kind and good man, as you seem to be. Although if you are, you must be the only such man in the world."

"Cara, cara! My dearest Roxane. You've seen little of the world, so how can you know what it's like? Let me show it to you." His fingers brushed her cheek, following the line of her tears. "You are dear and sweet and worthy. All of your life you have had bad fortune, but I have the power to change that. Please let me make you my wife."

The word wife struck terror in her heart; from what she had seen of husbands, they were a poor bargain indeed. The notion of seeing the world was equally scary. But what else could she do? San Francisco had not turned out not to be a happy place for her, and her prospects if she stayed here were worse than bleak. Even more terrible was the idea of returning to Missouri and facing a lifetime in prison.

She had never felt affection for a man before, yet this strange, wild-haired gentleman stirred something in her, something hopeful and even thrilling. Should she take a chance on him?

"Cara? Are you—"

"All right, monsieur. I'll go to Italy with you."

As soon as the words escaped from her mouth, she wanted to take them back. Yet she couldn't speak. Instead, she was drawn to put her lips on his. The kiss tasted of honey and cinnamon, of sunshine and spring rain.

She was sure he'd want to follow the kiss with more intimate activity—all men did. But he surprised her, as he'd done so often. He set her on her feet and stood up.

"We must go," he said. "Choose what you want to bring with you."

"Nothing from this chamber." She kicked the chemise she'd discarded on the floor. "But please, monsieur, may we stop in the Rose Room? I want to search for my treasure pouch."

"Of course," he said. "But it is time for you to stop calling me *monsieur*. My name is Alberto."

"Alberto," she repeated, the syllables skipping along her tongue like the notes of a song.

The Rose Room was dark, and Roxane lit a candle, just as she would do if Mr. Stregoni—Alberto—were a gentleman who had engaged her to entertain him there. The first thing she noticed when the flame flared was that Lady Celeste's bawdy Parisian prints were missing.

"One of the policemen must be a collector of fine art," she said to him. He was standing guard in the doorway.

The coins Thaddeus had tossed onto the Oriental rug were gone too. All the money she'd had in the world! Shards from the broken whiskey glass glinted in the candlelight. She hoped a jagged sliver had sliced the hand of the policeman who'd thought her meager fortune worth stealing.

She'd last seen her treasure pouch on the dresser, right before Thaddeus covered it with his top hat. The hat was now knocked on its side. Her heart sank.

"My pouch is gone, Alberto! What will I do?"

"I see something on the bed. Could that be it?"

She whirled around. Sure enough, there was the leather pouch, nested in the rumpled covers. She snatched it up.

"It's empty!"

She bit her lip and tried to blink back tears.

"What was in your pouch, cara?"

"Lady Celeste's amethyst necklace. She'll kill me when she finds out I let it get stolen."

"I imagine the loss of her necklace is the least of her worries at the moment."

"And my locket." Roxane's voice broke. "Why did they have to take that? It's worth nothing at all, except to me. Mama's picture! It was all I had to remember her—"

"Achoo!"

The sound of the sneeze startled her. "Who did that!"

"Not I," Alberto said. "I thought it was you."

"Achoo!"

"Someone's under the bed," Roxane said. It couldn't be a policeman, for why would a policeman hide?

She got down on her knees, holding the candle low so she could see. Its light revealed a mop of red curls.

"Fleur! Is that you? Come out of there."

No response. No movement.

"It's all right. You're safe. Everyone's gone. Well, except for Alb—Mr. Stregoni and me."

A moment passed and then Fleur wriggled out from under the bed. Roxane helped the girl to her feet. Fleur's small hands brushed dust off her corset but missed the smudge of dirt on her cheek.

"Oh, Roxane," she whispered. "I'm so scared. Whatever are we going to do?"

"What would you like to do, signorina?" Alberto came into the room to offer Fleur a protective arm.

"I—I want to go home!"

"Where is that?" he asked gently.

"Do you mean Sacramento?" To Alberto, Roxane added, "That's where her family lives."

Fleur's face lit up at the mention of the city's name, but she shook her head. "I've disgraced them," she mourned. "They'll never take me back."

"Let us give them a try," Alberto said. "Roxane and I are getting on a train in the morning, and Sacramento will be one of its first stops. We will take you with us, and if you like, we will go to your house with you and talk to your family. I am sure we can find an explanation that will satisfy them and they will welcome you with open arms."

Fleur's smile was brighter than the candle. "Oh, would you do that?"

"Go find some clothes to put on. You do not want to go home dressed like that."

Fleur hurried to the doorway, then turned. "I almost forgot. I found this under the bed."

She reached into the black lace at the top of her corset and drew out a length of ribbon. An object dangled from it—a tarnished silver heart.

"My locket! Oh, bless you!" Roxane hugged Fleur tight. "I thought it was gone forever."

Alberto said, "What about the amethyst necklace? Did you find that too?"

Fleur looked puzzled. "Amy—what?"

"A necklace with purple stones."

"No, just the one. I'll go get ready."

When she had dashed away, Roxane and Alberto searched the room from comer to corner, from ceiling to floor. No necklace.

"It's gone for good," Roxane moaned.

"That is all right." Alberto took the locket she was clutching and tied the ribbon around her neck. "You have the one that matters."

He drew her into his arms. She had just lifted her lips for a kiss when Fleur burst into the room.

"I'm ready. Let's go! Look, Roxane, I brought the book too. The ABC book. You can teach me the next letters while we're riding the train."

CHAPTER

47

Claire couldn't get away from the Burnham Mansion fast enough.

She picked her way through the dark maze of hallways and stairways to the ballroom door. She had no way to lock it behind her. With luck the police would assume the mysterious Cousin Thaddeus broke in this way.

She made herself walk calmly down the block to her VW. But her hands shook as she opened the door, fastened the seatbelt, put the key in the ignition.

She didn't want Ellie, or anyone else, to go through the trauma of stumbling on Thaddeus's body. But she couldn't use her own phone to call the police. They'd have too many questions she didn't know how to answer.

Van Ness Avenue was a few blocks away. A brightly lit commercial boulevard—she'd try to find a pay phone there. Then she'd go home, get into bed. She'd pull the covers over her head, curl into a ball, and stay there for a long, long time.

As she pulled away from the curb, a police cruiser came around the corner and stopped in front of the Burnham Mansion. Calling the cops wouldn't be necessary.

She drove away as quickly as she dared.

———•———

When Claire dragged herself into the apartment, Lindsay's boyfriend, Brad, was perched on the sofa, pulling the cork from a bottle of wine.

He raised the bottle in a salute. "Claire! You're just in time."

Lindsay came out from the kitchen and set two wineglasses on the coffee table. "Oh, hey! I was hoping you'd get here. Wait just a minute." She disappeared, returning a moment later with another glass. She gave Claire a hug, followed by a long searching look. "Are you okay?"

"I'm fine," Claire said quickly.

"My favorite cabernet," Brad said, pouring wine into the first glass. "Hope you like it."

The deep red wine reminded Claire of blood.

"Thanks, Brad, I'm sure it's wonderful, but I'm going to my room. I'm exhausted, and I have a headache. You two enjoy your evening."

She was glad Brad was here to distract Lindsay, who was sometimes too perceptive about Claire's moods. Normally she cherished her best friend's levelheaded counsel and warmhearted comfort. But not tonight. She couldn't tell Lindsay, or anyone, about what she'd gone through at the Burnham Mansion. Silence was essential if she wanted people to consider Simon's murder solved. No one would believe the truth—Claire hardly believed it herself. If rumors started to spread, she'd be in a hideous mess.

The suicide was faked. The death scene was staged. Did you hear about that crazy woman? She claims the killer was a guy from the nineteenth century who blasted through the time barrier. Anyone who's that far out of touch with reality ought to be locked up.

The only way to protect herself was to never breathe a word.

She shut her bedroom door and flopped onto her bed, intending to indulge in a misery wallow. It was Gram's foolproof cure for self-pity—allot a certain amount of time and spend it doing nothing but feeling sorry for yourself. No cheating. No reading or listening to music. Spend the whole time dwelling on your own gloom and wretchedness.

Claire set the timer on her phone for thirty, pulled her pillow over her head, and tried to banish the sight of blood and the sound of screaming.

She heard a snatch of jazz, the phone's ringtone. The caller ID read MIRABELLE BURNHAM.

Okay, she'd take the call. She owed Ellie some sort of explanation. If only she could come up with something believable to say.

"Claire! Thank goodness!" Ellie said. "I've been so upset. Where are you?"

"Home. I'm sorry I bailed on you."

"You vanished! What happened?"

"I, uh, started to feel sick, so I went for a walk. I needed air." Lame, but Claire couldn't think of anything better. "When I came back you were gone."

"How did you get out of the tower? You went up there and just—disappeared. I would've seen you come down. I was right there the whole time."

"Maybe you were looking out the window. I should have told you I was leaving. I wasn't thinking straight." At least the last sentence was true.

"I was afraid the murderer got to you. I went to the police and told Inspector Flaherty you'd vanished."

That explained the police cruiser. "Thanks for being concerned, Ellie. I'll let Flaherty know I'm okay."

After awkward goodbyes, Claire found the business card the homicide detectives had given her. To her relief, neither Flaherty nor Vargas was available to take her call. She left a message: she wasn't missing, she was fine, there'd been a misunderstanding.

She closed her eyes to resume her misery wallow.

The jazzy ringtone again—her sister this time.

"Oh, Claire! I was afraid I'd get your voicemail." Cassandra sounded like she was crying.

Claire felt a prickle of alarm. "What's the matter?"

"It's over. I kicked the bastard out."

"Peter? Did the police let him go?"

"He was cheating. Again. The last time I caught him, he swore he'd never do it again. That liar! That rotten, lying, unfaithful son of a bitch."

"He's done it before?"

"More than once. The receptionist at his office, some slut he met in a bar, even one of his clients. I don't know how he came up with this latest one, but when I went to pick him up at the Hall of Justice I saw her climbing all over him. So I drove away without him. When he got home, I booted his cheating ass out the door."

"I'm sorry, Cassandra." Claire bit her lip to keep from adding, *You're better off without that creep.* She felt a pang of guilt. What if she'd warned Cassandra about Ellie as soon as she suspected what Peter was up to? Or told Ellie that Peter was married, so keep your hands off? Would it have made a difference? Either way, Peter would have broken someone's heart.

"I can't stand this!" Cassandra wailed. "What am I going to tell the kids? And the house—I hate the thought of us rattling around in this huge place all by ourselves. You've done this, Claire, you've been through a divorce. What I am supposed to do? How am I ever going to get through it?"

"I'll help you. I'm coming right over. Everything will turn out okay."

She knew the last sentence was a platitude. Friends had tried to reassure her with the same banal sentiment when she caught

Zach in bed with Little Ms. Homewrecker. She hadn't believed it for a minute, but saying the words aloud now, she knew they were true.

———◆———

Another dead man, so soon after the last. My home is stained with blood.

Once again hordes of policemen, women too, are poking through these rooms, taking measurements, photos, and notes. I watch as they spread fingerprint dust and collect tiny scraps into bags. The commotion they create whips the energy into whirlwinds.

They don't know I'm here.

They're puzzled by what they're finding, unsure how to explain today's body. I could tell them how the man died, but I don't know how to reach out to them. Just as well. I wouldn't want to get my little friend Roxane in trouble. She killed him only to defend herself from dire harm, but would the police believe me if I tried to tell them so?

This house has seen too much death. My father, my mother, my son, myself. And this week, two strangers. This new one somehow looks familiar. He reminds me of my father's portrait, painted when he was young, which hung in the parlor. So handsome! I regret that I never saw him in his prime. When I was born he was already growing old. I was only twelve when he died, leaving my mother bereft.

Maman was always lonely. It was hard, living in a country that wasn't her own, even though she spoke English perfectly. Her friends were few and far-flung. The most cherished were the ones she called my tantes, my aunties—women from France, like her. They all lived in Maman's boardinghouse as young girls—or as she called them, jeunes filles. Though fate had scattered them, she sought them out after Papa died. As a girl I met them all, and their lives stirred my imagination.

I was fond of sweet Tante Fleur, married to a baker with a shop in Sacramento. They had seven plump, happy children. She read me stories and gave me cakes.

Tante Aurélie, pious and pinch-faced, frightened me. The wife of a hellfire-and-brimstone preacher in Fresno, she told me she loved me and hoped to save my immortal soul. She was always eager to tattle to God about my sins, even ones I hadn't yet committed.

Tante Yvette never married, though she was the most beautiful. She played the piano in theaters and concert halls. To her I owe my love of music and my willingness to practice on the squeaky old piano in our parlor.

Tante Véronique went to Washington, DC, on the arm of a congressman. He soon dropped dead—poisoned, it was whispered, perhaps by a political rival. When his bank account proved empty, she opened a boardinghouse like the one Maman ran long ago. I was charmed by the elegant house and the romantic young ladies who lived there. "What fun it would be," I told Maman, "to live in a place like this!" I was puzzled and disappointed when Maman cut our visit short.

My favorite was Tante Roxane, who came to see us from Italy. She told wonderful tales about her life there, though to my surprise, she claimed to have no memories of her childhood in France. Her husband's eyes, one silver, one gold, twinkled with fun. When he played the piano, the music was so lively I could've sworn sparks flew from his fingertips. The house rang with laughter when they were here.

How I long for laughter now!

The police are packing their gear; the medical examiner is loading the latest body onto a gurney for its trip to the morgue. I can only hope that the pall of gloom and bad fortune will go out the door with them.

Soon I'll be alone again. What's going to happen to this house? I've lived here more than one hundred years, but it's no longer mine, and the fact is, I'm no longer living. My grandchildren have no use for this place. It's a relic of a bygone time. Too big, too old. They'll tear it down, or remodel it into oblivion.

What a shame to see it go. The stories these rooms hold, the dreaming that took place here. The love and fear, the laughter and weeping, the hopes and desires—all vanished.

And once the house is nothing but a memory, where will I go?

The Place Called Forever. Is it time? Am I ready?

CHAPTER

48

"What a nightmare the last few days have been." Tess sounded weary and sad as she and Claire walked through the morning sunshine toward the Burnham Mansion. "Just think, less than a week ago this house was filled with people laughing, dancing, and having fun." She shook her head. "I still can't believe Simon's gone."

A hollow space opened in Claire at the sound of his name.

"I wish I'd had the chance to get to know him," she said. "He seemed like a wonderful man."

"He certainly was. It's a huge, huge loss." Tess sighed. "If only BAPA could save this house. It would be such a fitting tribute."

"Maybe this meeting will bring good news."

"I don't dare get my hopes up." Tess started up the front steps.

Claire took one step and then stopped. Her adventures in this house had been enough to last her a lifetime. She never again wanted to discover a bloody body or flip through time to another century.

"What are you waiting for?" Tess asked.

"Nothing." Claire climbed to the porch. No reason to think she wouldn't be safe here now. As long as she avoided the storage room and stayed out of the tower. And kept her distance from the black rose.

362

Tess pushed the doorbell. Ellie opened the door and flashed them a quick, nervous smile. "Come in. Everyone's back there." She wouldn't meet their eyes as she fluttered a hand toward the hall, "There's coffee if you'd like some."

Why was she acting uneasy? Maybe because she knew she'd won—Peter was hers. Facing his wife's sister, she felt guilty and embarrassed.

Good. She deserved to feel terrible.

The buzz of conversation beckoned them to the dining room. A dozen or so people stood in clusters by Granny Jo's huge mahogany table. Ellie's brothers were making the rounds, shaking hands. Tess joined a group of her fellow members of the BAPA board.

"Claire! I hoped you'd be here." Daniel Harding came up and shook her hand. "I brought your beautiful dress, just in case."

That awful Scarlett O'Hara gown—beautiful? Seriously?

He pointed to a corner of the room, where a dry-cleaning bag was draped over a chair. Mauve ruffles peeked from the bottom of the plastic.

The dress reminded Claire of her first sight of Roxane, standing on the grand staircase in her lilac gown and amethyst necklace. Claire glanced around, half expecting to see her among the gathered guests. "Thanks for taking care of it, Daniel."

"Glad to do it. Say, isn't that the same necklace you were wearing Saturday night? Very pretty."

"Yes. I wear it for good luck." Claire ran her fingers along the strand of purple crystals. She didn't mention that the luck she wanted today was BAPA's victory over his proposed condos.

At the card table where the coffee urn had been set up, she poured a cup. Turning around, she found herself face to face with Peter. His lawyerly suit and tie looked perfect, but he seeemed haggard. Shadows haunted his eyes.

"Claire!" He seemed startled to see her, and not pleased. "I didn't expect you to be at this gathering."

"Yet here I am," she said, proud of resisting the urge to toss the hot liquid in his face.

"I, uh, it's good to see you." Insincerity oozed from him. "I guess you know … How's Cassandra doing?"

"Wonderfully. No thanks to you."

In truth, her sister was miserable, caught in a cycle of weepiness, rage, and fear about the future. Claire had spent the past three nights at Cassandra's house, helping her deal with the reality of getting a divorce. Claire couldn't lessen the heartbreak, but she could guide her sister through the first painful steps—organizing paperwork, seeing a lawyer, fielding awkward questions from Willow and Jake. Claire was used to being the younger sister, the one who didn't quite have her life together. It felt strange to have her status shift, to be the person with assurance and expertise.

Richard Burnham stepped to the head of the massive dining table. His voice boomed out. "Take a seat, everyone. Let's get started."

Folding chairs had been arranged around the table. Claire sat next to Tess and took a deep sip of coffee, welcoming the warmth and the surge of caffeine. Peter ended up sitting right across from her, but he averted his eyes, making a point of looking anywhere but at Claire.

When Ellie came into the dining room, only one seat was free, between Peter and Daniel. Peter patted the table, inviting her to sit. To Claire's surprise Ellie scowled at him. She whispered something to Daniel, who slid over into the empty chair. Ellie took the place he'd vacated.

Now, that was interesting. Could it be there was trouble in paradise?

Everyone quieted, and Claire felt the energy in the house go still. Something seemed to be missing. Then she realized what was—an absence of whispers, of flutters stirring the air. Granny Jo's spirit, which always had hovered at the edge of Claire's consciousness in this house, was gone.

Whatever had made the old woman move on, Claire hoped she was content.

Richard clapped his hands, and eyes turned to him. "Thank you for coming. We're here because of this magnificent house, which has been in my family since the 1880s. My grandmother lived here her entire life. Now that she's gone, may she rest in peace"—here he bowed his head for a second—"ownership has passed to me, and my brother and sister. It's our responsibility—"

Marc Burnham broke in. "Cut the blather, Ree-*shar*. They all know the history."

Richard glared at him. "Yes, well. You also know we have two purchase offers on the table. The three of us met yesterday and made our decision. We brought you together to give you the news face to face."

Claire felt Tess tense up beside her.

"Both proposals are tempting. One would make the house a museum, preserving the past. The other would honor its history while bringing the property into the future. A hard choice, and we gave it careful thought. The vote was two to one. Marc's not entirely convinced yet, but Ellie and I agree it's best to accept Harding and Boyer's—"

Ellie jumped up from her seat. "Stop! I'm withdrawing my vote."

———•———

Ellie felt them all staring, their eyes pinning her to the wall like a butterfly.

"What the hell?" Richard's face turned red.

"I—I've changed my mind."

She sat back down, as surprised as anyone by her abrupt action. She couldn't believe how hard her heart was pounding. Didn't know how she'd found the courage.

She was sick of doing what others told her to do, of letting them define her. Standing up for herself felt good. She should have done it long ago.

"You—you can't," Richard sputtered. "It's been decided."

"Jeez, Ellie." Peter's voice, the low rumble she used to love. "Don't do something stupid."

"Are you sure?" Marc asked.

"I've never been more sure of anything."

She couldn't look at her brothers, and certainly not at Peter—she never wanted to see his face again. She stole a glance at Daniel, afraid of his reaction.

Ellie had spent a lot of time—very enjoyable time—with Daniel over the past few days. He was easy company, listening to her as if what she said mattered. He'd been a rock-steady friend through the horrors of the week—the discovery of another violent death in Granny Jo's house, the dealings with the police.

She hadn't told him how she'd vote, but it had become clear that selling the house to Harding & Boyer was in her best interest. Yesterday she'd announced her decision to her brothers. And tried to ignore Richard's gloating.

Later, deep in the night, she woke from a restless sleep and was startled to see Granny Jo standing by her bed, glowing faintly in the dark room.

"I love you, Mirabelle," her grandmother whispered. *"You know the right thing to do."*

A dream, but so vivid! All morning it had haunted her.

What had Granny Jo meant? Right for the house, right for her legacy, or right for Ellie?

"Ellie," Richard said now in that stern big-brother voice she detested, "this isn't the time to make a scene. We've agreed to sell to Harding and—"

She stood again, bracing her arms on the table. Her voice quavered. "This house is a treasure. Our family's treasure, and the city's too. I know Daniel's plan gives a nod to its history. But that's not the same as preserving it. Once it's gone, no one can ever get it back. So I'm voting to sell it to BAPA."

"Yes!" Marc leaped to his feet and slapped the table.

"Are you crazy?" Richard bellowed. "Think of the money you're throwing away."

"Money's not the only way to measure value. I'll manage just fine." She'd have to keep her job for now, and stay in the tiny, dull apartment, but her share of the sale to BAPA would let her pay down her old student loans and enroll in more college classes. Her life wouldn't change as quickly, but it would change for the better.

Richard started to say something more, but she cut him off. "This is what Granny Jo wanted. She told me so."

The BAPA representatives cheered. Claire and Tess gave each other high fives.

Best of all, Daniel reached over and took Ellie's hand.

She smiled when a faint whispered sound drifted past her ear: "Thank you."

———•———

Richard stormed out in a huff. Claire watched Peter slink away behind him.

367

While Tess and the other BAPA board members gathered around a jubilant Marc Burnham, Claire drifted into the hall. Ellie was there by herself, staring at the stained-glass window above the grand staircase.

"Ellie? I'm so glad you voted for BAPA."

"Oh!" Ellie spun around. "You startled me."

"I'm curious—what did you mean when you said Granny Jo told you what she wanted?"

"I … nothing. Just that I dreamed about her last night and—I knew her so well, Claire. She'd want her house to last forever. I thought what she desired wouldn't matter now that she's gone. But it does."

"I'm sure she's happy now, wherever she is. Simon's probably pleased too."

"I'm so sorry about what happened him," Ellie said. "That's part of why I was going to vote the other way. I thought changing the house into condos would make the crime scene disappear. But that's not true, is it? Simon's murder and the other man's death will always be part of this house's history."

"The other man," Claire said. "I heard the police think he killed Simon and was so overcome with guilt that he committed suicide."

"That's right. So horrible to think the murderer was a Burnham, even if it was some distant cousin I never knew about."

"Are the cops sure he was a relative of yours?"

"Thaddeus Birnbaum. Our great-grandfather's last name in the Old Country. The cops took DNA samples, and I'm sure they'll prove the family connection. Inspector Flaherty showed me a picture of his face. It looked exactly like the portrait of Isaac that hung in the parlor."

Good, Claire thought. People believed the story she'd concocted. A bizarre tale, but the truth was far more crazy.

Daniel walked up and handed Ellie a cup of coffee. "Thought you might need this." He slipped an arm around her waist.

"Thanks." Ellie looked at him with an expression that revealed gratitude and something more. Not love, but certainly affection.

"Ready to go?" he asked.

"Yes," she said. "Bye, Claire. Hope I'll see you again. Maybe at the opening of the BAPA museum."

Claire watched them leave. Apparently Peter had lost his wife and his mistress in the same week. She couldn't think of anyone who deserved it more.

———◆———

"Come on, Claire." Tess stood by the front door, her foot tapping impatiently.

"Just a minute." Claire laid the Scarlett O'Hara dress over the banister and climbed a few steps up the grand staircase. The vantage point gave her a good view of the foyer and parlor: the elaborately carved woodwork, the marble fireplace, the stained-glass windows that the sunlight turned to jewels.

How wonderful that all of this would be preserved. She was already looking forward to visiting BAPA's museum-to-be.

As she stood on the stairs, scantily clad young women scurried past her, accompanied by men whose eyes were filled with eager hunger. In the parlor, Lady Celeste sat in her throne-like chair, scribbling notes in her account book. Isaac stood beside her, whiskey glass in hand.

None of them were real. Not any more. Just images in her mind. Memories, hers alone.

That was one aspect of the Burnham Mansion's history that would never go on display. Once their daughter Josephine was born, Celeste and Isaac had taken great care to establish themselves as pillars of the community, dignified and respectable. A record of the bawdy house on Octavia Street might be moldering in some forgotten archive, but as far as Claire could tell she was the only person alive who knew about it.

One more secret she could never reveal.

Glancing up, she saw the wild-haired Mr. Stregoni leaning over the second-floor rail, beckoning to her. Roxane, beside him, offered Claire a sweet smile. What had befallen them after she parted company with them last night? Or was it more than a century ago?

Thank God she hadn't been trapped in the past forever.

"Claire!" Tess's voice rang out.

"Be right there." Coming down the stairs, Claire caught a whiff of spice-and-flowers perfume. A breath of air, feather-light, touched her cheek.

"Don't worry about my little friend. Thanks to that strange Italian fellow, she learned the power of love. Just as I did, from my darling Edouard."

"Granny Jo! You're still here—"

The riffle in the air fell still. The fragrance faded away.

"Claire?" Tired of waiting at the door, Tess had come up beside her. "Who are you talking to?"

"Just myself." Best to change the subject. "I bet you're pleased with the Burnhams' vote."

"Very!" Tess broke into a broad smile. "Such a beautiful house. I can't wait for the board to start planning. I was thinking we could call it the Burnham-Thatcher Museum."

"Great idea," Claire agreed. Then she whispered, "Take care of this place, Granny Jo."

She stepped toward the door and the bright sunshine outside. "I'm ready," she told Tess. "Let's go."

ACKNOWLEDGEMENTS

While the author is the person who puts the words on the page, many people contribute to the making and the magic of a book. I appreciate the generous help, intelligent suggestions, and kind support of numerous people. In particular I would like to thank the following individuals who each had a role in bringing this novel into the world: Paula Guran, Jonnie Jacobs, Rita Lakin, Bette Golden Lamb, J.J. Lamb, Camille Minichino, Wiley Saichek, Shelley Singer, Nicola Trwst, Judith Yamamoto, and Chelsea Quinn Yarbro.

For a look at a San Francisco Victorian mansion that will show what the Burnham Mansion might have looked like, visit the Haas-Lilienthal House on Franklin Street. While the two houses differ in many respects and do not share the same history, the Haas-Lilienthal House is of a similar size and era. Once a family home, it now open to the public as San Francisco's only Victorian house museum, and is well worth a visit. It is also the headquarters of San Francisco Heritage, a nonprofit organization whose mission is to preserve and enhance San Francisco's unique architectural and cultural identity. I had the privilege, a number of years ago, of being a member of the SF Heritage staff. At the time I was a newcomer to the city, and I greatly appreciate what the organization taught me about San Francisco's proud and fascinating history. Learn more at sfheritage.org.

Finally, my thanks to Charles Lucke, whose unwavering support and encouragement mean more to me than he knows.

ABOUT THE AUTHOR

Margaret Lucke flings words around as a writer and editorial consultant in the San Francisco Bay Area. She is fascinated by the power of stories and the magic of creativity.

Margaret writes tales of love, ghosts, and murder, sometimes all three in one book. In addition to *House of Desire,* she is the author of the novels *House of Whispers, Snow Angel,* and *A Relative Stranger* (nominated for an Anthony Award), and is the editor of *Fault Lines: Stories by Northern California Crime Writers,* published by the Northern California chapter of Sisters in Crime.

A former president of the Northern California chapter of Mystery Writers of America, Margaret teaches fiction writing classes for UC Berkeley Extension and other venues. She has also published two how-to books on writing—*Schaum's Quick Guide to Writing Great Short Stories* and *Writing Mysteries.*

She loves to hear from readers and writers and welcomes you to get in touch.

Website: margaretlucke.com
Newsletter: margaretlucke.com/contact
Facebook: Margaret-Lucke-Author
Twitter: @MargaretLucke